Love and the Dream Come True

Books by Tammy L. Gray

From Bethany House Publishers

STATE OF GRACE

Love and a Little White Lie
Love and the Silver Lining
Love and the Dream Come True

Love and the Dream Come True

TAMMY L. GRAY

BETHANYHOUSE

a division of Baker Publishing Group
Minneapolis, Minnesota

Published by Bethany House Publishers
11400 Hampshire Avenue South
Minneapolis, Minnesota 55438
www.bethanyhouse.com

Bethany House Publishers is a division of
Baker Publishing Group, Grand Rapids, Michigan

Printed in the United States of America

Library of Congress Cataloging-in-Publication Data
Names: Gray, Tammy L., author.
Title: Love and the dream come true / Tammy L. Gray.
Description: Minneapolis, Minnesota : Bethany House, a division of Baker
    Publishing Group, [2022] | Series: State of grace
Identifiers: LCCN 2022002386 | ISBN 9780764235931 (trade paperback) | ISBN
    9780764240096 (casebound) | ISBN 9781493437252 (ebook)
Subjects: LCGFT: Novels.
Classification: LCC PS3607.R39685 L677 2022 | DDC 813/.6—dc23/
    eng/20220120
LC record available at https://lccn.loc.gov/2022002386

Scripture quotations are from THE HOLY BIBLE, NEW INTERNATIONAL VER-
SION®, NIV® Copyright © 1973, 1978, 1984, 2011 by Biblica, Inc.® Used by
permission. All rights reserved worldwide.

Cover design by Susan Zucker

Author is represented by Jessica Kirkland, Kirkland Media Management.

Baker Publishing Group publications use paper produced from sustainable forestry
practices and post-consumer waste whenever possible.

22   23   24   25   26   27   28   7   6   5   4   3   2   1

For Tayler, Luke, and Lilli

Your family's bravery, steadfast love, and unyielding
perseverance inspire everyone who has the
privilege of knowing you.
Thank you for allowing me to share a glimpse
of your courage in this story.

ONE

Cameron

*M*usic used to be my breath, my muse, my one sure-and-steady force. It never quieted. Even when the sound muted and the melody faded into the walls and ceilings, still it continued in my ears, vibrated down into my core. Driving me. Feeding me. A siren of notes dancing through the hum of air particles and calling out as pure and consuming as the mythical creatures of the sea.

But no more. Now there's only a buzz, a low vibration whispering across my pores, carrying with it a concrete truth: the music, like everything else, has abandoned me.

I stare at my laptop screen. At the website of demos and the endless database of songs I neither wrote nor have any desire to perform. The label wants me to sell out. Wants a more current sound, generic, mass appeal—all key business phrases that make me feel nauseous.

My phone sits inches away from my fingers, and I grab it quickly, refusing to let Mark ignore me anymore. Rings blare from the speaker, and just when I think he's going to force me to leave another message, he picks up.

"Cameron! Hey, buddy, I was just about to call you back." His voice is the smooth silk of a master manipulator, which is probably why he's one of the most sought-after agents in the music industry. "Tell me you picked ten fabulous singles and we can put this baby to rest once and for all."

I press my lips together and try to keep my stomach from churning. "I've thought about their offer, Mark, and decided it's not going to work."

The pause on the other end of the line is deafening. I hear his chair squeak. Hear his tension sizzle through the invisible connection.

"I want to sing originals," I say when he remains silent. "I have more I can send you. They're more upbeat, catchy—"

"Cameron." He sighs, exasperated, and the hiss slithers into my bones. "They don't want original this time. They want hits. You had your shot at songwriting, and the album flopped. And hey, it happens, but this clinging to a fantasy is killing your career. The board nearly dropped you. The only reason they didn't was because—"

"I know. You don't have to remind me." I press two fingers against my temples and rub away the sting. My most popular song, "A Decade of Love," was used on the finale of an extremely successful reality singing show, sending it once again up the charts. An upward momentum my label has no intention of missing out on.

"Cam, I know you're having a hard time accepting this new reality, but our hands are tied. And really, it's not so bad. The label's letting you pick ten of the twelve songs for your next release when contractually they could be picking all of them . . . which they will if you don't give me something soon."

The thought burns through my veins. "And what if I refuse to make the next album? If we tell them it's my music or nothing?"

"Listen, buddy. It's been a rough year. I get it, so there's no need to make an impassioned decision now. Holidays are coming up, and I'm sure I can stall them till early January. Go meet a girl, skydive in the desert, take a hike through the rain forest or whatever you young Millennial kids like to do before making a life-altering decision."

He's trying to scare me into doing what he wants. It's been like this for years now. I'm just no longer willing to play the eager young artist. "You didn't answer the question, Mark. Contractually, what happens if I refuse?"

"Well . . ." His voice hardens, no longer the Pied Piper trying to get me to follow the flute. "If you refuse, you better be ready to pay out your contract, because that's where we're at, kiddo. Play or pay. Your contract says the music must be 'commercially acceptable.' And after the last album, you and I both know your originals will not fall into that category. So yes, you can refuse and walk away, but considering the financial losses they took on with you this year, they'll either sue or make sure no label ever touches you again. You understand what I'm saying, don't you?" When I don't respond, his voice presses in, tight and hard. "Your career will be over. Finished. The work we put into that last album, a waste. Your talent . . . a waste. And considering the history you shared with me when we first met, we both know you don't exactly have a lot to run home to."

A chill runs down my spine at his comment. I was naïve when I'd shared those things with him. Too young and sheltered to recognize this man was not a mentor like the ones I'd been raised with. Mark was out for himself, and I had to learn the hard way that I was only valuable if it meant he gained fame or money from my name.

Mark's voice lightens, returns to the rich, satiny coo he's known for. "So . . . take my seasoned advice and go away for the holidays. Rest. Regroup. Meanwhile, I'll do what I can to buy you more time."

I grind out an "okay" I don't mean at all.

"One great album, Cam. That's all it takes to get you back on top. Do it their way this time, make loads of money for both of us, and then we can go back and dust off those originals." He mutters something that sounds like an *I'll check in with you later*, and the screen on my phone goes black.

I shoot to my feet and walk away from my professionally decorated living room and the conversation that basically told me I have no options. Hardwood floors echo under my feet, a sound confirming that once upon a time, I'd arrived at greatness. I had the dream . . . all of it. A custom-built Nashville home far bigger than I needed. Interviews with talk-show hosts and entertainment anchors. A hit single that topped the charts. And a second album I was given full artistic freedom to produce.

What I never considered, even once, is what happens after the dream comes true. When the shiny Grammy starts to collect dust and its memory is slowly tarnished by unrecognized sales and irritated producers. When the agent who once stalked you stops returning phone calls, and suddenly you become the guy who's forced to play the game all over again. That's the part no one likes to talk about. The moment when you stare at the CDs and awards and framed magazine covers and wonder why any of it matters. Wonder how it's possible to have it all and yet . . . feel completely empty.

I ease open the cabinet in the formal dining room I've never once eaten in. The containers inside are no longer old shoeboxes but canvased cartons my decorator insisted were essential. I shouldn't be pulling them free. Not now. Not when I haven't dared to in over a year. But the resurgence of that song . . . that haunting, awful song . . . seems to be a string I'm bound to follow. I know exactly which box to reach for, exactly how deep the picture lies, exactly how much looking at it is going to rip at the festering wound that has yet to heal.

And yet seconds later it's in my hands and I'm staring at the five of us—Bryson, Darcy, Mason, Alison, and myself—arms interlaced, smiles warm, and hearts eager for the future ahead. We'd just graduated from high school a week prior and were heading out with our church for our final youth camp. The immediate pain that slices through my chest is worse than I expect. Worse than it was the last time I dared to look at their faces. Faces I haven't spoken to in years. Faces that mark betrayals we've never recovered from. I brace my fingers on each side, ready to shred the photo in half. My hands tremble, my heart begging me to end the misery and destroy this last tether I have to my former best friends. But I can't do it. Instead, I place the picture back inside, further down in the box this time, and slam the lid shut with a vengeance.

I scramble to my feet, my throat bone-dry, and head for the kitchen. Viciously, I open my massive stainless-steel fridge, filled with food only because I have a housekeeper who's paid to keep it that way, and grab a bottle of sparkling water. I suck down the cool liquid, desperately hoping it will calm the writhing storm inside. Only it doesn't. Instead, when the door shuts in front of me, I'm forced to behold another poisoned spear.

My sister's wedding invitation. My *baby* sister's wedding invitation. The little girl in pigtails who used to climb into my bed when she got scared and beg me to sing her to sleep is now a name etched in delicate script on thick parchment made to look distressed and aged.

I don't know why this event took me by such surprise. She's twenty-nine, the same age I was when I signed my first recording contract and left Texas without looking back.

Four years and three months ago . . . almost to the day.

And of course, it would be my luck that it's now, on the downhill side of my flailing career, that I'm forced to return home. I should have gone back the day after I stood on national television and accepted my award for Best Rock Performance. I've often wondered if my old friends were watching that night. If Darcy remembered the two of us, barely preteens, pretending to give and receive that same award using an old softball trophy of hers. If Bryson heard the name of the band that was once his crowning glory and regretted his decision to walk away. Or if either felt the sting when I intentionally left their names out of my acceptance speech. Probably not. After all, "A Decade of Love" was nominated for Song of the Year, an honor far higher than mine. And even though the title didn't win that night, its presence at the awards brought with it the ever-haunting truth that I would still be an unknown, unsigned artist if it hadn't been for that song—the one song on our entire album that I contributed nothing to—the same song that still to this day is why I have any future at all with my label.

Bryson's song.

I look over my shoulder at the open laptop on my coffee table and feel the heat rise in my stomach. I won't do it again. I won't sing someone else's music and pretend the lyrics don't rip me apart from the inside out. I've spent four years in the shadow of "A Decade of Love." Spent four years pretending that blasted song wasn't written for the girl I'd loved my entire life. The girl whose name I had been sure would be listed with mine on a wedding invitation one day. The girl who picked *him* over me.

My best friend and my band partner. Both ripped from me in one night.

Heat rises to my throat, and my chest constricts in an all-too-familiar way. I set my water bottle on the counter with a trembling hand and try again to swallow back the desert in my throat, nearly choking in the process. I know the agony that comes next, and the resentment I feel for both of them doubles.

A sting seizes my chest, and I press the spot with my palm, massaging the tender flesh. I suck in a deep, painful breath, trying to control the rush of adrenaline, but my heart races faster, sweat now beading on my forehead. Blood pumps in my ears, louder and louder as I fight for any sense of control, yet the fear comes despite the effort. It's intense, debilitating, and worse, I don't even know why I'm afraid, what has me so captive; I only know it's there, strangling me, trying to pull the life from my body. I sink to one knee, willing my eyes to focus on the red vase sitting carefully on my kitchen table, the one filled with fresh flowers and the promise of life. They blur and then come into crystal-clear focus. I count the petals, matching the rhythm to my breaths.

"You're fine," I whisper, going through the mantra I've been told to repeat. "You're in control. This is only a moment. It will pass."

It takes three full agonizing minutes until my chest no longer burns and my heart resumes reasonable palpitations. The techniques I've learned over the past couple of years have helped reduce the length and severity of the panic attacks, but this one is far too reminiscent of the first one I ever experienced four years ago. The one that came the very night I'd both lost and gained all my dreams.

Two more minutes pass before I'm finally able to stand fully, though my shirt is sticky and wet and my eyes sting.

Using the counter as support, I drag my wilting body to the far-left drawer and pull out the medicine bottle I constantly have on hand. I place the quick-dissolving pills under my tongue and wait until a manufactured calm pushes out the darkness.

It's the stress of a new album, I tell myself, burying the fact that I've had two of these attacks now in a week's span. Both coming after seeing that confounded invitation on the fridge. The one announcing an event that no excuse in the world will allow me to skip.

The piece of paper that forces me to return home.

TWO

Lexie

*M*usic is the perfect accompaniment to any mood. Good ones, bad ones, and all the little ones in between can be made just a little better by a catchy drumbeat, or a song that makes you want to shake your body until the room spins and your brain feels pleasantly light.

Today, more than ever, is the kind of day that deserves dancing.

I pick up my phone and scroll through my purchased music. All three of Cameron Lee's albums are staring back at me. The first he did with his church band when he was still on staff at Grace Community; the second was his Black Carousel album that catapulted him to the top of the charts and made him a household name; and the third is his latest album released only a year ago and his first one as a solo artist. The critics were harsh with this one, as were the fans, yet I click on the cover anyway. Maybe it's his blue eyes that still bring that schoolgirl crush to the surface or maybe it's the loyalty I feel for him, but I try to play this album as much if not more than the others. After all, someone needs to appreciate the obvious work he put into the arrangement.

The song choice is easy: track four. My favorite, and honestly the only song on the album that feels like him. The drum rolls, and then in comes an instrument composition that will one day be studied by musical prodigies. The complexity is what makes the song feel like Cameron's work, even if it is missing that soul-stirring depth he usually spins inside the notes. My shoulders bounce to the rhythm I have memorized. My smile comes big and bright as I pirouette inside my closet-sized bathroom, my thoughts returning to the fantasy that one day Cameron will sing to me for real and not just from my cracked iPhone screen. A fantasy that is as unlikely as the idea that he even remembers my name. To him, I was simply his buddy's cousin and his little sister's friend who hung out at the house sometimes.

But to me, Cameron Lee has always been a dream unfulfilled.

I was only fourteen when he went off to college and I've only seen him a handful of times since. Yet through his music, Cameron has shared a million little moments with me and some really big ones, too. He was in the car when I drove my daughter to school for the very first time, would calm me daily when the water heater broke and we had to take cold showers for two weeks, and has comforted me every year when December 10 hits the calendar, because it is the one day I let myself mourn for all I've lost. To allow for any more would be to spend my life walking backward, and that's simply not how I operate. Plus I'd unquestionably fall down the moment I tried.

"Mom!" my daughter yells from the hallway. "Fifteen-minute warning!"

I glance at the mirror and cringe. "Okay, I'm almost ready."

Not really. I still have to dry my hair, put on makeup, and find something to wear, but Morgan is a worrier and a time dictator and the complete opposite of me, which is probably why we've been butting heads lately.

Well-meaning parents warned me of the dreaded junior high years, of the hormonal roller coaster and the sassy monster that will take over my sweet baby girl. I didn't want to believe them. After all, Morgan's always had more spunk than most girls. But mostly I denied their cautions because the two of us have only had each other for the past ten years, and I still believe that's a bond no mood swing is going to break.

My eyes drift to the quote on my bathroom mirror, the one taped above the tiny round sink, and I wish my mother were here to give me advice on how to deal with my daughter's recent craving for space away from me. The edges of the paper quote are frayed, and the ink has faded some, but it still warms me with the same empowerment as it has since the day I read it in my mom's goodbye letter: *Do all the things you think you cannot do.*

"I'm trying, Mom," I whisper, feeling the loss of her with each and every passing day.

She was a sixth-grade social studies and English teacher, and she always quoted historical figures who had changed the world: C. S. Lewis, Bonhoeffer, Harriet Tubman, and this one, based on a quote from Eleanor Roosevelt. I have a journal of every encouraging word I can remember her telling me, and even though fourteen years have passed since I heard her beautiful voice, they still come back to me in pieces, and I continue to capture every word stored in my memory. She once said the greatest gift I could give her is to live out my life with optimism and faith, always looking forward, never behind me, and loving with all my heart. I turn thirty soon, and I pray I've made her proud by doing just that.

Today, the quote on the mirror is especially fitting. I glance at my phone sitting on the old Formica counter, and anticipation rolls through my stomach. My cousin Mason is at the title office right now, finalizing the purchase of my first house. The house the two of us bought together and will attempt to sell in less than six months. The house that will take me from a property-management worker bee to a full-blown entrepreneur doing exactly what I love to do—interior design.

"Are you kidding me right now?"

I jump at the irritated question and shift my attention to the doorway and to my daughter, who's manically tapping her foot on the linoleum. Morgan has always been an adorable little girl, but lately she's blossomed into a stunning young lady. Not that she's noticed. Morgan's idea of school prep is a ponytail and a clean T-shirt that's at least a size too big.

"You're still in your robe," she hisses. "And you're listening to Cameron Lee again, which you and I both know makes you even slower than your normal molasses pace!"

I pause the song and attempt to move faster, though added pressure always seems to have the opposite effect. "I can get ready in—" I glance back down at my phone—"nine minutes." I twist my damp hair and secure it with a large pronged clip. "See? Hair's already done."

"Mom, I've been late for school every day this week." Exasperation laces each word, and she crosses her arms as if I'm not already aware that she's annoyed.

Guilt lances me. "Not every day."

"Two out of three!" she barks, and we fall back into a pattern I wish I could say is rare, but it's not. Morgan is thirteen going on forty, and I'm, well, I'm responsible when I need to be. The rest of the time, I'm free. Because life's much too short to live it counting seconds and making lists. "And if I get five, I'll get lunch detention."

"Okay, okay." I flick my wrist to shoo her away so I can get dressed. "But you standing there growling is not going to make me move any faster."

"You have nine minutes!" She spins, and I hear her stomping through my bedroom. "Not a second more!"

"Got it." I rush around, trying to pick up the pace, and knock over two of my cosmetic cases in the process. This is ridiculous and unhelpful. I take a deep breath and attempt to get my already racing heart to calm. No such luck.

I restart the music and hope the sound of Cameron's voice will push the nervousness away. As usual it works, and the giddy excitement returns. I should feel a little guilty for inviting Cameron to our victory moment, especially since he and Mason haven't spoken in nearly five years, but I ignore that pinch of loyalty. Mason doesn't talk about the falling-out that occurred between him and his closest friends, so I see no reason why I have to sacrifice for an event that occurred ages ago.

Cameron's butter-rich voice follows me into my closet, and I sway to the sound. My clothing selection is bigger than one would imagine on my income, but I've become a master at consignment shopping. Sometimes a little stitch here and there can transform a piece of fabric, just like a little touch of color or the right throw pillow can turn a living room from drab to fabulous. *Life is an adventure, Lexie,* my mom would always say. *It can be someone else's existence you're coveting from the shadows, or it can be yours.*

"This one's for both of us, Mom," I whisper as I pull my newest find from the rack. Today isn't a wear-just-anything kind of day.

It's a conquer-the-world kind of day.

Morgan's hunched over the kitchen table writing in her notebook when I finally emerge from my bedroom in a swirl of perfume and bravado.

"Well, does this scream homeowner to you?" I spin on my heel to give her the full three-sixty.

She shoves her notebook in her backpack and stands so fast that the chair almost topples. "Finally. Let's go."

"Not until you stop and give me at least one gushing compliment." I spread my arms and wait. "Well?"

"You look the same as you always do."

"No, I don't!" I glance down at the gray pants I painstakingly tailored to fit every curve, and the silky top I paid way too much for considering it was used. "I'm wearing red today. I never wear red." It's usually too bold and flashy for me. I prefer pastels and florals, but not today. Men get power ties; well, I'm sporting my own power motif.

She concedes—likely because it's the only thing that will get us out of the house—and looks me over. "You look gorgeous and way too trendy for a mom."

That makes me grin. Very few of the kids in Morgan's eighth grade class have a mom still in her twenties. I'm kind of sad we'll be losing that shock factor soon.

I cup her cheeks and kiss her on the forehead. We're nearly the same height now, but she's still my little girl. "From one *gorgeous* woman to another, I say thank you."

Morgan's pursed lips break into a grin she tries to stop but can't. "I'm not gorgeous. I'm plain."

"Trust me, darling, you are anything but plain. Aphrodite herself would be jealous of those eyes." She has my sister's eyes. Large and so blue, it's like glaring at an endless ocean. My eyes are hazel and smaller, and while others might wish for something more dramatic, I'm grateful because they're also one of my mom's legacies.

Morgan blushes at my words, which of course makes her lips tighten again. "Enough of the gooey stuff. We need to leave now! And it didn't take you nine minutes, by the way. It took you thirteen."

"Okay, okay. Let me get my coffee."

"I already got it and put it in the car." She pushes me toward the back door, which is never a good thing because I'm forgetful on a normal day. I'm downright flighty under these conditions.

I sling my purse over my shoulder and get halfway through the kitchen when I realize what I'm missing. "My phone."

Morgan holds it up. "Right here."

"My keys."

"Got those too." She swings open the door that leads straight to our two-vehicle carport and jogs to the passenger side of my little Civic. "Your work bag is in the back seat, and I packed you a lunch today since I know you're going to be too house-obsessed to remember to eat." She disappears inside the car a second later.

I ease into the driver's seat, careful not to sit in a way that will wrinkle my blouse. "You're the best, you know that?"

"Yes, and you can show me your appreciation by actually driving me to school."

Shifting, I look at the rearview mirror as I roll down the driveway, turning the wheel in the opposite direction I should.

"Not again," she moans.

So much for hoping Morgan wouldn't notice. "It only adds two minutes to our trip. I counted."

"Two minutes in Lexie time is ten in the real world."

"I just want to see it, okay?" The house Mason and I are buying is only two blocks from my rental, which is on the fringe of one of the most sought after and historical neighborhoods in

21

Midlothian. Houses rarely ever hit the market, and when they do, they're snatched up in hours. They don't make neighborhoods like this one anymore. There are only two to three houses per block, with big oak trees and large lots. People still walk their dogs and wave at you from their porches. I knew the minute I became a property manager that I wanted to live in this area and immediately snatched the first rental I could afford when it became available seven years ago. It didn't matter that it was covered in paneling and had low popcorn ceilings, or that its lot was the smallest on the whole block. What mattered was that Morgan could safely ride her bike down the street. "I promise I'll speed on the highway to make up the time."

"Fine. I don't think I'll get there by the tardy bell anyway." She leans the side of her head against the window, and I already know why she agreed so easily. My newest project is only two houses down from the first person we met after we moved in, Betty Hardcastle. She was a recent widow who loved to cook for neighbors and adored my daughter the instant they met. She soon became a surrogate grandmother, and Morgan would often run there the minute she got home from school to help her bake or to play in the enormous tree house they built for their kids over fifty years ago. Two months ago, she passed away quietly in her sleep. A peaceful and deserving way to go for such a wonderful woman, but the loss left a hole in our hearts all the same. The house has been closed up ever since, yet Morgan still goes there often to visit the tree house. I let her because we all grieve differently, and I know one day it will either sell or be rented out, so why put restrictions on it now?

I turn the last corner and slow the car to a crawl. We pass Mrs. Hardcastle's house on the right and I feel our shared grief settle over the car.

The only relatives left in my daughter's life are me and my cousin, whom she only just met eighteen months ago, and I hate that I couldn't spare her the pain of losing another person she loves.

I press the gas a little until we're closer to what is about to be the culmination of all my dreams. The exterior of the house is grander than Mrs. Hardcastle's, with big windows and two dormers, but it's lacking the front porch that makes her place so picturesque. Mason plans to add one. He says it's a huge selling feature in these neighborhoods.

There's no sign in the neglected yard; this deal was done without real-estate agents and MLS listings. Maybe that's why I'm so nervous. A handshake and a bill of sale is feeling a little flimsy right now.

Morgan clears her throat, and as promised, I drive more quickly than I should, though even with the extra speeding, we still pull into the car loop four minutes after the tardy bell usually rings. She now must go to the front office and get a note and likely a lecture for something completely outside of her control.

"Sorry, babe. I promise I'll be less distracted tomorrow."

"No, you won't, but I still love you." She leans over and kisses my cheek. "Bye, Mom. See you after school."

"Bye! Have a wonderful day." I wave, but she doesn't look back as she hurries toward the double glass doors. I take a deep breath and move along, my stomach now a whirl of flutters I can't control. Mason should have called by now, at least with an update.

I do what I always do when I feel this way. I press the play button on my phone and let Cameron's beautiful melodies distract me from the unknown. The text comes two songs later.

Mason:
It's official. I hope you're ready to get your hands dirty.

I scream a victory cry into the air and turn up the volume until my eardrums nearly burst. And once again, my childhood-crush-turned-ridiculous-adult-fantasy-boyfriend is right there, celebrating this incredible moment right along with me.

~~

"Well, is it all you remembered it being?" Mason stands in the middle of the paneled living room with his fists on his hips. His face is scrunched as if he can see only the massive amount of work in front of us, while I'm beaming and touching the walls to ensure this isn't some kind of dream that will end with my alarm blaring.

"Are you kidding? It's so much more," I say, breathless. "Everywhere I turn, I see potential."

"So did I . . . at first." He sighs. "Now, all I see are dollar signs. I'm starting to wonder if this neighborhood will pull in the kind of final value we need to make it worth it."

"It will," I say emphatically. "I know every stretch of the housing market in Midlothian. We got a steal on this property."

His eyebrows form a V while he examines me. "Do you always see a skyful of rainbows or is it just for my benefit?"

"It's for everyone's benefit," I counter. Sure, I'm a perpetual optimist, but I like it that way. It makes life a much more enjoyable experience. "Our time on earth is much too short to spend it living in the doldrums. Look around. We are going to create something spectacular together!"

"Let's hope." His voice is dull, but I can see him fighting a smile. I follow him through the kitchen, living room, and entryway as he explains his plans for demo. The job is significant. We're tearing down walls, adding beams, moving the kitchen from the back of the house to the center. "Every day from this point on is critical, Lex. The price of construction material is skyrocketing, and with our doing this over the holidays, there's no room for error. Every day we lose will cost us in profit." He doesn't add that the delay will mean we have to fork out additional loan payments. For him, that's probably no big deal. For me, it will wipe out my already depleted savings. "Not to mention, you never know when this housing spike is going to bust, so we have to get it to market fast."

"Wow. So when you say 'no room for error,' you mean it." I chew on the edge of my fingernail, nerves hitting for the first time.

"Now that's more like it. Fear is healthy when approaching a six-figure renovation." He grins and walks over to ruffle my hair.

I push him away, though the effort doesn't budge his hulking frame, and smile back up at him. Mason's always been tall, reaching his full six-foot-two height back in the eighth grade. But now he's stocky as well, which adds an extra layer of intimidation. Growing up, we'd never been especially close, with him being four years older than me, and technically he's my first cousin once removed—his dad is my late grandfather's younger brother, if that makes any sense. Our families knew each other but weren't the type to hang out regularly, which meant the few interactions we did have were limited to the youth group at Grace Community Church and casual run-ins when our two social circles would intersect. After he graduated from high school, we pretty much lost touch.

It's funny how God brings blessings at the most unexpected moments. I'd randomly run into Mason at a corner grocery store eighteen months ago, and what started as a quick let's-catch-up lunch has now evolved into one of my most cherished friendships. Not only is Mason the only family I have left, but he's also the only person in my life who knows the heartbreak of how Morgan came to be mine.

"Alright then," he says after a few more seconds of silence. "Let's get down to business." He walks over to a stack of papers he left sprawled on the tile countertop—another thing that must go—and pulls out a long color-coded calendar that's made up of three sheets of printer paper taped together. "We need to coordinate our days now that we're partners." He winks at me, and I take a deep breath.

I know he thinks he doesn't need me. I'm the one who roped him into including me on this particular venture. But I am determined to prove otherwise. I know this market, and I've staged more rental houses than I could write down on a two-by-four. With my help, this house isn't going to simply turn a profit; it's going to turn the greatest profit he's ever seen. And then next time, it will be him begging me to be his partner.

"Now, what's your availability look like?" he asks, pen ready.

I stare down at his six-month schedule more than impressed. He's lined out all the lead times on countertops and appliances, the contractor dates and expectations, and his own time that's also split between this house and one more that is nearly finished. The only color not filled in is my time schedule. The goal is to have the house show-ready by the first of April. And with Midlothian being one of the fastest growing cities in Texas, I have no doubt we will immediately receive multiple offers.

I point to the weekend of the fifth, surprised to see his name on the calendar. "Cassie Lee's wedding is that Saturday. Aren't you going?"

"No," Mason says, his tone short and hard.

"But we could be each other's plus one." Sure, Mason was

Cameron's friend growing up, not Cassie's, but still. The Lees were the type of people who made you feel as if you were part of their family. And Mason had spent even more time there than I did. "Come on, Mason, it'll be fun." I poke his side, but he only glares at me before returning to the calendar.

"Not a chance. Trust me, Cassie will appreciate my distance. I don't exactly have the best track record when it comes to weddings." He scribbles something on the sheet, not bothering to expand on his little comment. "Is that it, or do you have other formal engagements I need to schedule around?"

I sigh, irritated he's trying to change the subject. "No, Mr. Grumpy. I'm basically free every weekend because I pathetically have no social life. And you can block out the week after Thanksgiving through Christmas. I'm taking all my vacation time to be your minion."

A small grin peeks through his sourness. "Good. And for the record, social lives are completely overrated."

"Only for hermits like you." I cross my arms, not yet ready to give up the battle. "Mrs. Lee is going to be really disappointed, you know. She asked if you were coming when I RSVPed."

"She'll understand."

"Is this because of your issues with Cameron? Don't you think it's been long enough that you two can kiss and make up finally?"

Mason's hand freezes on the paper. "Cam's whereabouts or actions do not drive my decisions. I'm not going because I don't want to. Plain and simple."

While I don't think it's that simple, I decide not to question his motivation. Instead, I go fishing, because even though the two of them haven't spoken in years, Mason is still my most reliable source for insight into Cameron's mind.

"But it makes sense, though, right?" I carefully bite at my fingernail, trying to be nonchalant about the question. "That he'd come to his sister's wedding? I know she'd want him to." My stomach flips at the idea of seeing him after all these years. Not that I've thought about it much . . . only every time I look at the invitation.

Mason scowls, and I realize I pushed it one question too many. "You have got to be kidding me."

"What?" I say, my breath hitching.

"You still have a thing for him. After all this time." He shakes his head, not so much irritated as confused. "Why?"

My face blazes hot. "How do you know I had a thing for him?"

"You weren't exactly the most subtle teenager. Every time Cam and you were in the same room, you'd start rambling in this giddy hyperspeed way that no one could understand, not to mention the tomato color your face would turn." He looks me over and presses his lips together. "Yep . . . that's the shade right there."

Mortification builds into indignation. "Yeah, well, so what? I have a wonderful imagination, Mason. And yes, it's true that Cameron Lee has been the star in my dreams since I was old enough to notice boys, and probably will remain there until I'm old and gray. But don't worry, I know it's as ridiculous now as it was back then."

"What's ridiculous is that you still see him as the ultimate catch." The slight edge to his tone feels both bitter and protective. "You can do better, Lex. That I can guarantee you."

And suddenly I feel bad for bringing the subject up at all. Mason's shoulders are now tight, and his mouth is set in a hard line. I bump his shoulder with mine, trying to ease some of the growing tension. "Well, be that as it may, a pretend perfect boyfriend is better than the actual reality that I haven't met anyone I would even consider seriously dating in nearly ten years. At least the former never disappoints."

Despite not wanting to, Mason chuckles. I think that's why we got close so fast. He's walking wounded in a way that he never shares. Whereas I refuse to be broken, despite all that's beaten me down. Mason reminds me what I'm fighting against, and one day maybe he'll decide to fight alongside me, too.

THREE

Cameron

My sister-in-law opens the door to my temporary rental, and immediately I'm hit with the musty smell of neglect and age. I knew coming home for Cassie's wedding and staying through the holidays would only be manageable if I had my own space. Lucky for me, Kelly is a seasoned real-estate agent with connections.

"Like I mentioned on the phone," she says, "this house has been empty for a couple of months. The owner, Mrs. Hardcastle, passed away in her sleep, and the family hasn't yet decided what they want to do with the property. I only knew about it because they called and asked me to give them sales comparables." She flips on the overhead light. It doesn't do much. Unlike my Nashville home, where vaulted ceilings and LED lights illuminate the space, this house has maybe an eight-foot clearance, old dome ceiling-fan lights, and windows completely hidden by heavy drapery.

Knowing my aversion to dark spaces, Kelly moves swiftly, pulling open the window coverings and apologizing when dust fills the air. "The family said they'd had the house cleaned, but I guess they didn't get to everything."

I walk through the small, crowded living room, lightly touching the sheets that protect the furniture. Framed pictures of the owner's family line the walls in ornate gold, all taken from a time when posed studio photography was the only way to go.

"We can find you something else," Kelly says, her voice hesitant. She's been handling me with kid gloves since the moment we hugged at the airport. I'd asked her to come alone, not yet ready for the bombardment that inevitably comes with my family.

"No. I like it. It's cozy." And I do. Nothing in this space reminds me of Nashville or the world I've been a part of for the last four years. There's no flash. No modern starkness. Everything, dated as it is, feels warm and comfortable. Plus it's private, a decent distance from my parents' place, and tucked in a neighborhood where the median age is likely sixty-five. The anonymity I'm searching for actually feels possible here.

"They were only willing to do a six-month lease. I asked for the three you wanted."

I brush her off with a wave of my hand. "Six is fine. My accountant will send a check this week."

She nods and walks over to a solid structure covered in dingy white cotton. She pulls up the cloth to reveal an ancient-looking piano stained a dark walnut color. "I'll have a tuning company come in if you want to use this while you're here." She slides back the keyboard cover and touches one of the ivory notes. A crisp flat sound radiates in the air, and it grates against my nerves.

"I'll think about it." I turn my back to her and walk toward the kitchen, eager to leave the now-suffocating space and the reminder that nothing in my life makes sense anymore.

What's worse is that Kelly can sense it. I see it in her eyes, in every careful word choice she makes.

Up until now, I'd managed to convince my family that I was good, thrilled even, with my new life. They'd come visit, and we'd spend a week sightseeing while I rambled on about concerts and celebrities. I'd make excuses for missing Thanksgiving and Christmas, and they'd protest but promise they were happy if I was happy. What is it about coming home that makes all the masks disappear? There's no use in even trying to fake it now.

"Caleb and I would love to have you over for dinner tonight," she says, optimism flowing through the invitation as she follows me to the tight opening that leads to a very small galley kitchen. The countertops are Formica, the appliances a cheap white plastic. Even more shocking, there isn't a stainless-steel accessory to be seen, or one that was manufactured after the turn of the century for that matter. Kelly scoots closer. "We could all catch up and, you know . . . reminisce about old times when you'd spend half your week eating all my groceries and arguing with your brother." She offers a sincere smile that feels both sad and hopeful.

I squeeze her hand, hoping it will take the sting out of my rejection. "Thanks . . . really, but I'd like to get settled. We're going to get lots of family time over the next few days." The wedding rehearsal is tomorrow night, and according to Kelly, Cassie's wedding is going to be massive. Over three hundred guests have already RSVPed, but thankfully most of them are from her fiancé's side, which is a relief. The last thing I want is to see hundreds of people who think they know me, or worse, want to talk about my failing career. "I do appreciate the offer, though. And the house, Kelly. It's a big weight off me."

She smiles at my gratitude. "You're welcome. Oh . . . before I forget." Her eyes brighten, and she reaches in her purse to pull out a folded piece of paper. "Cassie asked me to give you this."

I nearly cringe when I take the paper. Knowing my sister, it's likely filled with fitting demands and myriad appointments I have no intention of going to. But instead of a list, there's a quick line of delicate cursive that brings a warm wave of relief to my chest.

> *Your being here is even better than snuggles and lullabies. Thank you.*
>
> *Xoxo, Your baby sis.*

I swallow, ignoring the sting, and tuck the folded sheet in my back pocket. Kelly's eyes have filled as well, and I can tell there's so much she wants to say to me that it's crowding the space between us. She opens her mouth, but I don't give her time to speak. "I'll grab my bags from the car," I say a bit too eagerly. "And let you get on home before traffic picks up."

She nods, pressing her lips together. I'm grateful. I don't want a heart-to-heart. Not today. Just breathing and walking are about all I can stomach.

The air is cool outside, fallen leaves from a massive bur oak in the front yard crunching under my feet as I hasten to the back of Kelly's new SUV. I packed light. Two suitcases and a guitar case I haven't opened in months. I heave the instrument out, set it carefully on the street, and pause when an old familiar sound of a card snapping across tire spokes sends tiny pinpricks up my spine.

I look behind me just in time to see an adolescent girl whizzing by on a bicycle. It's just a flash of brown hair pulled back in a ponytail and faded jeans ripped at the knees, but it's enough to take me back twenty years. To a time when life was easy, and dreams were just starting to form. When Darcy and I would ride to our favorite playground and run around until our parents would send texts demanding we come home. We would plan the future. I was going to be a famous rock star and she would be a world-renowned veterinarian, marketing to the rich and famous, because of course we'd have to live in the same city. A tomorrow where we weren't together didn't make sense to either of us. And yet here we are . . . four years now without a word spoken between us.

I watch as the girl disappears around the corner and shake myself from the daze. Anger replaces the nostalgia. This is exactly why I haven't returned home. Because there is no memory here that doesn't include *her.*

Kelly presses her petite hand to my back. "Are you okay?"

"Yeah, I'm fine," I grumble, jerking my guitar from the ground. I'm not even in love with Darcy anymore. I let that fantasy go the minute I heard she and Bryson were married. So why, why do I still feel this gut-wrenching nausea every time her memory invades my mind? "You should get going. I've got it from here."

Kelly bites her lip, and suddenly I feel like a jerk.

"Thank you," I force out and walk over to wrap her in a hug.

She holds on the way a mother does when her son comes home from war. Maybe that's what she thinks has happened. That I've been wounded there. Forever changed. She doesn't realize it happened well before I ever left Texas. "Call if you need anything at all."

"I will," I promise and step back, giving her the most believable smile I can manage under the circumstances. It's enough to ease some of the tension in her shoulders and send her on her way.

I watch as Kelly drives down the street, stops at a stop

sign, and turns. The bicycle speeds by again, slowing as the young girl passes my new rental. She glares at me. Curious but also irritated, like I'm trespassing or something. I shake my head, realizing how ridiculous the assumption is, and lift my bags with both hands. If this is the depths my subconscious is going to stoop to in a mere two hours, I'm definitely in for a long few months.

After another round trip to the curb to retrieve my guitar, I shut the front door and breathe a sigh of relief that I made it to this point without one episode. I'd come close in the plane when we touched down but managed to talk myself to calm before the heart palpitations came. No one in my family knows about the panic attacks, and I intend to keep it that way. Maybe it's pride, or a resistance to their overprotective parenting, but no part of me is willing to lay my struggles out on display for judgment or input or "help" as they would call it.

I climb the stairs to the master bedroom, not sure what to expect considering the state of the main floor. The hallway is narrow, covered with the same brown carpet as the stairs. There are two smaller bedrooms on the right, each looking as if they haven't been slept in for years. The master is on the left, twice as big, and unlike the others it's been stripped bare. A new mattress lies on the bed frame, along with clean folded sheets. A gift from Kelly, I'm assuming. The en suite bath is tiny but functional, as is the one small closet. A chuckle bubbles in my throat as I try to imagine what my interior designer would say about the ornate maroon wallpaper with green vines running vertically to the ceiling. Ironically, knowing she'd hate it makes me like it all the more.

I set to work unpacking, not that it takes long, but it's a nice distraction. Especially when a text comes from Mark that he engaged with the label and they agreed to January 5.

Ten demo choices by then or they pick them all. I've already consulted a lawyer regarding the contract limitations, and basically he confirmed the same thing Mark warned of. Walking away is career suicide, plain and simple. Not to mention the financial blow the decision would cause.

The bed creaks when I sit, my hands lifting to rub my face as if the motion will somehow make the choice less impossible. But nothing comes except the resolution that I don't have the fortitude or the clout to buck the system. And yet I know, as sure as my reflection, that I also lack the strength needed to perform . . . well, anything right now.

Somehow, through the chaos and confusion, I have to find my love for music again. The raw, bone-crushing need to create no matter who hears the songs or buys the album.

I'm facing the battle of a lifetime and have no idea how to even begin the fight.

FOUR

Lexie

I stumble on my way out of the car, my completely impractical but gorgeous three-inch stilettos nearly breaking my ankles. The open driver's door luckily saves the day and keeps me from sprawling on the gravel in my party dress.

"I told you we were going to be late," Morgan says, her voice scolding as she watches me try to right myself before closing the door. "I came in four times and warned you, but no, you just had to curl your hair."

Yes, I did. And shave and change fifteen times. But one does not see the object of their teenage obsession after so many years without a significant amount of preparation. "We're not late. We still have seven minutes to get to our seats before the ceremony starts."

"Yes, and at this rate it's going to take us twenty." Morgan slams the door and comes to meet me at the path that will supposedly lead to the wedding gazebo. She's not stumbling at all, and the reason why makes me frown.

"Where's the boots I laid out for you?"

"They hurt my feet."

"So you wore tennis shoes instead?"

She casually lifts up the dress I forced her to wear and grins at the mangy sneakers on her feet. The very ones I insisted she throw out, since the seams have separated on both sides and have turned from white to a dirt-gray color. "You got to pick the clothes. I got to pick the accessories." Her satisfied smile widens when she glances back up. "Not all of us are trying to impress some guy today. A few of us are actually smart enough to dress for the environment."

"These shoes make this dress, and once we get to some grass, I'll be perfectly stable." I take another shaky step onto the flagstone. It's worn and slick. Not a good combination. "And I'm not trying to impress a guy. I simply wanted to look nice for Cassie's wedding."

"Please. You haven't spent that much time getting ready in a year. Not since the blind date you went on with what's-his-face."

I groan. What a waste of effort that night was. What's-his-face was a dud. A dud that wouldn't stop calling, and then he showed up at my house one night completely uninvited. That situation was the one and only time I called in Mason to intervene. I'm not sure what exactly he said to the guy, but he never called again.

My next attempt at a steady step falters, and Morgan, annoyed by our pace, wraps my arm around her elbow like a well-trained usher. I'm slightly embarrassed but grateful and lean into her as we walk.

"So, who is he?" she asks.

At this point, there's really no need to keep up the ruse. My girl is much too smart anyway. "No one you know." I sigh, the absurdity of the evening and my attempt at competing with the hordes of celebrity women he's been surrounded by hitting me over the head. "I don't really know him either. I used to, but it was a long time ago." A chuckle escapes my throat. "You're right. I look ridiculous."

She must sense the defeat because she squeezes my arm. "Actually, you look hot. Slightly drunk," she adds playfully, "but definitely hot."

Now I do laugh, not sure if I should be complimented or horrified by her description. "Thanks . . . I think."

The ground gets more level as we crest the hill, and soon after I'm able to walk steadily without assistance. Hundreds of white wooden folding chairs form a sea in front of us, and Morgan and I quietly slide into the back row, not even bothering to look for familiar faces in this crowd.

I crane in my seat, trying to see the front row, where the family of the bride is seated. It's a fool's quest. A mountain range of bodies blocks my view, some tall, some short, but none transparent. I fiddle with my necklace and work to keep the butterflies at a mild flight. It makes no sense, the anticipation I feel. Knowing my luck, I'll either never get to talk to him or end up embarrassing myself by behaving like a spastic lunatic, a habit I can't seem to kick whenever in Cameron Lee's presence. But no matter how many internal conversations I've had or fantasies I've stuffed down, my gut won't stop screaming that today is a turning point in both of our lives.

"I think I may be clairvoyant," I say to my daughter, needing to talk about the whirling of jumbled thoughts in my brain before they explode out.

She turns her head enough that I can see her smirk. "Why's that?"

"I have this premonition that something momentous is going to happen today."

"Two people are shackling themselves to 'death do us part.'"

I scowl at her description of marriage. "That's not what I mean." I may be intentionally single, but I've certainly never knocked the idea of a significant other one day. A part of me welcomes the idea of a partnership. Especially lately. "And for the record, marriage can be wonderful. If it's to the right person." My parents certainly showed that fact to be true.

"If you say so. I, however, am never getting married. Boys are gross."

"Yes, they are," I agree with a smile. I'm grateful my daughter hasn't made that switch from girly innocence to mature young woman yet. Goodness knows, I certainly don't feel ready to navigate teenage love, even while I know it's only a matter of time. One day, probably sooner than later, she'll have a crush, and her heart will pitter-patter when he speaks to her, and she'll dream of moonlight walks and stolen kisses, just like I did when I was her age.

Morgan tucks a stray hair behind her ear. It's a nice change to see her face. She's taken to wearing her hair down lately, parted dead center of her scalp. It's a striking look, but sometimes I think she's doing it to create a barrier. Ever since school started, she's barely made eye contact for longer than a few moments. And not just because she's been off and on mad at me. I can usually pinpoint those moments. It's the other times that feel gnawing because something in her eyes strikes me as shame, as if she's keeping something important from me. Which needles under my skin. We used to talk about everything. Now our discussions often end in her slamming doors and vowing never to speak to me again.

I touch Morgan's forearm and smile warmly at her. "You look really beautiful. Did I mention that?"

She smiles despite herself. "Only a thousand times."

"Good. Thank you for coming with me."

She shrugs as if I actually gave her a choice in the matter. "You're welcome."

"Mind if I slide in?"

I spin in my seat and look up toward the male voice asking the question. Despite knowing it isn't possible, I still feel a twinge of disappointment when the questioner isn't Cameron. "Um, sure. We'll scoot over." I tap Morgan's leg, and we both slide two seats to our right.

"Thanks." He unbuttons his jacket and sits, smiling at the both of us as he moves. "I'm Drake. Stephen's very fashionably late cousin." He gestures to the groom's side, which is completely full, and offers a hand.

I politely shake it. "Lexie. And this is my daughter, Morgan."

He reacts the way all men do when meeting us. Eyebrows rise while they internally calculate how they could be so off on my age. Usually it's enough to have them inching away, most not yet ready to take on this kind of responsibility.

Drake surprises me and squeezes my hand a little tighter. "Very nice to meet both of you." Our hands separate, but he edges closer. "And to think I almost turned around on the highway."

"Really? Why's that?"

"Because despite being a very fast driver, I have no ability to get anywhere on time. A vice my family will certainly remind me of many times in the next few hours."

My mouth quirks upward in solidarity. "What do you know . . . we share that same predicament."

His responding smile is actually kind of charming. "So that's why you're stuck out here in Siberia with me."

"Yes, but it doesn't seem like the wedding is starting on time, so . . . ." I draw out the word and focus on Morgan. "There was no need to stress after all."

She rolls her eyes and pulls out her phone. I watch as she clicks on one of her mindless time-passing games and return my attention to Drake, happy to have someone to distract me from stalking Cameron.

We go on to discuss our jobs, where we live, the house I'm currently demolishing. It's actually a very pleasant conversation, and I'm sort of disappointed when the music changes.

The crowd's murmur fades, and we shift to watch as ushers carefully bring the couple's grandparents down the aisle.

"Is he the guy?" Morgan's tickling whisper makes me jump.

I turn in her direction, my back to both the procession and Drake now. "What?"

"The guy you got all dressed up for," she mouths even more quietly.

"No. Definitely not." I eye Drake in my peripheral vision, trying for subtle. I guess in a way he's cute. Polished, that's for sure. But he's no Cameron Lee, and if anyone is going home with my number today, it's not going to be Cam's new cousin-in-law.

She leans in again. "Then why are you flirting so hard?"

"I'm not flirting," I whisper back. "I'm just having a normal conversation."

"I don't think he knows that, but then again, they never do." She bounces her eyebrows, her expression far too smug. "Who knows, Mom? Maybe you are clairvoyant after all and I just met my new daddy."

I smack her leg and shake my head slightly, putting a finger to my mouth. The daddy jokes have come more and more often. Part of me wonders if it's her way of asking about the man who shares her DNA. If so, she's going to have to get a lot more direct. That man is the last person I ever want to discuss with my daughter.

When I turn back to the wedding, I realize I missed Mr.

and Mrs. Lee's entrance. It's only their backs I catch now. A deep, rumbling longing yawns awake inside me as I watch them, hand in elbow, enjoy this monumental moment. My parents will never see me walk down the aisle. Will never give me away or light the unity candle as they are doing now.

I bite my lip in quiet admonishment. Sadness doesn't belong here. It's not fair to Cassie, and it's not what my mom would want.

"Don't let yesterday take up too much of today," she'd say, her list of inspirational quotes endless.

I let the words chase away the sorrow and watch as Cassie's husband-to-be walks out to take his place in the gazebo. His best man stands next to him, but that's the extent of the attendants. My heart warms at the sight because it feels very much like Cassie to keep the wedding party small. Despite the frill around us and the massive number of people here, my old friend is simple. She loves deeply and forever; her whole family does. It's nice after all these years to see that some things haven't changed.

The maid of honor walks by, followed by the most adorable little girl I've ever seen, whose deep dimples give away the Lee family connection. She drops rose petals as she passes, carefully watching them fall as if she has the most important job in the world. A tightness comes to my chest, and I slide my hand in Morgan's. She may never have worn fluffy white dresses, preferring overalls and mud-stomping boots, but it still takes me back to those days. Days that pass so fast you wonder if someone put life on fast-forward without your noticing. My little girl is a teenager. How in the world did that happen?

I swallow back the tears filling my eyes and stand with the audience when "Canon in D" floats through the air. As if I'm pulled that direction, I glance ahead and somehow get just a glimpse of Cameron through the wall of bodies. His face mirrors mine. The joy and the loss. They are such opposing emotions that it feels impossible someone would understand. But I do.

My pulse races, and my cheeks flare with heat as I cling to the vision of him. Cameron and I may not have spoken in over a decade, but we're no strangers. I hear his songs in my head. Hear the carefully chosen lyrics, the ache, the need that lines every note. Comfort surrounds me in those five seconds I get before his face is shielded again.

Stupid as the truth may be, I know a part of my heart will always belong to Cameron Lee. For the man I believe he is and for the role he's played in my life . . . real or not.

FIVE

Cameron

I pose for another canned shot, sweating buckets underneath my dress shirt. And not just because Texas didn't get the memo that November is supposed to be cold but also because the pictures never cease. We took nearly a hundred before the ceremony. Now they want all the same ones, only with the groom this time.

"Excellent. I'd like to get one more with the entire extended family," the photographer calls out, ushering aunts, uncles, and cousins from both sides out of the white folding chairs. We all cram in and give one last smile. The flash hits my eyes, and immediately my mouth relaxes, though my body seems to get more tense with the freedom. As miserable as the pictures have been, they've kept me occupied and protected.

Excitement buzzes in the air, as do comments about how lovely the wedding was and how perfect the happy couple are together. And I agree, even though needles continue to prickle inside my skin. Relief and dread come in equal measure when the photographer releases us to head over to the reception barn, where guests are already filling plates of buffet food. I agreed to stay for the dinner and first dance, mostly because the seating chart tucked me way back in a corner. My family has made every allowance they can to keep me shadowed, but I know from experience, nothing short of disappearing will stop the whispers and curious questioning. I've been mentally preparing myself for it all day, and yet still my feet shift back and forth, ready to bolt.

I'll endure the evening, though, and with a believable amount of cheer . . . for Cassie.

The family scatters like blown grass, myself included, as I walk toward the group of chairs covered with shade. I've been to Boots and Lace before, almost five years ago with an old girlfriend. January had given me a tour of the venue, pointing out her favorite tree and walking paths. The gazebo Cassie used tonight was only a block of concrete at the time.

My stomach twists with the memory. I'd been so young, so eager and ready for fame that I'd spent more time taking pictures for my social media following than actually enjoying the beauty around me. I wasted so much time looking ahead. And now I'd give anything to go back and shake the man I used to be.

"Cam?"

I turn at my sister's voice and watch as she picks up her billowing skirts and carefully takes two steps across the flag-stones to me. Cassie has always been pretty, but she's radiant today. Her long brown hair is curled in waves, and her cheeks glow with the excitement of new beginnings. Four years is not significantly younger than me, but it feels like a lifetime separates us. She's fresh with promise while I feel washed up at thirty-three.

"Do you have a second to talk?"

"For you today, I have whatever you need." I save her extra

steps and quickly stride in her direction, a smile once again on my face, though when I look at her, it comes naturally. She's happy. Genuinely happy. And despite being from old money and a bit socially awkward, her new husband is pretty great as well. He'll fit in nicely with the family. I stop when I get to her side, careful not to step on her dress. "How can I serve you?" I tease, resisting the urge to pull on one of the curly locks around her face.

She takes both my hands in hers, and there's a hint of moisture in her eyes.

My teasing fades into concern. "What's wrong? You're supposed to be nothing but blissfully ecstatic today."

"I am," she assures me, then swallows. "But I miss my big brother."

"I'm right here." I run a thumb across the back of her hand. "I promised you I'd stay . . . for a few hours at least."

"That's not what I mean. You're going back to Nashville."

"Not till after the New Year," I remind her, though why she's worried about my schedule is beyond me. "And besides, you'll be so wrapped up in newlywed joy that you won't even notice."

"I'll notice." She looks down at her jeweled slippers and back up at me. "I need to tell you something. And I need you to remember that you can't be mad at the bride on her wedding day."

I chuckle at the way she bites her lip just like she used to when we'd get in trouble as kids. "Yes, I know, Mom gave all of us the lecture this morning."

"Yeah, well, Mom doesn't exactly know what I did. Or didn't do, I guess."

"I'm not following."

Cassie blows out a quick breath and then squares her shoulders for an oncoming fight I have no intention of giving her. "You haven't come home in years, Cam. *Years*. It wasn't unreasonable that I didn't think you'd be here for this day."

I'm a little hurt by her lack of faith in me but brush off the emotion. "No, I guess it wasn't. Though I still don't get why you're worried about this right now."

She continues to chew on that lip, shifting from one foot to the other until finally she speaks again. "Before you agreed to come, I invited Darcy. And then after we got your yes, I was supposed to rescind the invitation, out of respect for you . . . but I didn't." She must have heard my sudden intake of breath, because she quickly continues, "I'm sorry, Cam, but she's like a sister to me and—" She pauses to sigh, and I can already feel the heat inching up my arms and into my neck. "Well, I saw her when I was walking down the aisle. She's here."

The words rip through my middle like a punch. More than a punch, a knife tearing right through the flesh. Tears well up in her carefully lined eyes, and despite the tension pounding against my temple like a sledgehammer, I work to keep my expression passive.

"I hate that I only see you once a year in some strange town." Cassie steps closer, apparently eager to explain her monumental betrayal. "And now that I'm married, it's only going to get harder to stay in touch. So you need to get over whatever it was that happened between the two of you. Because I'm not stupid, and I know no matter what lame excuse you come up with each year, you don't come home be-cause of her." Cassie's hands feel like ice inside mine as she squeezes tighter. "I know I'm ambushing you and I am really sorry for that, but I also knew this was the only way I could get you two in the same place at the same time." With that, she leans up and kisses my cheek. "I love you, Cam. Please do this. Please talk to her . . . for me." Then she picks up her skirt and carefully makes her way to her husband, who is purposely not looking my way. He must know, and I wonder who else participated in the entrapment.

I don't watch the two of them leave. I can't seem to do anything but stand there, my suit now suffocating with the shock pulsing from my chest. On instinct, I look around the outdoor venue, glancing from face to face to make sure Darcy's isn't one of them.

I squeeze my eyes shut and shove my hand in my pocket. My fingers curl around the small pillbox I stashed there, ready if needed. I hadn't wanted to use them today. They make me drowsy and often too relaxed to process everything going on around me. And today especially, Cassie deserves more than a half-present brother. Still, I rub at the plastic protecting the fragile escape and try to keep my breathing steady. *You're all right,* I chant in my head. *This is just a moment. It will pass.*

A heavy hand falls on my shoulder and I twist around, ready for a fight, half expecting to see Bryson's face staring back at me, rigid and unapologetic. But it's Caleb who's now backing away, his hands up in the air. "Whoa. Sorry, I didn't mean to startle you."

I shake off the adrenaline and try to regain my bearings before I fall apart in front of my brother. "You're fine. I'm just a little jumpy, I guess. Too many people."

He eyes me suspiciously but doesn't push the issue. Caleb and I have a unique relationship. We're the only two boys sandwiched between sisters, but despite there being a mere two years between us, we've never been especially close. I'm a dreamer, and he's a realist. Ironically, I've always kind of felt sorry for him. He seemed stuck to me. Grown up and married before I even finished college. And yet now I feel mildly envious. What I saw as stagnant is simply contentment. His life is simple, but he's happy. He loves his wife, his nine-to-five job, and has no aspirations of being anywhere but where he is right now.

I don't think I've ever felt that way, even on my best day.

"I thought maybe you'd like to grab our seats. This thing's going to be big enough that there's a good chance even someone like you might blend." He eyes the venue hopefully. Caleb hates crowds, another trait I never understood until now.

I should be able to do this. In four years, my family has asked nothing of me. They've sacrificed holidays and vacations to give me the space I needed, supported every decision, even the ones they didn't understand. I should be able to give them today. No matter how difficult. And yet I don't move. "I need a few minutes. I'll just catch you inside."

"You sure?"

"Yeah." I nod, fighting the nausea that hasn't stopped swirling since Darcy's name left Cassie's lips.

He'd have to be blind not to see I'm struggling, but Caleb isn't one to press his nose where it isn't wanted, and thankfully he walks away.

I revel in the silence, praying it gives me the strength I need.

A part of me wonders why she would come. The two of us didn't exactly walk away on good terms, both having all the ammunition we needed to annihilate each other with words, thus ending a twenty-nine-year friendship. But it's the other part of me that I loathe. It's the part that understands why she's here, that feels a mild sense of hope that we will find each other in the crowd. The part that still misses her after all this time. The part Cassie must have known still existed deep inside.

My mind begins a ping-pong of memories. Sleepovers

when we were too young to have any idea there was a difference between boys and girls. The kiss we attempted in my bedroom closet when we were twelve just because we were curious what it would feel like. Taking our first long-distance trip after getting our driver's licenses and then holding her hand when she called her mom to tell her she hit a curb and busted the tire. Graduating from high school and college. Seeing her at my first gig when I finally decided to join Bryson and his band. And then the beginning of the end, watching them kiss and knowing I couldn't support the pairing. And finally the goodbye in her bedroom. Hearing her tell me she wanted out. That she didn't even know who she was without me. That all this time she'd felt suffocated by me.

You'd think that would be the worst, but it wasn't. Despite my resentment, despite his taking the girl I loved, the worst is still the memory of Bryson telling me he was quitting. Watching him walk away from Black Carousel and from our brand-new signing contract. His hand outstretched, his placating words as he told me the band was mine. Then his arm dropping when I refused to shake the hand of the man I now considered an enemy.

I guess that was better than the alternative. If I'd seen the long-term impact at the time, I might have punched him. But I didn't recognize the genius behind his gesture. He'd willingly given me his future and taken mine in the process.

That night I'd driven away with my head pressed to the tour bus window and vowed never to think of either of them again.

My word isn't worth much these days, I guess, because the flood of thoughts is suddenly deafening. Four years of careful denial and locked-away emotion are now beating their way through every one of my senses.

My heart races as I feel the desperation coming on. I need

to get myself under control before I'm any good to my family in there. Despite the cooling air, I rip off my suit coat and welcome the release of pent-up heat.

Coat fisted in my hand, I walk toward the parking lot and the rented car that will take me away from this place. I know I can't leave, but I also don't know how to stay here and be a bigger person than I am.

Sweat beads on my forehead, and I push my strides faster. Not quite a run, but close.

I don't even see the collision coming until it's too late. Until her body is pressed against my chest and my arms are snaking around her to keep us both from falling to the ground.

"I'm so sorry," I croak out, the surprise and alarm somehow jolting my heart back to a normal rhythm. I feel a strained chuckle form in my throat as I pull back and she rights herself. "I wasn't paying attention."

And then she looks up, and my world goes back to tilting.

"Cameron." It's a question and a statement in one. Her eyes are wide, first with shock and then with a pain I recognize down to my core. "I . . . I was hoping I'd run into you . . . just not quite so literally."

Leave it to Darcy to make a joke out of this. I should laugh. I would have, years ago. But all I can do is stare at the woman who ripped my heart out. She hasn't changed at all, unless being more beautiful than I remember counts. Her chestnut hair is longer, maybe four inches, and her skin darker like she spends a lot of time outside, but her face, her eyes, especially those electric bluish-green eyes, are exactly the same.

Her smile fades when I don't respond, and her hands clutch a small stuffed animal like a stress ball. "How have you been?"

I fight for calm, fight for the man who's stood in front of thousands and performed, even when exhausted and so sick I could barely sing. I'm strong enough to do this. "Good," I finally say, though there's little volume in my words. "What about you?"

She swallows as we both struggle to navigate this completely unfamiliar awkwardness between us. For nearly thirty years we could say or do anything around each other with no worry. We had an unspoken language. An ability to read each other's thoughts and feelings. Now just speaking feels like a monumental accomplishment. "I'm good," she finally says. "I'm working with a nonprofit rescue foundation. We just expanded our facility."

Darcy's love for dogs exceeds anyone's I've ever known. "That's great. I'm happy for you." I step back, planning on this being the end of our forced congenial conversation. "Well . . . I . . . need to . . ." I point behind me to the parking lot and try to come up with some kind of excuse.

"I saw you on TV," she blurts out and removes the space I'd gained between us. "Congratulations. A Grammy is huge." She smiles at me, and I'm taken aback by how my heart twitches, the ice that's hardened over four years trembling a little. "And your Jimmy Fallon debut was incredible. I laughed so hard, Piper started howling. She is known for her sense of humor."

I can picture it. Her curled up with her little dog in her lap, giggling as Jimmy and I did a voice battle that of course he was always going to win.

"Thanks." My voice is softer now, and I fight the urge to smile along with her. "You can't imagine the teasing I endured afterward. Especially from Caleb."

She laughs, sweet and gentle. A laugh I've heard a thousand times. Could it really be this easy to pick up again?

After so many years of silence? She must sense my question because her smile fades, and she watches me with a sorrow I understand all too well. "Cam . . . I . . ." But her words are stopped by a miniature figure slamming into her legs. The *oomph* she sighs nearly breaks the rest of the ice between us, and on instinct I reach out in case she needs steadying. She doesn't. She heaves the toddler into her arms as if she's done it a million times and turns him to face me. "This is my son, Charlie. Charlie, this is one of Mommy's oldest friends. Can you say hi?"

Charlie watches me with his mother's eyes but doesn't say hi. He sticks a thumb in his mouth and sets his head on her shoulder, his gaze never leaving mine.

My throat aches with a fire I didn't think was possible. Except for the eyes, he's the spitting image of his father. Dark curly hair, olive skin, and that stubborn set to his mouth that no doubt has made parenthood a challenge.

Darcy lifts the animal in her hand, and the boy takes it eagerly, rubbing the cloth over his face with a sigh. "Sorry. He didn't get much of a nap today."

I need to say something, want to say something, but the minute my voice returns, a shadow covers our little threesome.

"Sorry, babe. He got away from me." Bryson's jog is mild and halts the minute our eyes make contact. "Cam." Unlike Darcy, he doesn't smile. Instead, he reaches his arm out and wraps it around his family possessively. A simple gold band on his left hand gleams in the setting sun.

I want to growl. Want to shout a curse and remind him that the family he's now clinging to is supposed to be mine. I don't. Instead, I lock my hands into fists and stare at the man who stole my life. "Bryson." My voice is cold now, the softening that began with Darcy's smile long gone. Tension builds between us, and it rockets my heartbeat again. I can't stop it this time. Not without help. There's too much anger. Too many unsaid words between us. "I need to go grab something from my car for Cassie," I say, backing away. "I'll see you at the reception." It's a lie I'm not even trying to hide. I'm not going in there. Cassie can hate me, but she'll just have to understand.

Darcy watches me retreat with a regret I refuse to try to interpret. This was her doing. All of it. I won't mourn what was lost. I refuse to give either of them the satisfaction.

I turn around and continue down the hill, my chest burning so badly my knees nearly buckle. I can't do this here. Not in plain sight. I search for shelter and find an alcove in a brick retaining wall. My eyes have gone blurry, and it's all I can do to stumble forward until I'm completely hidden and my back is pressed against the hard masonry. Cold from the bare ground seeps into my pants, and I kick my leg straight to access my pocket. It's a struggle, but I get my hands to function enough to grab the pillbox and fumble with the tight clip. Finally it opens, and I toss the pills to the back of my throat. My eyes squeeze shut while blood pounds in my ears. It echoes like a broken speaker, the vibrations sending a shooting pain into my temples. I cradle my head, my eyes stinging from the agony, both physical and emotional.

"Um, mister . . . are you okay? Do you need me to call 911?"

The voice is muted through the ringing in my ears, but it still startles me. I glance up, expecting to see someone standing over me. There's no one. I turn my head, and seated two feet away on the other side of the alcove is a girl. One that can't be older than twelve or thirteen. She has a half-eaten plate of food in her lap and is staring at me apprehensively as if she'll be expected to perform CPR any second.

"No," I whisper, still fighting the nausea clawing up my esophagus. "I just need a minute."

"You sure, 'cause your face is sort of green. And I'm one of those sympathy pukers. So if you hurl, I'm going to as well."

A bubble of laughter forms in my gut. "I'm not going to throw up." At least I hope the pills kick in fast enough to thwart the usual reaction. I take two more deep inhales and let my head fall back against the wall. A tingling has started in my limbs, the first sign that the medication is taking effect. Soon my pulse will be normal, my muscles relaxed, and the roller coaster of irrational fear will fade into a memory.

She's quiet while I take the few seconds I need and perks up the minute I turn my head in her direction. "Sorry. I didn't know anyone was out here."

"Obviously," she deadpans, then gives me the same look my public relations rep does when I haven't worn the appropriate attire for the occasion. I can't even imagine what I must look like now. My shirt is drenched against my back, my pants dirty and wrinkled.

Poor girl must think I'm a psychopath. "I didn't mean to frighten you." I attempt to sit up straighter, but my legs shake and tremble. Oh well, at this point, what's five more minutes?

"You didn't frighten me. I've taken self-defense classes with my mom three different times." Simple. Direct. Much too much like another adolescent girl I once knew. "Not that you're much of a threat . . . at least not right now." She waves a hand at my disheveled state and somehow zaps away any lingering awkwardness.

That is until she starts studying my face like a dermatologist. "What?" I lean away from her cautiously.

"I know you." She studies me closer, then snaps her fingers. "Yep. I wasn't sure at first because you were hyperventilating and all, but now I'm certain it's you."

"You know me?" She's vaguely familiar, but I can't place from where. Maybe because her hair is like two shower curtains over most of her features.

"Yeah. Your face is on my mom's phone all the time." She sets down her plate and clarifies. "She's a big fan. Has all three of your albums. Even the indie one."

I groan. Great, just great. "Let me guess. 'A Decade of Love' is her favorite."

If she deciphered the venom in my voice, I can't tell. She simply shrugs. "I don't know. They all sound the same to me."

I chuckle. "Thanks."

"No offense or anything. I'm sure you're a great musician. I'm just more into rap. Lecrae, NF, Tedashii, that kind of stuff. Mom's strict about what I listen to." She rolls her eyes. "She's strict about everything, but those artists have been"—she air-quotes—"approved."

Maybe it's the absurdity of the situation, but somehow this blunt kid is actually making me feel better. "Where is your mom now?"

"Who knows?" She sighs. "She's one of those super chatty butterfly types. You know, the kind who can walk up to any stranger and dazzle them with a hair toss."

"And you're not a hair-tossing dazzler?" I ask, grinning.

She grunts a laugh that is anything but ladylike and pulls her knees to her chest. I immediately notice the tennis shoes.

I point to her feet. "Nice sneakers. I bet half the women here are wishing they'd done the same thing."

"Thanks." She clicks her feet together three times and sits up proudly. "I thought so too." Her phone buzzes at her side and she picks it up, reads, rolls her eyes, and texts back. "I swear my mom has Spidey sense. It's like she knows the minute I talk about her." She sets her phone down. "I told her where to find me, though I didn't mention you. It will be fun

57

to watch her face when she realizes I'm sitting with the great Cameron Lee." Her eyes brighten. "She's going to flip. I'm telling you . . . the woman is borderline obsessed."

Fantastic. The last thing I need right now is a gushing fangirl to end what is becoming a miserable evening. "Sorry, kid. We're going to have to save the introductions for another time." I scramble to my feet and brush off the dirt clinging to my pants. "I need to get back, and you should too. It's getting dark."

"I'm not a baby. I'll be in high school next year." She scoffs, and I realize I've somehow offended her. "And I haven't been afraid of the dark since I was seven."

"I didn't mean . . ." I stumble over my words, having no idea how to articulate what I want to say. "It's just that you really shouldn't make a habit of talking to strangers, especially hidden out here. The world is not always . . . kind."

"Hey, you crashed *my* party. Not the other way around." She stands too, abandoning her plate. "And what else was I supposed to do when a guy falls down and looks like he's about to go into cardiac arrest?"

Once again, laughter bubbles in my chest. Real laughter. The kind I've forgotten exists. "You go find another grown-up to help. Or did your mom not teach you about 'stranger danger'?"

She crosses her arms in defiance, but I see the hidden smirk. This girl apparently likes to argue. "I don't know. Why don't you ask her yourself?" She lifts her chin. "She's right there."

I swallow a groan, knowing I'm now stuck playing the gracious star for the next ten minutes, and turn around. But the figure stumbling over the rocky path is not exactly what I pictured the girl's music-obsessed mom to look like. This woman is . . . well, stunning. Her dress rises a little as she walks, exposing slim bare legs that end elegantly in sexy black heels.

"See what I mean . . . dazzling."

The kid's right. At least the part I can see is. Her face is down, concentrating on the ground like it might swallow her up. Her dark hair is thick and long, hanging down to nearly the middle of her back. The dress she's wearing is enough to stop traffic, though somehow she makes it look classy.

"Is this your way of torturing me for forcing you to come? I'm flailing around like a baby giraffe." The woman's voice is soft, laced with humor, not anger, and strangely very familiar. It curls in my stomach like I've somehow stumbled through time. I know why the minute she looks up and our eyes meet.

"Little Lexie?" My voice is barely recognizable. It's too elated, too surprised. How is this even possible? I turn from her to her teenage daughter and try to reconcile the pairing. The last time I saw Lexie was at her and Cassie's high school graduation, and she certainly didn't have a kid.

Lexie halts a few feet from us, and her eyes flit from mine to her daughter's face. "Cameron." She says it like I'm choking her. "I . . . um . . . hi." She exhales in shared wonderment. "How are you? I saw you during the ceremony and wondered if we'd get to talk, but wow. You're here"—her forehead wrinkles—"with my daughter."

Yep. It's definitely Lexie. Down to the flush in her cheeks, bright eyes, and nervous babble. Why I feel so relieved, I have no idea, but some unknown force moves me forward.

I don't stop, don't take her hand cordially or say a quick hello. Those actions all feel too small for the gratitude I feel that some things . . . some people never change. Before I can stop myself, I pass all bounds of social etiquette, take her into my arms, and hug her like a lifeline.

SIX

Lexie

In my dreams, I'm eloquent and debonair. In my dreams, I don't fall off my shoes trying to walk or flush beet-red the minute he says my name. In my dreams, I don't nearly choke when he hugs me or clumsily smell the collar of his shirt.

But this is not my dreams. This is real life. And somehow, Cameron Lee has his arms wrapped around my waist, his chest pressed against mine, and his perfect, sensual, beautiful mouth inches from my ear.

"It's so good to see you," he whispers, and torturous goose bumps fill my neck and arms. I should say something, but I don't trust my voice not to sound like a croaking frog. He releases me and steps back, grinning. "How long has it been?"

Eleven years and five months, almost to the day. But who's counting? "A while," I finally manage to say without so much as a crack. I nearly high-five myself for the accomplishment. "Why aren't you at the reception?"

"I, um, well, you know how those things go. No one misses you as long as the bride and groom are there." He shoves his hands into his pockets but doesn't stop looking at me, like he's meeting me for the first time.

It's glorious and unnerving, and I find myself fidgeting first with my dress, then my hair. "When did you fly in?" There. Perfectly normal question. Not even a hint of spaz.

Cameron's smile widens, and my favorite feature appears, the one that only comes when he's truly happy. Two delicious dimples in the sides of his mouth. "Thursday."

"Oh, good. You've had some family time, then." I glance to Morgan, and her furrowed brow makes my fingers tingle. Maybe I'm not doing quite as well as I think I am. Perfect. Now I'm fidgeting even more. And why isn't she saying anything? I give her the *help me* glare, but she only grins and shakes her head. Oh, she is so going to pay for this.

"Lexie Walters." He says it like he still can't quite believe his eyes. "You look all grown up."

Butterflies surge in my stomach. Was that a big brother type of comment or an *I'm a man, you're a woman* comment? I can't tell. I play with the ends of my hair and pray I'm not making a complete fool of myself as I flirtatiously glance up through my eyelashes. "Yes, I am."

A heated silence ensues, until Cameron clears his throat. "So, um, what are you doing now? You were going to Tarleton for business, right?"

"I was, yes, but it didn't quite work out." I try to keep my voice chipper, especially with Morgan listening to our conversation. I don't want her to ever feel responsible for my life detour. I'd make the same decision a hundred times over if it meant keeping her. "I'm in property management now. It's a good fit for me."

His expression warms. "I can see that. You've always been really good with people." He sighs, and I try my best not to giddy-scream that not only did he remember me, but he actually has an opinion on my personality. "Time is a crazy thing, isn't it? Cassie's married. You have a daughter." He gets that same expression I saw during the ceremony. Happiness laced with loss.

I feel my heart swell. Feel the need to wrap him in my arms and tell him everything's going to be okay. Tell him I'm here for him if he needs a friend, because I know. I know exactly how it feels to be lost and alone.

"She's quite a kid," he says in a chuckle and glances at Morgan, who crosses her arms like she's ready to defend whatever is coming next. "Very honest."

I press a fist to my mouth, my face heating up more. "Oh, gosh. What did she say?"

Cameron's laughter is a balm to my cheeks, and I find a way to look up at him, even though it makes every bone in my body want to melt. "Nothing too incriminating."

Morgan glances at him like she's surprised he doesn't give me more details. There's a hint of respect in the look, and despite my desperate desire to ask for a line-by-line transcript of the conversation, I let it go. Morgan's not the kind of girl one wins over easily. It took Mason nearly six months of browbeating before she treated him like more than an intruder.

"She didn't mention your husband, though. Will he be wondering where the two of you are?"

Am I hallucinating or did Cameron's voice hitch on the word *husband*?

"No. Not married," I say quickly, unwilling for him to get the wrong impression for even a second, and show him my very unadorned left hand as if he needs proof. "No boyfriend either. Single. Very single." Morgan's eyes widen to the size of saucers, as if I'm right at this moment growing an extra head. I may as well be. My face burns so hot I almost see heat waves flowing from the surface of my skin. "I mean, not that you asked for that much detail." Oh. My. Word. I need to be muzzled. Right now.

Cameron grins again, and I'm sure he's trying his best not to laugh at me. Honorable as always.

"So, are you heading back?" I look behind me at the reception barn, my heart fluttering. In my dreams, we danced all night. Fast ones, slow ones. It made no difference. He twirled me around, and we laughed because it made us both stumble. I tossed my shoes in the corner, but Cameron was so light on his feet that it didn't matter I was spinning barefoot. People made circles around us, clapping as he channeled Patrick Swayze and lifted me high above his head. Then, when we were drenched with sweat and beaming with so much happiness it spilled into the air around us, he walked me to my car. His hands gripped my cheeks as he told me he'd always secretly loved me and then kissed me good-night.

I feel my hand on my chest at the same time a contented sigh escapes my lips. It awakens me. Brings me back to the present and the two giving me blank stares. Morgan's is horror-filled. Cameron's is confused, but there's still amusement there.

I pray for the ground to swallow me whole. "Sorry. I just remembered I forgot to do something at work, and it took me out of the moment for a second." I find a smile through the utter embarrassment. "Um, the reception. Are you going? Stephen and Cassie had just finished the first dance when I came out here."

When Cameron's mouth tightens and he looks down at his shoes, I realize I've said the exact wrong thing. But it's too late. The energy bouncing between us has fizzled, the air now tense with unspoken words. He's hurting and I don't know why. Cameron's always been close to his family.

The schoolgirl drunk on fantasy kisses disappears, and I

feel my protective side come soaring to the surface. Morgan calls it my "lioness face." The one I get when anyone dares to hurt someone I care about. "Or we can just stay out here. Enjoy the beauty and this great weather for a while."

"Actually . . . I think the night is probably over for me." He glances at Morgan again. They share a look of understanding, and I catch a glimpse of compassion in her expression. "I'm not feeling all that well."

I grip my tiny purse, trying not to sound completely disappointed. "I have Motrin and allergy medicine if you need it."

Cameron only smiles, but it's weak. Fake. No dimples. No sparkle to his eyes. "Thanks, but neither of those is going to cure my issue." He picks up his rumpled jacket from the ground and steps close to Morgan, hand outstretched. "Morgan. It was nice to meet you."

She grips his hand and quirks that sarcastic brow of hers. "I guess this means we're not strangers anymore."

He shakes his head the same way I do when she somehow wins an argument I didn't even realize we were having. "I guess not." He takes a step closer to me, stops for a lingering second, then squeezes my arm. "Please tell Cassie I left and that . . . I'm sorry." The sadness in his voice leaks through my skin and makes my heart hurt. His hand releases its pressure, slides delicately down my arm, until his fingers wrap around mine. "It was really good to see you, Lexie." A quick tight squeeze and that's it.

No dance. No confession of love. No good-night kiss.

I watch him walk away, back straight, shoulders hunched, until the top of his head disappears down the hill.

Frustration scours me. Makes my skin tingle and my breath come in short, angry spurts. Why do I do this to myself every time? Dream the impossible? Let myself believe for one achingly wonderful minute that the fantasy might just happen.

"What . . . the heck . . . was that?"

I spin around to face my daughter, who obviously found her voice box again. "What do you mean?"

"Are you kidding me? Did you not hear yourself?" Her mouth opens and closes in awed wonder. "You were a freak, Mom. A total and complete raging lunatic." She presses her hand to her head as if trying to combat the image of me completely blowing it. "Where was the hair flip and the whimsical flirting smile that makes men drool?" Her grunt of laughter makes me bury my head in my hands.

"Oh stop. I feel stupid enough as it is."

But she's doubled over, her laughter filling the air with a sweet noise that's too addicting to fight. I giggle. A little at first. Then a lot. And we're both adolescents now. Her teasing me while I try to smack her arm and make her take it back.

And then a new pain hits, because there was a time when my sister and I would do the same thing. Over the same silly crush I can't seem to let go of. But maybe this is why. These feelings are safe. Familiar. They are the only good thing that's still here from a time when we were a family of four. Before my sister abandoned us. Before my mom and dad left this earth. Before Morgan.

"Well, Mom, I will give you this," Morgan says, patting my back. "You certainly know how to make a lasting impression."

SEVEN

Cameron

T shut my front door with a defeated groan and lay my jacket over the closest armrest. Being home—or in this house, I guess—slightly improves my mood. The sting of failure is a little less biting, and the resolve to move forward still lingers in the air, reminding me there's more to come than disappointment and ghosts of the past.

My cuff links are the next item I shed, setting them carefully on the dining table still covered with a dust sheet. I'd meant to remove them all, but I've barely been here long enough to sleep the last two days, let alone exert the effort needed to make this place feel lived in. I grip the edge of the table with both hands and breathe a huge sigh of relief.

It's over. This day—the crowd, the dread pooling in my gut for weeks now—is finally over.

Maybe now my family can settle into some kind of normalcy instead of the tiptoeing around, which hasn't ceased since they first said hello. The reunion had been less invasive than I expected, likely due to Mom and Dad having Cassie to focus on, but I still got the array of questions. How am I doing? Am I getting enough sleep? And the one Dad always seems to slip in there: *"How's your spiritual life?"*

I shake my head and push off the table. My spiritual life has been nonexistent for a while now. Not strained like it was for years when God refused to answer my prayers, but flat-out extinct. Of course, I didn't say that to my father, who serves as an elder at Grace Community. No, to him I said the same as I have for years now—I'm struggling but hanging in there. I'm sure he wonders the same thing that I do. Can one still call it struggling after this many years, or is that last flicker of faith snuffed out for good? It feels gone, but so does everything else I once cherished, so how can I really judge?

I roll my sleeves while I make my way to the refrigerator, flipping on lights as I go. It takes three different switches before I find the right one. Mom sent me home with enough food last night to keep me fed for a week, and Kelly had already stocked the fridge with mineral water and the basic essentials. I grab a fresh bottle and walk toward the stairs, ready to put an end to this forever-long day.

But a flickering light stops me in my tracks. I pause, glancing out the back window that I hardly noticed until now. It's large, four huge panes of glass, and all are in desperate need of a good exterior cleaning. I step closer and try to peer through the dirt smudges. I must have accidentally turned the outdoor lights on. A halo of cream attempts to highlight the porch but barely shows a railing and three steps. Across the yard, there are pockets of dangling lights, probably from a string of them that has mostly burnt out.

For the first time ever, I unlock the bolt and pull on the handle. It opens easily, not like the front door that requires a push and sometimes a good swift kick. I open the screen that's also locked and make my way to a porch structure so grand it feels impossible that I didn't know it was there.

My breath hitches as I take in the full view of the property. It's gorgeous. The yard is easily an acre or more in size and dotted with beautiful English gardens and large trees and evergreens. I slide my phone from my pocket and turn on the flashlight, hoping to see more than the haze the dirt-coated lights provide. My gaze pauses on the tree farthest away. I step down from the porch onto a pathway made from flagstones. There's something in that tree, but I can't quite make it out. My flashlight looms in front of me, revealing just enough to keep me from tripping.

Finally, I reach the bottom of the trunk and look up. It's a house. Not a small fort or a box of plywood like most tree houses; no, this thing is elaborate. Pitched roof, walk-around deck, two windows with shutters, and an arched doorway. I can't tell the color, but I imagine it's very likely painted something equally as picturesque. Whoever built this thing did so from scratch and with a lot of sweat equity. Probably the man in most of the pictures inside the house. The one with a broad smile who always seemed to be hugging someone right when the photo was snapped. A man who had a full life, with a wife and kids, and probably never once thought he was doomed to be lonely forever.

I place a hand on the ladder but stop mid-step as I consider my attire and the likelihood of running into some sort of animal or insect in the dark. Explorations will have to wait for tomorrow, but I feel a hint of something rise in my chest at the thought—anticipation.

It's odd, but before tonight, it'd been over a year since I felt the sensation, and now it's come twice in less than two hours. The first shockingly when I realized it was Lexie Walters stumbling toward us.

I step back, running a hand through my hair. My physical reaction to her was . . . unexpected. Not that I didn't enjoy Lexie's company growing up. I did. In fact, she was the only friend of Cassie's I could stand to be around. The others would giggle and talk nonstop about boys and hairstyles like silly little lumps on the couch. Lexie was different. She'd jump at the chance to play a game or go outside or even help my mom in the kitchen.

She affected all of us, especially Cassie, who often saw the world as half empty. Lexie was perpetually cheerful, optimistic, and complimentary. She made you feel as if you could conquer the world and almost expected you to do it. But she was a kid. Likable, but still a kid.

Tonight, there was nothing childish about her. Her skin was delicate and soft. Her eyes, wide and full of a compassion I actually believed was real. I hadn't wanted to let go. Hadn't wanted to leave, especially after she made a point to emphasize her singleness.

I feel a rare smile come at the memory. And just as quickly force it away. Pursuing her would be selfish. If history has proven anything, it's that I'm incapable of deep meaningful relationships. Someone like Lexie deserves more than the shell of a man I've become. Maybe in a different dimension. One where I hadn't spent nearly thirty years loving the wrong girl.

Heat rises up my neck and flushes my cheeks. I don't want to be out here thinking of Darcy. She's not supposed to exist in this place that only five minutes ago felt like a sanctuary. My strides quicken as I return to the house and slam the back door hard enough that it bounces open again. I need to return to the plan. Focus on the music and find myself again.

I grab my laptop and tear off the table's stupid white sheet, now mocking me that even this place belongs to someone else. My cuff links scatter across the floor and probably under some piece of furniture that hasn't been moved in a decade. I don't care that they cost a small fortune or that I painstakingly went to three different jewelers to find the perfect pair. None of that stuff matters anymore. I'd pay any sum of money to make the echo in my head disappear. To hear the music like I used to. To feel passion and happiness again.

But neither of those emotions can be bought, so I'm back to square one. Back to the only route that feels even a little promising.

My computer screen brightens, and I immediately pull up a search engine. If I am to find my old self again, I must remember what it feels like to be that person. And what I loved most back then was being onstage. I click through my favorite music venues in Dallas and find a good indie concert for next weekend. I need the desperation of a band not yet signed. The eye of the tiger. The hunger that only comes when your dream feels both a breath and a mountain away. It's a feeling so invasive, so penetrating that it touches every person in the room, and more than ever, I need to submerge myself inside of that yearning.

I check out their website and study the layout and marketing, both of which are subpar, and feel a sense of compassion for the young men. There's so much to know, so much I wish someone had taught me before that first contract. And especially before that second one. The one currently clamped around my neck and threatening to squeeze.

I shut the laptop and thread my hands over my head.

This pursuit is a long shot. I know it, but I have no other options or ideas. I close my eyes and sigh, exhaustion setting in. My heart knows to pray. To seek guidance and help when all feels so jumbled. But my head can't seem to allow it. It's not just Darcy and Bryson I'm angry at. I'm angry at God, at myself. At every step I took that I felt sure was in God's will at the time. Now I stand at a cliff, teetering over it, barely balancing as I wait for the inevitable fall.

Why would I ever go back to the One who led me to this horrible place to begin with?

I wouldn't. I don't. Instead, I stand up, turn off each and every light, and feel grateful that tomorrow brings a new day.

EIGHT

Lexie

I've never been especially good in the kitchen. Sure, I've tried printing out recipes or attempting those mouthwatering dishes that pop up on my social media page, but rarely have I found success behind an apron. Morgan says it's my propensity to get bored within ten minutes of starting a task. I chalk it up to becoming a mother at nineteen. Survival mode isn't usually the easiest time to develop a new skill.

But despite the barely edible, slightly burned, or simply so-disgusting-you-have-to-trash-it meals in my portfolio, I still feel guilty for once again feeding my daughter fast food. "So, we should probably talk about what the next few weeks are going to look like. Between work and the house, I'm not going to have a lot of free time." Mason and I have already made great progress in a short amount of time—ripping out carpet, tearing out paneling, and busting through walls—but there is still so much to do.

"Tell me something I don't already know," she says, a mangled piece of burger winking at me from her overstuffed mouth. "You've barely been home since you bought that stupid house."

Her comment makes the guilt I've already been dealing with triple. "Well, you could always help us," I offer.

She rolls her eyes like I just suggested she jump off a cliff. The first day, Morgan thought it was fun to beat away at the Sheetrock but has since opted to stay home alone in the evenings. I don't like it, but I also don't think it's fair to ask her to sit in a house with no internet or TV.

"Come on, Morgan. Come with me tonight. Be a part of this new venture with me." Which is what I had hoped would happen. That Morgan and I would bond over paint-color choices and dusty clothes. Instead, she's only pulled further and further away. Even when we are together lately, she'd rather be on her phone than talk to me. "We used to do everything together. Remember? We'd have spa days and watch movies. This is different, but we'd still be together." I hate that I am practically begging my daughter to spend time with me, but I'll resort to just about anything at this point.

"We haven't had a spa day since I was ten," she groans. "But that's the problem. You still see me as this little girl. I'm not."

My insides twist with anticipation of yet another argument. "I don't see you as a little girl."

"Really? Then why do all my friends have the internet on their phone? And social media? You say you love me, but you won't even give me the basic tools for a reasonable social life."

And here we go again, the real issue finally coming to the surface. "Morgan, we have been over this a million times."

"I just don't understand why you don't trust me. I've never done anything to make you think I'm going to do something bad."

"It's not about trust." And it truly isn't. It's about her emotional health. "And not all your friends have unlimited access. I know for a fact that Melissa's mom is just as strict about her daughter's phone as I am."

"Nah-ah," she whines. "Melissa's mom lets her have email."

"You have email."

"Through the school laptop! They block every address that comes in outside of the district."

My eyes narrow, a flutter of concern in my stomach. "And who do you need to talk to that isn't at your school?"

"Half the kids at youth group."

My shoulders relax. "Then have them text you."

"You monitor my texts."

I simply shrug, feeling no need to apologize for being pro-tective. "If it's something I shouldn't read, then you have no need to send it."

She snarls and returns to her burger, adolescent metabo-lism winning out over the need to argue. And even if she were to try to go to the mattress on the issue, it's pointless. I won't budge on the internet rules—for far more reasons than just cyberbullying and "like" count obsession. I've seen the work of the beast firsthand. It's how my sister met her no-good, cheating, bottom-feeding boyfriend after Mom got sick. The one who got her into drugs and alcohol. The one who took her depression struggles to a life-threatening level. The one whose inevitable abandonment of their relationship left her permanently scarred.

Morgan's had enough in her life working against her. She doesn't need to add images of fake perfection to make her question the, yes, unconventional but solid, loving household we've established.

"Someday you'll understand why I'm so protective. In fact, I have no doubt they will do studies on your generation and show exactly how damaging all those apps are for you."

"Whatever. I don't even know why I bother." She pushes her plate away and stands from the table.

"Where are you going? We're not done talking."

"I want to ride my bike before it gets dark."

I lift a brow. "To where exactly?"

"Nowhere. Just around." Her face flushes, a dead giveaway that she's not telling the whole truth.

And worse, I know exactly why. "Morgan, I've made my stance on this subject very clear. Nanni's house is rented now." A fact I confirmed last week when I saw a new mattress being hauled through the front door. A cleaning crew was there the next day and then a locksmith, making my spare key obsolete. I haven't met the new renter, who supposedly moved in last week, but I did hear from the neighbors that he was young and male. Two more reasons why my daughter will not be hanging out in the backyard. "I'm sorry, but you cannot go to the tree house anymore."

"But his car is gone. I checked when we drove by there on our way home. And the side gate is unlocked."

How am I even having to explain this to her? "I don't care if it's wide open with a welcome mat. You don't go trespassing through some stranger's backyard with or without him being home. It's not our property, and it's not safe."

"Might I remind you that you didn't say one word about my wandering at the wedding or talking to a certain guy whom I've never met before. Or does that exception only apply to rock stars?"

Humiliation pushes away the growing annoyance, and I rest my head in my hands. I feel too tired to fight. Too disappointed to pull up even one of my mother's cheerful quotes. I only got ten minutes with him. Ten horrifically embarrassing minutes and then Cameron was gone. Along with all the anticipation I'd been clinging to. He probably hopped the first plane out, lounging in first class with a mimosa and telling stories about his sister's crazy friend who wouldn't stop blushing. If I hadn't had the house to focus on yesterday, I might have died of embarrassment. At least Mason was kind and didn't chant "I told you so" while we worked. In fact, he didn't mention the wedding at all—a gift I'm forever grateful for.

"What do you want me to say?" I sigh, looking back up at her.

"I want you to recognize how hard it is for me to just sit at home all day. At least when I had the tree house, I felt like I wasn't in prison." She crosses her arms and pouts like a toddler, and sometimes I wonder if we are going backward. It sure has felt that way lately.

And maybe that's why the last of my patience snaps. "You know what? You're right. You have been home alone far too much. You're going with me tonight."

"But, Mom!"

"No. Sorry. You've made your point loud and clear. You don't need to spend another night alone in this house."

She must know she's on the verge of an even more severe punishment and opts to keep her mouth shut as she grabs her plate from the table and storms off to her room.

I lower my head to my hands and question every decision I feel so unqualified to make. I hate arguing with her, especially this close to the anniversary of when both of our lives were forever changed. She may not remember the years of perpetual nightmares, wet beds, and separation anxiety, but I still do, and in full vivid clarity. Her thirteen-year-old brain can't register that while for some, the holiday season is magical and cathartic, for us it always equals pain and strife.

I've learned to recognize mine, fighting against the sadness at every turn. Morgan doesn't remember enough to know the darker reason behind her extra bit of sass and emotion. But it comes anyway, like an unwanted package delivered right on schedule.

Mason runs his forearm across his brow to wipe at a fresh sheen of sweat while I once again haul splintered wood and crushed tile out to the construction dumpster in the driveway. We've moved to the bathroom. The next stop on our demolition tour. The downstairs living and dining rooms are practically gutted, minus a few support posts that will also go away once the new beams go in. Kitchen work is next and by far the hardest, but Mason says we're right on schedule, so fingers crossed.

I return with a bottle of cold water for each of us and a desperate need to get off my feet. "Let's take a break. My lungs feel like they might explode, even with this stupid dust mask on."

He nods, takes a long swig of the clear liquid, and drops his sledgehammer onto the bashed-in floor. We walk out of the confined space. It's a full bathroom, tiled floor to ceiling in glossy pink squares. There are already two larger bathrooms upstairs, so we're turning this one into a nice half bath, which is much more practical considering the size.

Mason drops down to sit on his large white Yeti cooler, the same one I just pulled the drinks from. He's as exhausted as I am, probably more so. He's worked twelve to fourteen hours a day this week to finish up his other house while tearing apart this one. No wonder the man has no girlfriend or even friends for that matter.

"We should stop. It's nearly ten," I offer, as much for him as for me.

He shakes his head. "You can go. I'll finish up."

My hackles rise. "I'm not leaving you here alone. If you stay, then I stay. We're partners."

"I know we are." He glances to the stairs. "But it's not just you I'm worried about."

"Oh." I stare at my gloved fingers.

"Lex." His voice is tentative, which is very unlike my cousin. I look back up, and his expression is a sweet mix of discomfort and concern. "I'm not exactly the most attentive person when it comes to charting other people's feelings, but even I could sense the tension when you two walked in."

"Yeah . . ." My stomach flips and tangles. "She's mad at me."

"Why?"

"Because I'm a terrible mom who spends my life trying to protect her. You know, horrible things like that." I force a smile I don't feel at all. "Truth is, holidays are hard . . . on both of us."

"Because of Annie?"

"Annie . . ." I dip my chin and pull at the leather covering my fingers. "Wow. I haven't thought about that nickname in years. She stopped letting us call her that in junior high. Said it was too babyish." She'd been Annaliese ever since. My older sister is named after our grandmother on my dad's side. Mason's aunt. Supposedly, there used to be large gatherings and Sunday dinners before the patriarchs passed, but I'd been too young to remember any of it.

"Sorry. I didn't mean to make you sad. It's just always what I called her." Mason and my sister are closer in age, having only a year between them. They played as kids and even had a few electives together in high school. That is, until she dropped out her senior year, exactly two months after Mom passed away.

"It's fine. I like thinking of how she was back then."

"She looks just like her." He stares again at the stairway, and I know he's referring to my daughter. And she does, more and more each day. It's both wonderful and haunting. His voice hesitates again, his eyes swinging back to mine. "Does Morgan ever ask about her?"

My mind stills on the question, and I shake my head quickly. "No. And I see no reason to bring up a situation that will only make her feel abandoned and unwanted."

"Lexie . . . she's thirteen." His voice holds admonishment, and my stomach twists. I don't like the turn of this conversation at all. "She's becoming a young woman with I'm sure a ton of emotions and questions. You should be concerned that she's not asking them."

"We're not like you, okay?" I stand and take in a frustrated breath. "We don't focus on the negative or on things in our past we can't control. We press on. Look ahead. Find beauty in today. That's what my mom taught me, and that's what I'm teaching my daughter."

"Okay, sorry I asked." He lifts his hands in surrender, likely not used to my defensiveness or the sharpness in my tone.

"No. I'm sorry," I say, that heavy weight falling on me again. "I guess I'm in a mood today."

"Correction." His tone is lighthearted, but it still feels like I'm being lectured. "You've been in a mood for *days*. I'm guessing the wedding didn't go quite as you hoped."

I know without asking that he's referring to Cameron and the fantasy that will never be. "Great. Now I'm stupid *and* moody."

"You're not stupid."

"Oh no . . . I am. Trust me. You weren't there. I was in full form." I roll my eyes at my own absurdity. I shouldn't care that Cam skipped out of the reception. Or that I didn't get the dance I've always dreamed of having. I should be grateful for what I do have. A beautiful daughter and a great life. And yet somehow I can't seem to shake the sorrow I feel.

But I must, because there is no place for it, not right now. I force a halfhearted grin, hoping it will convince Mason to drop the subject. "At least the night wasn't a total bust to my ego. There was this handsome, successful guy who practically begged for my number before I left."

Mason smirks and leans a shoulder against the wall. "Did you give it to him?"

"No." I sigh, somewhat wishing I had. It might help this lingering sting. "I don't want the suit-wearing, city-commuting, pick-up-women-at-a-wedding guy. I want the guy who will make me hot chocolate and sing to me when I'm sad." Two things Cameron did when Cassie and I watched an especially sappy movie that hit way too close to home after my mother died. He'd been home visiting from college, and in my memory he's covered in shining white armor. "And anyway, Morgan needs stability . . . now more than ever."

Mason wraps me in a side hug and kisses the top of my head. "You're a good mom, Lex. Annie's made a lot of mistakes, but giving you Morgan was not one of them."

Tears fill my eyes and begin spilling over. I'm too tired to fight them, and I press my head into Mason's chest. He's been given the fairy-tale version. The one I cheerfully try to believe on the good days. But the truth is far less sympathetic, and I once again push the dragon away before anger and pain destroy all the progress I've made.

On December 10, it will have been ten years since I saw my sister's face. Ten years since we spoke together or hugged or shared our grief with each other.

It will mark ten years of wondering if she's even still alive.

Some anniversaries we welcome. We have parties, blow out candles, and plan romantic candlelight dinners. Not this one. This one might just break whatever strength I have left.

NINE

Cameron

Six days have passed since the wedding, and while I hadn't meant for this backyard project to become a full-scale overhaul, somehow replacing one string of outdoor lights became two, then five. I'm now on my seventh box of new dangling lights and moving into territory that was completely unlit prior to my three return trips to the local hardware store.

I connect the final string and climb down the ladder to stand back and examine the swoop and height. This definitely would have been easier with another set of eyes, but it's invigorating to do it on my own. Working with my hands is not a practice I've ever made a habit of doing. I always considered it a hazard, too much of a chance at slicing a finger or bruising a bone. My hands were for music. They had to dance across the strings of my violin, had to sprint up and down the neck of a guitar without pain or thought or hesitation. How wonderful that they now feel valuable, important after so many months of unuse.

I walk the area, face upturned toward the sun, my eyes

following each string, mentally taking measurements until I reach the tree that started my fury of creative energy.

The morning had started simple. A steaming cup of coffee, a step through the back door to see the yard illuminated by the rising sun. The disastrous run-in with Darcy was in the past and I'd survived. It was a fresh beginning. A new dawn . . . one of promise and hope. I'd set my coffee cup down, walked the ten feet or so to the tree house, and climbed as eagerly as a ten-year-old to see what had been clothed in darkness the night before.

The ladder was still sturdy, hammered into the bark for maximum support, the wood sanded and stained. If rot had ever occurred, I couldn't detect it. Step after step I'd climbed, twelve feet high into the air, until I scrambled on top of the landing. The rustic porch I'd barely seen with my phone's flashlight the night before was safely lined with a hardwood railing that hadn't been stripped of bark or sanded. It matched the branches, nearly blending in.

The entrance door was made of stained cedar. Arched on top and knotted throughout. The handle was cast iron, dark and textured. I'd turned it, my heart racing with a childlike wonderment.

But the door had been locked. I'd tugged on the knob, shook the structure, but it was futile. The owner's family had obviously chosen to keep this one spot sacred. No strangers allowed. I'd moved around the porch, pressed my face to the dirty window, and tried to peer inside. But again I was denied the splendor of youthful exploration. Tiny lace curtains obscured any possible clue as to what lingered in the small room.

I slid to the ground, laughing at how ridiculous I'd become. It was only a tree house and yet I felt this deep sense of disappointment. But it was there, my back against the railing of the porch, twelve feet above the ground, that I saw the power cord. Electricity carefully run not just to the inside of the tree house but to the first string of lights, long ago burnt out and never replaced.

A new beginning after all.

And I'd taken full advantage, passing nearly a week immersed in restoration. It wasn't just the lights. I'd pulled weeds, trimmed dead branches, replaced rotted furniture, installed tiki torches and a portable fire pit. It's silly. I'm only here until a little after the New Year, not even long enough to enjoy the hours of labor I've invested. But it doesn't matter.

My chest is full of the wonderful outside air. My head clear even if for just a fleeting moment. I've made this, and it's beautiful. The first truly wonderful thing I've created in a very long time.

Sweat and dirt coat my shirt, and now that the final task is done, I feel the filth surrounding me. Discarded boxes lie across the walkway. I grab all three and break them down into compacted cardboard. I walk backward to the side gate, taking in the final product one more time, before turning around. Thank goodness it's trash day. I've already filled the large black container to the brim and have two more stuffed contractor bags lying next to it on the curb.

I catch the eye of my new neighbor, Mr. Stallworth, the second I step out into the front yard. He came by to visit two days ago and gave me all the information I could ever want on each person who'd died on this street in the last decade. My parents taught me to be polite to all elders, so I stood there for nearly forty minutes and nodded my head. I hurry my steps to the edge of the lawn, willing him not to come over.

After a quick wave that hopefully says *In a hurry, can't talk*, I shove the strips of cardboard down into the trash bin and smack my hands together to shake the remaining dirt from my gloves before pulling them off. I spent a lot of years rolling my eyes at my dad's many lectures on work ethic, but I have to give him this one. There is a great sense of accomplishment that comes with a hard day's work. I feel good. Alive.

I raise my head and take in the neighborhood that's temporarily mine. It is rather charming. Every house is unique, and each lawn is impeccably maintained even without a homeowner's association dictating it. A guy came by in a truck yesterday and placed American flags in front of each house. They flap in the breeze, declaring victory with every swish. I breathe it all in, the quiet, the calm, the strength of everything around me, and feel surprisingly at home.

Until that haunting bicycle click tickles my ears, and I spot her again. The same girl who zoomed by the day I moved in. The same tight ponytail, same faded sweatshirt, same piercing stare, only this time she slows as she approaches. An eerie sense that I know her hits me, and she must wonder the same, because she halts right in front of my neighbor's house, her scrawny legs straddling the bike dead center in the middle of the road. I feel an odd sense of protective energy and look both ways to make sure she isn't in any danger. By the time my gaze falls back to her, she's already moving toward the curb with purpose.

"Hey, Mr. Stallworth!"

The man practically bounces down the stairs, which is no easy feat at seventy years old. "Morgan! Where have you been hiding?"

"Oh, you know. Mom keeps me locked away." She drops her bike to the ground and runs over to hug the old man.

Morgan? And then it hits me. That smirk, that sarcastic tone, those curious eyes that are watching me like a hawk.

It's the girl from the wedding. Lexie's daughter. I barely recognize her with her hair now pulled from her face.

An immediate jolt of anticipation surges through me. I'd considered calling Lexie more than a few times, even went so far as to pull up Cassie's contact to text her a plea for the information. But then good sense would kick in and I'd shove the phone back in my pocket and return to the task at hand. But now her daughter is standing in front of my neighbor's house, discussing baked goods with a man who is obviously no stranger.

Mr. Stallworth turns to me, his hand affectionately still on Morgan's shoulder. "Have you met our new neighbor? He's renting Betty's place for a few months." Both their faces turn grim at the mention of the late owner of this property, but the grief fades quickly, neither willing to dwell on it for too long.

"Yeah, I've met him." Morgan rests a hand on her hip and tosses me a look that feels a lot like a dressing down. "And if I'd known it was you, I would have come talk to you way sooner. I can't believe I wasted a whole week!" On her tiptoes, she gives the old man a kiss on the cheek, then strolls my way. "I have a proposal for you."

"For me?" I glance at my neighbor, now completely uncomfortable.

"You may as well say yes now," he hollers. "She's just gonna bug you until you do." He shakes his head affectionately and works to climb the steps back onto his porch.

She stops a foot away and wrinkles her nose. "You look disgusting, by the way."

"Yeah, well, I've been working." I run a hand through my hair and feel the dirt caked on each strand. And then I'm annoyed that I let a teenager make me feel insecure. "Aren't you supposed to be in school?"

She shrugs. "It's Veterans Day. We don't have school."

Makes sense. Though it still doesn't explain why she's in my neighborhood. And how she knows Mr. Stallworth.

As if she can sense the question, she answers, "I live a couple blocks over. I saw you moving in last week with your *lady friend*." She grins now, and I don't miss the implication in it.

"Kelly's my sister-in-law," I correct, though why, again I don't know. She's a kid. I have no reason to justify myself or my choices. And yet, for some reason, the idea of her assuming I'm attached bothers me. "Where's your mom?"

"We'll get to that. First, we need to have a sit-down."

My brows shoot up. "A sit-down?"

"Yeah, you know, like in gangster movies where they go back and forth to negotiate terms. A sit-down." She brushes past me and bounces up the stairs to the front porch. I can tell by her ease that she's done this many times before. She plops down into the hanging swing and gestures to the wicker love seat across from it. "Come on, dude, time is money."

A chuckle explodes in my chest. "How old are you again?"

"Thirteen. But Mom says I act like a forty-year-old."

I take the steps slowly, my eyes still searching the street for exactly the person she's speaking of. "Does Lexie know you're here?"

"She knows I'm out riding my bike, and we'll tell her all about our new agreement . . . *after* we talk." Her mouth sets, and I have a feeling she's already had this conversation many times in her head. She looks too ready, and this whole thing feels very premeditated.

Still, I play along and sit on the dusty old couch. A *crack* sounds and I stand again, thinking better of it. I look up for the first time at the neglected space. Cobwebs line the corners and rafters. Dirt and dead leaves coat the ground. Maybe my work outside is not finished after all. I spy the chains holding up the swing Morgan is moving back and forth on with persistence. I don't want her tossed to the ground with a *crack* of snapping metal. But the chains are shiny and new. The wood's worn but doesn't appear to be structurally unsound.

Satisfied at her safety, I opt to lean my back against the wide square pillar and cross my arms. "Okay. What are we negotiating?" It takes effort to swallow my grin, but if the kid wants formality, it's the least I can do to oblige her.

She takes a deep breath, and for a second I see her true age reflected in her anxious gaze. Whatever she's about to say is important to her. It takes me back to childhood, to my sister pulling us all into the living room to show us her newly choreographed dance. She had the same nervous determination. The hint of fear that one or all of us would say the wrong words and dampen her dreams. We never did. And something in my gut tells me I won't do so now either. Not if I can avoid it.

"Nanni, um, Mrs. Hardcastle, was my friend. She babysat me from the time I was little until the very day she fell asleep and didn't wake up again." Her eyes gloss over, and I feel a punch to my gut. Feel an odd desire to comfort her the way her father would. But I stay rooted because I'm not her father, or her brother, or even a close family friend. I'm little more than a stranger.

"I'm sorry for your loss," I say, my voice losing the pretend edge it had originally. "From the pictures, she seems like a wonderful lady."

"She was." Morgan wipes each eye with the bottom of her palm and sits straighter, once again focused. "But that's not why I'm here. I'm here to discuss use of the tree house."

My breath halts in my chest. "The tree house?"

"It's in the backyard." Her forehead wrinkles. "You haven't been back there?"

"I've seen it."

"Well, then you understand why it's important to me. It's been my special place for years now." She clasps her hands in her lap, her voice getting stronger and more articulate. This is obviously the part she's practiced. "And I know Nanni would have put that in a will somewhere if she had any idea her time was so short. So, my proposal is this: you let me use the tree house on weekends and holidays; I'll go through the back gate; I won't disturb you in any way; and as payment, I will mow the yard and rake the leaves once a week." She nods, indicating she has said her piece. "Well, what do you think?"

I open my mouth to speak and then close it again. Her proposal isn't unreasonable, though I have significant concerns about a young girl being seen going in and out of my backyard. Perception is nearly as harmful as reality. But even if I could get past that part, the other more immediate problem I have no solution for. "The tree house is locked. The family must have closed it up after she died." I feel guilty, like I'm somehow to blame for the predicament. "I'm sorry. But it's not usable."

She hesitates, then slowly pulls at a string around her neck, freeing something from inside her hoodie. A small metal key dangles at the end. Black. The same color as the lock. "And if it was usable?"

I feel my palms start to sweat, a sense of being cornered shaking the air around me. "Then . . . I would have to think about it," I say slowly. Morgan is probably too young to realize the difference between her options when Mrs. Hardcastle lived here versus her options with a male renter. There would have to be very clear, visible boundaries and protections in place for both of us. But I would let Lexie take the lead on this one. If she's as protective as Morgan claims, then I likely won't have to be the bad guy. "And discuss the idea with your mom."

Morgan's face splits into a huge smile. "I was hoping you'd say that!"

My brow furrows again. "You were?"

"Heck yeah. I mean, come on. If you were all eager to let a young girl hang out in your backyard unsupervised, then you'd be creepy. And then I'd really be out of options. That's why I waited so long to come by. I even had Mr. Stallworth spy on you the other day and give me his report." She beams, apparently feeling proud of herself. "He said you had kind eyes and were very polite, by the way. But once I saw it was you, I realized that all my surveillance this past week was pointless."

My head begins a slow pound. "And why is that?"

"Well, because you were lecturey with me the other day about safety. It reminded me of my uncle—well, I guess he's my third cousin or something like that, but he acts like an uncle. Plus, well, my mom is usually an excellent judge of character. And she *definitely* likes you." Morgan hops up. "So, let's go."

I feel like I've just been spun in a circle sixteen times with a blindfold on, and now Morgan wants me to stumble around in a game of capture the flag. "Go where?"

"To ask my mom. She's right over there, working on the house." She points to the notably unsightly old home that's obviously being renovated. It stands out on the block, even without the large dumpster sitting in the driveway.

At the mention of Lexie, my head clears a little of the fog Morgan's rambling produced. "That's where you live?" I've never seen a car parked overnight. Just the white work truck that comes daily and parks along the curb, but never stays.

"Oh no. Our home is that way." She points in the opposite

direction. "Four houses down and two blocks over. You can barely see it from the road. It's tucked back behind two big burly trees. Mom says we're the redheaded stepchild of this neighborhood, so they like to keep us quiet and out of sight." She chuckles at the inside joke that I imagine is one of many between the two of them. "The other eyesore I'm referring to is where Mom decided to channel her inner HGTV host. She calls it a flip or something."

I shouldn't be surprised. Lexie has never been predictable or conventional. Whether it's good or bad fortune that Lexie lives this close, I haven't quite decided. Though my pulse seems to have an opinion. It ticks higher when I peer down the street, wondering why she would take on such a massive project by herself. "She's there? Right now?"

Morgan nods. "Yep."

I should hesitate more than I do. "Okay. Wait out here. I need to shower first."

The less-than-subtle kid waves a hand in front of her nose. "Yes, you do." And then she sits back down on the swing. Her eyes lock on her phone screen a second later.

I step forward and disappear into the house. A sense I've just been clobbered with a baseball bat haunts me but doesn't seem to stop my rushed bolt up the stairs.

TEN

Lexie

We're behind schedule. Two days to be exact, and it's my fault. Mason isn't saying so; he's not saying much at all, but that's how I know he's stressed. I was supposed to be helping him every night this past week, but work has been ridiculously busy. I've barely had time to pick up Morgan and stuff some dinner in our mouths between mitigating crises and trying to get my properties transferred. Sometimes I wonder if vacation is really vacation at all if you spend the weeks before working twice as hard just trying to take the owed time off.

At least I have today. Well, sort of. Veterans Day is an official holiday for us, but it comes with a caveat: we have to keep our phones on us at all times for emergencies. I've already had one that pulled me away for an hour.

"I'm so sorry," I say, shoving my fingers back in my work gloves and praying the phone stays silent.

"It's not your fault." Mason swings the sledgehammer at

the upper cabinets with a fury that makes me step back a little.

"It feels like my fault."

He sighs and runs his arm across his dusty, sweaty forehead. "I should have scheduled more contingency. I didn't expect the bathroom to take so long."

We'd run into multiple problems in that space. Mold, old termite damage, a leaking pipe. Mason was able to navigate through the mess and fix all the issues, but I know the work would have gone much faster if I'd been around to help.

"So where does that put us, time-wise?"

"Tight. We only have fifteen days to finish the kitchen, demo both upstairs bathrooms, and frame out the new kitchen walls, if we have any hope of not having to reschedule the plumbers."

I bite my lip, remembering Mason's warning at the beginning. The plumbers were one of those critical-path items. If they got pushed back, every other trade got pushed back. "Okay. Just over two weeks. We can do it."

He opens his mouth, probably to remind me that it's taken us almost that long to do much easier demo, but instead he swings the hammer at the next set of cabinets. Sometimes I think Mason likes this part best. The slamming and hitting. He always seems to be in a better mood after he's knocked out a wall or two.

I stay back until he's finished and then get to work on my assigned task—debris removal. He slams. I pick up the mangled wood, fill a wheelbarrow to overflowing, then roll it out to the dumpster. We continue this way until all but one upper cabinet is left.

Mason offers me the sledgehammer. "Care to do the honors?"

I take it, more than eager to get out my own frustration.

Arms positioned in an unpracticed softball pre-swing, I squeeze the rough wood handle and twist, putting my whole body and meager strength into the knockdown.

It's effective. Too effective. The cabinet shatters on impact and flies from the wall, along with a strip of Sheetrock and layers of chipped paint. Splinters dance over me, filling my hair, stinging my cheeks, and coating me with the same dirty gray dust that has turned Mason's hair from a rich brown to a dull taupe.

"Oops," I squeak out, staring at the destruction at my feet, my arms now frozen at my sides.

I half expect Mason to growl, but he surprises me with a chuckle and a hearty slap on the back. "Nice work. I was beginning to think you didn't have it in you."

"Have what in me?"

"A temper." He winks because we both know I actually don't have a temper at all. On the rare occasions I do get really angry, it comes out in tears and obsessive cleaning streaks.

"You're really not mad at me?"

He sighs. "Lex, I couldn't be mad at you if I tried. But if you don't stop yapping and get to work, I might very well send you home."

In other words, I'm being a distraction instead of a help. "Noted." I nod purposefully without another word and toss the mangled wood into the wheelbarrow. It's nearly full . . . again.

Mason crawls under the sink, and I hear the buzz of the drill. Soon the sink shifts, and the counters pop. A good sign. Maybe these won't be anchored into the studs like the one in the bathroom. We had to cut out three inches of wood to remove it. And of course it was the one wall we had wanted to keep intact.

"Mom!" A bang from the front door slamming comes next.

"In the kitchen," I call back to Morgan, glancing down at my phone. Wow. She's actually done as I asked and checked in on the hour mark. Ten minutes early even. In fact, she's been pretty great all week. Extra helpful, kind, slow to argue, even with me dragging her to four different houses that will be new listings on Monday. She's buttering me up for some big ask, I'm sure, but I don't care. I'm going to enjoy every minute of the manipulation.

She rounds the corner, and just as I'm about to offer her a compliment on her time management, my gaze falls to the man behind her.

"You'll never guess who moved into Nanni's house!" She halts and does her best *The Price Is Right* model pose. "Meet our new neighbor . . . the infamous Cameron Lee."

My heart rattles the moment we make eye contact, and then horror fills my chest as I watch his gaze travel over my dusty double braids, stained overalls, and ugly black steel-toed boots that Mason insists I wear. "You're the handsome single guy down the street?" I blurt out before my brain tells my mouth those words weren't meant to be uttered out loud.

Cameron smiles, that deep beautiful one that haunts my best dreams. "Apparently."

There's a mumble from under the sink, but I can't process it. I can't process anything but the reality that Cameron is here . . . in the flesh. Did he not go back home after the wedding?

"Lexie!"

I jump at Mason's shout and immediately turn in his direction. He has both arms holding up the counter while his head is doing its best to keep the teetering sink from falling. I rush over, grab the stainless-steel basin, and lift it out.

With a feat of strength I can't comprehend, Mason somehow manages to stand and restabilize the tilting section of heavy tile. He spins, face flushed. Deep red grooves cut across his biceps. "What the—"

"I'm so sorry. I didn't hear you."

"This is a construction site, Lex! You have to pay attention. I nearly crushed my arm."

So much for Mason's theory that he can't get mad at me. He's definitely there, and now that I've experienced it, I know it's a first. This version is completely different from his norm.

"I'm sorry," I say, very much missing his usual silent broodiness.

"It's my fault," Morgan jumps in. "I distracted her."

He glances toward our guests, registering them for the first time. It's right then that two old friends-turned-strangers catch their first glimpse of each other. Mason curses. And not the under-his-breath kind. The kind that has Morgan's eyes going wide and a smirk crossing her lips.

Cameron's back straightens. "Nice to see you, too."

The mishap in the kitchen is a distant memory now. Mason's focus is one hundred percent on the man in front of him. "What are you doing here? You should be halfway back to L.A. by now." The tone is both condescending and cold enough to bring goose bumps to my arms.

"It's Nashville, and I'm staying in town through the end of the year." He glances from Mason to me. "I didn't realize you two were—"

"Cousins," I blurt.

Cameron reacts much like he did at the wedding, brandishing that amused grin that always seems to appear after I speak. "Yes. I remember the family connection. I just didn't realize you two were working on this project together."

"Oh, well, yeah," I stammer, hoping he can't see how mortified I am. "Mason and I are business partners now."

Morgan waves a hand. "Yes, great. You know him, he knows you. We all know each other," she says, her voice rife with annoyance. "Now can we please get to the whole reason I dragged him over here?"

Mason crosses his arms, his eyes still on Cameron. "Yes, please enlighten us."

Morgan hesitates and glances at me for guidance. She's not used to Mason taking a position of authority. I'm not either, though I wouldn't mind if he did. I trust him completely, but in this case he doesn't seem to have any objectivity.

I step forward, laying my hand gently on Mason's back. "I've got this."

"That . . . I doubt," he says, letting out a bitter huff. He turns to give me his make-this-quick scowl and then heads back to the sagging counter without another word to our guest.

My face heats as another round of embarrassment washes over me—this time at my cousin's less-than-cordial behavior. I plant an everything-is-normal smile on my face and turn back to Cameron. "You should know you've had all the women on this street in quite a tizzy." I wince at the sound in my ears. My voice is too cheery, especially under the circumstances. But I can't seem to stop the need to overcompensate for Mason's dismissal. "You're all they've been talking about for a week now, and their theories were quite entertaining."

That glorious grin returns. "Were they?"

"Oh yes. Let's see. One was that you are a recent divorcé who's fighting for custody of his kids. Another that you recently got out of some kind of white-collar prison. And my favorite, you are new to the witness-protection program." Encouraged when he laughs, I change my voice to match Mrs. Volta's next door. "I mean, why else would a single guy need a home all to himself in this neighborhood?"

A hammering ensues—loud, obnoxious, and completely unnecessary. But Mason's intent is clear: *take this conversation somewhere else*. I point to the sliding glass door that's already open to give us a breeze.

Morgan rolls her eyes and stomps out. "This is ridiculous. I just need five minutes."

"And you'll get them," I promise, following her. Cameron takes the rear, and I try not to imagine how much worse my appearance is from the back.

He slides the glass door closed, and immediately the noise quiets.

"I'm sorry about Mason." I pull off my gloves and try to tame the mass of wispy hair that's pulled free of my twin braids. "It's not you. He's just under a lot of stress."

"Oh, it absolutely is me," Cameron says, his tone not up for negotiation. "And you don't need to apologize for him."

Morgan obnoxiously sighs. "Good gracious. You guys have more drama than Netflix. Can we please get to the point?" She slams her hands against the sides of her legs. "Cameron—"

"Mr. Lee," I correct.

"Cameron is fine. Preferred actually."

Morgan grits her teeth, then forces a polite clipped voice through them. "Cameron *Lee* agreed to let me use the tree house. He just wanted to verify it was okay with you."

The flinch I see from Cameron tells me he didn't exactly agree. I wait to see if he'll contradict her sentence, but he doesn't. Instead, he shoves his hands into his pockets. "We both—" he looks at Morgan, and she averts her eyes guiltily—"wanted to make sure you were completely comfortable with the idea."

Morgan's pleading, hopeful gaze shoots right through my heart. Her obsession with that tree house has gotten nonsensical. Borderline concerning. I try to understand. She's told me a thousand times why. It's comfortable, familiar, an escape all to herself. Part of me had hoped this renter situation would keep me from having to be the bad guy and putting an end to it all. But my daughter is apparently nothing if not resourceful and determined.

Still, my gut says I need to proceed cautiously. "Please give me and Cameron a minute alone to discuss it."

"But—"

"Morgan," I warn, using my best mom tone. "I can either tell you no now, or you can give me a few minutes to think about it."

She clamps her mouth shut and spins around. A second later, the door slides closed again, giving Cameron and me the privacy I wanted.

"I'm so sorry she ambushed you," I say in a deep exhale and turn back to him. For a brief second I forget he's my childhood crush and speak without any of my usual fluster. I guess that's one of the joys of motherhood; it trumps every other identifier. "I don't understand why that tree house is so important to her, but . . . it is."

"Nah. I get it. I have three siblings. I would have killed for a place like that."

I don't remind him that Morgan is an only child. Instead, I warm at the memory of all the years I spent with the Lees. Loud, chaotic, but always kind and full of love. I felt it at the wedding, too, and like it did when I was younger, it soothed a deep longing in my heart. The same longing I'm sure all kids feel who have lost their parents way too young.

"It's absolutely okay if you don't want her to use it. You can blame it on me."

Cameron shakes his head, watching me in that awed we've-just-met expression again.

"What?" I ask.

"It's just surreal. You're a mom, and you're so good at it."

The compliment comes so matter-of-factly that I feel my-self flush immediately. "Oh, thanks."

"How did . . . ?" He hesitates, then slowly continues. "How is it that you have a thirteen-year-old I've never met?"

Appreciation slides over me. I've been asked a version of that question a thousand times, but never this way. Like he feels cheated that he didn't get to know her when she was little. "I wasn't the one who gave birth to Morgan," I say, be-cause I refuse to put it any other way. "She was three when I got her."

Surprise colors his expression. "She's adopted? But . . . you look so much alike."

My heart swells. I love hearing that. "Thank you. We're related. Just not in that way. Technically, I'm Morgan's aunt. Annaliese is her birth mom." The words sting coming out. She's my daughter in every way that matters.

Cameron's silent as he digests the information. Another reaction I appreciate. He doesn't bombard me with intru-sive questions or try to backpedal as if he's brought up some deep fracture in my life. He just stands there contemplating and then graciously moves on. "I don't mind Morgan using the tree house, but I think for perception's sake and for ev-eryone's comfort, it's best that either you be there or I make myself scarce."

"Cam, that's asking way too much of you. I couldn't kick you out of your own house."

"It's technically not my house." His natural flirtatious tone comes out, and back are the flutters and young girl fantasies.

I feel the heat rise up my neck and do my best to push it back down. I'm a parent for crying out loud. "What if we compromise? Instead of leaving, you hang out on the front porch. This neighborhood has eyes everywhere, and honestly, I don't feel totally comfortable with her being there all alone."

"Deal." Cameron reaches out a hand, and I take it, hesitantly, because there will be no way to pretend while touching him. His fingers squeeze mine and linger. Not long enough for my satisfaction, but longer than warranted.

Giddy laughter rolls in my stomach as that pesky hope rears its head again. I've had enough platonic handshakes to know this one was definitely more. How much more, I don't know, but I'll take a centimeter if that's all I can get.

"So, um . . ." He flicks his head to the sliding glass door. "Should I give her the good news, or do you want to?"

I turn to see my teenage daughter with her lips mashed against the glass. A silly smile on her face. "I have a strange feeling she already knows."

We walk toward the house, and she has the door open before we make it a foot away. "Well, can I go?"

"With permission—"

She cuts me off with a whoop and a hug that nearly upends me. "Thank you!" She plants a wet, sloppy kiss on my cheek. "You're the best mom in the world."

My heart dances with pleasure. I'll never tire of hearing those words.

"So can I go there now?" She glances from Cameron to me.

"It's fine with me," he offers when I don't answer right away.

Cameron really is an especially good man. "One hour," I say firmly. "Not a minute longer."

"Yes, ma'am." She rushes to the door after another quick hug and waits, bouncing on her toes.

Cameron laughs at her eagerness, and it brightens his face. Chases away the heaviness he seems to be carrying these days. Suddenly, he's younger, with dreams and excitement. "I guess that's my cue," he says, his voice returning me to the present.

"Thank you again."

"Sure thing."

I watch them go and marvel at the sight of the two of them bantering back and forth as they cross the street. Slowly, I shut the door and head back to the kitchen.

Mason has the counter in shattered pieces on the floor. I make quick work of scooping up the mess.

"It's going to end badly," he says, his voice no longer angry but resigned.

I know exactly what he's referring to, but I ask anyway. "What is?"

"You and Cameron."

"There is no me and Cameron." I keep working, unwilling to let Mason dampen my mood. "Not yet at least."

"Well, there will be. I've known Cam for most of my life. And I know exactly what the man looks like when he has a new fascination. And you, Lexie, are it."

A smile bursts through my attempt to stay nonchalant, and the pieces of countertop in my hands fall back to the ground. "You think so?"

"What I think . . ." Mason's scowl deepens. "What I know is that you are in love with a fantasy, Lex. A memory. You have no idea of the man he's become."

"Then I'll just have to get to know him better," I argue.

"Let me save you the trouble. Cameron needs to be worshiped and adored. And you have a tendency to ignore anything that is unpleasant. That combination is lethal, and one, if not both, of you is going to end up disappointed and heartbroken."

"Well, so what?"

Mason's eyebrows shoot up. He wasn't expecting that reaction.

"My heart's already been broken. Three times." I cross

my arms, my voice taking on the same dark tone his has. "I survived those. And you know what? I'd take the pain all over again if it meant one more day with any of them." Tears sting my eyes. "I don't care if Cam has a week or a month or a day. If I can be a part of his world even for a second, I'm going to take advantage of the opportunity."

We stand there, eye to eye, and for the first time I feel like the older cousin. The wise one. The one who's lived far more life.

Mason shakes his head but doesn't say another word.

ELEVEN

Cameron

The bar is dark, small, and crowded. It's a scene I've been a part of for years and yet it feels suffocating now. I move sideways through the bodies, a baseball cap low on my head. It's unlikely anyone will recognize me, and even more unlikely it would matter if they did, but I still don't want to risk the chance. For once, I want to fade inside the walls and be a silent observer.

The band hasn't taken the stage yet, and the music popping through the speakers irritates my ears. The bass is too high, the mix of sound distorted through old speakers. I find a corner tucked in the back and wait. Maybe this wasn't such a great idea. Maybe I'm fooling myself thinking I can go back in time and fill this void in my life.

Two girls stumble out of the bathroom, giggling. They seem too young to be allowed in here, but that's probably because I'm too old. I press my fingers to my temples and try to rub away the buzzing in my head. It's been constant and unyielding since Morgan waved goodbye and trotted back to the house her mom is renovating.

My lips curl upward at the thought of Lexie. Red-faced, covered head to toe in dust, her hair braided like a schoolgirl's, and then there were the overalls. I chuckle and it releases some of the tension shooting across my skull. Even with her attempt to look like a hillbilly, she was . . . well, adorable. Inside and out. Everything about her appeals to me. Her charm, her wit, the way she looks at me as if I'm super-human. I shake the niggling thought away. I can't, won't, go there. Besides, she'll soon learn like all the rest that I am in fact flawed, deeply, unchangeably, and I couldn't bear seeing the disappointment in her eyes.

The lights flicker and then out rushes the young, eager band. I feel their excitement, from the atmosphere or from my own memory, I'm not sure, but it's there, deep in my chest, my stomach turning in anticipation. Not jealousy, though, which I'm a little surprised doesn't exist at all. I don't want to be up there, working the crowd, exuding an energy that's either deep inside or forced. I don't miss the pressure, the stage, or the fame. Just the music. That's what has my skin tingling and my nerves dancing. I want to be swept away by the sound, to forget everything else.

The lead singer tosses back his hair the same way Bryson used to and welcomes the crowd already starting to push closer to the stage. He winks down at two cheering girls and counts out the beat.

Sound envelops the room—drums, both guitars, and the piano all at once. It makes me cringe, the demand and harsh-ness of it all. They should have faded the entry, should have hung out the strings and only tapped the cymbal. The song is a cover, though roughed up to give it their own unique twist. They should have left the score alone. This version is pain-fully harsh.

I watch as the lead guitarist fumbles over the chords,

working to keep up with a pace that's way too fast for the melody. He bites his lip, studies his hands. He assumes no one is watching him. But he's all I can focus on, the only one even remotely interesting up on that stage. And then suddenly it's not some stranger up there. It's Mason, tall and lanky and devoid of the sixty-plus pounds of muscle he's packed on since I last saw him. Regret and shame fill me. He's changed so much, not just in physical appearance but in his countenance. His scowl was so unfamiliar I almost didn't recognize him.

Mason had been like Lexie when we were younger. The first to welcome a new friend, perpetually optimistic, kind. He'd been my sidekick for years, totally content to stay in the shadows, until the day Bryson dreamed up Black Carousel and invited Mason to join him. He'd never been in the spotlight; not next to me, who'd grab it unceasingly. But to everyone's shock, Mason loved it. It didn't matter that he wasn't very good or that Bryson nagged at him constantly to improve. He just loved being a part of something greater.

And I stole it from him.

I scrub a hand over my face, the familiar heaviness settling deep inside me.

Sure, Bryson had been the one pushing me to join the band for years, and yes, Bryson was very likely going to fire Mason sooner rather than later. But his choices shouldn't have mattered. I'd made a promise to Mason that I wouldn't join Black Carousel unless he was one hundred percent on board, and I did it anyway. Not just without his permission, but behind his back and without so much as an explanation or heads-up. No wonder the guy left town and hasn't talked to me since. I deserve his hatred.

The song ends, and the guitarist looks as relieved as I am. But the feeling is short-lived as they move into another relentlessly pounding piece. How did these guys even get booked? They're terrible. It's another cover song, another butchering of someone else's talent. I clench my fist, forcing myself to stay and listen. This outing was supposed to help me find a tiny measure of joy. Not take me down a memory lane of all my failures.

After two more minutes, I can no longer stand to be here. I move to leave, to spare myself this mockery they're making, when finally something new tickles my ears. An original, written by none other than the guitarist who's kept my attention since they walked out onstage. For the first time he looks excited, and I ease back into my corner, cautiously optimistic.

The song has promise at first. The drums roll and linger at the tips of the notes. It's pleasant, inviting. But soon the song shifts, the chords mashing together like two trucks in a head-on collision. I focus, work to separate the notes, figure out why they feel tangled. It's what I do best, deconstruct and reconstruct sound. Mold it, caress it, lovingly place it where it belongs. It's artistry, like a jeweler with fine metals.

I concentrate harder, force the background sound to fade into the sticky concrete floors. The whole of the sound is working, but inside, at the core, something is off. I can feel it, ingest it with every breath, and yet it circumvents me, rushes away before I can grab hold and demand to know what exactly is broken.

They end the tragic piece with a riff I cannot stand, and yet I nearly beg for them to begin again. To rewind, redo. To give me the chance to grasp what is missing. But the band gives me no such reprieve. Instead, another cover song is introduced, and my legs nearly buckle. I push through the crowd, my heart pulsing with the need for escape. The previous song chases me now, mocking me—out the door, down the street, and into my car. I speed home with a fury, cursing at the radio because it does nothing to replace the manic frustration in my head. I barely make it next to the curb before the nausea comes and releases on the pavement outside my house. I'm grateful it's dark, after ten, and well past the time when my kindhearted but far-too-involved neighbors would be peeking out their windows. Still convulsing, I tear myself from the car and stumble down the sidewalk like a drunk man, though I haven't touched a drop of alcohol since my first year on tour.

"Just get inside," I mumble to myself. "It's always better inside." In this house, in this small haven carved out in the middle of Texas.

But tonight, my front door offers no sanctuary. My hands shake on the handle, my feet numb as they furiously pound up the stairs. I have to get this cursed thing out of my head, now before it ruins me. I slam open the bedroom door and tear the suitcases out from under my bed. My music pad hasn't been touched in months, and feeling the paper beneath my fingertips is like a cold glass of water after an endless drought.

The pencil burns against my skin as I furiously write out the melody they sang. The harmonies are next, in perfect precision against the black notes I've scribbled. Two pages, then three. When all the verses are out of my head and on paper, I search for the broken piece like a detective, touching each note, humming the rhythm, then crossing it out and changing what isn't right. Only the changes aren't right either. I rip the paper in my attempt to erase my latest fix and try again. And again. And again.

I feel the void of the solution staring at me, hands cupped around its ears, tongue out, hips swaying back and forth as if to say, *You can't fix me; you can't fix you.*

I tear the page from the book, mash it up into a tight ball, and fling it across the room with a cry so fierce I'm surprised it doesn't set off my car alarm downstairs. My chest rises and falls in heavy agony as the ball rolls across the floor. I collapse onto the bed, head in my hands, and wait for the blackness to swallow me whole.

It doesn't, probably because I want it to.

Tears sting my eyes as exhaustion spills over me. But sleep is out of the question. I stand, body and mind both so weary it takes sheer adrenaline to lean down, pick up the music pad, and start all over again.

TWELVE

Lexie

Everything hurts. My back, my legs, even my elbows for crying out loud. There are muscles I never knew existed screaming at me as I roll my tortured body out of bed. Mason and I stayed at the house and worked until three in the morning, attempting to make up some of the lost time. We're supposed to meet up again at eleven, but I'm not totally sure I won't crumple into a ball of tears when I put those horrible boots back on.

Light shines through my sheer curtains, indicating I need to check the time. Morgan is staying at a friend's place for the afternoon and evening, a birthday outing ending in an overnight slumber party, though Morgan has never before participated in that segment. I half expected her to ask, beg even, to do so this time, and I'd even prepped myself to say yes, to let the reins loosen just a bit. But she didn't mention a word. And I, of course, didn't either.

I glance down at my phone and groan. I need to move. Need to get her gift wrapped and have her ready and dropped off before the endless hours of hard labor begin.

"Morgan!" I yell, attempting to sit up and succumbing back to the horizontal position. "I need coffee . . . and pain medicine." This last sentence comes out as a childish cry, and I won't lie that it's tempting to do just that. Cry and moan and refuse to move. But then Mason's unyielding, determined face fills my memory, and I shove the covers back again. The man had been an absolute bore all night. It didn't matter if I tossed jokes in his direction or turned up the music and danced like an idiot. Nothing fazed him. He just pounded and pounded at the walls and floors without so much as a grunt in my direction. Whatever memories or feelings that the reunion with Cameron had stirred up, they'd obviously not been the favorable kind.

Oh well, I can't dwell on Mason's struggles, not if he won't share even a piece of his pain with me.

The only person you can control, Lexie, is you. Don't spend your life as a grumbling spectator in someone else's story.

Mom's voice in my head draws away some of the fatigue. It's enough to push my legs over the side of the bed, my feet hitting the carpet with just enough momentum to draw me upright. But not for long. I fall back, my quads cramping as I sit down on my slumping mattress.

"Morgan!" I cry out again, praying she's already up. For years, she'd pop in at five or six a.m., ready with the sun to start her day. Dragging me out of bed with little hesitation or remorse. So, where's my little early morning riser now that it benefits me?

My door cracks, and soon I see her nose peeking through. When she's sure I'm decent, the door widens to reveal my beautiful, fantastic daughter fully dressed and carrying a hot mug of coffee in her hand.

"You are my absolute favorite person in the entire world," I say, hands outstretched.

"Only because you taught me how to make coffee when I turned ten." She sits next to me, and I study her face. She, at least, looks well rested. She'd been out cold when I got home last night, an open book lying on her chest. "You better drink this quick," she says, shoving the mug into my waiting hands. "You look . . . wrecked."

I take a long sip and sigh. "I feel wrecked. Mason must have a battery pack somewhere under his skin that he recharges on the hour. The man never stops."

"It must be in the genes," she snorts, implying I'm not much better. She's probably right.

"So, what big plans do you girls have today?"

"Melissa's mom is taking us ice skating at the mall, and afterward we're heading to the movies. Then we're going to open presents and do karaoke. I can text when they're starting to settle for the night."

"Unless . . ." I can't even believe the words are coming out. "You want to . . ."

"No." She shakes her head. "Maybe next time."

"Okay." I'm both surprised and relieved. "Well, it sounds like either way you're going to have a ton of fun. I'm really glad you guys have gotten close this year. I like her family."

"Yeah. Me too." She plays uncharacteristically with her fingers, looking small and insecure. An image as rare as it is unnerving.

I run a hand over her head. "Is everything okay, honey?" She glances at me, and I feel a punch in the gut. It's the same expression she had as a toddler when I caught her climbing the pantry shelves to get to the cookies. Shame mixed with resolve. She's keeping something from me. I've known it for weeks now, but I can't seem to break through the shell she's raised around her. "Morgan," I say in my softest, gentlest voice, even though I can feel my insides tightening. Mason's words haven't stopped haunting me since he uttered them. Maybe it is time to discuss my sister or at least open the door for Morgan to ask. "I know I've been a little distracted lately, but you can always talk to me . . . about anything."

For a moment, she seems to contemplate it. I even notice her lips part slightly, and then her expression shuts down and my darling sarcastic girl is back. "You need a shower. Bad." She stands and picks up the pile of clothes I left on the floor beside my bed. "I'll throw these disgusting things in the washer. I don't want you mixing them with my stuff."

"Thanks, baby," I say, and feel a little relieved we didn't go headlong into the past. Despite Mason's warnings, I have to believe in the strength of my relationship with Morgan. She'll come to me when she's ready. And I'll be here, eager to mend whatever hurt is causing that pain in her eyes.

She holds the clothes out away from her body and pauses when she gets halfway over the threshold. "Hey, do you mind stopping at Cameron's house on the way? I left a couple of books I had borrowed from Melissa in the tree house, and I promised I'd give them back tonight."

The idea of seeing Cameron sends a jolt of unfettered energy through me. "Yeah, um, sure." I'm on my feet now, touching my hair and marveling at the filth. "Don't start those clothes yet. I need to add my sheets, as well."

She laughs. "No kidding, and a bottle of bleach."

I wave a dismissive hand at her and head for the shower, wondering just how much Mason is going to tease me when he sees I put on makeup this morning.

I knock on Cameron's door, hoping he doesn't think I'm being intrusive by showing up unannounced.

"This is totally unnecessary. I can just run around the back and grab them," Morgan says, her arms crossed with impatience.

"It's courteous to let someone know before you traipse through their backyard."

"Yeah," she snorts. "That's exactly why we're knocking on his door."

I ignore the comment and reach up to knock again, only this time the door opens and my breath hitches at the sight in front of us. Cameron's hair sticks up at all angles around his face, and his eyes are veined with stress and fatigue. He wears a T-shirt, but it's inside out. And his feet stand bare on the laminate floor.

Morgan gasps. "Whoa. You look worse than my mom did this morning." I reach out and pinch her. "OUCH! What was that for?" She rubs the spot on her arm with far more drama than necessary. I barely squeezed.

Cameron shields his eyes from the sun, confusion covering his sleep-lined face. "Lexie?"

"We woke you. I'm so sorry." My apology seems to break him out of the haze, and he lowers his hand, then glances from me to my daughter. "I would have texted or called," I continue in a rush, "but I don't have your phone number."

His brow creases further, and Morgan rolls her eyes, apparently done with the niceties. "I needed to grab some things from the tree house, and Mom felt it necessary to hound you for permission. So that's why we're standing on your porch right now, okay?"

"The tree house?" Cameron attempts to rub the sleep from his eyes, but it only makes the redness grow around the rims. The poor guy is barely coherent.

"You're obviously busy. We'll come back later." I take a step away from the door and gesture for Morgan to do the same.

"But—" she begins.

"No, no, it's fine." He shakes his head as if working to come out of his stupor. "Do whatever you have to do."

Morgan doesn't wait for me to contradict him but rushes past us both through the front door. I hear the back one slam seconds later. We're definitely going to need to have another conversation about boundaries.

"Sorry. She's a little too comfortable in this house."

We stand in awkward silence for a moment. He still seems to be waking up, and I'm totally unsure how to proceed considering Cameron's disheveled state.

The weirdness continues for another achingly long thirty seconds, until finally he reacts and moves from the entrance. "I'm sorry. Come in."

I walk past him hesitantly. The two of us have never been uncomfortable around each other, but then again, Cameron has never been quite so exposed before. Despite spending many nights at his childhood home, I was never privy to the unapologetic filth most teenage boys are known for. Cameron always looked and smelled amazing. In my memories, he even had that starlike sparkle whenever he smiled.

He shuts the door, and my gaze travels around the room, bringing both comfort and grief. Nothing has changed since the last time I was here, with the exception of a few draped cloths tossed to the corner. Most of the furniture is still covered, minus the couch. The one Cameron apparently crashed on last night. The cushions are mashed down, and a lone blanket lies on the floor as if he'd tossed it off in a hurry.

"I like what you've done with the place," I quip, hoping to ease the heaviness I feel emanating from him. If this torturous silence is going to end, it's obviously going to have to be me who does something about it.

"Yeah. I, um, haven't had much time." He runs a trembling

hand through his hair, leaving the tangled mess to stick up even higher on his head.

Again the room is bathed in silence. It needles beneath my skin, revs up my adrenaline. "Hey, do you want some coffee?" I offer, praying for something that might break him out of this frozen state. "Because I would love some."

"Desperately," he groans, his arms falling to his sides. Finally, life flashes into his eyes. "But I used the rest of what Kelly brought over last night."

"Hmm. So I take it you haven't found the stash yet?"

"The stash?"

"Yes. The former lady of the house had a tendency to hide the good stuff, where even a crew of housecleaners likely missed it." I spin, grateful to have a mission. Mrs. Hardcastle was a caffeine junkie. She was known for her blackest coffee and boxes upon boxes of vanilla wafers, which she'd dip in her cup and consume with delight. I pass through the dining room and halt, the sight an explanation in itself. Papers lay strewn everywhere. Some crumpled in balls throughout the room, several scattered across the table, half scratchings and half legible. Compositions. But not the delicate, precise ones Cameron used to create while lying on his stomach on the living room floor. These are frenzied, harsh, and violent. "What are you—?"

"It's nothing." Cameron rushes to the table and quickly pushes the stray pages into a stack. "Just a project I'm working on."

The disgust in his voice is palpable. This so-called project is neither wanted nor enjoyed.

I continue to the small galley kitchen, kicking aside more crumpled, rejected pages as I go. A new Keurig sits on the counter, the box of pods beside it empty. I squat down to the cabinet beside the fridge. The long narrow one that's at least

three feet deep. Tucked in the back, just as it has been for
the past seven years, is Mrs. Hardcastle's old electric perco-
lating coffeemaker. "There it is," I say proudly as I pull it free.

Cameron joins me, and I subtly notice him toss an armful
of mashed-up paper balls into the trash. "What is that thing?"

I grin, looking up at him. "The worst cup of coffee you've
ever tasted, but you'll be awake for a week."

To my delight, I get a grin back. It softens the lines on his
face, loosens the tightness in his shoulders. I notice small
paper cuts on nearly every finger but don't mention it. Instead, I stand and try not to look indelicate as I crawl up onto
the kitchen counter.

"What are you . . . ?" He moves closer as if he needs to be
there to catch my impending fall. "Be careful."

I stretch and pull open one of the two tiny cabinets above
the refrigerator. The ones no one ever uses because they are
impossible to reach. Of course, Mrs. Hardcastle had a trusty
stepladder and a very mobile thirteen-year-old at her disposal.
"I'm good. I just need to . . ." I reach to the back, feeling
around the space because I can't see anything, until finally
my fingers make contact with the old metal container. "Yes!"
I slide it free and ease down from the poor Formica counter,
breathing a sigh of victory.

Cameron examines the item in my hand that's probably as
old as Mrs. Hardcastle herself. "A lunch box?"

"Only on the outside." I flip the lock and pull out the
pungent dark roast coffee that is so familiar it warms me and
grieves me at the same time. I miss her. It's not the biting
pain like it is with my parents and sister, but it's there, a void,
nonetheless. Mom used to say those voids were signs of a full
life. One spent knowing and loving lots of people. I cling to
that idea now, and it pushes back the tears.

I go about the task of filling the pot with water and measuring grounds. "It will take about seven minutes to brew. And when it's done, be sure to remove the basket or you'll be chewing on grounds more than drinking the coffee."

"That sounds way too complicated." He leans a hip against the counter, eyes me in a way that makes my skin tingle. "Stay and have a cup with me?"

My chest heaves with pleasure and that oh-so-familiar longing I may never get rid of. "I'd love to, but Morgan has a party I need to get her to."

He glances out the back window. "I don't see her complaining."

"No, I guess not." I press the start button and hear the hiss of water beginning to boil. "All set."

"Come on. I want to show you something." There's color in his cheeks once again, and his eyes have lost the dullness that made the normally sparkling blue look gray and ominous. Even the redness has subsided a little.

"Okay." I follow him to the back door and watch as he slowly opens it, as if waiting for a grand reveal. When I see the vast change in front of me, I realize that's exactly what he was doing. "Wow," I say, more as a breath than a word. The screen closes behind us, but I barely register the sound. The entire yard has been transformed. Trees trimmed, rotting decking replaced, new lights strung in a crisscross pattern across the entire expanse of yard, new furniture, and is that . . . I move closer to the steps . . . yes, a fire pit. "You *have* been busy."

He chuckles, and I nearly slap my forehead. There are a million things I could have said that would have been far more eloquent than that.

"I mean, it's remarkable, Cam. Really." I turn to face him and soften at the way his body has relaxed. The way the hardness that's grown in the past ten years retreats and reveals the boy I so desperately thought I loved.

Morgan pops her head out of the tree house. "Is it time to go?"

I check my phone and note that, yes, it is time to leave, but I don't want to. "We have a few more minutes."

"Awesome." She ducks back in, and I feel him come closer. He stops when we are side by side, still perched on the edge of the porch.

"What's it like inside there?" he asks, curiosity seeping from his voice.

"You haven't seen it?"

He shakes his head. "It was locked when I went exploring."

"Ah yes." I nod, then point to the frog figurine on one of the new side tables. "There's a key ring of spares in there. Or there was at one point. I know the locks got changed, but I imagine the tree house one is still good."

"I don't want to invade her privacy." He shoves his hands into his jeans pockets and leans back against the porch post as if he needs the extra support.

"It's really no problem. Morgan won't mind at all." Well, maybe she will a little, but she'll get over it.

"That's okay. I'm good right where I'm at." He leans his head back, staring out into the distance with palpable relief.

I watch him, his eyes unfocused, his body a breath from collapse, and wonder how it's possible he's changed so much. "That, um, project you were working on. Is it for your next album?"

"No. My label isn't interested at all in my creativity. They want a robot. Not an artist." He closes his eyes and shakes his head slowly, almost as if he's afraid to move too much. "Maybe they're right. Maybe it's time to just . . ." His voice fades, and once again he's lost inside himself.

His lids remain shut, and I wonder if he even realizes he's shared such an intimate admission. But exhaustion can do that to a person. Break them down, shatter defenses. It's how I bonded with Mrs. Hardcastle so fast. She'd come over to welcome me to the neighborhood with a batch of cookies. Morgan had been sick all night with the flu, and I was barely well enough to make it to the door. When it opened and I saw her smiling face, I broke down in tears. She mended us both back to health for the next two days. We'd been like family ever since.

The rich smell of her coffee percolates through the open back door, and my throat tightens. I glance at Cameron, practically sleeping on his feet, then at the tree house, and for the first time I truly understand Morgan's insistence on remaining attached to Mrs. Hardcastle's home. I feel her presence, too. That soft touch to the cheek. The sweet way she'd always make me feel supported and validated, especially when it came to being a mother with no one to guide me.

"Do you remember when Cassie decided to take possession of your room?" My hands tremble at the idea of revealing what I'm about to share, but I suck in a determined breath and force the words to continue. "She'd said yours was bigger and had better windows and that it wasn't fair you got to have it when you already had an apartment at school."

His eyes flutter open. "I remember. We fought about it for a week. She'd thrown out all my music."

"Well, not exactly. I may have salvaged a few, well, actually all your recordings." The words linger between us, and Cameron stands a little straighter, registering my admission. There'd been dozens of demos. Some instrumental, some ear-piercingly horrid as he learned the recording equipment, and some so heart-wrenchingly beautiful they could bring one to tears in an instant. "I was supposed to bring them out to the trash bin, but instead I rummaged through the bag and rescued every note you'd created."

His eyes blaze into me now, part terrified, part . . . I don't know what to call it, regret maybe?

I reach out and take his hand boldly, squeeze his fingers between mine. "You are more than an artist, Cameron. Your music has strengthened me when I had nothing left to hold on to. It's comforted me when I was sure I would break." I glance toward the house, as if I can still see the torn-up pages lying on the table, and back to him. "A robot couldn't have done that."

Cameron's eyes fill so fast they blur in front of me. He doesn't say a word, but his hand grips mine hard now, clinging to me and my words.

"Mom! We have to go!" Morgan's shout shatters the moment. "Melissa's texting me like crazy."

Cameron turns away, and I can only guess that he doesn't want Morgan to see him so vulnerable.

I swallow before answering my daughter, working to keep my voice light. "I'll meet you out front. Go through the gate." Morgan will pick up on Cameron's emotion in an instant if I let her near us. I turn back to Cam. "Looks like I'm going to have to take a rain check on the coffee."

He doesn't move, just stands there rigid, head lowered, arms a shield across his chest. I step back and wish things didn't feel so uncomfortable, even though I know it's my fault that they do. I've crossed a line. Pushed too hard. Inserted myself into his life as if we were best friends, not two people who haven't spoken in years.

He didn't ask me to come here. Didn't ask for my intrusion into his life and his music.

I open my mouth to apologize, then stop because I'm not sorry that we had a real moment. I want to know him. The man he is now, even if he doesn't seem to want to share this version. So instead of saying more words, I lay my hand on his arm in a gentle goodbye and see myself out the front door.

THIRTEEN

Cameron

I wake to sunshine late Sunday morning. I slept for nearly twenty-four hours. It was the sleep of the dead, dreamless and peaceful. A sleep I hadn't had in months, maybe even in years.

My hand automatically reaches for my phone on the nightstand. I'd put it on *Do not disturb* Friday before the concert and had yet to lift the isolation. As soon as I do, a flood of notifications hits. My parents, my sister who's back from her honeymoon, my agent.

Immediately, I set the device facedown, unwilling to ruin this moment with a fire hose of stresses. Instead, I revel in the ache of not moving for so long. Revel in the way my head feels free of the noise, of the song I was finally able to fix after Lexie and Morgan left. It'd only taken minutes. One glance at the page and there it was, the half-step mistake. I'd collapsed into bed soon after, exhausted.

I shower and dress in record time, or at least record time for me. There is no dragging of my feet. No bemoaning the endless hours ahead. I'm actually looking forward to the day. And to Lexie.

A shot of adrenaline hits at the thought of seeing her again. She was a light in the darkness yesterday. Driftwood in a sea of black, churning waters. I need to thank her, to explain why her belief in me opened a chasm of hope. For the first time since Darcy walked out of my life, I felt like someone saw me. Understood me. I hadn't realized how debilitating that loss had been until the moment Lexie squeezed my hand.

I bounce down the stairs and halt, my own eyes seeing what she must have for the first time. Papers are still discarded everywhere, and the burnt, bitter coffee still sits untouched in the carafe. It's already eleven. If Morgan keeps to the schedule she outlined, they will be by after church. A mere hour and a half from now.

Not wanting this mess to be how Lexie pictures me, I rip through the first floor, tearing off dust sheets, cleaning, and vacuuming. The kitchen doesn't need much since I've been living off leftovers and takeout, but I clean anyway. I want her to see the difference, to feel the change just as I have.

Almost precisely on cue, the doorbell rings. I rush to open it, the anticipation so intense my hands tremble. I press my palm to the frame, bend over the way I used to right before taking the stage, and breathe in and out until my pulse quits its sharp hammer against my wrists. Once in control, I open the door, only to be met with the harsh pang of disappointment.

"Well, you certainly look better." Morgan stands alone, her voice as snappy as ever, holding a shoebox-sized storage bin in her hands. "And it's a good thing, because Mom said I had to leave immediately if you didn't."

I work to find a smile. "Where is your mom?"

"Where else?" She sighs and gestures with her head toward the renovation down the street. "But she asked me to bring you this." She extends her arms and pushes the box into my hands. "She said they were yours and to say thank-you for letting her borrow them for so long."

"Thanks." I examine the container. It's clear, and inside are old SD cards and USB memory sticks. "Did she say what they were?"

"Nope." Morgan bounces on her tiptoes, impatience setting in. "Listen, I only have an hour, and the clock started when I left, so can I . . . ?"

I pull my eyes from the gift. "Sure, go ahead."

"Awesome." She practically jumps off the porch and jogs around to the back gate.

True to my agreement with her mother, I shut the front door and settle into the swing on the porch out front, glancing back at the house down the street twice before deciding not to walk over. With Mason there, it wouldn't be the conversation I want anyhow.

I slowly open the container, my breath hitching when I see the first scribbled label. My music.

It's like a step through time. I pick up each one, note the date, and hear the songs in my head. The technology gets smaller in size and larger in memory with each passing year, until it stops altogether the year when I could store the massive amounts of data in an imaginary computer cloud. She'd really kept my music? All these years?

I carefully place the lid back on the box and pull out my phone. In two clicks I order the accessories I need to download the songs and shortly after get the notice they will be in before five o'clock tomorrow.

Listening to my old songs has to be better than watching subpar bands onstage. This weekend's fiasco proved that concretely. And these would be my words, my compositions, my dreams laid out for me to relive. Fear suddenly replaces the excitement, and I lower my head to my hands, my pulse a quick beat once again. What if I still don't feel anything? What if the void never leaves?

I bolt to my feet, agony surging with the unknown, and refocus on the filthy porch. In seconds, I have my broom and a trash bag, grateful for the distraction.

~☙

I had every intention of declining dinner tonight. Cassie and Stephen will be there, and I haven't totally forgiven her for what she put me through at her wedding. But I also know that if I had stayed at the house any longer, I would've walked down the street and very likely made an even bigger fool of myself with Lexie. If she'd wanted to see me, she would have brought the box herself, not sent it with Morgan.

I rub at my neck, agitated that I can't get her out of my mind, and knock hard on my parents' door. The last time a girl had me this tied up in knots, she'd devastated me.

Cassie's beaming face is the first thing I see past the now-open entrance. "You came!" she screeches, rushing out to knock me over in a hug. "I thought you might still be mad at me."

"I am still mad at you." And yet my arms encircle her, pulling her close. Despite all effort, I've never been successful at resisting Cassie's charms. None of us have. It's the superpower of the baby in the family.

"No, you're not. And besides, you didn't come to the reception, so I already got my punishment." She leans back, her eyes meeting mine. "I really am sorry."

Her sincerity completely zaps any residual frustration. "You're forgiven."

"Good!" She leaps from my arms only to grab my hand, pulling me inside the house so familiar I could walk through it blind and still know where to find everything. "I can't wait to tell you all about our trip. It was so romantic and peaceful."

"Save the details for Catherine." I groan, wishing more than ever that our oldest sister was here to be a buffer. Cassie has an unbearable habit of oversharing.

She giggles. "Fine. But you have to look at our snorkeling pictures at least."

"That I can do."

My dad and Stephen are already seated at the dining table when we walk in, and Cassie rushes off to help Mom with the dinner.

"You made it," my dad says with a hitch of surprise. Apparently, no one expected me to show up tonight. "I was beginning to think I'd imagined you coming home for the holidays." His words are a not-so-subtle reminder that I've been a ghost since the wedding. The neglect wasn't intentional, just part of the survival.

"I've been busy," I say, pulling out a chair opposite Stephen. He smiles, and it's both nervous and apologetic. Poor guy apparently doesn't know what it's like in a big family. Drama and bickering are part of the DNA. He'll learn soon enough. Cassie is the best at it. "You should come by and see the backyard. I think I've hung about a hundred lights."

"Aren't you just renting the place?"

"Yeah, but who knows? Maybe . . ." I trail off when I notice the spark of hope in my father's eyes and regroup. "Maybe all my work will help Kelly get the contract. She'd be able to sell it quickly in that area for sure. And she did go out of her way to get the place for me to begin with."

Dad tries to hide his disappointment, but I don't miss how

his chest falls. "Yeah. No, that's good." He reaches for his water glass and swallows down the liquid.

This new politeness between us is unnerving, but I prefer it to the alternative. Dad is the investigative type. He digs until he finds the problem and then won't stop meddling until it's fixed. Physical, mental, spiritual, it doesn't matter. He's a pro at it. And truthfully, if I thought he could fix me, I'd tell him everything, but he can't.

Mom and Cassie coming in, arms full, saves us from the lingering silence. Dad and I both jump up to relieve them of the serving dishes and set them carefully down on preplaced hot pads. Cassie takes a seat next to her husband, and I'm warmed by how he pulls her in and kisses her temple. Stephen may not be the most charismatic or talkative guy I've ever known, but he obviously adores my sister and that's good enough for me.

"Well." My mom sighs, her eyes glistening as she looks between me and my sister. "I think this special night calls for a special prayer. Cameron, honey, will you do the honors?"

The entire table looks at me expectantly, and I fight the rising panic in my chest. "Sure," I croak out, and we all bow our heads the way we did at every dinner I remember growing up.

Luckily, the words come out clear and unstilted. Muscle memory, I guess. When I say amen, they all repeat the word, and soon the sounds of passing dishes and moving utensils replace the heaviness in the air.

Conversation ensues, Cassie driving most of it as she gives detail after detail of their trip to Cozumel. I listen, asking questions where appropriate, and enjoy the fact that no one is focused on me. The topic shifts to the wedding, and Mom gives insight into all the old friends they saw and what each person is now up to. My back stiffens as I process each name she mentions in passing, noting the absence of the very one who has spent nearly as much time at this dinner table as I have. I shouldn't be surprised. My family knows better than to mention Darcy to me by now. Once it's clear Mom isn't going to dredge up the past, I settle back in my chair, silently enjoying the food on my plate.

"And goodness, Lexie sure has gotten beautiful. When was the last time you two had seen each other?" My mom's question is for Cassie, but I look up anyway, my attention now one hundred percent focused on the chatter around me.

Cassie swallows before answering. "A couple months ago. We ran into each other at that coffee shop on West and talked for almost an hour. She's exactly the same." She shakes her head, and the motion is laced with admiration. "A complete optimist despite everything."

"Seems so unfair," Mom pipes in. "Losing both parents so young."

I'm riveted now. "Lexie's dad died? When?"

"Not long after graduation. Nine months maybe?" Dad says. "She was off at college, and after a few days of not being able to get ahold of him, she called the police. They found him in his kitchen. He'd had a brain aneurism."

"Oh . . . I didn't know." My chest aches for her loss. I still remember the months after her mom's funeral. The dullness in her eyes. The way she'd tried to smile even though it was obvious her heart was broken.

"Which one was Lexie?" Stephen asks, contributing for the first time to the exchange.

"Short black dress," Cassie quips.

Stephen's eyes light with awareness. "Does she have long dark hair? And is working on some house renovation?"

"Yes . . ." Cassie raises an eyebrow. "Should I be concerned that you know all of that?"

I narrow my eyes, wondering the same thing. Not that any

guy would have missed those legs, but still, the groom should be an exception.

Stephen immediately flushes. "What? No, gosh no. I wasn't asking for me. That's just how my cousin described her." His jumble of sentences proves his innocence, and Cassie laughs, apparently enjoying his fluster. "Drake's been hounding me for days about getting her phone number. I guess they hit it off or something."

"Really? Oh, that would be awesome. We could double-date." Cassie reaches down for her purse, and lightning flashes through my veins.

"I think if Lexie wanted him to have her number, she would have given it to him." I don't realize I'm clutching my fork until all eyes land on me. I hadn't meant for the words to come out so forcefully, but the idea of some guy harassing her makes my skin crawl. Slowly, I release the utensil and try to relax my tone. "I mean, she isn't exactly shy."

"No, she isn't." Cassie releases her purse without retrieving the sought-after phone, and something intangible releases in my chest. "Nor is her daughter, but I don't guess you've met her yet?" Cassie's oncoming smirk is slow and far too insightful. "Or maybe you have?"

We engage in a silent showdown. She's fishing and doing it in front of Mom and Dad, so I have no choice but to swallow the hook. "Yes," I finally say. "We ran into each other at the wedding, and ironically they live in my neighborhood. Morgan's . . ." I'm at a loss for words to describe the bold, sarcastic teenager who makes all others seem incredibly dull. "Well, she's a pretty cool kid. Unique."

"Sounds a lot like Lexie," Mom says warmly. "She was always so polite and helpful."

I snort out a laugh. "I wouldn't exactly call Morgan polite.

The kid's all heart and instinct. She'd take down a giant if she needed to."

Mom's eyes turn glossy, and she reaches down the table to squeeze my hand. "I miss that smile, Cam."

I hadn't realized I was smiling, but the gooey eyes of my mom and sister prove I am.

"In case you're wondering, I'd be thrilled," Cassie says. "Lexie's a remarkable human being."

"I'm not wondering anything, especially since I'm leaving right after the New Year," I remind her.

"If you say so." Her voice is not only smug but also laced with challenge.

"I'm confused," Stephen says, glancing between me and my sister. "Are we or are we not giving Drake Lexie's number?"

Cassie winks at me and turns to her husband. "No. We most certainly are not."

FOURTEEN

Lexie

I stand in the center of the old kitchen, soon to be a laundry room, and feel pretty darn proud of us. Mason and I killed ourselves all weekend, and not only have we made up the lost days, but I've even had him laughing a time or two. Now we have two weeks until the plumbers come, and there seems to be a distinctive light at the end of the tunnel.

"So what's next?" I ask.

Mason tosses another pile of swept-up dirt into a large black trash bag. "We head upstairs and demo the last two bathrooms. Then we start framing walls. If we make the kind of progress we did in the kitchen, we could actually get done early." He grunts a laugh of disbelief. We're both still stunned at the ease of the kitchen demo. No leaks. No surprise piping. Even the laminate floors came up without much fuss. It's as if the kitchen knew deep down it had spent its life in the wrong location and was eager to move.

The new kitchen we've designed is located at the center of the house, which will dramatically change the flow and function of the entire space. It's going to be breathtaking, especially once we put in the wall of sliding doors that will span the entire back of the house.

"Maybe . . ." I draw out the word, hoping to soften Mason up a bit. "Since we did so much this weekend, we could take tonight off?" I'm still in my work clothes and have had dreams of sweatpants, long baths, and hours of sleep. "I'll even take you to dinner. My treat."

Mason runs his forearm across his brow, and for a second I think he might actually consider the idea. But the moment fades, and instead he picks up his toolbox. "I had a big lunch, so I'm good. You should go, though. I know Morgan would enjoy some time with her mom."

"Don't even try that tactic with me." I cross my arms and scowl, though there's not a lot of heat behind it. "We've been over this more than once. If you stay, then I stay."

"I'm not working a full-time job right now, am I? Nor do I have a teenage kid. You've earned a break, Lexie."

I hear Morgan stomping around upstairs, and guilt nearly makes me grab my keys and go home. But it's just for a season, I tell myself again. An investment in our future. Sacrifices come with the territory. "Looks like it's overalls for me. I'm just going to run Morgan home and change." I walk toward the stairs, ignoring Mason's you're-being-too-stubborn-for-your-own-good glare, and yell, "Morgan, let's go!"

"Coming!" She flies around the landing, backpack in hand. "What's for dinner?"

"We'll decide in the car."

She bounces down the stairs, and the noise of her footsteps nearly drowns out the hard knock on the front door. I pause, and it comes again. Three knocks this time. "Mason, are you expecting someone?" I call back to the kitchen.

"Nope."

Morgan heads for the door, but I stop her. The only people who come to this house are takeout delivery people and solicitors. If Mason didn't order anything, then it's very likely one of the many salesmen who frequent the neighborhood preying on the vulnerable senior population. "I'll get it. You go say goodbye to Mason."

When she's out of sight, I swing open the door, expecting a stranger. Instead, it's Cameron standing there with his back to me. His hands are pushed down into his pockets, his feet restless as if he hasn't quite decided whether to stay or go.

"Hey, what are you . . . ?"

He turns, and the smile he gives me chokes the rest of the words from my throat. He's a new person today compared to Saturday. Gone is the pallid tone in his skin, the red-rimmed eyes, the defeated stance. "I saw your car pull up," he says quickly. "I thought maybe I could talk you into dinner."

"Morgan's with me." I step outside and close the door tightly. Cameron's presence always seems to put a burr under Mason's skin, and I'd rather not deal with the aftermath of another confrontation.

"Of course. Both of you, I mean. And Mason, too, if he wants." The last part comes out strangled, but I'm still impressed he offered. "Mom sent me home last night with more food than one human being could possibly eat. I figured I'd share the wealth."

A home-cooked meal. My mouth waters at the thought. "Did Morgan tell you I'm a terrible cook? Is that why you're here? To save my daughter from another night of fast food?"

His smile grows wider. "No, she didn't tell me that, but I'm good with saving both of you if you'll let me." I'm taken aback by the easy air about him tonight. It reminds me of the old

Cameron, and my buried teenage heart begins beating faster. My feet ache to follow him and indulge in a wonderful night of his company, but I made a commitment and I can't leave Mason here alone.

I open my mouth to regretfully decline when the front door opens behind me.

"Oh, it's just Cameron," Morgan calls out and hops down the steps to stand next to me. "Hey, what's up?"

I look behind me, and Mason is standing inside the doorway. He folds his arms in front of his chest and leans against the frame like a protective older brother.

"I came to see if you guys wanted some dinner," Cameron says before I have a chance to defuse my cousin.

"You included," I add, still watching Mason, hoping the invitation will lessen the scowl on his face.

He glares at me, and I know he has no intention of doing anything with Cameron tonight or ever. "Do whatever you want." He pushes off the doorframe. "I did give you the night off."

A sick feeling churns in my gut when he shuts the door a second later. His words and his tone were not saying the same thing.

"Was he serious?" Morgan beams. "You're not working tonight?"

I look between the two hopeful faces in front of me and then back at the one I can no longer see behind the closed front door. An impossible situation. One that inevitably hurts someone.

"I can swing a dinner," I finally say, conceding. My cousin will stew while I'm gone, but he's already admitted to not being able to stay mad at me.

A grin lights up Morgan's face as she turns to Cameron. "You're good luck."

The comment seems to pour over him like melting sunshine. His eyes grow warm and affectionate. "I think you are, as well."

"Then let's go, pokies. I'm hungry." She bounces to the car to drop off her bag. "I'll be in the tree house. Call me when dinner's ready," she says, running ahead of us. In that moment she looks like a little girl again, eager and wide-eyed. It's the hardest part about this age. One moment she's my baby, the next she wants me to back off and give her complete freedom. Neither feels right.

I join Cameron on the sidewalk, and we trail after her.

"How was work today?" he asks after a long beat of silence.

"Good. This is my last week, so I'm mostly tying up loose ends."

"You're quitting?"

"Oh no. I'm just taking all my saved vacation time. I'll go back after Christmas."

"Wow. That's, what . . . six weeks?"

"Five. We get a week off at Thanksgiving and a week off at Christmas, with each of us rotating an on-call day for emergencies. I'll take the three weeks in between. To help Mason with the house," I add.

"Makes sense. That's quite a project you've taken on."

"I know. But it's all going to be worth it in the end," I say, mostly to remind myself. I was late paying two bills this month, missed an important meeting at work, and walked around all day yesterday with two different shoes on. Organization has never been my strong suit, and that character flaw is coming back to bite me now.

We stop in front of his house, and he hesitates before walking up the steps. "I want to thank you. For my music."

"You're welcome. I thought maybe . . ." I stop and decide I'd better give him some backstory or I'll sound like a complete stalker. "When my mom got sick, she found this old record player. She'd saved all her favorite music from when she was a kid, and on the bad days she'd listen for hours to oldies that would make your ears bleed." I smile at the memory, grateful to have all those albums buried in the closet. The record player quit working years ago, but I don't have to hear the music to think of her. "Those songs were her lifeline, a reminder of better times." I wonder again at the dangers of giving him so much truth but decide to press ahead anyway. Time is too short, and I want him to know how much he's influenced my life. "Your music has done the same for me. And I don't know, but I thought maybe they could do something similar for you, as well."

His expression turns soft, much like it did when Morgan said his being around brought good luck. It makes me wonder how long it's been since Cameron had someone encourage him. "I'm not quite sure what they are to me yet, but I've been listening to them most of the afternoon. Well, cringing as I listen is more like it."

I laugh because I know exactly which ones he would consider cringeworthy, and ironically those are some of my favorites. "Don't be too hard on yourself. Everyone has to start somewhere."

"I guess." He sighs, and I wish I could read him better. There's so much happening behind his eyes, so much I know he's not saying. "Well, we should probably get you fed." A barrier erected, I realize. He's not yet ready to trust me. And that's okay, I suppose. For now, dinner can be enough. He spreads his arms out. "After you." There's pride in his voice, eagerness even.

I know why as soon as I walk inside. All the dust sheets are gone, the living room clean and inviting once again. "I hope you didn't do all this just for us."

"Maybe a little. But also for myself." He steps around me,

and I follow him to the kitchen. A rich, buttery aroma fills the air.

"Smells delicious," I murmur, leaning against the counter while he pulls a large pan of chicken from the oven. "Can I help you?"

"Nope. You're my guest tonight. Go make yourself comfortable." He gestures to the back door, and again I see the eagerness to please. "We're eating outside."

"Fun." I push off the counter, my heart dancing because this entire evening feels like more than a thank-you. I step outside and halt when I see the new patio table. Fresh flowers sit in a vase on top of white linen. But it isn't the fancy setup with chargers and tall, elegant glasses that makes my hand cling to my chest. It's the fact that there are three place settings already set. Morgan wasn't an afterthought. She was part of his evening from the beginning.

The screen opens, and Cameron pushes through with two large platters in his hands. I move aside and watch as he cautiously sets each down, careful to keep the aesthetics of the table intact. He's an artist in every way. Beauty is his muse.

"Morgan," I call. "Time to eat." She appears quickly and clambers down from the tree house. "Go wash your hands."

Cameron stands behind a chair and pulls it out for me. I sit and wonder when I'm going to wake up.

Dinner turned into a blur of words, mostly from my daughter, who pestered Cameron with question after question about life on tour, celebrities he's met, the favorite places he's played at, and on and on. Cameron graciously answered every single one, even though at times I saw his shoulders tense or noticed he'd swallow uncomfortably. Not all those memories were positive, but he answered as if they were, often with the

same charisma he displayed when being interviewed by entertainment reporters.

Our plates have been empty for a while now, and the sun
has set, leaving the backyard a gloriously lit oasis to look out
upon. I should politely take my leave. I've already stayed an
hour longer than I meant to, resetting the timer on my watch
twice. But apparently, ending the evening is a discipline I
can't seem to conquer.

"Anyone want dessert?" Cameron offers, and I pull my
eyes away from the hanging lights and back to him.

"I don't. I'm stuffed," Morgan says, throwing her napkin
on her plate. And she should be. The girl single-handedly ate
half the pan of chicken. "Can I be excused?"

"Not until we clean up."

"Okay." She groans and eyes Cam. "We would've been fine
with paper plates, by the way. It's pretty much all we eat off
of."

Cameron laughs, and my cheeks flush with embarrassment. His mom would be horrified by the idea of serving dinner on anything but elegant dishes. "You're both my guests of
honor, so no clean-up duties tonight." He winks at her. "And
next time I'll remember the paper plates."

Her eyes perk up as she holds her breath, waiting to see if
she can so easily be allowed to skip protocol.

And sadly she can be, because truthfully the idea of a few
moments alone with Cameron feels like a rare treat.

"Far be it from me to argue with the host," I concede, and
she's out of her chair before I change my mind. I turn back to
Cameron. "I, on the other hand, insist on helping you clean up."

"Not a chance." He leans back in his chair and watches
me curiously. "Besides, now that it's just the two of us, you
can tell me more about you and what all you've been doing
the last ten years."

"Me?" I brush off the question like it's ridiculous. "Compared to what you just shared, my life is incredibly boring."

"There's something to be said for boring." His voice sobers a little. "Lately, I'm finding the idea of a simple existence a lot more appealing."

"Why is—?"

"Nope." He shakes his head. "We are not turning this conversation back to me. I want to know about *you*, Lexie."

"There's really not much to tell." Even as the words come out, I know they aren't accurate. There is a lot to tell, but it's also not a time in my life I like to focus on. The past hurts, which is why I don't spend any time there. But the stubborn set to Cameron's jaw tells me I'm not getting out of this exercise even if I want to. "After I got Morgan, I came home to find a job that had flexible hours. And thankfully, I had enough money saved to keep us fed and sheltered." I pause, the sting of that time coming back in full measure. The money had been from Dad's estate, split between Annaliese and me. I shudder to think of what her half went to. "We made it through that first year," I continue, wanting to move on in both word and thought. "And then I finished my associate degree online and got in at the property-management office I work at now. It's been pretty much the same ever since."

"That must have been really difficult without family to help." His voice turns soft, compassionate. "I heard about your dad. I'm really sorry."

"Thank you." I swallow down a sudden spark of grief and smile at him. "Despite everything that's happened, though, we've been very blessed. We found our rental house a few years later and met Mrs. Hardcastle. She was God's chosen surrogate grandparent for sure." I glance around the beautiful backyard Cameron has created. "She would have loved what you've done out here."

He doesn't comment, and I realize I've once again directed the conversation back to him. He doesn't let me get away with the detour. "You mentioned needing a lifeline earlier. Is that when you were talking about? That year after Morgan came to live with you?"

I'm amazed he listened so intently. It's a new facet of Cameron's personality I'm not quite accustomed to. He used to flip from thought to thought, moving at a constant speed, always needing the next big event or project. This version seems to sit still more, listen closer, and truly cares about the answers given. And maybe that's why I also settle back in my seat. Why it feels totally safe to share the deepest parts of my life with him. "Yes, it was a really hard time. Dad hadn't even been gone a year yet, and Annaliese . . ." I fade off, pushing down the pain that always comes when I think of my sister, and skip past the worst parts. "I had no clue what I was doing. It's truly a miracle Morgan wasn't taken from me." My mind catapults to those twenty-plus-hour days when sleep was a wish and survival the only thing keeping me upright.

He reaches across the table and takes my hand. "I know what it feels like to be all alone, Lexie. I'm sorry you've ever had to feel that way."

The heat of his palm against mine makes my heart swell again. The hope comes, thick and heavy, that maybe these feelings I have aren't one-sided after all. "That's just it. I wasn't completely alone. I had my faith, the strength my parents instilled in me, and your music. I know your voice so well at this point that I could pick out your signature on any song." I trace the line of his finger leisurely, inviting him to do the same. He squeezes my hand instead and eyes me with such compassion and concern that I want to reach out and smooth out the frown in his brow. To assure him that despite all that's happened, I am not a broken bird that needs her wings fixed. "Don't look so stricken." I smile reassuringly at him, yet he continues to watch me with intensive scrutiny. "That was a long time ago. I'm happy, Cameron. I have Morgan, which makes it all worth it. I don't waste time looking back."

"Good. I'm glad you've found a way to do that. Most people aren't that strong." His voice is soft and filled with an admiration I don't really deserve.

"I am serious about being able to find your signature," I say, wanting to leave this subject and all the stirrings it causes deep inside. "You should test me."

His brow wrinkles. "Test you?"

"Yes. Play me any original song from your first two albums, and I bet you I'd be able to pinpoint exactly what you added to the composition."

"Any song?" His eyes dance with mischief.

"Yep. Any song."

"And what are the stakes?" His voice purrs, a challenge dropped in my lap.

I fall silent while a bucket of wishes spills out in my mind. If only he knew how many things I want to ask for, especially when I feel so confident in my abilities. "If I guess correctly," I say, "then you have to sing for me." It's an easy request, but something I've dreamt about more times than I care to admit. "And I get to pick the song."

His smile fades into a line. I watch as he bites his lip, contemplating my request. "You can ask for anything and that is what you pick?"

I nod emphatically. "Yes, definitely."

"Okay. But one song is too easy for such a prize." There's a tremble in his voice I don't quite understand because he almost sounds terrified. "We'll do three. And if you pick out my signature in each song," he adds, "I'll sing for you." It's a statement, but there is no surety in his voice. "And if you don't, then you have to promise you'll come over again for dinner."

My heart leaps. A win-win either way. But I don't tell him that. "Who picks the songs?"

He ponders the question, probably wondering how serious I am. "We each get one, and then we'll flip for the third."

"Tell you what, you sing me two songs and you can pick all three."

"You're that sure of yourself?"

"Absolutely."

My confidence seems to surprise him, but he nods, accepting the terms. "Alright, it's a deal." He pulls out his phone, presses the screen a few times, and sets it on the table between us.

The first song is so easy, it's laughable. But I play along, enjoying the amusement in his eyes as he watches me bounce in my chair along to the music. This is from his Grace Community album. Track five.

He pauses the phone when it finishes, and I smugly give him the answer. "You wrote the entire thing . . . except for the bridge."

"Yes," he says slowly, disbelief lingering in his voice. "Brent added it hours before we recorded the CD. How did you know?"

"That part is too commercial to be your work," I say. Brent has been the worship pastor at Grace Community for fifteen years. I practically have his signature memorized, as well. "Next."

This time Cameron's eyes narrow, and his lips curl. Competitive energy sparks between us. I love that he's going to at least try to challenge me. He pulls up Black Carousel's album—the one that catapulted him to a household name—and presses track two.

This one is Bryson's work. Hard and fast and angry. I'd heard him play it before, when Mason was still in the band, but this version is just slightly different from what they sang back in the day. A layer of strings was added to the second verse and chorus. This version also has a gorgeous harmony that the first lacked.

I pause it before it's finished. I don't need to hear the rest. "You added strings and the harmonies. You also changed the lyrics on the third verse."

He falls back into his chair, stunned. "You're right again. How—?"

"Well, I sort of cheated on this one. I watched Mason perform it once . . . right before he left the band. You made it much better," I say quickly when his gaze turns guilty. I nearly kick myself under the table. I know better than to invite my cousin into this conversation.

Cameron remains still, contemplative. And then he sits up, wordlessly, and presses another song from the same album.

"A Decade of Love" pours out from the speaker. He watches me listen, intently, as if he's cataloging every response I make.

My confidence wanes. This song has always confounded me. Cameron's voice is beautiful. Smoky, dreamy, sensual, but it's never felt quite right to me.

The song fades to silence, and Cameron turns off his phone. "Well? What part did I write?" The edge to his voice tells me this is more than an innocent bet. He truly is testing me.

I decide to go with my instincts, even if it means a blow to my pride, and raise my hands in surrender. "You win, I guess. I don't hear your heart in this song at all. Only your voice."

Cameron freezes, a storm filling his eyes. Surprise, hurt, anger. Every emotion plays across his features. I can't tell if

I'm right or wrong in my guess, only that whatever it is, the answer is a sword to his chest. He swallows and then carefully, as if each word slices his tongue, answers, "You're right. I added nothing to this song."

There's no joy in my victory, though I'm guessing my defeat wouldn't bring any different result. "Why did you pick it, then?"

"I don't know," he sighs, running a hand through his hair. His tone is distant, detached.

"I'm sorry." I'm at a loss as to what to do or say to make this better. "I feel like I've upset you."

His gaze flashes to mine. "No. You didn't." Tenderness plays across his expression, the storm receding as quickly as it came. "You are . . ." He pauses, not finishing the thought. "Can I show you something?"

"Sure." I stand when he does, still shaky from his oscillating emotions, and follow him back into the house.

He pulls out his laptop and logs in, leaning over the table versus sitting down. I watch as he navigates through a website, then clicks a highlighted link. "My label wants me to choose ten songs from our database of demos. I've narrowed it down to about twenty. This one is probably at the top." He clicks again, and music follows. He stands fully now and crosses his arms. The stance feels defensive, and I can't help but wonder why he's choosing from other people's work when there's an overflow of music within.

Cameron's an artist. He lives to create, not regurgitate someone else's handiwork.

Still, I try to listen with an open mind. To give him the courtesy of doing what he's asked me to do.

When it's finished, the air feels weighty with silence.

"Well, what do you think?" He bites his lip again, unsure. It's surreal to watch. Cameron nervous about music? Has the world turned completely upside down?

"It's good. Probably a big hit."

He seems to pick up on the lack of excitement in my voice. "But?"

"It isn't you. The depth. The originality. The emotion. It isn't there."

"I don't think any of that matters."

My breath catches. "Of course it matters."

"No," he says firmly. "It doesn't. I had an album with depth. One I poured my soul into. Fans hated it." He stares up at the ceiling. "If it wasn't for 'A Decade of Love,' I would still be an unknown, struggling, wannabe artist. And as you pointed out, I had nothing to do with that song."

I step closer, my heart aching to physically comfort him. "Your career is more than one song."

"No, it isn't." He laughs humorlessly. "I'm a fraud, Lexie. I've climbed to the top on someone else's back. And every time I try to take control and regain my life again, I fail." He looks at me then, and all the emotion I've seen periodically through barely open cracks comes spilling to the surface. "I haven't picked up an instrument in three months. Haven't sung a note. I feel like the music betrayed me and I have no idea where to go from here."

The admission guts me as much as it does him. I lose any last resistance and take his hands in mine. They're cold and shaky. He turns his face away, and I sense the humiliation in what he just admitted. If only he could see himself the way I see him. If only he understood what I know still exists underneath all his baggage and hurt.

"Cameron." Boldness leaks into my voice. "Look at me." I squeeze his hands harder until finally he does. Tears glisten in his eyes, and my resolve doubles. "You are not a failure. That last album, your label, critics, or whoever. They do not define you."

"It's not just them who believe it. I feel it." He closes his eyes. "I gave everything to those songs. Made sure each and every note was perfection. It makes no sense that the album didn't succeed." His voice rises, and he steps back, releasing me. I see the resentment replace the hurt, the tightness in his mouth, the slant of his eyes.

I hesitate over whether to give him a truth he apparently can't or doesn't want to see. Yes, his one and only solo album was technically perfect, but he's lying to himself if he thinks he poured his soul into it. Maybe his time, his blood, sweat, and tears, but not his soul. But my telling him as much won't change his perception. He has to hear it. He has to feel the difference, or my words are pointless.

"Do you have that box of songs I gave you?"

His brow wrinkles, but he turns and pulls the container out of the buffet near the dining table and hands it to me. I sort through the array of songs until I find the one that sends my heart into my throat. "This is my favorite song you've ever written," I say, extending the SD card that's so worn, the Sharpie label is only illegible black ticks. "Compare this song to every one on your newest album and tell me if they're the same."

He looks down at my offering but doesn't take it. Maybe he's not ready to admit the truth to himself yet. I guess I understand. We all have those times when the illusion feels more like home.

I set the card carefully on the table. When he's ready, he'll find what he's looking for. "Well, I should probably get Morgan home and change into my fancy overalls."

"I'm sorry, Lexie. Tonight was supposed to be about you, and once again I turned it to me." He watches me, the apology leaking from his voice. "Stay. We'll go back outside and have some dessert." But his offer is flat despite his best efforts.

"Thank you, but I really need to get back and help Mason."

He swallows, and then a hint of a smile breaks his solemn expression. "Yes. I imagine he is picturing my head as he swings the sledgehammer."

Probably so.

We walk to the backyard together, neither of us returning to the earlier conversation, and I call for Morgan to come down.

Cameron offers to walk me back to my car, still parked on the curb near Mason's truck, but I decline. He hasn't yet recovered from our conversation, even though he's putting on a very good show. He banters with Morgan, smiles when appropriate, and pretends. I now realize that's all he's been doing since our reconnection at the wedding. I just hadn't seen it until tonight. And now that I have, it's all I notice. The slight clenching of his jaw, the hard line of his shoulders. Every small, controlled gesture that tells me he's one breath away from falling apart. But he's practiced at this game. Enough to bid us goodbye without my daughter even noticing a difference.

I watch him watch us leave for only a brief second before turning around. Where this puts us, I don't know. I can't seem to reconcile the Cameron that is with the person he used to be. The boy of my childhood was light, fun, and every breath in his body was dedicated to music. For the first time, I wonder if Mason might be right. If maybe I have been blind to the man now in front of me.

Morgan whistles as we cross the street.

"You're in a good mood," I say, glad that at least one of us is leaving happy.

"What?" She turns as if just noticing I'm with her, and red flushes her cheeks. "Oh yes. I had fun over there." She charges ahead and rushes to the front door. I watch her disappear, and an old familiar churning plays in my stomach. She's been so delightful lately, so considerate and helpful. Is it wrong to wonder if maybe she, too, is pretending just like Cameron? Am I missing a gaping wound in her, too?

I stop at my car and lean my back against the door. My stomach twists like a wrung-out towel, and my chest aches for my mother's advice. I don't often let myself wallow in her absence, but lately I seem to be struggling to stay optimistic. I feel like I'm juggling a hundred little things and any minute now one is going to crash at my feet.

As if my thoughts are prophetic, a scream comes a second later. My head whirls to face the open front door, my heart a hammer against my rib cage. I rush forward, chasing after the anguished voice, and burst into the house. The foyer is empty, as is the living room. "Morgan!"

"Upstairs. Hurry, Mom. It's Mason. He's . . ." Her words are swallowed by a sob.

Fear clutches my throat, cutting off my air supply, but I run anyway. Up the stairs, down the hall, and into the small bathroom I was supposed to be helping destroy.

The world narrows into a small tunnel. My big, burly, stubborn-as-a-mule cousin is laid out on the floor, unconscious. Blood trickles from his brow. The ladder he obviously fell from is now tipped over and embedded into the wall.

Flashes of my father in the kitchen fill my mind. I never actually saw him, but I've imagined the moment over and over again.

"He's still breathing," Morgan squeaks out between guttural sobs. "I also checked his pulse like you showed me. It's weak, but it's there."

My vision returns, my father's body fading away as Mason's replaces it. Morgan's on her knees next to him, her hand clutching his. I see that three-year-old girl all over again. The gripping fear, the anguish, the black hole of doubt.

I slowly move toward them, keeping every panicked emotion clamped neatly in my chest. I can't break down. I have to be strong for her. Gently, I place both hands on her arms and pull her to standing. She acquiesces quickly and moves aside. I take her place next to him.

"Morgan, go downstairs and call 911. Don't come up here again until they get here, okay?"

She nods, tears streaming into her mouth, and then rushes from the horrific scene.

I move aside the hair on his forehead, checking for more injury. It's sticky, plastered to his forehead by sweat and dried blood. His lids flicker a little and slowly start to open. Then a wince of pain flashes so sharp against his face that he clenches his jaw and pulls in a seething breath.

"Don't move," I say quickly. "Tell me what hurts."

"My back," he moans, and the sound is barely audible. "I . . . I think . . ."

"Shhh. Just relax." I take his hand and press it to my cheek. I feel his pulse race now underneath my touch, the pain undoubtedly increasing. "We're getting you help, okay? I know it's hard, but try to stay still."

Guilt knifes through me. I abandoned him here, all alone. I knew what we were doing was dangerous. I knew he needed help and yet I left anyway. Selfish . . . so incredibly selfish. My vision blurs with tears, distorting Mason's broken body in front of me. "I'm sorry." I squeeze his hand, my heart crying out to the Lord to make this horror go away. "I'm so, so sorry."

FIFTEEN

Cameron

I'm halfway through the dishes when I hear sirens, distant at first and then louder and louder as if they're barreling right down my street. A slow churning hits my stomach. I've met most of my neighbors now, and the thought of any one of them being in trouble raises the hair on my arms. I wipe my hands, toss the towel onto the counter, and hurry to the front door. Red flashes split through the front windows, and my speed increases, turning the lock with fumbling fingers.

The noise becomes deafening when the door opens. I see the EMT and fire truck, and my heart seizes in my chest. I take off running, not thinking, not bothering to shut the door or grab my phone. Lexie. Morgan. Their names fly across my skin, the pure rush of panic as intense as if they were my own family.

I barrel through the open front door of the house they're renovating, my head on a swivel, searching. I spot Morgan immediately. She's huddled by the stairs, tears streaming down her face. She rushes forward, nearly knocking me over with the force of her desperate hug.

I will my heart to stop pounding, will my voice to stay even and calm. "What happened? Where's your mom?"

"She's with Mason . . . He fell." She sobs against my shirt, and I pray she doesn't notice the relief in my rigid body. Lexie's okay. She's not hurt. My head swims with dizziness, but I fight through it. Fight against every instinct that tells me to rush upstairs.

Instead, I do the one thing I know Lexie would want more than anything. I hold and comfort her daughter, assuring Morgan that their cousin will be okay and that the paramedics are here, and they know exactly what to do.

Voices and the clanking of metal grabs our attention, and we watch as the EMTs carefully descend the staircase with the stretcher. I move out of the way, bringing Morgan with me. With each step, Mason groans at the jarring. I fight the instinct to run to him. To be the friend I once was and not the stranger I've become.

When we were ten, I fractured my foot jumping off a flying swing. It was June and I had to wear an awful, heavy boot for six weeks. No swimming, no running, no summer fun. Mason had his mom drop him off at my house every day just to keep me company. He didn't even really like video games, too sedentary, but he played them anyway, side by side with me on the couch.

More memories fill my brain, and in each there's one commonality—Mason's loyalty. It never faltered.

My nerves prick with each drop of the stretcher's wheels, and I watch horror-struck at the immense pain it causes my childhood buddy. When the paramedics make it halfway down, I catch my first glimpse of Lexie trailing behind them.

Her face is ashen, her body trembling. She flinches with

each of Mason's cries of pain, and I swear more blood drains from her face with each slow step down the stairs. I lean down and whisper into Morgan's ear. "Go to the living room and wait for me. I'm going to check on your mom."

She nods a little too easily, and I'm gutted with the expression on her face as she turns away. The spirited, hands-on-her-hips sarcastic ball of fire is gone, replaced by a dazed, empty shell that seems to explain all I've observed of her and Lexie's dynamic. Morgan is not nearly as tough as she pretends to be.

As soon as the stretcher is off the stairs and heading out the door, I hurry to Lexie and meet her at the bottom of the staircase. She jolts when our eyes meet, and I realize this is the first moment she's been able to focus on anything but Mason's writhing body.

I take her hands in mine. They're icy cold and clammy. I don't have time to get a word out before she pulls them free and searches the room for something.

"They're taking him to Methodist Hospital, and I have to get his insurance card and driver's license." Her voice is far more controlled than her frightened body should allow. "And Morgan. Where is she? I need to get her some clothes and get her to Melissa's house. My phone." She moves past me, looking again for her daughter. "I need to find my phone. I need to get his car. His dog. Oh no. He probably needs to be let out. And work . . . I need to get . . ."

I chase after her and block her frantic movements. She finally, for the first time, looks me in the eye, and I'm hollowed out by the guilt and panic I see in them. "Lexie. All these things will happen. We'll make sure of it, okay?"

She swallows and nods. Her lip trembles, and I wonder how long it's been since she didn't have to be the one in charge. The one who fixes everything and everyone. My guess is it's been far, far too long since she's been the one who was taken care of.

"Do me a favor. Take a deep breath."

She does, and it's shaky as it passes her lips.

I place my hands on her shoulders and pull her to me. "Next, I'm going to hold you. Not for long. Just for two minutes." She's stiff when our chests meet, but I don't stop. I slide my hand up her back while my other hand tightens around her waist, and I pull her to me the same way I held Morgan earlier, easing her head to my chest.

She collapses into me, and I barely react in time to hold her upright. Lexie doesn't cry like Morgan did. She just holds on. My embrace tightens, and I squeeze my eyes shut, struck by the fact that I want to cry in her place. It's been so long since I've allowed myself to care this much for anyone that I honestly wondered if I was even capable of it anymore. Yet with her, it feels impossible not to care. Not to want to shield her and Morgan from life's hardships.

As promised, I slowly release her after the allotted two minutes, and my heart aches with the desire to pull her back to me. It's only when I see the color has returned to her cheeks and her eyes clearing that logic and reason take precedence. "What can I do to help you?" I ask, my voice steady. My arms fall away.

She closes her eyes and breathes in and out. When they open, her gaze is focused and alert. "Could you shut up the house and take care of Mason's dog? He can stay in the yard tonight. You'll just need to make sure he has water and food." She glances around again and spots her purse on the floor in the entrance. Probably where she dropped it when she rushed inside. "I'll text you the address and get his keys for you." She stops halfway to her handbag and glances at me, startled. "I don't have your contact information." She shakes her head like it's a crazy thought, and I agree. In this world where nearly every relationship we have is forged through technology, how is it possible that we've never interacted that way?

She moves quickly and efficiently, sending out any necessary texts, including the first one ever to me. Morgan seems to calm as she watches her mom take control, but I still go to her and wrap a comforting arm around her shoulder.

"We should have stayed here," she says, verbalizing the guilt I know Lexie feels, as well. "I shouldn't have pushed Mom so hard to take a break. I didn't realize how dangerous . . ." Her voice cracks, and she stops.

I squeeze, again attempting comfort that feels almost foreign. "If I've learned anything, Morgan, it's that life is made up of a whole bunch of should'ves. But I've yet to find a time machine to change any one of them. Or a crystal ball to prevent more in the future." She glances up at me, thoroughly listening, taking in my counsel in a way that makes me want to be worthy of the trust she's giving. "My advice is simply to learn. Learn from every moment and hope that as you do, the should'ves get further and further apart."

I listen to my voice, wondering where the wisdom came from. Certainly not my own life. I've immersed myself in should'ves for so long that I could list them by date, time, and place.

Lexie comes into the bare living room with all the items she needs to take care of her cousin. "Go get in the car," she says to her daughter, who immediately obeys. To me, she nods like a seasoned professional as she places Mason's keys into my hand. "Thank you. Just call if you have any questions."

I itch to pull her back in my arms, to kiss away the sorrow in her eyes and the sharp determination in the set of her mouth. "It's all under control," I say, working to appear just as competent as she seems to be. "You just go be with Mason."

She offers a half smile, turns away, and shuts the door behind her.

There are many facets to this woman, I'm learning, most of which I've already had the privilege to see. Her kindness, her humor, her unending optimism. This one pummels my chest in a way I don't expect: her strength.

She doesn't need me to save her. Not even in this moment.

I didn't go to the hospital last night, mostly because I felt pretty sure that my presence would upset Mason and, in turn, cause Lexie more stress. She texted this morning that he was doing okay and had been admitted as of midnight last night. He'd fractured his back in two places and suffered a mild concussion. He was scheduled for surgery today at eleven, and the prognosis looked good for a full recovery. She then thanked me for my help and let me know she had the dog covered now, so I didn't need to go back over there today.

That was two hours ago, and yet the information dump continues to nag at me. There was no invitation in her words. She didn't say *don't come to the hospital*, but she might as well have. I know Lexie isn't a kid anymore—her life alone makes that glaringly obvious—but this version feels far too cold and mature for the woman I'm only just getting to know. She's pulling back, and I have no idea if I want to let her or break down the hospital doors and shake her out of this new cocoon.

I turn off the fifth demo I've listened to this morning and toss my headphones on the dining room table, frustrated. I still have eight more songs I need to pick, and yet all I can think about is whether Lexie is really as okay as her text implies, and if Morgan slept at all last night or if she stared at the ceiling for hours like I did, playing the should've game again.

I stand, slide my chair out with irritated aggression, and ignore the SD card Lexie placed on my dining room table last night. I've been ignoring it all morning, but now it seems to be pulsing, filling the room with accusation and doubt. I don't even know which song she was referring to. The frayed label has no more than a few black lines at this point. And I certainly don't want to compare the sound to my newest album. I haven't listened to one note on that piece of junk since the radio stopped playing the songs only a mere three weeks after release. "A Decade of Love" stayed on the Billboard Hot 100 for a solid year. Not one song from my newest album even broke the list. What I thought had been the culmination of all my years of sacrifice and unyielding ambition had turned into my greatest failure. No amount of wanting to please or to understand Lexie will make me relive that nightmare over again.

And yet I can't take my eyes off the plastic.

I see it when I pass by. See it when I'm in the kitchen refilling my coffee. See it again when I open the back door. I even see it when the door is closed and I'm standing on the back porch, facing the completely opposite direction. I squeeze my eyes closed and growl because yes, even now, the confounded thing is still invading my thoughts.

My stomach sours, and I toss the remnants of coffee left in my cup onto the grass in front of me. I know this feeling. I've dealt with the scars of it my entire life. It's my curse, my weakness. I have no ability to compartmentalize. Once a thought or feeling or obsession takes root, it's unrelenting in its battery.

I slap down my empty cup on the wooden rail and storm back inside. My fingers brush quickly across the table, grasping the SD card with both bitterness and resentment. I'm back in my chair seconds later, hooking up the adapter I need to listen to the music. I place my headphones back over my ears, wishing they'd also drown out the manic slamming of my heart against my rib cage.

In college, I took an entire semester course on Beethoven, studied his compositions, his family, and even his disability. So many others in my group thought his deafness was a tragedy, but I secretly envied his ability to shut out the world and just play. To not be plagued repeatedly by the noise around him. I feel that same envy now. I wish I couldn't hear the notes coming through, wish I didn't remember exactly where I was when this song first penetrated my mind. Wish I didn't feel the sickening tumble in my gut as I wholeheartedly praised a God I've all but written off.

I only make it to the second verse when my headphones go flying. I grip the edges of the chair, my heart racing, my eyes filling with remorseful tears that feel more like acid than saline. I barely feel my legs as I rise from the table and grab my keys. I don't know why I'm going where I'm going, and yet I can't seem to stop myself from starting the car and slamming the gearshift into drive.

Ten minutes later, I'm at Grace Community Church. I didn't need to finish the song Lexie claimed was her favorite. The notes haven't stopped clawing inside my brain since I slammed my computer shut. They were the last lyrics I'd written as a praise team member nine months before I walked out of this building and never came back. The last notes I penned to paper before months of writer's block and confusion and frustration took hold of every action and decision. And if I were to be truthful with myself, they were also the last verses I crafted from when my heart still trusted God to guide me. Every song since has been mine and mine alone.

I turn off the ignition and walk to the worship center. I never returned the key when I unceremoniously quit and wonder if they've changed the locks since my departure. I slide in the metal and twist. The bolt turns, just as easily as it did nearly five years ago.

The lights are off, but sunlight streams through the many glass doors illuminating the stadium seating. Easily two thousand people would fill this room on a Sunday morning and listen to us play. When I first started with the band, I'd been in awe, struck by my good fortune to have this kind of opportunity to share my love for both God and music. Then the years passed, and a stirring for more took over. I started counting people, feeling frustrated and disappointed when there weren't more. How naïve I'd been thinking numbers would change the heart. I've played for tens of thousands of fans in too many cities to count and yet here I am, back again. Broken in more ways than I ever thought possible.

I walk slowly to the stage entrance, my fingers tingling with each hesitant step. Part of me wants to run away, slam the doors, and forget all the memories of this old life. The other part is clinging now to the song in my head. The words washing over me with tenderness. My love had been strong. My trust, unfathomable. My faith had been genuine. Relief quickens my steps at that realization. I think, in the deepest parts of my soul, I've questioned if it had been.

Stage lights spark to life the minute I flip up the switches on the wall. I feel the familiar buzz of electricity dancing across my skin as I step out onto the platform. I used to come here when I was hurting and confused, which became all the time in those last few months at Grace Community. I'd sit at the piano, close my eyes, and just play. I wouldn't think. I would just feel and dream. I eye the piano in the corner but make no effort to go to it or sit down. I don't want to touch the cool ivory or press my foot to the pedal. I don't want to go anywhere near it.

I close my eyes and look upward, inhaling the smell of the wood, hearing the sound of cheering fans, tasting the sweat from the kind of performance that makes your insides sizzle.

The brush of soft falling steps from behind jars me from my wanderings. I spin around just as the intruder steps onto the stage, and then I'm thrust back in time. January Sanders—well, not Sanders anymore, I imagine—stands in front of me. She hasn't changed at all, minus the rounding belly and the glow that tells me the life she ended up with has been a good one. Her dark hair is still long, well past her shoulders, and her delicate features, almost ethereal, seem to warm when she sees me.

"How did you . . . ?"

"Cameras," she says, pointing to the sanctuary ceiling. "We rock-paper-scissored to see who would come talk to you first."

I swallow, still rooted in place. I'd taken her on this very stage and sung to her. I thought she'd been an answer to prayer. I'd even convinced myself I was falling in love with her. "I take it you lost," I say, my voice dry and scratchy.

Her brows wrinkle. "No . . . I won." There's a lift in the last syllable. A question.

I don't answer. Only turn and stare out at the empty chairs. She and I parted on good terms, but the church and I did not. Her being here means she kept her position. I can only imagine the things that have been said about me since I left.

She steps forward, closer and closer, until she's standing at my side. She's quiet, relaxed, and we both say nothing. That also jars me. She used to need to fill every moment with a quip or sarcastic remark. A façade, I realized too late. I guess she doesn't need the mask anymore. Must be nice.

"So, when is the appropriate time to ask for your autograph?" she says after a moment.

My chuckle comes out of nowhere. Okay, maybe the girl I knew is still in there somewhere. "I only do signings on Thursdays now. You'll have to track me down then."

She snaps her fingers in an *ah, shucks* motion, then turns to face me. "When did you get back in town?"

I'm relieved the question is simple, but not surprised. What January and I had was never deep. It'd been an escape for both of us. "A couple weeks ago. My little sister got married."

"Oh. That sounds fun."

It wasn't, but I don't tell her that. Instead, I let my gaze fall to her rounded stomach. "Looks like congratulations are in order."

She instinctively places a protective hand against her middle. "Thanks."

"First one?"

That gets a snort. "No. I have a thirteen-month-old little girl. Lacey." Her smile is endearing, even as she rolls her eyes. "Leave it to Dillon to be an overachiever." She produces her phone from a hidden pocket and taps the screen before handing it over.

I stare at her family. Dillon's sporting a smile I didn't know he had in him and holding a truly adorable little girl with two front teeth and a delighted, gummy grin. I'm not surprised by the rush of happiness I feel for my old friend. After all Dillon went through, it's a relief to see his world come back whole. What does surprise me is how much I want to reciprocate the gesture. To show January a picture of Morgan with her sassy smirk, and Lexie with that open, welcoming soul that makes anyone she meets love her immediately. But I don't get that luxury, so I simply pass back January's phone and say, "She's beautiful," with total sincerity. "I'm really happy for both of you."

"Thank you." She reaches out and squeezes my hand as if she can see how bad I'm hurting. Our eyes meet, and it seems we've been catapulted to an alternate universe where she's the strong, steady one and I'm the forever lost soul.

A throat clears and we jump, both our hands dropping as if caught, though why, I'm not sure. There's nothing left between January and me but a bond of friendship.

I glance toward the backstage the same time January does, and we each react differently to our intruder. I tense, she relaxes.

Pastor Thomas steps closer and watches me with the same penetrating gaze he's known for. His discernment has always been uncanny, and I'm definitely not thrilled to be on the receiving end. He's not a tall man, but his presence is formidable. Even in his forties, he's fit, thick-chested, with large rounded muscles on his arms and stocky legs.

"Come see everyone before you leave," January says before she excuses herself. Her lack of surprise grates on me a little. She's obviously been sent ahead to soften the blow.

Pastor Thomas doesn't speak, and I find the silence only ratchets up my unease. I cross my arms, ready for the admonishment that is undoubtedly coming.

"I'll give you my key before I leave today," I say coolly, jumping ahead of the request.

He nods, straight and simple. "That's fine, but I'm more interested in why you decided to come in the first place."

I blow out a breath that's shaky at best. I ache to talk to him, yet sort of hate myself for the desire. So many times when I was on staff, I'd see people leave the church, often with chips on their shoulders, blaming everyone else for their issues. Then months or even years later, they'd come back, their lives broken, and expect Pastor Thomas to comfort them and fix all their problems. I'd made a comment about it to him once, but he hadn't agreed. Instead, he said, *"If they didn't feel they could come back when they needed us the most, then I really did fail them."*

The memory sends a jolt to my heart and makes my throat burn. I dip my head, fighting for control. Why does his presence bring so much shame? His hand lands on my shoulder, firm and comforting. And then I hear him start to pray.

Fiery hot tears burn against my closed lids, but nothing seems to keep them at bay. I hadn't seen how much I'd really lost on my journey to fame. The people, yes, I'd mourned them many times. The peace and comfort of home and family also stung regularly. But now I feel the greater death, the part of myself I'd all but forgotten existed. My integrity. My conviction. Each one was handed over again and again with choices I did not have to make.

"I'm sorry." The words grind out, hot and heavy. "I shouldn't have left the band the way I did." I'd barely given them a week's notice. Didn't bother to find a replacement for the following Sunday. Didn't even show up for practice that last week on staff. No wonder my old bandmates still won't talk to me. I'd thought they resented my fame. How arrogant of me. What they resented was my selfish, hasty departure.

"I forgave you a long time ago," he says so quickly and easily that I believe him. "It's human to want to forge your own path, Cameron. And unfortunately, very painful when we wise up and try to stumble back onto God's. But I'm here for you, however you need me. I know it's been a while, but I will always be your pastor and your friend."

I swallow twice, fighting for calm. "Do you mind if I stay here a little longer?"

His hand slides away. "Take all the time you need. I'll keep Margie from barging in here to tackle a hug out of you."

I'm grateful for the imagery. It makes me smile, pushes

161

back the heaviness just a bit. I hear his footsteps as he departs and also when they stop.

"Keep the key," he says. "Obviously, no one's missed it."

The gesture is a grand one, especially for a man who is so extremely careful with security and safety. It means he still trusts me. Still respects me. Though why, I cannot fathom.

I glance back at him. "Thank you. For this and for the years I got to work under you. I learned more than even I realized. I should have said it when I left, but pride wouldn't let me." When I see a bit of sorrow sneak past his shield, I know I was one of many in his congregation who have hurt him over the years. And also one of many he graciously forgave.

My gaze returns to the empty room, my heart pounding with the need to make another apology. One so much larger and important than the last one. I fall to my knees, grip the back of my head in surrender and agony, and finally, without agenda or expectation . . . I pray.

SIXTEEN

Lexie

I detest hospitals. They remind me too much of sickness and decay, and my mom wasting away one day at a time. I'd sit with her during chemo treatments, watch as the poison that was meant to save her also wrecked her insides. I refuse to let Mason experience any of that torment.

I float around his room, adding another flower arrangement to the ugly laminate countertop. I brought pillows with me this morning, as well. Bright and cheerful ones, along with a throw blanket I carefully place over the small couch that can turn into a bed for guests if needed. The space is still sterile and cold, but as I spread the curtains wide, letting in a burst of sunshine, I do feel relief that the room reflects life a whole lot more than death.

"What are you doing now?" Mason groans, irritable as ever. He's hooked up to an IV that keeps him trapped in his bed. It feeds saline, antibiotics, and very likely strong post-surgery pain meds, though they have done nothing to improve his mood. "Good grief, woman. Go home. You're driving me crazy."

"I love you, too." I blow him a kiss and finish straightening the curtains. It was my fault he fell. My fault he stayed broken on the floor for over thirty minutes. I chose living out a stupid, childish fantasy over my own cousin. Never, ever again. "I've already told you I'm not leaving until you're discharged. I don't trust you not to catch a cab and go home like nothing ever happened." Mason and I have already argued the subject round and round, and I'm determined to out-stubborn him.

He shuts his eyes and heaves a deep, grating breath. "What if I agree to your terms? Will that be enough to make you leave?"

My hands still, and I turn around. "Maybe." A willingness to negotiate is not common with him.

"Okay." He turns his head to me since it's the only part of his body he's allowed to move right now. His back is braced and has to stay that way for another twenty-four hours. "I'll go to your house to recover for one week if you give me three hours without your incessant optimism and relentless decorating."

I cross my arms against my chest. "Agree to ten days, and I won't come back until tomorrow morning."

"Ten days is ridiculous."

"No, it's not. The doctor was clear. You're not supposed to bend from the waist, lift more than ten pounds, or even twist your torso. We both know you'll do that in the first five minutes if you go home." Mason grumbles a sigh while I storm to the side of his bed. "This is serious, Mason. They said you were lucky, that if you're careful you will have a full recovery. But if you're not, you could not only reinjure what they fixed but also make it far worse. You can't grit your teeth and bear through it this time. You have to let the bones heal." He turns his head away from me, and I take his hand. "Ten days. Then you'll have your post-surgery checkup, and we can reevaluate at that time." I squeeze his callused fingers. "Please, Mason. I know you hate relying on people, but we're not just anyone. Morgan and I are your family."

He turns his head back to me, and my throat tightens at the softness in his expression. He can pretend to be harder than steel, but God gave us a gift when he reunited us, and I know Mason feels it as much as I do. "Okay. Ten days. But there will be no coddling, understand?"

I nod once.

"I will follow doctor's orders, but that doesn't make me an invalid. The new brace will allow for complete mobility, so I do not need a nurse or a mother. I can and will take care of all my basic needs. And . . . you will not use my going there as an opportunity to ease your unnecessary guilt." His brows shoot up, his expression clear that he worries I'll overcompensate. "Those are my conditions. Do you think you can handle them?"

I chew on the side of my nail because I'm not totally sure I can. But the terms are fair. And mostly, they keep Mason in my sight. "I can."

"Okay then. I'll go home with you and Morgan for ten days." He pulls his hand away. "Now close those curtains and get out of my room before I change my mind."

I press my lips together to keep from smiling at my victory and grab my purse. I don't shut the curtains. I don't even walk close to them. Without me here, Mason needs all the sunshine he can get. "I'll be back in the morning."

He's still snarling about the light when I reach the hallway. I stop first at the nurses' station and tell them where I'm going and how to reach me if he needs anything. Then I start making lists again, adding one item after another with each step to the elevators. I need to temporarily convert Morgan's room, get Mason one of those clawed reaching devices, add handicap handles in the bathroom, and stock the fridge. I'm manically typing each thing into my phone when the elevator doors swing open. I glance up from my phone, briefly, and then my heart tumbles into my stomach.

"Cameron?"

He steps free of the closing doors while I stay rooted in place. I haven't let myself think of him at all. A punishment, after thinking about him too much caused this nightmare to begin with.

"Hey," he says carefully, concern etched in his voice. "How's Mason doing?" Cam's polished today. Designer jeans, a crisp polo shirt, and model-worthy hair. Yet his eyes still carry that weariness I'm just now starting to realize is permanent.

"Good. The surgery went really well. Less damage than first suspected. They think just six weeks of recovery if he's careful."

Cameron smirks. "What are the chances that he will be?"

I roll my eyes. "One hundred percent if I have anything to do with it."

He's carrying a large plastic takeout bag with handles. When he sees my eyes glance downward, he lifts his arm. "For you. And Morgan." I carefully take the offering and look inside. There are at least ten plastic containers of prepared food. "The worst thing about hospitals and recovery is that you're stuck eating fast food for weeks. I thought this might free up some time and keep you girls healthy, too."

It's such a thoughtful gesture I don't know what to say. "Wow, Cam. This is perfect." Especially with Mason hopefully getting discharged tomorrow. "We will certainly eat it all."

"Good. And just say the word, and more will appear."

I think back to the way he held me in his arms the other night. The way he allowed me those two minutes to just stop and breathe. And then he'd taken care of the dog and now the food. How could I have ever questioned if he was still the same amazing man he's always been? "Thank you, but you've already done so much."

"Funny. I feel like I haven't done anything at all." He runs a nervous hand through his hair, then pats it back into place. "How are you holding up?"

The elevator dings and opens to a group of five. We're standing right in the exit path and move toward the waiting area to give them all room to pass by. I take a seat at one of the empty tables and set the food on the bare surface. Cameron follows, lowering himself into the chair across from me.

"I feel responsible," I admit after a long sigh. "I feel like I've been neglecting my commitments, which isn't fair to Mason. We were supposed to be partners, and I bailed on him."

"He told you to go. I was standing right there."

"I know, but still." I stare at the tabletop, the weight on my chest continuing to smother me.

He reaches out and squeezes my hand. Warmth flows from his fingers to mine, and I wish so badly that our evening hadn't ended the way it did. Everything feels mildly tainted now. "You didn't do anything wrong, Lexie. If anything, your quick thinking kept him from being even more hurt." His voice turns earnest. "And look at all you've done since. You've been here nonstop for days. You took care of his house, his dog, all his insurance paperwork. Those are big, important things he never even had to stress about. Mason is so lucky to have someone like you in his life. And if for a second he thinks his fall is your fault, then he's an idiot."

I swallow down the ache in my throat. "He doesn't think it's my fault. He's told me like five times that he was the one who stepped too high on the ladder, knowing how tight and dangerous the space was." I chuckle before I start to cry. "But he definitely doesn't consider himself lucky, either. He says I'm driving him crazy. He basically kicked me out."

That gets a deep smile out of Cam, so much so that both dimples appear. "And you let him do that?"

"Well . . . I did negotiate his staying with me first, so I guess I sort of won. I just wish he would let us love and care for him the way family is supposed to." The way Cameron's looking at me makes my cheeks heat, and I quickly brush off my words. "I'm probably being too sentimental. Mason tells me that all the time."

"No. You're perfect. Just the way you are." He slides his hand further over mine, caressing the soft skin by my thumb, and every nerve ending in my skin becomes gloriously alive. "Lexie . . . I think we need—"

My phone vibrates obnoxiously in my purse, drowning out Cameron's words and the growing cadence of my heartbeat. I glance down at my open handbag and see Morgan's face, along with the time.

"Oh, shoot. Shoot, shoot, shoot. She's going to kill me." I snatch the phone and answer, "I'm almost there."

"Almost here as in you haven't left yet or really almost here? Like you're about to turn into the car loop almost here?" The aggravation in her voice brings a whole new level of guilt. I've done this way more times than I care to admit.

"I'm not about to turn into the car loop," I say, grimacing.

"Mom!" she screams into the phone. "I cannot believe you forgot me again. I told you three times this morning that it was early release today! Three times!"

I slide my purse onto my shoulder and stand, mouthing

an apology to Cameron. He can no doubt hear her shrieks through the phone and is also on his feet, his lips twitching in an attempt to hold back laughter. "Just get some homework done and I'll be there in a minute."

"I don't have homework. It's Thanksgiving break, remember?"

Cameron hands me the bag of food I'm about to forget as well, and I back up, waving at him. I rush to the elevators, trying to ignore the disappointment roaring inside. Whatever Cameron was about to tell me was undoubtedly going to be better than what I'm going to be pelted with on the long car ride home.

SEVENTEEN

Cameron

Twatch Lexie disappear behind the closing elevator doors and press my fingers to my temples, grateful for Morgan's interruption. The things I was about to say shouldn't be said. They're selfish. A request for more when I can give back so little. It's just become impossible to be around her and keep my steadily growing feelings locked inside.

I continue to stand in the waiting room, debating my next steps. Mason would want me to leave him alone. Of this, I have no doubt. Which is why I've hesitated and waited, each passing day a reminder that I need to make things right between us. The time at Grace Community was an awakening—walking down the familiar halls, feeling Margie's bone-crushing embrace as if I'd never disappointed her, even signing a few autographs for the new staff members, who saw me as more of a legend than a coward. I'd gone there expecting the act to break me, and instead it seems to have sparked something inside to life. Hope, maybe, that restoration is possible.

With a new determination I'm still not quite used to, I step toward the hallway. Doors line each side, and I quickly glance at each last name written in black on small whiteboards. When I see Mason's, I stop. The door is slightly ajar, and the lights are all on. I pause to listen for a nurse or any other indication he isn't alone but am greeted with only silence.

Slowly, I push the door inward, just enough to let me pass by. Mason comes into view immediately. His eyes are closed, and his bare feet practically hang over the edge of the bed. I'm grateful he doesn't look small, even in this setting.

I walk closer to him, and he must hear me coming because his shoulders tense.

"Finally," he grumbles, his eyes still closed. "Can you please shut those curtains? My head is killing me."

I quickly make my way over to the windows and pull the drapery shut. Lexie's handiwork is all over this room, which causes a longing deep in my chest. Designer pillows, fresh flowers, two hardback books stacked on Mason's side table. She wanted him to be comfortable, to feel loved. It's written on each and every special touch of color.

"Thanks," he says with a guttural relief. "Now the lights, please."

"I think it might be a bit awkward for us to talk alone in the dark."

His eyes flash open the minute I speak and his brows turn inward, irritation etched in the lines in his forehead. "What are you doing here?"

The way he grimaces and keeps his lids slightly closed sends a jolt of pity through me. I go to Mason's side and turn on one of the small table lamps. Then I walk back to the door and flip off the bright overhead lights. The room goes dark, minus the slight aura around his bed. "Is that better?"

Mason nods and lets out a long breath. "Is Lexie gone?"

"Yeah," I say, coming forward, watching him with more perception this time. "You didn't want her to know how much pain you're still in, did you?" He doesn't answer, but he doesn't need to. The truth is written all over his face. "Do you want me to get a nurse?"

"No. Not yet. If you're going to trap me here and make me have some kind of heart-to-heart, I'd like to have all my faculties."

I chuckle slightly as I lower into the open chair near his bed. "How do you know that's what I'm planning to do?"

"You forget how long we were friends."

Loss settles in my rib cage. "No, I don't."

His lips tighten, a defensive move against me, I'm sure. I suppose I understand the need to be guarded, though I hate it.

When I don't say anything, Mason lifts his hand in a waving motion. "Well . . . go on, let's get this over with."

Once again, I'm taken aback by this new version of my old friend. He's so cold, so . . . "You know who you remind me of now? Bryson." The words come as fast as I think them, and Mason grunts a laugh. I don't think it's funny at all. I think it's a tragedy.

"I'm guessing that's not a compliment coming from you." He turns his head toward me, looks me dead in the eye, and grins maliciously. "How's Darcy, by the way?"

It's a low blow, intended to wound. And it does. Her name is a sharp jab to my heart. "I have no idea," I say back with equal heat. I work my jaw, forcing myself to stay seated, and release the words I came here to say. "I'm sorry I took your spot in the band." The apology grates as it comes out, even though it's true. I'm just still trying to recover from his earlier arrow. I can feel the tingle in my skin, the short breaths, and building nausea in my gut.

Mason looks at the ceiling. I wish I could still get a read

on him, but there's too much sharpness now, too much buried anger to have a hint of what he's thinking. "My anger was never about Black Carousel," he finally says. "Though I guess for you, that's all it's ever been about."

Another jab, this time to my character. "Then what?" I demand. "If not the band, why the hatred?"

He's quiet, pensive, and I almost think he's going to stay that way and give me no opportunity to make amends. "I admired you so much growing up," he whispers. "Your drive, your talent. The way you could create masterpieces out of nothing. I remember wondering why you even bothered with any of us. We were all so ordinary compared to you."

His memory is distorted. I'd clung to every one of them. Darcy, Mason, even Bryson at times . . . they were sure ground. Unshakable.

"And then the night of my twenty-third birthday party, Bryson told me his grand idea about forming a band and how he wanted me to be the first member." That admission makes my back straighten and my jaw clench. Mason must sense the tension because he turns his head to look at me once more. "You didn't know that, did you? You thought we'd pulled the idea together on a whim. Just a couple old friends trying to retain their youth."

I don't say anything, can't seem to find the words at all. That party had been a surprise. The first birthday we'd all celebrated together since returning to Midlothian. It'd been closer to a reunion than a true birthday, but we'd still showered Mason with gag gifts and a two-layer cake. Five friends, ready for that launch into real life. Five friends who didn't have secrets and betrayals between them yet . . . or so I thought.

"Bryson didn't want you to be a part of the band," Mason continues, his voice holding no softness, no remorse at all for shattering yet another illusion in my life. "He told me that five seconds after asking me to join, just in case I had any thought to include you. He said you'd take over and make it about you. I didn't care either way. It was just nice to be a part of a dream; it didn't matter whose it was. So, we waited . . . almost a year, practicing under the radar. And then finally, when you were committed enough to the praise band to not care about our silly little venture, Bryson decided it was time to go public." Mason's chuckle is cruel. "Man, did he know you well."

The air crackles with an accusation I can't argue against. Here I sit, the proud owner of a Grammy with *Black Carousel* etched in gold. And even though the band broke up after that first record and I went solo, the award will forever be proof I'd done just what Bryson expected. Resentment blazes through me. "Bryson's the one who fired you. Not me. He's also the one who quit, knowing I wouldn't walk away from the contract he'd placed in front of me." I work my jaw, the words razor blades in my mouth. "I didn't steal your band, Mason. Bryson sold it, his payment for ripping away my life."

Mason outright laughs. "You still don't get it. You still think Bryson somehow orchestrated your entire future."

"He did."

"No." His voice calms, and I watch as he shakes his head in both sympathy and resignation. "He simply gave you what we all knew you'd take. The music. The fame. It's always been your first love. Always. We were your friends, we loved you. But we were never naïve enough to think you would choose us. Now, Bryson working that to his advantage? Well, the guy is shrewder than I am, that's for sure."

I detest the admiration in his voice. The acceptance of Bryson's sins over my own. "If you thought so little of me, then why bother leaving town? Why act as if I betrayed you when I took over as lead guitarist?"

"I guess I realized I didn't admire you anymore. Knowing a person's flaws and then being on the receiving end of them, well, it's different. Integrity matters to me; I just didn't know how much until I saw how little you had."

Those words are the sharpest and most painful yet. Probably because they are the only ones he didn't say with the intent to injure. These were his truths. And mine as well, because everything he accused me of is accurate. I had no loyalty to him. Sure, I felt guilt more often than not, but never remorse. Even these last four years, I've been too consumed with my resentment toward Bryson and Darcy to even recognize that I'd inflicted the same pain on Mason. Funny how loss sometimes only comes after seeing what you've tossed aside. Mason is the kind of friend you get once in a lifetime. And even if we find a way to make peace, I know the bond between us will likely never again be the same.

"You're right," I say, acid pouring through my veins, dissolving all the bits of clarity and hope I'd gained the other day. "I traded our friendship for my chance at fame. I knew the cost when I said yes to Bryson that night, and I willingly paid it. And I can see how that wouldn't be forgivable. But for what it's worth, my apology is sincere. I really am sorry."

"The crazy thing is I want to believe you." He chuckles humorlessly. "I want you to be the man I thought you were, but deep down we both know you only want to make nice for Lexie's sake."

Irritation circles around the earlier conviction. In one sense, he's right. Lexie is why the two of us reconnected, why we even have the opportunity to have this conversation. But my apology is not for her. If that were the case, I would have done it weeks ago. No. Today is about making amends to the people I hurt. Just like I had with Pastor Thomas. "I'm not here for Lexie. I'm here to somehow make restitution for the pain I caused you."

His flinch comes with a hiss so sharp I'm surprised I don't see blood. "Don't insult me. I've known you too long and I'm way too aware of how you look at her. You're worried I'm going to mess up whatever it is you two have going right now. It's the whole reason you're fumbling for some kind of truce between us. Well, don't bother, okay? I've made my opinion of you very clear." Mason turns his head away, looking now at the opposite end of the room. "You're not good enough for her. I know it. You know it. I'm just waiting for Lexie to wise up and see it for herself."

"So there's nothing I can say to make you believe that I've changed? You'd just throw away years and years of friendship? Offer no second chances?"

"I don't trust you, Cam. Not your intentions or your word." He turns back to meet my gaze, and it's ice cold. "If you really cared about Lexie, you'd remove yourself from her life before you rip it apart any further than you already have."

I sit there, my heart pounding. "How have I messed up her life?"

"Are you serious? Are you really so self-absorbed that you can't see the hell we are in right now? We're already over budget, and every time I turn around, there's one more thing at that house that needs fixing. Lexie has sunk every penny she owns into this venture with me, and while I can afford to end up in the red every once in a while, she can't. And now with me down . . ." He slams his palm on the bed, frustration pulsing from him. "You've been nothing but a terrible distraction since you got into town—to the both of us. And to what end? What is your plan here? Play house for a little while, act like a daddy to Morgan? Make promises to Lexie about the future that you absolutely won't keep? To you, Lexie is this fun, beautiful, and interesting holiday fling you get to add to your arsenal. But to me, she's family . . ." He chokes up on the word. "And I'll be the one left here, watching the aftermath of her heart smashed to pieces."

"I didn't mean . . ." I can't find the words. Can't even digest the extent of the lashes he's just leveled on me. "I had no intention of making her life worse. Of hurting her."

"Save the speech for someone who might actually believe you." His voice quiets, pained in a way I've never heard from my old friend. "Turn off that light when you leave." He closes his eyes, wincing in the process, and I know our conversation is over.

Slowly, I rise to my feet, still reeling. "I'll let the nurse know you're in pain."

I spend the rest of the day fleeing from Mason's words. First to my dad's office, then all around town doing meaningless errands, cleaning the house, replacing the lights on the front porch, and now I'm in the backyard, pulling weeds and watering the trees. But even the oasis I've created can't stop his words from catching up to me. They fall on my shoulders, a steady press, like the setting sun almost lost to the horizon.

"If you really cared about Lexie, you'd remove yourself from her life before you rip it apart any further than you already have."

I close my eyes against the strain of his accusation. I want to prove him wrong. Have spent the day trying to justify every interaction, searching for evidence that I've been more than a wrecking ball to her life.

Instead, I've only stirred a beast. Felt the panic yawn

awake and the sickness strangle me as soon as I accepted that Mason had been right—from the minute I hugged Lexie hello, our friendship has been completely centered around me. Had I even asked about the house? Cared that she was drowning? Noticed her stress at all?

I eye the prescription bottle sitting on the iron side table. I've kept it in reach all afternoon. Ready for when the attack would come. It's been on the fringe all day. Its claws tapping at my mind, inside my chest. Hungry to prove that coming home was fruitless. To prove that despite my steps forward, I've made no real progress at all.

I ball my fingers into a fist and try counting away the worry, the fears, the tingling that's already started at my toes and is working its way up my legs. Taunting me.

A throat clears from behind, and I spin around, startled.

Lexie watches me tentatively, as if summoned right from the heavens. "I was taking a walk and saw your lights were on. When you didn't answer the door, I figured . . ." She smiles when her eyes flick to the water hose drooped in my hand. "You're getting all wet."

She steps closer to help, and unadulterated fear grips my throat. "No, I've got it," I choke out. I'm too close to the edge for her to be here. One foot already scooting toward the cliff. I turn off the sprayer and grab the hand towel I'd haphazardly tossed over the back of the chair. I can hardly pull my eyes from hers, and yet I feel my insides coil and twist each second she stands there watching me. Waiting. Expecting me to be a better man than I am.

"You're not good enough for her. I know it. You know it. I'm just waiting for Lexie to wise up and see it for herself."

Mason is right. I have to stop . . . whatever this is between us. I swallow down the part of me that wants to fall into her arms and cross mine instead. "Did you need something from me?" My voice is flat, distant, a clear indication that I don't want her to stay.

She presses her lips together. The tingles are at my knees now, and I feel them tremble, feel my muscles going weak. She doesn't seem to notice or care that I'm pleading for her to leave with every ounce of my being. "You were going to tell me something at the hospital. It seemed important."

I shake my head, my throat now ash. Nausea has pooled in my stomach, and it's taking every muscle in my back to keep from retching on the grass by my feet.

"Cameron . . ." She steps forward, two, then three foot-falls, and I can't move. Can't back up the way I should.

Instead, I close my eyes. "Lexie, I really need you to go. Please. Now." The weight on my lungs is suffocating, and my breath falters, comes in the quick manic rhythms of a man on the edge of hyperventilating. I feel her warm hand on my skin, feel her fingers drag across my forehead.

"Your skin is so clammy," she says, her voice shifting from tentative to nurturing. "Cam, are you feeling okay?"

"Please, Lexie . . . I don't want you to see me like this." My voice is barely a whisper because I already know it's too late. I can't stop it. I pull away from her, back up as many steps as I can, then fall to my knees, hurling my guts out. I've barely eaten all day, so it's more dry heaves and water than anything worse. Still my body shakes violently. I glance up only enough to get my bearings, to search out the bottle that I immediately see is more than an arm's length away. Giving up, I return to my heaving, pressing a hand against the pain shooting across my abdomen. And then I feel her again. Feel her kneel close beside me, feel her hand rub the muscles along my back.

"It's okay. Breathe. In and out."

I cling to her words, try to obey the calm she's projecting. I feel the towel on my face, wiping away the sweat and mucus.

Then the press of a pill at my lips. I open enough for her to slide both tablets in. She's still holding me, rocking me, when tears spill over my eyelids. I feel shredded by her watching this. Seeing me so broken and weak and disgusting.

She's too good. Too kind. Mason's right. I'm going to destroy her just like I've destroyed everyone . . . including myself.

EIGHTEEN

Lexie

Cameron's been inside the house for twenty minutes now. *"I need to clean up,"* is all he said to me the moment he could scramble to his feet. He didn't look back when he walked away. Didn't look at anything but his feet.

My knees bounce as I sit, waiting. I know he wants me to go, but I can't leave now. Not without talking to him about what happened. Restless, I pull my phone from the back pocket of my jeans and check in with Morgan. My walk was only supposed to be fifteen minutes and I don't want her worrying.

> **Me:**
> Checking in. I went to Cam's and may be a while.

> **Morgan:**
> Big surprise.

She sent a laughing emoji. Then kissing lips. I roll my eyes.

> **Me:**
> Stop. It's not like that between us.

Morgan:
Whatever.

Me:
I'm right down the street if you need anything.

Morgan:
When are you not just down the street?

I ignore her comment and the familiar stirring of guilt.

Me:
Let's get ice cream when I get back. Just the two of us.

Morgan gives me a thumbs-up, and I put the phone away. Good timing, too, because Cameron finally emerges from the house. He's obviously showered and has replaced his jeans with joggers. The long-sleeved T-shirt he wears hugs his chest, though it's impossible to make out what that might look like because his arms are tightly folded.

"You didn't have to wait on me," he says with that same absent voice he tried with me earlier.

I stand from the lawn chair. "I wanted to."

The air between us is different now. Equal. I no longer see Cameron as the unreachable fantasy I'd once created. If tonight showed me anything, it's that he's human and wounded and as real as any other person.

He sighs and walks over to the fire pit, resigned, it seems, that I'm not leaving without a conversation. "Are you cold?"

"A little."

It takes him only a few seconds to get the propane going, and fire pulses from the center bowl. I step closer to the heat and to him.

He slides into the chair next to mine, a fact I'm grateful for because there were options farther away. I sit too, silently, giving him the time he apparently needs to speak about what I just witnessed.

"I'm so sorry you had to see me like that," he says, lowering his head into his hands. "I never wanted you to."

I fold my hands in my lap and turn in his direction. "When did the panic attacks begin?" He looks up at me, his brow furrowed, confused that I recognize what he just went through. "My sister used to suffer from the same thing after my mom died. Even if I hadn't seen the medicine bottle, I know the signs. Hers were a little more violent, but otherwise similar."

He blows out a thin breath. "Did they ever go away?"

How I wish I could tell him yes, but I don't even know if my sister is alive, let alone if she's finally healthy. "I don't know. She dropped out of school and ran away six months later. When I saw her last, she seemed okay, but the visit was only a couple of days." Two days. Two days that forever changed my life.

"Is that when you got Morgan?"

I nod, slowly, the memory coming back so fierce it sends a sharp pain right to the center of my chest.

My lingering silence doesn't go unnoticed, and Cameron shifts in his seat. "You don't have to tell me more if you don't want to."

"No, it's okay." He's right. I don't want to go into details about that weekend, but since I'm asking him hard questions, it seems only fair that I let him ask some, as well.

"It happened two weeks before Christmas. I was at college finishing up finals when Annie, being the spontaneous girl she's known to be, showed up with rosy cheeks and a Santa hat on. I was thrilled, of course. She'd been in and out of contact for over a year, and I hadn't seen Morgan in person since my father's funeral." I swallow down the boulder in my throat as I picture Morgan's innocent face that first night. She called me "Exie" and twisted my hair into tangles that I oohed and aahed over.

"Annaliese and I picked up as if she'd never been gone," I continue. "Late-night movies snuggled under a blanket, stories of Mom and Dad and our Christmas traditions. We even went out and bought a small tree with all the decorations we could afford. It was the happiest we'd been since before our mother had died. And I remember optimistically thinking that we could start our own traditions . . . our own family, just the three of us." I choke on the words, my nose stinging, the back of my throat a painful ache as I fight the oncoming tears. "She disappeared in the middle of the night. I woke up the next day with Morgan sucking her thumb beside my bed, crying for her mommy. I had no idea where she went, only that she left behind a terrified toddler, an overwhelmed, heartbroken nineteen-year-old, and a note that said 'I'm sorry' in messy blue ink."

Cameron draws back, his breath sucking in. "What did you do?"

"I survived," I say, grateful to have the story done and over with. "She only had a pay-by-the-month phone that no longer worked, so I waited until the new year, hoping she would be in touch. After she didn't call, I had to make some hard decisions."

"Is that when you dropped out of college?"

"Yeah. Morgan was . . . well, let's just say there would be no getting a babysitter. She wouldn't even leave my side for months. Slept every night in my bed for . . . years. My dad had left me some money, so I used that. Then when it became apparent that my sister was never coming back, I petitioned for full-custody guardianship. Annaliese never responded to the notices."

"What about Morgan's father?"

"I have suspicions but no proof of who he is. Morgan's birth certificate only has Annie's name on it, so there was nothing we had to do on that end."

"But what if he ever showed up? Or if Annaliese came back?"

A shiver runs down my spine at the questions that have caused more nightmares than I care to admit. "They'd have to take me to court, but yes, they could potentially take her away from me. Neither legally gave up their rights, so . . ."

"No one would ever consent to that madness." His voice is so protective and appalled it makes me smile at him.

"No, I hope not. But that's the toughest part. I love my sister, but I fear her, too. Part of me wishes she would call, and the other part prays she never does. That probably makes me a really terrible person."

"You are definitely not a terrible person, Lexie. Trust me on that. I've seen enough in the industry to know."

His words fall with a heaviness between us, and I scoot to the edge of my chair, closer to him and to the warm fire. "Is the industry what caused the attacks to start? Life as a celebrity?"

"I wish it were. I'd love to be able to blame the fame for all my problems." He hangs his head, his hands trembling. "But unfortunately, they started before I ever left Texas." His head pops up, but he doesn't look at me, just the fire, as if remembering every moment of that time. "It was my last concert in Dallas. Well, an audition more than a concert. We were trying to get picked up to be the official opening act for Firesight's tour. We killed it that night. Every beat was perfection. Our synergy unmatched. It was so extraordinary that I was shaking when I got offstage. Only it didn't lessen as the adrenaline wore off; it just got more intense. Then the nausea hit, and I barely made it to the bathroom. I thought I'd caught a stomach bug, until it happened again the day I signed the record contract. After that, it became a daily thing, sometimes even twice in one day. I honestly started to think I was going insane."

"I'm so sorry." I can't imagine the fear he must have dealt with all by himself. Annaliese had been young, still under our dad's care. He'd taken her to doctors, counselors, whatever she needed.

"After about two months, I broke down and told my new agent everything that was happening and then some." He blows out another stream of air. "Mark got me hooked up with a doctor while I was on tour. That's when I got a name for the episodes, some coping strategies, and medicine." He glances at me and attempts a smile. "Believe it or not, this is me in a good place. I've only had three since being home."

I knew of one other. I'd seen him the day after, had seen the wreckage the attack had left behind. But the first . . . "Cassie's wedding," I say softly.

He nods, and so much makes sense now. His disheveled state, his unwillingness to go to the party. "Morgan saw me," he admits. "She was worried about having to do CPR." The last word comes out with a chuckle. It makes me laugh, too. "In hindsight, I credit her for pulling me back from the brink that day. She's a truly amazing kid, Lex. And you're an incredible mom. I'm even more in awe now that you've shared your history."

"Thanks." Silence falls between us again, but I want more. Want him to know that I truly do understand what he's going through. "After my mom died, my sister became deathly afraid of anything medical. Pharmacies, hospitals, dentists, even the grocery store would do it sometimes. Is that how it is for you?"

Cam sits up, rubs the back of his head. "It's not really places for me. I thought for years that it was just music-driven. The pressure maybe, of performing or recording, but I don't know. Lately, it's sporadic, or at least it has been since deciding to come home. It's like the demons from my past and the music are so intertwined right now that I can't really distinguish between them anymore. And the more I touch each wound, the more muddled it all becomes."

Guilt lasers through me. "I'm sure I didn't help when I pushed you so hard to listen to your old songs the other night. I'm sorry. I had no idea."

"No, Lexie, this is not your fault at all." He scoots to the edge of his seat, our knees nearly touching. "If anything, I'm the one who should be apologizing. I've dropped myself into your life. A life you have fought to create despite all the trauma you've been through. And I have done nothing but mess things up for you."

"That's not true. We'd be living on fast food if it wasn't for you." I pray he can feel the lightness in my voice, see how much I want to pull him out of this obvious spiral into self-loathing. "Cam, you have been nothing but generous to us since you got into town. Letting Morgan use the tree house, helping us the other night after Mason's fall, coming to the hospital, making Morgan and me that fabulous din-ner."

"Yeah . . . that dinner." He presses his fingers against his forehead. "I can't even sing the songs I promised you."

"I don't care about that."

"But I do. My word should mean something. And it hasn't for far too long." He stands slowly and sighs. His new calm is more unnerving than his usual emotion. "I just think you and I need to keep some distance between us. Morgan can still use the tree house, don't worry about that, but whatever was starting to spark here." He points between the two of us. "I think we need to stop it."

My lungs deflate like he just pricked them with a needle. Of all the things I thought might come out of his mouth, these words were not even possibilities. "Is that what you wanted to tell me at the hospital?"

He presses his lips together and crosses his arms again. "No."

"Then what was it?"

"It doesn't matter."

My heart thunders in my chest, and I stand, my eyes steady on his. "Yes, it does."

"No, it doesn't," he growls, exasperated. "Because what I was going to tell you today would have been catastrophic. It would have been selfish and wrong and completely irresponsible. You deserve someone far better than me in your life." The look in his eyes gives me all the answers I need. I see the longing, the desire, even the respect he has for me.

It's now or never, and I refuse to let this moment go without admitting the truth. "Cameron, I've had a crush on you since I was thirteen."

His brows arch in surprise. "What?"

"I was excited to go to Cassie's wedding because she's my friend, but I couldn't even sleep the night before anticipating that I might see you there. Because even though we hadn't spoken in years, you have remained a huge part of my life. Whenever I have a victory or a loss, I listen to *you*, because your lyrics, your music, they are inside of me as much as they are inside of you." I step closer and ignore him when he shakes his head, silently begging me to stop moving. "And now that I've gotten to know the man you are now, that girlhood crush has turned into something far deeper. Far more substantial." I'm in front of him now, close enough that our bodies are inches from touching. "Telling me that you feel even an ounce of what I do would not have been cata-strophic; it would have been a dream." My fingers trail a line up his arm. Goose bumps follow my touch, and his body goes rigid from the internal battle I know he's fighting. He's been fighting it since the moment we saw each other again.

"Lexie," he whispers, shutting his eyes, "I'm leaving, and even if I wasn't, I'm no good at long-term relationships. I've proven that time and time again. Just ask Mas—"

I place a finger over his lips. "I don't care about your past or about you leaving. If I spent my life waiting on the perfect scenario, I'd never live. There are no guarantees. No prom-ise of tomorrow. I know that better than most. If a couple of months is all we can have together, then I'll take it."

He stares down at me, his hands finding their way to my waist, pulling me all the way until our chests meet. "I don't want to hurt you." The fierceness in his tone matches the fierceness in his eyes.

"The only thing hurting me right now is you holding back. These imperfections that you think make you unworthy, they just make you human." I grip the front of his shirt, willing him to hear the truth inside my words. "I'm not asking you for promises. I'm just asking for *you*."

I see the moment he surrenders. The moment he lets me have all I've ever wanted with him. His leans forward, his voice a soft whisper against my lips. "Then you're asking for a broken man." His breath mingles with mine, his refusal to close the tiny distance between us a sure sign he's giving me one last chance to walk away.

"We're all a little broken." And with that I press in, taking the kiss I've wanted for weeks now, for years really. Only fan-tasy has nothing on reality. In fantasy, your imagination is lim-ited to what you know or have seen on TV or experienced in the past. This kiss is beyond all my limited dreams. My whole body is tense with desire, straining toward him. I feel feverish, weak, light-headed.

He pushes back my hair and deepens the kiss. We stagger to the nearest tree, and I pull his body to mine. My fingers slide up the back of his shirt, touch the lean path of muscles through the threadbare material. I'm lost in the feel of him, lost in the raw emotion of loving this man for a lifetime. I pull him even closer, ignoring the equal force of him pulling away. Not this time. I won't let us fall backward. Won't let him go.

"Lexie . . . stop," he pleads as if I'm physically hurting him. "What I'm feeling for you is already too much. I can't . . ." He braces his palm against the trunk, pushing away enough to keep a halo of space around me. His chest rises and falls while his breath comes fast and shallow.

We stay there, silent. I watch him calm down. Watch his eyes slowly flutter open. Watch his beautiful mouth curl into a timid smile. "I have less than two months," he says, his voice rough as he gently touches his finger to my mouth, tracing a line over the very spot his lips just warmed. "How will it ever be enough time?" The ache in his tone is enough to make me wonder if his fears of getting hurt were his and not mine.

I take his free hand and bring it to my heart, my fingers cupping his. "My mom used to tell me to be grateful for the little things in life. That when you add them all together, they are much grander than the big things we think we need." I kiss the tips of his fingers. "I'm guessing time works the same way."

He brushes a hair from my cheek. "Then we'll just have to take advantage of every minute."

"Yes, we will."

He shakes his head like he can't really believe we're standing here. "Are you absolutely sure you want this?"

The tenderness in his tone makes my heart melt all over again. Only this time the flutters aren't for the boy who speared me with his dimples and took residence on every page in my diary. This time, my heart beats for the man in front of me. For the real and true bond we share every time we're together. For his broken heart and my slightly battered one. For what this time together could mean for both of us.

"Yes. I'm absolutely, positively sure." And just in case words aren't enough, I cup his face gently with my hands and show him again exactly how I feel.

NINETEEN

Cameron

I walked Lexie home not long after we kissed. A part of me didn't want to. The same part that had to pull myself away from the goodbye on her doorstep. The part that could spend every minute of every day with this amazing girl.

That ever-blurring line was officially crossed tonight. There's no going back. No pretense that friendship is the only thing between us.

Mason had been right about my denied feelings. He'd seen it, just like he'd seen me years ago. But I won't prove him true this time. I won't hurt her or disappoint her. Not just to prove a point, but also because I think doing so would break my heart more than hers. If tonight showed me anything, it was how incredibly strong Lexie is. At nineteen, she'd become an overnight mother, and instead of breaking, she conquered. How at thirty-three could I continue to sit in self-pity? The idea feels as laughable as it does pathetic.

I shove my hands into my pockets, the brisk cold like sharp needles on my face. Our houses are only two blocks from each other, but the trip had been considerably more enjoyable with Lexie at my side. We'd held hands, fingers laced, childlike almost in its sweetness. I haven't felt that kind of innocent delight in years. Haven't wanted to be with someone on such an emotional, spiritual, and physical level since . . . well, since Darcy. And she hardly counts, because she was never real, only an illusion.

But Lexie is real and in a lot of ways knows me on a level Darcy never understood. The music, that part of me, Lexie gets. She doesn't just placate my artistry, but loves it, desires it as much as she desires me. She makes me feel as though maybe it isn't such a curse after all.

I'm determined not to ruin this relationship like I have all the ones in the past. We'll take our time. Get to know each other. Mason was right to worry. My history with women has always been to jump in too fast and then cut ties and run, leaving heartache in my wake. I refuse to do the same with Lexie. We'll be friends first. Honest to a fault. And when I return to Nashville, it will be without guilt and without pain for either of us.

Maybe by then the crush she's had will be satisfied and she'll be ready to send me packing. I shake my head at the thought, disliking how my stomach twists at the prospect, and focus on the memory of her touch. The silken way her fingers pressed against my skin, the softness of her beautiful lips.

She saw all my worst parts tonight and still wanted me.

Wind whips through the trees, and leaves fall in a smooth floating rhythm down to my feet. I halt my steps, my eyes fixed on the brown dry foliage. Then I glance upward and watch as the wind strips more leaves from the branches.

My heartbeat ratchets higher, my eyes closing to make sure I'm not imagining the sound. No, I'm not. It's entwined through the rustling, the hiss, even the slight tap of a branch against the windowsill of a nearby house. A melody. Clear and soft and hypnotic.

The buzzing in my head, the one that scrapes across my veins with furious persistence, is momentarily . . . silenced.

I suck in a breath, maybe my first real one in months, and don't move for fear the music will disappear again. But it only grows in volume, beckoning me, welcoming me home after crossing a long stark desert.

My feet move again, faster than before. I'm only four houses away from my own, and the music seems to be following me, dancing and swirling alongside the sidewalk, a smile across its face, hope in its eyes. The same hope I feel bubbling up inside of me.

I need to feel it. Need to ingest the notes, press them against my lungs. I'm practically running when I hit my front door. I tear across the threshold and up the stairs. The guitar I brought with me is buried under my bed. Intentionally stored out of reach and out of sight. I drop to my knees, then to my stomach, and reach my fingers into the darkness until they make contact.

The instrument still lies in its original black case, old and chipped. I hadn't brought the guitar from Nashville to play it, but to return it to its original owner—my father. The wood had felt warped beneath my fingers the last time I'd played. Like I'd ruin its legacy by simply holding it with the dirt now permanently stained on my hands.

The case finally slides free of the bed and I stare at it, still on my knees, fear once again returning. The last time I'd allowed myself to play, the pain had nearly crushed me. Now I ache to touch the strings. I look toward the ceiling, questioning the sudden motivation. Was this His forgiveness? His gift back to me after I'd squandered it away so completely?

Or was it Lexie? Her acceptance of my faults, her kindness and care that came with zero expectations? Or maybe she, too, is a gift.

I don't know the answer and quickly realize I don't care. Whatever or whoever brought me to this moment, I'm so grateful for it that I brush the layer of dust from the case top, flip up the two locks on each side, and gingerly lift the lid.

The smell immediately punches me in the stomach, the musty velvet, the aged wood and oil I'd recently rubbed over its grain. I wait for the panic to come, to trap me inside the fear of never being good enough, but the nausea never makes an appearance. Not when I clasp the neck or when I free the instrument from its holder. Not even when I rise and sit on the bed, cradling the wood in my lap.

Instead, I feel a stirring inside, a hope that I will once again be the artist I used to be. I breathe in, bring the melody to my mind, let it spill over me the way it did all the way home. I relish the gentle touch, feel it caress my face.

And then I dare to pluck the strings, to play the first chord by my hand in nearly one hundred days. My heart leaps, desperately praying that I finally found the cure after all this time. But the sound is off, broken. The melody reeks of amateur clichés, of commercial jingles and horrific band practices. Where is the softness, the brush of airiness dancing along my ears? What is this dark, bulky, ear-piercing noise coming from my fingers?

My hand clamps the strings, silencing the last of the vibration.

How could I have been so wrong . . . yet again?

Slowly, I get to my feet, stare down at my inept fingers, and firmly place the offending instrument back into its case.

I step onto my front porch trying to put last night's musical failure behind me. I'd been stupid to think one or two good moments could change years of decline. My life has never worked that way.

With my Bible in one hand and cup of coffee in the other, I make my way to my newest furniture purchase—a single chair tucked in the corner that gives me a full view of the neighborhood. It's the same routine I've engaged in every morning since that day at Grace Community. I still haven't actually opened the Book, but holding it already feels like a giant step forward. It's been years since I've touched a Bible and wouldn't even have this one now if my mom hadn't slipped it in along with one of her many food deliveries. She's more subtle than my father but persistent all the same.

There was a time when this morning's routine was easy. Enjoyable even. I'd study pages of verses. Turn the Psalms into music. But I'm not the same man I was back then. I've seen too much. Done too much to approach this time without fear and trembling. Years ago, I would have deemed a man like me unworthy of forgiveness. Maybe I still do.

I set the Bible on a nearby table and fold my hands together. At least praying has become less stilted. I bow my head, and just as I'm about to begin my routine of asking God to help me find my way back to the man I used to be, a squeak from the screen door has my head lifting back up.

Morgan stands on the front steps in jeans and a thick coat. I check the time, confused by her unexpected appearance. Mason gets released from the hospital today, and I have no doubt that Lexie is going to need all the help she can get.

She remains quiet, her expression dark and pensive. "Is everything okay?" I ask.

She shrugs. "Yeah, it's fine. Mom's being manic about

cleaning, so I got out while I still could." She drops down onto the porch swing and slumps.

I'm surprised she doesn't run straight to the tree house, which is her normal behavior. Usually, I barely get a quip of a hello before she disappears. But I sense something is off today. Maybe she still hasn't recovered from seeing Mason fall. I clear my throat, not totally sure of my next question. I've always loved children, had been very active with both of my nieces and younger cousins until recently. Yet teenagers are different; that strange combination of budding adult and child that even they can't quite distinguish between. "How are you doing with all that's happened? You were pretty upset the other day."

She lifts one shoulder and drops it again. "Mom says we're not supposed to focus on bad things. She quoted something about the dark night ending and the sun rising again." She rolls her eyes, and I press my lips together to keep from grinning.

"Well, I don't mind if you talk about it," I offer. "And I guarantee you won't get any motivational speeches from me."

Her shoulders perk up slightly as she seems to contemplate my invitation. "She's not my real mom, you know." Morgan watches me as if she's testing the truth behind my words. "She's technically my aunt."

I swallow down my unease. A discussion about Mason or even a fear of death, I was prepared for. This, not so much. "I know. She told me."

"Really?" Morgan's brows shoot upward. "She doesn't normally tell anyone." She's quiet for a second and then begins again. "When I was in the second grade, I told all my friends at school that she was my aunt Lexie, not my mom. When we had our first parent-teacher conference, she found out what I'd been telling everyone." Morgan shakes her head.

"She cried for like a week. I didn't mean to hurt her. I was . . . mad, I guess, that my real mom wasn't there."

Helplessness grows at the inadequacy I feel discussing this subject with Morgan. "Did you tell Lexie how you felt?"

She shakes her head adamantly. "No way. The subject of my real mom is off-limits in our house."

"Morgan, I strongly doubt that."

"Well, yeah, Mom hasn't said so out loud, but you don't see her face every time I even hint about her childhood. Or bring up sisters. It crumbles and then she's depressed for days."

I'd think Morgan was exaggerating, only I've seen that same expression when Lexie told me the story of Annaliese's departure. Still, ignoring something this huge doesn't sound like the Lexie I've gotten to know. She's been exposing every one of my insecurities since that first day at the wedding. "Your mom is a lot stronger than you're giving her credit for."

"Not when it comes to this. There's this look of betrayal she gets when I ask questions, and then I feel awful and un-grateful. She gave up so much for me." Morgan wrings her hands together and bites her lip. "But is it really so wrong that I want to know where I come from?" Her eyes gleam from un-shed tears, and I feel a gut punch of compassion for her.

"No," I say. "It's not wrong."

She studies her hands again and blows out a long stream of air. "I'm gonna go in the tree house now," she says, standing. "You won't tell my mom about this conversation, will you?"

I hesitate to answer, having no idea what the proper proto-col is for this kind of thing.

"Please, Cameron. She's so stressed right now with the house and with Mason's fall. It will wreck her."

Hurting Lexie is the absolute last thing in the world I want to do. I nod at her daughter. "I won't say anything."

Relief seems to relax her entire frame. "Thank you. I feel

a lot better." She grins, and I can see that gleam in her eyes that usually comes right before a spearing comment. "And because you were so cool about it, I'll give you a little inside scoop. Mom was singing in the shower this morning and drew hearts on the fogged mirror." She opens the screen to leave, still smiling. "So, whatever you're doing . . . it's working." She turns then and takes off in a childish run toward her hideaway.

I shake my head as I watch her disappear up the tree, wondering if there will ever be a time when a conversation with Morgan won't leave me completely stupefied.

TWENTY

Lexie

*G*etting Mason settled in was a lot more fun in theory than in reality. Instead of only having to deal with one grumbling housemate, I now have two, and they seem to feed off each other's foul moods. Of course, Mason has a good reason. He's in constant pain and hates being dependent on anyone. Morgan, I guess, has good reasons, too. She's a teenager, hormonal, and I did commandeer her one place of privacy—her room. At least I'm making up for it a little bit. I've doubled her treehouse time, with Cameron's permission. Which is where she is now. It's where I wish I was as well, especially since I haven't interacted with him beyond texting since he dropped me off at my house three days ago.

I quietly shut my bedroom door, not wanting to disturb Mason, who only went to sleep a few hours ago. I've heard him the past two nights moving quietly around the house. I'm one of those who can fall asleep quickly and easily, so it doesn't bother me when he wakes me at three or four in the morning. I just worry. Especially since I don't think his back is the reason for the insomnia.

His door is closed when I pass by and make my way to the other side of the house. I feel grateful relief until I walk into my kitchen and see him already seated at our small round table, coffee cup in front of him. The first couple of days home were hard. All three of us had to learn boundaries, but once we got past the initial shock of a third person in the house and Mason's pain decreased, we've all been a lot happier.

"Morning," he says, his eyes tired and dark. He sits uncomfortably straight, but I'm happy to see him using the new brace the surgeon gave him. It gives much more range of motion than the first one and also keeps him from accidentally moving in a way that could harm the bones. "I made coffee."

"Thanks." I pull open the fridge and grab my morning yogurt and blueberries.

It's ten on Monday and it feels odd that we aren't knee-deep in mangled Sheetrock by now. This entire week was supposed to be dedicated to framing walls and prepping for the plumbers. Instead, the house has sat untouched for five days.

I lower myself to the chair across from him and have to press my lips together to keep from checking to see if he needs anything. He's told me repeatedly that he will ask if he does and to stop treating him like a houseguest.

"I've made about a dozen calls," he says, getting past the niceties and right to the point. "Best I can get us is a skeleton crew of two guys next week."

"But aren't the plumbers coming then?"

He tips his head to the ceiling. "They were supposed to, but without the walls framed and the upstairs bathrooms still a mess, they're only going to be able to do a fraction of what we need." His sigh is stressed and tired. "I'm just going to wait and see what they say. Who knows, maybe the overlap will work somehow."

I press the cool plastic cup against my fingers. "Do you still have that list of what all needs to be done?" We'd sat down together his second night here and revamped the schedule based on Mason's inability to work for at least six weeks. That's also when he wrote out every task we were going to have to pay for now. He'd offered to take on the additional expense, citing that his injury should not impact me negatively. I, of course, refused. I'm not his charity case. I'm his partner, and if I've learned anything over the past ten years, it's how to make ends meet when finances get tight.

Still, the list was daunting. A full page and that was just to be ready for the plumbers. "I saw a few things that I can do in the interim." Mason begins to shake his head, but I cut him off. "If you want me to respect your independence, then you need to respect mine, as well. I'm not naïve. I know I'm not a tradesman, but there were a lot of items on that list that we've done before." My voice rises, ready to battle. "I'm off work, and Morgan is out of school, so I don't have to worry about picking her up. It's a waste for me to just sit around this house, especially when you refuse to let me help you with anything."

It pains him, I can tell, but he nods. "Okay. I'll highlight a few things that would be doable for you." Slowly, he stands, wincing twice, and I physically have to hold on to the chair to keep from jumping up to get it for him. It takes triple the time it should, but eventually Mason returns to the kitchen with a paper in hand.

We spend the next ten minutes scrutinizing each job, Mason using another paper to detail each task, including chicken-scratch drawings so there's no confusion.

When we finish, I almost feel prepared. "Thank you," I say, taking both lists and folding them carefully. "Now, please, you look exhausted. Go back to sleep, and I'll give you a complete rundown of my progress when I get home."

He rubs his eyes, fighting the truth that he literally looks one second from toppling over in his chair. "I guess a few more hours would be nice."

"And Morgan's going to Melissa's house today, so you'll have total peace and quiet."

His hands fall away, and his stare is so full of appreciation and softness that it makes my throat burn. I can tell he wants to say something, that maybe for once he wants to let me past that ridiculous four-inch armor he has, but instead he rises to his feet again. And simply lays a hand on my shoulder as he passes by. "Let me know how it goes."

I press my palm to the top of his hand. "I will."

He shuffles down the hall, slow and broken, and it's enough to spur me into action. I text Melissa's mom and ask her to pick Morgan up at Cameron's house instead of mine. Then I text Morgan that they're on the way. I spend the next ten minutes searching for my overalls, which un-fortunately I find in a heap behind the bathroom door. And then it's the mad hunt for other clothes I don't mind getting ruined. A search that takes far longer than it should, since all of Morgan's belongings are in my room now instead of hers. I groan, hoping this isn't an omen for how the day is going to go. Finally, I'm sufficiently dressed and pull on my dusty work boots. My hair is already in a tight ponytail, so I leave it alone. I brush my teeth, stare at my flushed complexion in the mirror, and sigh. Vanity has no place in my life right now. If I'm going to do right by Mason, I'm going to have to learn to be Superwoman with a hammer.

I grab my keys, the lists, and two energy drinks. Maybe I

should bring three . . . just in case. Arms full, I toss everything into my car and continue my internal pep talk on the short drive to the house. *You can do this. You can tear down tile and detach sinks. You are strong and capable of anything.*

As I park along the curb, I see Cameron sitting on the front step, waiting for me. "Is Morgan okay?" I call through the open window.

"Oh yeah. Your friend picked her up before I ran to the coffee shop." He stands, holding two to-go cups, and heads down the sidewalk. "I thought you might need some reinforcements." I quickly get out of the car, abandoning my slew of drinks. He passes a cup to me. "Cinnamon latte, right?"

"Yes, thank you." I take a small sip. Perfection. And a luxury I very rarely give myself. A six-dollar cup of coffee is not often in the budget.

Cameron shifts on his feet awkwardly, and it's completely adorable. He's wearing old faded jeans and an equally faded T-shirt. He also has on work boots, brand-new judging by the gleam of the leather.

A smile grows on my lips, wide and appreciative. "Is the coffee the only reinforcement you brought?"

He seems relieved at my perception. "Well, I'm no carpenter, but I do come with an extra set of hands if you'd like some help."

"Are you kidding me? I need an army of help at this point." Not to mention that it means we get to spend the entire day together.

I take another sip as we stand there, smiling, awkward. It has been days since we've seen each other, and texts just don't have the same impact.

But instead of leaning down to kiss me like I want him to, he pulls his gaze away from mine and to the house that stands vacant in front of us. "Should we go in?"

"Um, yeah. Sure." I walk past him to the door but pause before sliding my key inside the lock. The memory of Mason strapped to the gurney comes so swift and debilitating that I nearly drop the metal key ring to the ground.

A warm hand presses against my back. "Lexie, you okay?"

"Sorry." I shake my head, but still can't seem to get my fingers to work. "I haven't been back to the house since Mason fell." I swallow. "I guess the memory is hitting me a little harder than I thought it would." It had been the same with my father's house. From the moment I stepped past the threshold, the childhood memories were replaced with ones conjured in my mind: my father's gray skin, his broken body, his soulless eyes. Being there was like swallowing staples. And now I feel them return, sharp and cold against my throat.

Cameron gently detangles the keys from my fingers and takes care of opening the door. He doesn't push me to go inside, only stands there beside me and waits patiently. I take two deep breaths, tell myself to get over it, if not for me, then for Mason, and step inside. But rather than finding traces of the horrific night littered on every surface, there's only a clean and tidy space in front of me.

"Did you . . . ?" I trail off, because of course he did. I'd asked him to close up the house for me. But the work he had to have done was well beyond my request or expectation. "Cameron. Thank you so much."

He flips on the light. "It was the least I could do," he says, unaware of how odd it is for me to have a partner in a crisis.

We walk quietly through the barren entrance toward the stairs, and my nerves prickle with each step. I want him to touch me. I don't want to spend the next eight hours making small talk when we've become so much more.

I set my cup on the stairs and then remove his from his

grasp, as well. In two steps I'm next to him, my chest pressed against his, my head tilted upward. "You didn't kiss me hello."

His hands immediately find my waist, and the smile I dream about finally appears. "I wasn't sure if you wanted me to." He swallows. "You've been a little distant since we last talked. And Mason, well, I thought he might have changed your mind."

Ah, so that was it. I brush a finger lightly over his cheek. "I have definitely not changed my mind. I've just been preoccupied. I'm sorry."

He shakes his head like my apology is unwarranted, and finally, ever so gently, he presses his lips to mine. My eyes close as I melt into the fantasy once again. I'd almost convinced myself it wasn't true, that I had conjured the whole evening. But this is real. His mouth, his breath, his hand now wrapped around my back is very, very real.

We pull away, and his gaze caresses my face, lingering, watching me with awed surprise. "How did I never see you before now?" I snort a laugh as soon as the words leave his lips, because they feel like both an insult and a compliment, though I know he only meant it as one of those things. His face blanches in horror, as if just realizing his error. "Forget I said that. I didn't mean . . ."

"No, it's okay," I tease. "I was just your little sister's friend. An annoyance at best."

"Never." He pulls me closer and nuzzles my neck. "If anything, I'm the one who doesn't measure up. You are like sunshine in my hands. And I feel like any moment now you're going to realize you don't belong there and slip right through my fingers."

My face heats with the admiration in his words. "Trust me. You have nothing to worry about. I have a long list of deal breakers, and you've already passed every single one."

"You have a list?" His brow creases, worry forming a line on his forehead. "What's on there?"

I smile because he's beautiful, especially when that hint of insecurity flushes his cheeks. "Why does it matter now? I'm putty in your arms, can't you see that?"

He steps back, his voice hitching. "It matters because I don't want to break them in the future."

"Cam, I was kidding when I said I had a list. I meant more an idea of expectations."

"Okay, then start there."

The ridiculousness of his reaction nearly makes me laugh, but then I see his mouth tighten, see his body tense with every moment I don't answer. "You're serious?"

"Yes," he says with complete surety. "I want at least three."

"Three?"

"Yes, three things that are deal breakers for you."

"Alright, fine. You win. Let's see . . ." I still think this is absolutely stupid as I search for the three key things that have ended more than one relationship. "Okay, I have it. Deal breaker number one: any guy I'm with has to share my faith and live it out in both his speech and actions."

"That's a good one." Cameron nods, his mouth easing from its earlier tightness. "Number two?"

I run my fingertips along the light hair of his forearms, wishing he would relax. "Deal breaker number two: I need to look forward to being with him." I shrug because for some that may seem shallow, but if I don't enjoy his company, then how can I promise a lifetime to him?

He leans down and runs his lips over my forehead. "That's how I feel about you. I look forward to seeing you from the moment I wake up."

"Ditto," I whisper. Even when he's sad or when I see the ache that lingers inside, I still want to be there, next to him. Cameron encompasses his surroundings. Feels every-thing and everyone. An artist who breathes in the world and breathes out a song.

"And the last one?" His lips have trailed down to my cheek, making my mind nearly too fuzzy to answer.

"Deal breaker three, and the most important. The one that wipes all the others away."

He pulls back so our eyes meet, his stare intent and ready, as if whatever it is, he'll climb a mountain to meet it.

"Don't look so worried." I bite my lip to keep from laugh-ing. "It's simple, really. Any man I'm with has to love my daughter."

His brow creases even tighter. "That's way too easy."

"You'd be surprised." I remember the first time I saw him with Morgan. The way she watched him. Tentative but also with respect and admiration. I remember how he held her as she cried when Mason fell and how many hours he's spent on his front porch just to give her space while also giving me comfort. Maybe all those things are easy for him, but that just further proves how extraordinary he is. "What about you?" I say, my throat suddenly burning. "What are your deal breakers?"

"Similar to yours," he says a little too easily.

"Hey, you're the one who started this little exercise." I punch his arm playfully. "You can't take my answers."

"Okay. I guess that's fair." His eyes turn weary, and I see prior hurts in them. Heartbreak. Betrayal. "There's really only one." I feel him retreat, emotionally and physically. We're no longer touching, and the separation chafes at my skin.

"Tell me what it is." I take his hand, pulling him back to me. He reluctantly comes, head bowed.

"I won't tolerate lying. A little one, a big one. By omission or by any other excuse they might come up with." His sigh is shaky, painful. "I want the person I'm with to respect me enough to be one hundred percent honest. No matter the cost."

I step closer, cradle not just his hand but his entire forearm to my chest, and look him square in the eye. "I swear I will never lie to you."

His eyes soften, and tenderness leaks into his stare. "And I already love your daughter." He wraps his hand gently around the back of my neck and pulls me close. I expect a kiss, but instead his forehead touches mine and we stand there, me clutching his arm, skin searing skin, breath crossing. "Are you absolutely sure my leaving isn't another one of those deal breakers?"

"Yes, I'm sure," I whisper. I don't fear heartbreak the way he obviously does. I don't fear anything but chances not taken.

Reluctantly he lets go, and we each drop our hold on each other. The air is rife with intensity, but I would expect nothing less from a man like Cameron. "We should probably get to work, huh? If I know Mason, there's some kind of plan laid out in chronological order." He glances around, looking half ready for someone to jump out of the corner and catch us together.

I bite my lip, my cousin the very last person on my mind, though he should have been at the forefront. I guiltily pull the folded paper from my pocket. "He made me a list complete with instructions."

Cameron looks it over, and his eyes widen, his lips pressing together to hide his unease. "Can I be honest without completely jeopardizing my masculinity?" He runs a hand through his hair. "I have no idea what half of this means."

"Don't worry. I do . . . a little." I loop my arm through his and tug him toward the staircase. "And what we don't know we'll figure out together."

"Together, huh?" He stops and looks down at me, his eyes calculating. Then he leans down and brushes a soft, lingering kiss over my lips. "I like the sound of that."

～⁹

We spent the day talking a lot more than working. And kissing. Yes, there was lots and lots of kissing. But between those stolen moments and the rare beat of a hammer, we just got to know each other again. Not the heavy things this time. Not the panic attacks or my life after Annaliese disappeared. Instead, we shared the fun stuff. I told him all about the first vacation I took with just me and Morgan. He told me about his house in Nashville and the spastic designer who would practically slap his hand when he'd try to change something. We shared guttural laughs when we detached the sink and old stale water sprayed him in the face. Luckily, it only lasted a second since the main water valve has been turned off for weeks now.

We're both dirty, grimy, flushed, and happier than two kids at Disneyland. Or at least I think he is, as well. His dimples haven't disappeared all day.

Cameron tosses his crowbar onto the pile of shattered tile. "I'm exhausted."

"Me too. Let's take a break."

We walk down the hallway until we find the one carpeted area without debris. Our drinks are still there from earlier, as is our discarded takeout.

I go to pick up my bottle when he grabs my hand and pulls me to his chest, his lips dipping to tickle my neck. "How do you do this day after day?"

I'm giggling like a schoolgirl when I say, "I drink lots of energy drinks."

"I have a better idea." He kisses me, swallowing the sound

of my laughter. It's slow and gentle, lingering. His fingers graze the loose hairs at my temple, his touch reverent. My stomach dips, this kiss the most intimate we've shared. It feels deep and emotional, and so full of longing that it radiates off us both. His release is slow, our gazes locked on each other as he pulls away. A storm brews behind his eyes.

I run a finger down his cheek. "What's wrong?"

"I had a talk with Mason at the hospital," Cameron says, letting go and leaning his back against the wall. "He mentioned the house renovation was in some peril . . ." He trails off, his eyes fixed on the mess down the hallway. "I'm sorry I haven't asked about it. Haven't offered to help before now." Regret steams off his words, and I get a very sharp suspicion that Mason talked about far more than just this house.

"What did he say to you?"

"Nothing that stuck apparently." Cameron shakes away whatever thoughts began to haunt him and smiles, broad and honest. "But he is worried about you and about this renovation."

I bite my lip, my stomach turning for an entirely different reason this time. While Cameron and I have been here all day, we wouldn't exactly get an award for the greatest efficiency. "Mason can be more intense than is warranted. He's a bit of a pessimist."

"He didn't used to be." Cameron bends over and casually hands me my water bottle from earlier, but I can tell by the way he stiffens that the changes in Mason bother him.

"I know." I rub the plastic between my palms, feeling the need to explain. "I think something traumatic happened in Austin."

Cameron pauses mid-drink and lowers his hand. "Like what?"

"I don't know any details. But he was there for two years,

and he *never* mentions the city or old friends. The only thing he ever talks about is working with his dad's buddy, who taught him how to do all this stuff." I spread my arms and look around the destruction. "He battles his demons with every blow. Silently hurting. And since he won't let me help him, I just pray and hope one day he opens up."

"Sounds like you two have gotten really close since he's been back."

"He's my best friend," I say simply. Truthfully.

Cameron's quiet for a second and then looks down at his dirty boots. "Mason doesn't have a lot of respect for me any-more," he says wearily. "And I can't really blame him. I let him down." His sigh is heart-wrenching. "He's not going to be happy about the two of us."

I walk over and take Cameron's hand, an act of reassur-ance I can tell he needs. "I love Mason. And yes, his opinion matters a great deal to me." He looks up, that unsettled dark-ness once again in his eyes. "But not where you're concerned. In regard to you and me . . . I have no doubts."

He tugs me close. I expect another kiss, but instead he simply holds me tight as if I might very well disappear. He presses his forehead to the space between my neck and shoulder, breathing me in. I close my eyes, welcoming the warmth, the feel of his back underneath my fingertips.

And suddenly I don't care that we barely made a dent in the bathroom today. I don't care that what we have is tempo-rary or reckless. It's just him and me. And I'll take it . . . no matter how painful it will be when it all disappears.

TWENTY-ONE

Cameron

I'm far too eager to see her. Too eager to touch her and kiss her and to show her the surprise that will be here in less than ten minutes.

I pace the empty rooms across the bottom floor of the house we stayed at for nearly eight hours yesterday. My muscles should hurt, should be strained and tight with overuse, but the only thing taut in my body is my chest. The anticipation whirling in and out of my rib cage.

Finally, the door swings open, and in walks all the light in the universe. "I'm the worst person ever," she says, dropping her bag to the floor. "I totally misled him . . . on purpose. I sat in the living room last night and let Mason come to the conclusion that we got most of the bathroom demoed. All the tile, even the floors. I practically nodded when his eyes widened, and he asked if we'd done the whole thing." She covers her face with her hands and shakes her head miserably. "I couldn't admit the truth."

I don't hesitate, not even for a second. Not when it's all I've thought about since saying goodbye last night. I stride over, peel her hands from her face, and kiss her good morning until she goes limp in my arms. I feel drunk on the smell of her. Drunk on every moment we shared yesterday, every story, every kiss that was forbidden when we were supposed to be working.

Being with her is the closest I've come to the euphoria I used to get from the stage and the screaming fans. Only this glorious adventure doesn't hurt. It doesn't make me burn with regret. It's just light. Light and beauty and the essence that is Lexie.

"What if I can guarantee right now that not only will we finish yesterday's work, but every item on Mason's list?" I ask, practically beaming.

"I'd say you have far more faith in us than I do."

"Not in us." I hear the crunch of tires and spin her around to face the still-open front door. "In them."

She gapes as a second truck parks, and then a third. "What did you—?"

"I brought some stronger reinforcements this time."

"Is that . . . your dad?" She glances over her shoulder at me and then back to the four men, each in old jeans and work boots, strolling up the sidewalk.

"Yep." I point to the man to his left. "And the gray one is my uncle Henry, Dad's older brother. The other two are Bill and Aiden. Bill is Dad's best friend. And his son, Aiden, as luck would have it, owns his own construction company, so he has all the cool tools. Needless to say, some favors were called in."

"But how do they even have time to do this?"

"Ah, you know Dad. He always shuts down the office this week. Likes to give his employees family time." One of the many benefits of owning his own company. Dad was always around, spending time with us, investing in our lives. There's nothing he loves more than feeling like we kids still need him. "Uncle Henry drove in this weekend and said he didn't have anything better to do. And, well, Bill and Aiden love Mom's cooking, so trading a Thanksgiving meal for a day of labor was an easy sell."

"I don't . . . thank you." She practically chokes on the words, her shock still apparent in the stunned set of her shoulders.

I lean down, whisper gently in her ear, "You're welcome." My own temperature rises when I see the responding goose bumps and feel the shiver that runs through her body.

Dad barrels into the house with a bold hello, and I step back from her, putting a more appropriate distance between the two of us. People have always told me I look just like my father. Same coloring, same height, same deep dimples. But Dad is a better man, a stronger man. Uncompromising in his convictions and decisions. A lot like Caleb actually. He glances around the space, his head nodding in appreciation. "Well, this is quite a fine place you have here, Lex. Don't suppose you'd mind if we pitch in a little today, do you?"

"Mind?" Lexie squeaks out and then hugs my dad so tight the man blushes a little. "I'm beyond ecstatic." She presses her hands to her cheeks, her voice still laced with disbelief. "Thank you so much."

He lays a hand on her shoulder and turns her toward his companions while I stand back, watching. I know that look on his face. It's the same pride he gets when introducing his children. And it seems right that Lexie would qualify, considering how often she played at our house when we were kids. "Boys, this is Lexie, one of Cassie's best friends growing up."

Bill is the first to shake her hand, and she lunges and hugs him. In fact, she embraces every one of the men as if they are all family and coming over to hang out for the day. Aiden, who's a year older than me and recently divorced, lingers a little too long for my liking, but I don't feel that usual twist of jealousy. With January, and especially with Darcy, the feeling of possessiveness would gut me regularly. Like I needed to defend what we had, hold on with white-knuckled fury or risk the bond being severed. But watching Lexie charm each person in the room, make them feel appreciated and important and cared for, the strongest emotion I can muster is amusement. And admiration. It's as if I know in my heart without question that Lexie is safe. I trust her. Fully and completely.

Aiden takes the lead and follows Lexie as she walks him through her and Mason's vision for the property. They study the construction plans laid out on the empty dining room floor. She also gives him two lists. One far longer than what we were working toward yesterday. He reads and nods, saying very little. Lexie gnaws on her lip, trying not to interrupt, but I can tell it's killing her to wait. She's practically bouncing on her toes.

I start toward her but halt when a piece of my heart splinters as if chipped off by the sudden rush of memory. Of Darcy telling me I smothered her. Of her admitting she was fleeing the country just to get away from me. My back tenses, and I push the insecurity away. Lexie is not Darcy.

As much out of pride as out of her apparent need, I stride forward and place a hand on Lexie's back. I feel her melt into me. Feel her body relax, and my own warm, when she turns and smiles at me. A thank-you for being there. My stomach unwinds, and I feel stupid for questioning myself in the first place.

"Well, I think we should have no problem getting this taken care of for you," Aiden says, glancing up from the piece of paper. He smirks at the three men still chatting together.

"Of course, we're dealing with a crew of geriatrics, so no promises. Their knees will likely give out before lunch."

"My knees are iron and steel," Bill says with equal jest. He, like my dad and uncle, are still in their fifties. They don't even qualify for senior discounts yet. "And besides, you're lucky to have us. Half your Millennial generation has never even picked up a hammer."

Aiden ignores his dad and smiles back at Lexie. "Don't let them out of your sight. Dad prides himself on being a closet architect. Next thing you know he'll be smashing walls you don't want smashed." When Lexie's eyes widen, he quickly adds, "I'm kidding. They're actually really skilled."

She releases a sigh of relief and gives Aiden the kind of smile that could melt a giant's frozen heart. "I'm genuinely overwhelmed. How can I ever thank you?"

He glances up at me, and I don't miss the understanding in his eyes. He can see why I called in these favors. Why Lexie was worth the IOUs that would one day be cashed in. "No thanks necessary. Any friend of Cam's is a friend of mine." Aiden and I have known each other since grade school. We didn't have a lot in common, so we were never that close, but he's a good man.

I reach out my hand to shake his. "I really appreciate your coming."

He nods. "We're just going to grab some supplies out of the truck and then we'll get started."

As they all head back outside, punching and pushing each other like teenagers, I grab Lexie's hand. The downfall of this favor is that we won't have a second alone together today, and after that earlier uncertainty, I need to feel her in my arms. I pull her to the back of the house and into a small room, hidden from our guests. Her back pressed against the wall, I lean in and kiss her, long and slow.

She wraps her arms around my neck and giggles when I move from her lips to her neck. "You better enjoy this kiss," she says, breathless, "because it's the last one you're getting today."

I nuzzle her with my nose and feign surprise. "You'd really deny me? After saving the day?"

"You made a phone call. *They* are saving the day."

I fall back and place my hand on my heart. "You wound me."

"Ah . . . poor thing," she teases, patting my cheek playfully.

I gently take her hand in mine and kiss the inside of her wrist. She watches me with a tenderness I don't deserve, and yet I seem to be the only one she wants. It's both glorious and terrifying. And I want to milk every second, to have her next to me as much as this limited time will allow. "Come to Thanksgiving," I whisper.

"What?"

"You and Morgan. Come with me to Thanksgiving," I say louder this time, wanting to make sure she knows I'm serious. "My parents will love seeing you. And Cassie and Stephen will be there. We can even drag Mason along if you want."

Her brows pinch together. "You mean like show up as a couple? Or as friends?"

"I don't know about you, but I don't kiss my friends. Plus I'm obviously not very good at staying away from you." I lean down to nuzzle her neck, but she pushes me back, biting her lip.

"I'll have to tell Morgan first."

"I'm pretty sure she's already figured it out. The girl is ridiculously perceptive, and come on, you did admit to being enamored with me for the past sixteen years."

Her face blushes hot and red and she covers it with her hands. "I cannot believe you brought that up."

"I love that you had a crush on me. I find it adorable." My

voice lowers as I brush my lips across her forehead. "I find you incredibly adorable."

She smiles up at me, and just when I'm about to lean down and resume my favorite pastime, my phone buzzes in my pocket. Regretfully, I pull it free, turning my gaze from Lexie for only a second.

Dad:
Stop distracting Lexie and come upstairs. We have questions.

I snort out a laugh and show her the text.

Horror crosses her expression as she tries to pull free.

"Nope. Not until you agree to come on Thursday."

"Yes, fine. Okay. We'll go." Lexie shakes her head, her cheeks flushed, her eyes bright with delight. "And you, sir, better behave the rest of the day." She points. "I mean it." She takes my hand and pulls me from the room, both of us laughing as if we're thirteen and just got caught by my parents. Which I guess we kind of did.

There have been so few good days in the last five years that I stopped expecting much more than quiet survival. Happiness or joy was not even a dream to consider.

And yet I know, without question, that today is going to be different. Today is going to be a really, really great day.

TWENTY-TWO

Lexie

"Cam just pulled up," Morgan says as she leans against the frame of my bathroom door.

"Already? I was supposed to have ten more minutes." I glance up at the mirror, my eyes wild, my heart racing. Red splotches are covering my neck and face, making me look like a blotchy mess. Cam has never even been inside my house before, and now we're . . . well, I don't even know what to call our relationship. The whole thing is so surreal.

"Wow, Mom. You're, like, totally freaking out."

"I am not freaking out." I fumble for my makeup brush and cover my face with another layer of loose powder. I am freaking out. I'm so nervous I have hardly been able to eat in two days.

"It's just Thanksgiving."

"No, it's also meeting his family—"

"I thought you've known his family forever."

I drop my brush onto the counter nearly covered with cosmetics and press my palms on the cool tile. "Yes, I have, but this is different. I'm not going as Cassie's friend. I'm going as his date. And . . ." I turn and look at her. "How are you so okay with all of this? Aren't you supposed to rant and rave about this sort of thing?"

She shrugs. "I like Cam. And it's good you have someone besides just me. Someone special to you."

Her words form a knot in my chest. "You'll always be my priority, though. You know that, right?"

She rolls her eyes. "Yes, I know. I'm just saying that Cam is a good man. And I approve, wholeheartedly. Besides, aren't you always going on and on about how we need to seize every opportunity and welcome the people God places in our lives?" Her speech is mocking and overexaggerated, but it's enough to pull me from my stupor.

"You're right." I sigh and grip the countertop. "I'm being dumb."

"Yes. And a bit neurotic."

I laugh, and so does she. I'm not often the one to panic, but Morgan always seems to know what to say when the rare occasion happens. Ironically, the words she often chooses are my own, or really, my mom's.

The doorbell ringing splits through the house.

I shoo her toward the door. "Go get that so Mason doesn't have to get up. I'll be out in a sec."

She pitches her brow. "Which version?"

"The sane one. Now hurry."

She backs away, a grin on her face. She seems happy today. Relaxed. Maybe because Cameron said the gathering was outside and casual, so there was zero argument about her jeans and tennis shoes. I, on the other hand, have put on eight different outfits. The line between not trying too hard and *I came here straight from the bed* is very thin, and I've struggled to find the balance.

I step back, taking in my appearance one more time. The

winning look is dark jeans with a thin long-sleeved blue sweater, large hoop silver earrings, and my hair loose around my shoulders. I spray some perfume, spin to let the droplets fall over the entire area of my shirt, and decide it's as good as it's going to get.

Cameron is strolling through the small living room, glancing at framed pictures, when I emerge and shut my bedroom door. I do not want him to see the mass of rejected clothing covering my bed.

"Hey, sorry I kept you waiting," I say, slightly breathless. We haven't seen each other since the guys came on Tuesday and stayed till nearly nine o'clock working. Aiden had to call in a couple of guys from his crew to push us over the top, but we'd gotten it done. The entire list. Everything we needed to do before the plumbers come on Monday.

Cam glances up, sets down the frame of me and Morgan he's holding, and smiles in that way of his that has the heat rising again on my neck. "Definitely worth the wait." He steps closer and kisses me softly on the cheek. "You look beautiful."

I pull back instinctively and glance at Mason on the couch. He doesn't notice. He's too busy being stubborn about not going today and watching some pregame football program.

Cameron must sense my unease because he clears his throat and backs away. "Your house is lovely."

I tilt my head at the way his inflection rises at the end of the sentence. "You sound surprised."

"Not really. Okay, maybe a little." He grins sheepishly. "You and Morgan kind of talk about this place like living in it is a hardship."

"That's because this house has low ceilings, terrible plumbing, and abysmal lighting. But it's home, so we make the best of it."

"Well, I can definitely see why you're so good at your job. It feels elegant yet comfortable in here." He looks around at my hard work, and I relish the appreciation in his gaze. We've never had a lot of extra money, but I've always done my best to make the little we have feel warm and inviting.

"Thank you." We stand there a little awkwardly, probably because of my earlier hesitation to touch him. He doesn't say it, but I can sense a stitch of hurt. "I'm sorry. I'm being weird, I know," I blurt out. "It's just that I've never, well, brought guys around them before." My gaze darts between Mason on the couch and Morgan mindlessly playing on her phone, so he knows which *them* I'm referring to.

"I understand." He squeezes my hand but lets go right away. I'm not sure I'll ever get used to his easy affection. How little he hesitates to touch me whenever he can. And maybe it's the many, many long years of singleness, or maybe it's just him, but I crave the contact. So much so that I already feel the sting of it being gone. "If it makes you feel any better, I've never brought a date to a family function, either."

My eyes widen. "Never?"

He shakes his head. "Nope. Only friends."

"Ugh. I wish you hadn't told me that."

Cameron's laugh is quick and endearing. "Why?"

"Because . . ." I step closer and lower my voice. "I don't want to disappoint your family."

"That, Lexie, is not possible. You are probably the only wise decision I've made in the last four years."

My entire body warms with those words, and the last of the lingering unease fades away. "Thank you." This time, I'm the one who takes his hand, and he lightly brushes his fingers across my cheek.

"So, how did Morgan take the news?" he asks, his hand dropping. "Am I in for a horrifically tense car ride?"

I shrug, realizing that the only person making a big deal of today is me, and I need to stop it before I ruin the entire thing. "She thought us dating was great. You have done the impossible and won over my daughter."

His smile widens like a proud parent. "Well then, we better get going so I can continue the trend."

We make our way back to the living room. Cameron heads to the door, where Morgan waits impatiently. I watch as he ruffles her hair, the way she hits his arm away but smiles at the affection, and I have to look away. We're both getting far too comfortable with Cameron being around. I reach the couch a step later and place both hands gently on Mason's shoulders. "Are you sure you won't come with us?"

"Yeah, Mason. It's weird that you want to spend Thanksgiving by yourself," Morgan adds. We've been tag-teaming all morning, but it hasn't been effective.

"I'm not by myself," Mason says for the third time today. "You two will be back later, and I expect a feast of leftovers." I go to stand next to Morgan, and when we both stare at him with pleading eyes, he sighs. "Listen. I would go, but I've been to these things before, and trust me. Lounging at home will be much easier for me than watching everyone else play volleyball and basketball while I sit there immobile."

Guilt wrenches my insides, and the look on Cameron's face makes me think Mason's words do the same to him. "I'll make sure Mom hooks you up," he says to my cousin with a hitch in his voice. "She's been baking for days."

"Thanks. And tell your dad they did a bang-up job at the house. Lex brought me by yesterday, and I couldn't be more impressed."

Cameron's shrug almost looks embarrassed by the praise. "It was nothing."

"No, it most definitely was not nothing. It was a huge help

and something my old friend would have thought to do." When Mason looks at Cam, it's the first time I've seen him do so without hostility. In fact, there's even a hint of respect in his tone. "And it's appreciated."

I feel a sting in my throat but swallow it down. One thing about Mason, he gives it straight, good or bad. You always know where you stand with him.

"Well, we should probably go." I walk back over to my couch-bound cousin and give him a quick kiss on the cheek. "Call me if you need anything."

"I will. You girls have fun."

The mood as we get into Cameron's car is quiet, not his usual weariness, but more reflection as if he's lost in memories. Good ones, it seems, because his smile is genuine as he turns on the radio and eases down the driveway.

We make it out of the neighborhood and onto the highway when Morgan finally breaks the silence. "Okay, so give me the scoop. Who, what, and where is this little shindig you're dragging us to?" I turn my head to see that she's scooted up as close as she can to the front, her head between our two seats.

"Get your seat belt back on," I say.

"It is on." She pulls at the strap and lets it fall. The thing is pulled as far as it can go from the seat. "So spill. I like to go into places prepared."

Cameron laughs in a way that feels like a release of whatever thoughts were holding him captive. I don't know if Morgan intended this reaction when she asked the question, but part of me thinks maybe she knew Cam needed someone to pull him out of his head. "The 'who' is my entire family. My mom and dad. My oldest sister, Catherine, her husband, and their two daughters. My brother, Caleb, and his wife, Kelly. The one you saw at the house with me."

Morgan nods. "Do they have kids, too?"

"No. Not yet." The way he says it makes me think that choice hasn't been theirs. "And then Cassie and Stephen, who you already know from the wedding. Then it's my uncle and his entire family, which is two of my cousins, their spouses, and five grandkids. One is close to your age. Bailey. She just turned fourteen."

"Holy smokes. That's more than twenty people!"

"Probably closer to thirty. I left out the friends who will likely stop by, as well." Cameron chuckles. "We like big events in my family."

"Apparently," she says and glances my way. "I guess I understand now why you were freaking out earlier."

My cheeks catch on fire, but Cameron squeezes my knee and continues. "It will be fun. You'll see. We always have a big volleyball game going, football, basketball, dominoes. Whatever you want to do. Dad and Mom have five acres so there's plenty of room."

"What about piñatas and tug-of-war?" she asks, her voice hitching with unfettered excitement.

"Not in the past, but hey, I'm open to any new tradition."

Morgan settles back in her seat, a smile plastered across her beautiful face. "You know what, Cam? This might actually be fun."

He turns and winks at me, but I can't seem to dislodge this creeping unease. Piñatas and tug-of-war? She'd said them like they were random ideas, but memories I haven't explored in years dart through my mind. Pictures of Annaliese blindfolded, Mason laughing as he tugs the rope opposite us. I couldn't have been more than six or seven the last time our families all got together. But the picture is now vivid, as if Morgan's words cleaned an old cloudy window.

I glance at her one more time but keep my questions at

bay. She's too happy today. And who knows why she made that connection. It could be coincidence, or Mason could have mentioned the gatherings in passing, I suppose. I sit up straighter, determination stretching my spine. Today is going to be fun, and I am done letting all my insecurities ruin it.

Upon entering the Lees' house, we were bombarded with so many hugs and hellos that I didn't have time to worry even if I still wanted to. Morgan and Bailey sparked an immediate connection, probably because they were at least eight years older than any of the other kids there. Cam was swallowed up by family members who haven't talked to him in years while I found my way to the kitchen and offered his mom help. She declined, sending me right back out and telling me to go enjoy myself.

I'm now fully loaded with a lemonade-punch concoction while I make my way down the stone walkway to the back-yard party in full swing. A buzz comes from my purse, and I pause to check the caller ID just in case Mason changed his mind. It's the same number that called an hour ago, and once again I send it to voicemail, which will give whoever it is our company's after-hours number. I'm not the agent on call today, so I'm definitely not dealing with holiday emergencies.

I drop my phone back in my purse and continue to the last place I saw Cameron and Morgan. Two long decorated tables have been set up near the path, and I stop to admire the beauty of Mrs. Lee's handiwork. They are both covered in linen and adorned with festive orange and yellow décor centerpieces. The place settings are fancy gold chargers holding thick paper plates that look far too much like porcelain to be real. I'm about to pick one up and make sure it really is disposable when I hear a familiar voice behind me.

"Mom's gone a little over the top since Cameron's home this year. I swear she's put as much effort into this gathering as the wedding."

I turn around and quickly hug my childhood friend. "How are you?" I ask, squeezing her tight. "How was the honey-moon? And married life?"

We release each other, and Cassie blushes. "Nice. A little weird sometimes. Especially the whole sharing-a-bathroom thing."

"I can't imagine," I say, even though the idea sounds wonderful. It isn't the same by any means, but after getting past the rocky start, having Mason around has been nice, even with his gruffness. There's always someone to talk with, to share burdens and funny stories.

"But really, he's great." A smile blossoms that makes Cassie glow and takes her from gorgeous to downright stunning. "I'm so lucky."

"He's the lucky one, I'm sure." I catch a glimpse of Cameron right as I finish speaking, and my heart leaps just like it used to when I was a kid. He's standing in between Morgan and Bailey, laughing as he pushes them out of the way every time the ball comes in their direction.

"He's pretty lucky, too," Cassie says softly, apparently watching me watch them.

"What?" I force myself to turn away from the scene, and urge that pesky, wishful part of myself that longs for more time to disappear.

"Cameron." She flashes a glance at her brother, who's now getting a taste of his own medicine. The girls gang up and tackle him, all three falling to the ground. "This is the happiest I've seen him in years."

"Yeah?" And that one comment is why I'll take the six weeks we have left and relish them. I turn to my old friend, blushing much like she did. "He makes me pretty happy, too."

But her response is not what I expect. Instead of our falling into giggles and boy-talk like we did when we were teenagers, Cassie's mouth goes tight, her eyes turning sorrowful. "I'm in a weird spot because I love my brother more than anything. And you're one of my closest friends. Not to mention that you two are adults and definitely don't need my opinion or interference." She looks out at him again, swallowing. He's surrendered to Morgan and Bailey's punishment and is slowly pulling himself up from the ground, grass covering his jeans. "I should just shut up, mind my own business, and try to freeze time or something."

"But . . ." I offer, knowing the word is right around the corner. Cassie and I have always been completely open with each other, and I can't imagine the two of us changing now.

"But . . ." She sighs, turning away from the giddy joy in every one of Cameron's movements. "I can't freeze time. Nor can I pretend not to know the things that I do." She shakes her head and looks at the ground. "I don't want you to get hurt. And I feel pretty certain you're going to be if you walk into this thing with him blind."

The air stills in my chest, but I force my lungs to work, to expand and contract like they're supposed to. Cassie, like Mason it seems, is determined to play the relationship police. "Cassie, I've survived the loss of both my parents, my sister, and my childhood in a span of three years. I've raised a daughter and made a good life for both of us. You don't have to protect me. Cameron and I have been completely honest with each other."

She glances back up, her eyes glistening, and nods. "I'm sure you have. He wouldn't want it any other way. But it's not secrets that I'm worried about. It's the parts of himself he refuses to deal with that always seem to cause the most damage."

Despite knowing I shouldn't ask, I can't seem to stop the growing curiosity. "And what do you think those things are?"

She sighs as if making a decision and then quietly says, "Cam has never gotten over Darcy. Even I didn't realize the extent of his feelings until I saw his reaction when I told him she was at the wedding. And then after I got home from the honeymoon, I called her to find out what really happened between the two of them because I was so sick of his evasions on the subject." She pauses, and I know I should stop her from telling me more. From telling me secrets that Cameron obviously didn't want me to know. But I don't. Instead, I take a breath and listen when Cassie says, "He professed his love for her the night before his last concert in town. She turned him down and chose Bryson. That's why he's never come back home. He can't stomach the idea of them together."

"Oh" is all I can say. Cameron had told me that his first ever panic attack had come the very next day. He'd said the demons from his past and the music were too intertwined to separate. How had I not thought of Darcy? They were inseparable growing up.

"He hasn't contacted her," Cassie quickly adds, as if that makes her words more digestible. "Not even after they spoke at the wedding. But that's part of what has me so worried. Cam has a bad habit of jumping in way too fast. He feels everything, all the time, so when something feels good, he grabs on ferociously as if it will erase all the rest of his issues. But it never does, because, like I said, he feels *everything* to his core." She sighs as if even the emphatic words can't express how much. "I'm telling you this because what you see right now, this glee, this euphoric happiness, it's not going to stay. No matter how awesome you are or how much I know he cares for you." Her brow creases, concern lacing every word. "The truth is, until Cam makes things right with Darcy and deals with the circumstances surrounding why he left town the way he did, he's never going to be whole. Functional maybe, but never whole." She squeezes my hand. I know it must feel like ice against hers. "And you, Lexie, deserve to be loved by a man who's whole."

I immediately feel like a traitor. This was an entire piece of Cameron's past that he got no say as to whether it was shared with me or not. I stay quiet, completely unsure how to respond without inviting more intrusion into Cameron's privacy.

She bites her lip. "What are you thinking?"

"Honestly, I'm a little confused as to why you're telling me all this. Do you not want us dating?"

"What? No. I love the fact that you're dating. I encouraged it." Her voice turns almost desperate. "I think you might be the only one who has any chance at fixing him."

The word *fix* grates against my skin and I can't tell if I'm more offended for myself or for Cameron. "Your brother doesn't need fixing."

"You don't understand how bad the last four years have been." Cassie presses her palms to her face and shakes her head before dropping her hands. "I want the real him back. The one I grew up with. I know he's still in there, past this empty shell of a person he's become."

I swallow down another defensive retort. Cameron is anything but empty. One just has to look into his eyes to see the overflow of emotion. But Cassie is just being Cassie. And despite her misguided efforts, she's saying all this because she loves him. "Cassie, while I know your heart is in the right place, I think the best thing you can do for Cameron is to let him figure things out on his time and in his way."

Her anxious expression softens into an embarrassed chuckle.

"Is that your polite way of telling me to butt out?" I simply shrug. "Okay, fine. Not another word." I raise an eyebrow, and she laughs harder. "Seriously. I promise." She makes a locking motion on her mouth and throws away the key.

"Thank you." We turn back to the volleyball court and both get a wave from her brother. He motions for me to join him, and I hug Cassie one more time. "Enjoy this precious season with your husband. Don't miss it by focusing on problems that aren't yours to solve."

She takes my hands after releasing me. "You've always been so wise, but I think motherhood has made you even more so."

I don't tell her it isn't motherhood specifically that's done it, but life itself. Tragedy, loss, victories. They all shape you, either positively or negatively, and often it's your choice which one. I ease down the path to where Cameron waits for me and walk straight into his arms, kissing him quick and purposefully.

His entire face lights up with affection, and he cups my cheek, leans down, and kisses me one more time.

Cassie's concern was exactly what I needed to pull myself out of the fog I'd been in all morning. This time with Cameron is a gift. Short, long, it doesn't matter. I'd broken my own rules, focused way too much on the things that could go wrong. There is so precious little time, and I am going to take my own advice and not waste any of it.

The rest of the day was perfect. Laughter, food, family. It was all so wonderful and warm that I closed my eyes the entire way home, wishing I could bottle the feeling and drink it whenever I needed a pick-me-up.

Cameron follows us out of the car, intent on walking us to the door.

232

I stop him halfway up the sidewalk. "Morgan, will you take the food inside for me, please?"

She heaves the overfilled bag into her hand and trudges forward. "Gladly. The last thing I want to watch is you two sucking faces out here. Believe me, I got my fill at the party."

I should correct her sassiness, but instead I giggle, watching her with a silly grin on my face until she disappears inside.

Cameron wraps his arms around my waist and pulls me close. "I wouldn't want to fail her expectations," he says, grinning, right before pressing his lips to mine. Sure, we were affectionate today, but not like this. This kiss is long, slow, and much too delicious to subject others to it.

When he releases me, we both sigh because our bodies and are minds are definitely not on the same page right now. Our minds tell us to stop, to go inside and say goodbye. Our bodies remind us that we are two consenting adults and that his house is gloriously empty.

Thankfully, one of us has mastered the art of mind over body.

"I should probably go," Cameron whispers.

"Yeah," I say, though I don't want to.

"Thank you for coming with me today."

I squeeze his hand. "Thank you for inviting us. I had a wonderful time."

He kisses me again and then begins to walk away. I tug on his hand, not letting him go. He acquiesces far too easily, yet it's not more kisses I need, at least not right now.

I stop him before he can pull me close again. "Cameron, wait . . . I need to tell you something first."

"Okay . . ." He studies me, and I feel a ripple of tension run through him. "I'm guessing from the grimace on your face that it's not going to be something I want to hear."

"Cassie talked to me—well, told me some things today about you and Darcy."

His jaw clenches so hard I'm surprised I don't hear his teeth crack. "That's it. I'm officially going to throttle my little sister."

"Don't. She means well. She's worried about you."

"What did she tell you?"

I repeat our conversation, every word, because he has a right to know. "I'm sorry," I say when I'm done.

"How are you the one who's sorry?" He lets go of my hand and runs his through his hair, his voice tight with disbelief.

"Because I should have stopped the conversation earlier. That wasn't her story to tell."

That long-suffering weariness returns to his eyes, and I wonder if maybe I shouldn't have said anything. But I promised him I'd never lie or omit information, and I keep my promises.

He lets out a long sigh. "Lexie, I—"

I press my finger to his lips. "If you want to talk about it someday, then okay, but not because you feel obligated to counteract your sister's conclusions. What she told me does not affect *us* in any way. I just felt it was wrong for you not to be aware that I now know something so intimate about your life."

He takes my finger gently in his hand and brings it away from his lips. "I'm glad you don't need to hear what happened, but I want to tell you. I've wanted to for a while, but I didn't want my past anywhere near the two of us." He pauses as if still trying to form the words he needs. "Cassie has a bad habit of setting the narrative when she doesn't understand what's going on, and in this case she's flat-out wrong. I'm not in love with Darcy anymore." His voice comes with such hard conviction that I have no doubt he's telling the truth.

I swallow as a rope uncoils in my stomach. One I didn't even realize was there until he said those words.

"And our fallout did not stem from the fact that she broke my heart four years ago," he continues, apparently determined to give me the whole story despite the late hour or that we're still standing in my driveway. "I always knew the feelings were one-sided, even when I hoped they would grow. It was the lies that broke us. The way she slowly pulled away and cut me out instead of being honest with me. That's what felt like the greatest betrayal, because she didn't just omit the truth about what she was feeling at the time, she left me . . . too slowly for me to be completely sure what was happening. And then when I would say something, she'd pretend everything was fine, as if I was being paranoid."

I hear it now. The bite in his words. The anger still tangled in whatever he used to feel for her.

"At the time, Darcy was my world." He looks down at me, an apology in his eyes.

I squeeze his hand, assure him that his talking about a former love is not hurting me.

He shakes his head as if still admonishing himself for being young and naïve. "Every thought I had revolved around her and the music. They were intertwined, one feeding the other. So when she disappeared, she took pieces of the music with her, and I never really got them back." This time he looks at me, his gaze straight into mine. A promise that his words are truth. I brace myself for whatever feels this important to him. "And that is the lingering pain that Cassie still sees. That's what I've wanted to explain to you every day since you held my hand on the back porch and told me my lyrics touched your life. I just didn't know how to articulate it without implying something more. The feelings are too jumbled to call it love or romance or longing for one person. Her

departure represented an entire part of my soul that I probably should never have given to her, but I did. And because of
that decision, I've spent the last four years trying and failing
to find the music in myself again." He runs a finger along my
cheek so gently I feel an unexpected wave of emotion. "That
is . . . until I met you. And you gave me pieces of the music
back. In that box of old recordings, in your memories, even in
the silly game we played."

I swallow, the enormity of what he's shared clinging to my
heart.

"For the first time in years, Lexie, I'm far more interested
in looking at my future than being stuck in the past. And I
don't want to be that guy who lives life with resentment and
bitterness and what-ifs trailing behind him anymore. You've
taught me that."

I blink, trying to keep the tears at bay, but it's pointless.
They come, spilling over, one by one. To be able to give him
such a gift after all his music has given me is too overwhelm-
ing to put into words. And I'm grateful I don't have to.

Cameron wraps his arms around my back, and I'm pulled
into a tight all-encompassing hug. I feel his breath on my
hair, feel his lips trail down the top of my head to my heated
cheeks. And then he's kissing me, deep and unashamed, as
if I'm his sun and moon and stars. There is no up or down
or reason at this point. All I can do is fall. And that's exactly
what I do. I fall for Cameron Lee all over again.

And for the first time, I begin to wonder if maybe this
thing, this special, unexpected, wonderful thing between us,
is more than a temporary fascination. I begin to wonder if
maybe . . . it's love.

TWENTY-THREE

Cameron

Something inside me released after that night in front of Lexie's house. The agony and pain began to dissolve, not completely, but noticeable all the same. There was a freedom that came from exposing that sensitive, vulnerable part that involved Darcy. I'm not sure I even understood the full source of my anger until I'd laid the feelings out for Lexie to see. And see them, she did, and if even a part of me thought my confession would make her bolt, Lexie had proven without question that she is just as perfect as I believed her to be. If anything, it's brought us even closer.

Though Mason and the house seem determined to keep us apart. The plumbers have been on-site daily for over two weeks now. And since Mason insists on monitoring every second of their work, and Lexie insists on making sure her cousin doesn't reinjure himself, our interactions during day-light hours are limited to texts and quick phone calls. We've only gotten to have a few moments of alone time together since Thanksgiving, and her absence feels like a grater across my skin.

I assume Morgan's feeling the same way based on how she describes her current life woes to me. Since that first conversation when I gave her permission to speak her mind, Morgan has completely taken advantage of the guiltless sounding board I offered her. She's never mentioned her mother again. Has stayed firmly in the shallow end, but even that's become a ritual of sorts. As soon as she finishes her allotted tree-house time, she joins me on the front porch and unleashes the floodgates. Yesterday, it was about Mason drinking all the milk and how her mom won't say a word about it to him. And worse, the doctor won't release him to drive for another week, so she's stuck sharing a bed for another seven days with her mom, who apparently kicks like a madwoman in the middle of the night. I usually just listen and try not to laugh at her misery. It seems to work. She always leaves here appearing lighter than when she walked up.

My lips quirk upward as I wonder what she'll tell me today. She's been in the tree house for nearly half an hour, so I fully expect her to come through the back gate any minute now. I glance through the screen toward the renovation two doors down, scanning the many cars parked along the curb. Maybe when Morgan's done, the two of us can find an excuse to go by the house and try to talk Lexie into a late movie. Morgan's mentioned three releases she's dying to see. Of course, that list was followed by a grumble about how she's stuck at home all the time now so what does it even matter.

I pull my gaze from the porch screen and back to the book in my lap. The pages lie open, thin and light against the tips of my fingers. I still haven't found the strength to read blocks of Scripture, but I have been flipping through, stopping at verses I highlighted when I was in high school. Looking back, I can honestly say that time was the peak of my faith. The future was wide open, and I believed God could do anything He chose to. It would never have crossed my mind that my path would diverge so far from His. But it had, one bad decision leading to the next one.

The rumble of an engine peels my gaze away from the open Bible and to the red truck inching its way down my street. The thing's a beast. Extended cab, large all-terrain tires, wheels that had to have cost thousands, and a lift kit that makes the cars nearby look like miniature toys. I haven't seen a truck this obnoxious since . . . The thought falls like a rock to the pit of my stomach as I watch the truck park behind my rental car, its cab barely fitting under the swooping oak in the front yard. I know who it is without even seeing him open the driver's door and step out. Bryson.

I slam my Bible shut and glance to the passenger window for only a moment to ensure a certain somebody is not with him. She, thankfully, is not.

The truck door closing fires a shot of adrenaline through me as I watch him come into view from around the bed of the vehicle. I wouldn't have recognized him if it wasn't for the dark unruly hair or that arrogant strut he's had since junior high. Gone are the black clothes and combat boots. Instead, he wears faded jeans and a heather-blue T-shirt I know Darcy had to have chosen for him. It's her style, soft and etched with some unique saying or picture that likely made her laugh at the store. I know. I had a drawer full of Darcy shirts before I swept them into a trash bag.

He pauses when he sees me watching him, and we both stare through the mesh. If he's here to tell me to stay away from his wife, he's six weeks overdue. But I have a sick feeling that Cassie is responsible for this unexpected visit.

Bryson reaches for the screen door, and it squeaks maliciously as it opens. A groan not unlike the one splitting across my chest. He doesn't speak, but neither do I. He simply watches me as he enters and sits, unwelcome, on the new wicker couch I just put here. I wish I hadn't bothered. Wish he was lounging on the old rotted one that was one sit away from collapsing. He laces his fingers together, sets his elbows on his knees, and watches me. My eyes dart to the same gold band he was wearing at the wedding, and the contempt that has only built over the last several years bounces with blazing heat between us.

Memories smash against my brain to the first night he asked me to be in the band. It'd been a flippant comment, said in jest, or so I thought at the time. I'd blown off the request until he asked again six months later. That time I'd told him no, flat out, no hesitation at all. Then he asked again, and again, until finally, at one of the lowest points in my life, I said yes. We'd been goofing around, playing old songs that were supposed to take my mind off January's deception. But Bryson had secretly recorded our jam session. Then he'd played it back for me, along with one he'd done with Mason. The two were unnervingly different. Bryson had looked me in the eyes, much like he's doing now, and said, *"I guarantee you we'll be signed within a year."* He'd been right. Only it hadn't taken a year. Just six months and a knife in my back.

"What are you doing here?" I say, though it sounds much more like a growl.

Bryson leans his back against the couch and crosses his arms as if I'm the intruder here and not him. "I thought it was time we talked."

"I have nothing to say to you."

"Yeah, you made that pretty clear at the wedding."

Silence falls again, heavy and electric. I feel trapped in my seat, and yet the energy bouncing inside my skin is enough to light my entire property.

"She still grieves the loss of you," he finally says, his voice rough and uneven.

His words are a punch so painful, I have to swallow to keep from choking. There's no question who *she* is. Darcy is a wall between us as solid as if she were standing right here.

"I didn't get the connection until recently," he continues while I clench my teeth so hard that they hurt. "It was just part of who she was. She would wake up in the middle of the night, and I'd find her outside with the dogs, distant and lost in her head. But then it stopped. And I thought that was it. She just had to get used to being married, used to all the change she hates so much. But then Charlie was born, and the insomnia began all over again. Only this time, she'd go to his room, watch him sleep, and cry. I figured it was the transition or hormones. And sure enough, after six months, she started sleeping through the night again." He works his jaw, clenching and unclenching his hands. "But then we ran into you at the wedding. And wouldn't you know, she hasn't slept through the night since."

Heat races down my arms, my fingers tingling. I want to punch him for telling me these things. For pretending Darcy hurts for our broken friendship as much as I do. But I remain silent, unmoving.

Bryson continues watching me, surprise flickering in his eyes. "You don't have anything to say?"

I shrug, cold and indifferent. "You're the one who made her choose between us. The fallout's on you."

Bryson shoves his hands in his hair, anger threatening his calm façade. "I knew coming here was a mistake."

"Well, no one invited you, so you're free to leave anytime." The bite in my voice is enough to make his breath hitch.

"You really don't care anymore? You're that empty?"

I just stare at him, willing my blood to still, willing my face into the nothingness I became for years because of him.

"Wow. Cassie said as much, but seeing it firsthand is . . ."

Is that pity in his voice? The idea makes me want to roar, makes me have to clamp down on the swing not to jump from my seat. "Betrayal tends to do that to a person," I snap.

Bryson finally exposes the man I know he still is and grinds out a guttural defense. "When are you going to wake up to reality, Cam? Darcy was never yours!"

"I'm not talking about Darcy!" I explode back, and the air shifts between us. I immediately want to take back my words, want to find that cold, calm person I'd been when he first walked in. In that one sentence I'd said far more to him than I ever wanted to. But it's too late now—the words come, harsh and uninvited as they spill from my lips. "You said we would do it together. That we were going to create music the world had never heard before. That the two of us were an unstoppable force." My chest burns as I point to him. "Those were your words. Your promises. And I stupidly believed you. I sacrificed everything, including myself, for *your* dream. And the one thing . . . the one person I wouldn't have given up, you ripped from me anyway."

"Oh, bull, it was your dream, too!" he yells back. Then he stops, takes a deep breath before speaking again. "You didn't do any of that for me," he says, lethally calm now. "You did it for you. At some point, Cameron, you're gonna need to man up and take responsibility for your own actions. Stop making me the villain in your life."

"Stop? How? I can't get away from you." I bolt to my feet, the tension far too intense for me to stay seated. "You're intrinsically tangled in my life. And I have to relive that nightmare all over again every time I sing that cursed song!"

"You don't think I know that?" He matches every one of my movements until we're face-to-face, shouting at each other. "That I don't see your fingerprints on each royalty check? That you're not a ghost in my wife's eyes that I have to face every day?" He braces his back against the porch post as if removing himself from the growing aggression between us. "You don't think that the words you said to her don't still haunt me? That I wish I'd never overheard you two fighting that day?"

I don't have to sort through buried memories to remember that argument with Darcy. It had seared more than just my heart. It had wrecked all the trust we'd ever built between us. My anger had exploded as I told her all the ways Bryson would inevitably fail her. And I believed every word; I still do.

"I look at my son." Bryson's voice is hitched now. Vulnerable in a way that has me stepping away from him. Has me sitting back down. "I see the innocence and adoration in his eyes, and I wonder when I'm going to ruin it. I'll be holding Darcy and wonder when she's going to wise up. Wonder when she's gonna realize that someone like her should never love someone like me." He looks at me then, his eyes glistening, and I can't speak. Can't move because this man in front of me is not the guy I've loathed for years. "I keep waiting for a bomb to detonate my life and prove you right—that I'm incapable of love. That I have no hope of being a good father and husband." He stands straighter, his voice and body growing more controlled. "So yeah, I admit, when I saw you at the wedding . . . when I saw you talking to the two most important people in the world to me, saw the way you still looked at her . . . I felt that bomb go off. Felt threatened in a way I hadn't since the day you got on that tour bus. And I hated you for it in that moment. Probably as much or more than you hated me." He sighs, and when our gazes meet, it doesn't feel like a battle anymore. It feels like a surrender from a man who would rather die than admit defeat. "Whether you realize it or not, Cam, I'm not the only villain in this scenario."

He pulls open the screen to leave, then pauses. "Darcy's never changed her number. Not even when it was compromised and she'd get five to ten spam calls a day. She refused. Just in case you might one day call."

We stare wordlessly at each other and when I don't respond, he shakes his head and turns away. I watch him go in stunned silence. Watch his hands slide into his pockets, watch his shoulders sag as if our interaction did not go the way he wanted it to.

As soon as his truck drives off, I lower my head to my hands and press my palms into my eyes, trying to control the way my body has begun to tremble. He was hurting because Darcy was hurting. Hurting from my silence. My inability to let go of all the pain she'd leveled on me. I had loved her for so long, I don't even remember a time when I didn't. I'd designed every future with her at the center. And when she disappeared, a part of me did, too.

"Cam . . . are you okay?"

I jerk my head up at the small, quiet voice next to me. Morgan stands inside the porch, next to the door. I hadn't even heard her come in.

"Yeah, I'm fine," I say, but the words come out in a croak. "How long have you been here?"

"On the porch? Only a few seconds. On the side of the house listening to you two yelling . . ." She bites her lip and shrugs. "A while."

I close my eyes in silent admonishment. I should have thought about the time. I knew Morgan would be finishing soon. I glance back at her, keep her gaze so she understands my total sincerity. "I'm so sorry you had to hear that. We should never have been arguing so openly." I've seen the way Morgan retreats and crumbles in times of chaos and conflict. She loves too deeply to brush off her feelings so easily. I get it. I get her. I'm exactly the same way.

"Who was that?" she asks, finding her way to the couch that Bryson just vacated. A little spunk has come back into her voice. More confident that I'm not about to fall apart. And surprisingly, I'm not on the edge of a panic attack. There is no residual tingle, no rising nausea, no fear of any kind. Only the heavy press of questions and decisions I can't quite reconcile.

I shake my head, realizing I never answered Morgan's question. I need to focus, need to push every word of that conversation off this porch. "That was Bryson. He's the one who started Black Carousel."

She makes an o with her mouth because she knows exactly what that means for me. Lexie has made her listen to our songs again and again. "And Darcy?"

"Darcy is his wife and . . . an old friend of mine." It's the word *friend* I choke up on more than *wife*, which surprises me enough that my brow furrows.

"You're in love with his wife?" she blurts out, her eyes wide as saucers. "Does Mom know?"

I can't help the chuckle that comes. "First off, I am not in love with Darcy. At all. Not even a little. And second, yes, your mom knows all about my past with her." And she would know about today, too, and hopefully be able to offer some kind of advice. Maybe she could help me understand how I even begin to process seeing the hardened, invulnerable man I once knew lay every one of his emotions bare at my feet.

"Cameron."

I flinch at my name and shake the thoughts away again. "What?"

"Did you hear what I said?" Her voice is sharper now, annoyed.

"No. I'm sorry, Morgan. I promise, I'm listening now."

"Good. Because I was telling you that Mom likes you a lot. And she really needs you to be there for her." Morgan looks down and plays with her fingers. "I don't want her to be alone."

Guilt singes me as I watch her struggle with my hurting her mother and admonish myself again for my inability to compartmentalize. "Hey." Morgan glances back up at me, and there are tears in her eyes. "Your mom will never be alone. She has you and Mason and me. I promise, what you overheard is not going to affect any of that."

"Okay," she says, but there's no assurance in it.

"Are you sure it's okay, because you don't seem convinced?" She swallows like she's considering my words, so I press in more. "Come on, Morgan. I think we've gotten close enough that you can trust me by now."

That makes her smile, but it fades too quickly. "I do trust you." She bites at her pinky nail. "Probably more than I've trusted anyone besides my mom."

I suck in a breath, the weight of that admission sitting heavy on my shoulders. I've let so many people in my life down, but I will not let Morgan appear on that list. "What's going on?" I ask, seeing the deeper scars behind her insecurity.

"What do you mean?"

"You look upset, and while I'm guessing you didn't like hearing me argue with my old bandmate, I doubt it would bring you this level of distress." I hesitate because I don't know if this subject is one I'm allowed to bring up or not. "Is it about your birth mom again?" Her eyes widen, no doubt surprised by my boldness, but then she shakes her head. I can't tell if she's lying. We've always been so honest with each other that I have little experience in that area. "Then what? Lexie?" Again, her face goes just slightly paler, and now I'm really starting to worry. "Morgan . . ."

"I have this friend . . . at school," she finally blurts out. "She asked for my advice, and I don't know what to do."

Surprise overtakes me. Junior high drama is not what I was expecting to hear. "Okay . . ." I swallow down the immense feeling of inadequacy. "I'll help if I can. But I think your mom would probably be a better resource."

"No!" Her adamant horror leaves nothing to interpret. "I already know what she'd say, and she'd probably do something crazy like call this person's mom or something. And you can't tell her, either. You promised our conversations were safe."

"Morgan . . . calm down. I'm not going to say anything."

Relief spills from her eyes. "Sorry. It's just . . . this is a really big deal for my friend. And if it's managed wrong, it could all blow up in her face."

A hole forms in my stomach as she gnaws at her pinky again, and I have a sneaking suspicion that the "friend" she's discussing is her. I have no idea how to navigate my role here. But I also don't want to miss this opportunity to help Morgan if she needs me.

When I nod for her to continue, she does, rushing the sentences. "So my friend has this really big secret she's keeping from, um, another friend of ours. And it's not a dangerous secret, but it's one she knows will upset her friend. And will probably change their relationship forever."

"Does the secret involve another person?" She nods, and I want to throw up. "A boy maybe?"

"A boy?" She blanches, surprised, but then smiles like my figuring it out gives her permission to tell all. "Yes, a boy," she says more adamantly. "So, my friend likes this boy a lot, but her other friend won't approve, so they've been sneaking around, you know, so they don't have to deal with the fallout of her friend's emotions. But now they want to go public so they can spend more time together, but this friend doesn't know how to tell her other friend because it's been a secret now for so many months. Which means she's going to be even madder than she would have been if she had just told her what was going on from the beginning." She takes a breath. "What should I tell her to do?"

I press my fingers to my temples, both in shock and in protective rage. A boy. Morgan has been seeing a boy secretly behind her mom's back. I'll strangle the kid. And how did this happen? Where have they possibly been meeting? If he laid even one hand on her, I'll . . . I close my eyes as the truth slams against my chest. The tree house.

"Cam? You didn't answer me. Should she tell her?"

I look up, trying to get my shuddering breath under control. "Yes, she should. Sooner rather than later. Secrets always come out, Morgan. And they hurt a lot more when the one who's been lied to finds out from someone else. Trust me on that one."

She bites her lip and nods. "I know. That's what I think, too." She takes a deep breath and then exhales. "Thanks." She stands. "I have to go. Mom texted me fifteen minutes ago to get back and, well, I'm late." She smiles optimistically. "Want to come with? She never gets as annoyed when you're there."

I shake my head, trying to unclench my teeth. "Sorry, kid. You're on your own this time."

"Okay, fine." She bounces out of the porch as if our talk freed her from the burden. And maybe it has. Because I feel like it's now around my shoulders, pressing me down, clasping its hands around my neck.

I bolt to my feet and go inside once Morgan is halfway down the street. It takes ten strides before I'm out the back door and fumbling with the frog container for the spare key Lexie told me about. If there has been a boy in the tree house, I'll be able to tell. Teenage boys all have a scent about them. It's how I caught on that Cassie had been secretly dating this punk in high school. His body odor had lingered all over her car. That time, the decision to tell our parents had been easy. And I'd managed to do it anonymously. But this time, Morgan would know, and she'd never trust me again.

Key fisted in my hand, I make the climb up the trunk and onto the landing. The door is locked as usual, which makes so much more sense now. I slide in the key, pull open the door, and prepare my heart for the worst-case scenario. But . . . there's nothing, not one whiff of teenage-boy stench. Only a beautiful, girly reading nook lies in my line of vision. A bean bag sits in the corner, dented, but not with the weight of two bodies, only one. An iPad lies near, plugged in and charging. Morgan has a few water bottles sitting in a pretty silver bucket—Lexie's touch, I'm sure. And a small lamp with pink beads on the shade sits on a stack of books. Innocence and youth are the only essence in this lovely place.

Relief has me collapsing on the round furry rug in the center of the small space. I'd jumped to the wrong conclusion. Projected all my raging emotions from Bryson's visit onto that sweet young girl. Embarrassment rattles in my chest. Morgan simply wanted my advice, and I'd read way too much into her questions. And of course I did. I have no experience being a father, no business interfering in Lexie's parenting.

I run a shaky hand through my hair and exit the sacred space. I feel like both an intruder and a hypocrite. I'd told Morgan to trust me and then I didn't trust her. Carefully, I shut and lock the door, and decide in the future to take her at her word.

TWENTY-FOUR

Lexie

I've never been so grateful for quiet. After weeks of jackhammering and construction noise, closing the door behind the last plumber leaving for the day is a monumental relief.

I roll my shoulders, the weight of the day weighing down on me, and move into the living room to lay out my latest project boards. The original ones I'd put together had to be scrapped due to the limited availability and exorbitant prices. Mason wasn't exaggerating when he said material had skyrocketed. Gone were the marble countertops and hand-scraped hardwood floors. Still, I am satisfied with the compromises I made and especially with the new price tag.

I hear Mason's approach before seeing him. The shuffle of his feet, the shortened length of his stride. All reminders he is still very much in pain despite the weeks of healing. Learning he still wasn't cleared to drive had sent him back into a spiral of moodiness and hostility. Not toward me, thankfully, just toward every other person who dared to step foot into this house. Which is probably why Cameron never ventures here during the day. I feel a faint smile at the thought of him, but it fades quickly. Even thoughts of my childhood crush can't alleviate the sadness today brings.

"Wanna tell me why you're so quiet today?"

"I'm not quiet," I grumble. And I have no intention of verbalizing the significance of this particularly nightmarish day to him or anyone. I've just been mentally checking calendar boxes in my head for a month now. "Besides, you've been too busy snarling at the plumbers to notice me anyway."

"Oh, I've noticed. You haven't barked at me once for moving too much." Mason stands near the wide opening to the living area and leans a forearm on the frame. "Did something happen with Cam?" he asks, his voice sharp, as if he's been waiting for this very conversation.

"No. Things with Cam are fine. It's Morgan," I add because I'm going to have to give him something. And really, she is the reason behind my turmoil.

"What did she do this time?"

"Nothing," I say, my heart squeezing again. That's just it. Morgan did nothing to deserve being abandoned exactly ten years ago today. I don't even know if she remembers. She didn't say a word this morning, even when I prodded. "Hey, come take a look at this new tile I picked and see if you like it."

"You don't want to talk about this, do you?"

"Not especially." The bite in my tone is not for him. It's for the hollowed-out place in my heart that I have no capacity to ignore today.

Mason's eyes narrow, but he doesn't push. Instead, he walks over, takes a hurried glance at my finishing board, and crosses his arms. "These look expensive."

"Exactly, but they're not. I mean, not crazy expensive."

He rubs his eyebrow and sighs. "Lexie, we are so far beyond budget—"

"I'm very aware of the budget limitations, Mason," I say, cutting him off. "You've more than drilled our situation into my head. You need to trust me on the design side as much as I trust you on the construction. It's the only way this partnership will work." I feel my voice get stronger, the need to feel like I'm in control of something right now swelling up in me. "I know what sells. A renovation is pointless if the finishes don't meet the expectations of the market price." He nods because he knows deep down I'm right, which feels kind of good. "Do you need a ride home?" I ask, seeing the exhaustion on his face.

"Nah. After today's fiasco, I could use the fresh air."

I rub his arm to show my support. The plumbers had to jackhammer through the slab this morning to fix a pipe, and Mason nearly burst out of his skin when he heard the news. This was supposed to be the last Saturday they worked, and now we're pushed another three days. To his credit, Mason remained calm, though the tension still showed in his shoulders. "I'll see you at home, then. I still want to finalize the paint colors."

"Sounds good," he says and squeezes my shoulder on his way out of the room.

"Mason?" He turns, and the weariness in his eyes reinforces my next words. "It's just a house." Sure, it represents a dream and a future. But there will always be another structure to purchase. Another chance to try again if this one fails.

"I know."

"Do you?"

He rubs the back of his neck, and I can see the struggle in his eyes. It's more than a house to him. It's control when he has none. "Yeah, I do." He smiles, the first one I've seen in days. "See you at home."

As much as I love hearing him call my house his home, I

can't stop the churning that comes to my stomach the minute the front door shuts. Mason and I have different issues. He refuses to come out of his pain, and I refuse to jump into mine. The problem today is that it's chasing me, and I'm running out of places to hide. I do my best to focus on the house, on visualizing the final product that will make all this strife worth the effort, but my mind keeps drifting back in time.

I hold up more paint swatches against the wall, trying to see how the light changes the only slightly different shades. My phone rings from the corner where I dumped my things, and I consider ignoring it for a brief second. It's probably just Morgan asking what's for dinner. A common call that seems to come right around this time. I drop the tiny squares and make my way over to my bag. Morgan is at the house, studying for her midterms, and I should probably warn her of Mason's return and his subsequent mood.

But the caller isn't my daughter. It's once again a number I don't recognize. I send it to voicemail, but my fingers hover over the device, a surge of fear rising up inside that makes no logical sense.

Mom used to say I had flawless intuition. That I could sense change coming and would react much like an animal before a big storm. I'd felt it the night my mom told me she was sick, and again the day before Annaliese ran away from home. The only time it had failed me was ten years ago. That night I'd had no idea what was about to happen.

I tap the screen to view a list of missed calls. The same number comes up six times since Thanksgiving. I work the tension out of my back, trying my best to rationalize my nerves.

I've had clients before who refused to deal with any other manager. Surely this is the case here. Why else would they

ignore the clear instructions on the voicemail that I am on
leave and to call the office for support?

Still, I touch the digits, memorizing them as if they are
somehow critically important.

"Lex?"

I nearly drop my phone as I spin around to face the front
door and view Cameron easing it shut behind him. My throat
aches from the shock of the interruption, and I internally
growl at myself to get control. I will not let this dark anniversary ruin me. Not again.

So, to Cameron I offer a glorious smile and a "Hey," which
comes out much too high-pitched.

"Well, are there pipes running through walls and hot water
to spare?"

"We have something far better . . . a new hole in the slab."
I sigh, exhausted, and point to the rectangular cavern he
must have missed. "When they ran the cameras, they found
a collapsed sewage pipe. We had to tear up the downstairs
bathroom and part of the hallway."

"Oh no. Lexie, I'm sorry."

"It's okay. At least I'm taking the news better than Mason.
I have no doubt the man has a list going of all the things that
have gone wrong since starting this project. He's even taken
to calling the house our little money pit." I work to keep my
smile in place. "This is just one more obstacle we are going to
have to overcome."

"We should all be so lucky as to have your optimism." He
walks over and envelops me in a hug I know I need but find
it's more a liability right now than a help. I'm much too close
to breaking down, and I don't want to talk about my feelings,
which is exactly what he will ask me to do if I lose control.

I disentangle from his arms. "Well, I wish my optimism
would help me make a decision."

"Anything I can help with?"

"Maybe." I reach down for my three paint options and put them against the wall.

He scrutinizes each one and finally points to the far-left swatch. "I like that one the best."

I examine them all again and find I agree with him. "Thanks. Me too." I place our choice on the board and feel a rush of relief. "It's nice having a boyfriend who's an artist. Mason simply grunted and asked the price tag."

"Is he still around?" Cameron glances around the empty house. "I was hoping we could talk."

And obviously he didn't want to do so with an audience. "Mason left a little while ago." I pause, trying to decipher if I'm reading into his tone. "Is everything okay?"

"Yes. I mean . . . I don't know." He shoves his hands into his pockets, clearly uncomfortable. "Bryson came to see me today. Apparently, Cassie isn't the only one bent on interfering with me and Darcy." Cam's mouth is tight when he says her name, but gone is the usual bitterness. Now he just sounds tired. "He wanted me to know in some roundabout way that she misses me."

I digest his words, on the impact they very likely had on his just-now healing heart. "That must've been pretty awkward."

He grunts with a laugh of agreement. "That's putting it mildly." I'm quiet as he stares at his shoes, his mind still racing, it seems, from what had happened. "Since junior high, Bryson had been this egocentric, hotheaded rebel. He didn't care about people. He just used them in whatever way he needed to get what he wanted."

I wonder if Cameron realizes he's using past tense, but I don't miss it. "And now?"

He shakes his head as if he's still trying to believe it himself.

"Now he's, I don't know, I want to say soft. But he fought back when I yelled, so that's not it either. He was just so . . . open. About his life, about his insecurities. I still can't quite believe it."

"Four years is a long time," I say. "People change."

"Yeah, you're probably right." Again, Cameron sighs, and the heaviness seems to fill the space between us like thick smoke. "He wants me to call her. But I just don't know if I can."

"Can what? Talk to her?"

"Forgive her." He says the words like a prayer. Like he's asked for the strength to do it many, many times before and come up short.

I slide my hand in his and lace our fingers together, warm and sure. "I think you already have or you wouldn't be here talking to me about it."

Cameron looks at me, his eyes searching mine. "And how would you feel if I did call her? Not that I've decided to, but before I even considered the option, I wanted to check with you first."

Warmth spills into my chest at the consideration. "You don't have to ask my permission."

"I know, but reconciling with her is not worth it if I lose you in the process." He glances down at his shoes again, breaking eye contact. Is he embarrassed, ashamed, or maybe just afraid of my reaction? He shouldn't be. I don't feel threatened by Darcy. Well . . . not significantly threatened anyway. It stings that she still has this kind of impact on him, but memories are just that . . . memories. They aren't real. For years I wished they were. Wished they could bring back my mom and my dad and my sister, but memories are only there as a gift so that you don't forget the special times. To live in them is a tragedy.

"I'm not going anywhere." I touch his cheek until he looks up again. "Darcy has always been a huge part of your life. This isn't news to me. In fact, it's possible you'll never fully be whole without resolving things with her." I don't miss the fact that it's Cassie's words spilling from my lips, even though I'm not sure I believe they're true. But she certainly does, and Cameron seems to want them to be. "Bryson's right. You should call her."

"Lexie." His voice turns soft, unconvinced. "Are you sure? If this bothers you at all, please tell me. I don't want to take you for granted. Miss some hidden part that's hurting."

I feel my chest constrict and feel my lips nearly form the words that cry out how today is killing me slowly inside. How I miss my sister and my parents so much it's nearly dropped me to my knees. How I'm worried about Morgan and the way she keeps pulling further and further from me. But I can't succumb to the pain. I won't survive it.

So instead I press my lips to his and pull him in so tight, it almost knocks us both from our feet. Cameron has always been my place of relief. My escape from turmoil. My beautiful fantasy world that nothing harsh or broken can touch. And today is no different.

TWENTY-FIVE

Cameron

I stare down at the stream of messages I'd initiated earlier that morning, my stomach a sea of anticipation. It had taken me five days to make the decision to text Darcy. Five days of distracting myself with Lexie and Morgan. Five days of convincing myself that this one indulgence would not destroy the healing that had taken place since coming home from Nashville.

Me:
Bryson said you wanted to talk.

Darcy:
He did?

Me:
If he's wrong, that's fine too.

Darcy:
No, I do want to talk, but in person. Not texting where I can't read your tone.

Me:
You used to be able to read it just fine.

Darcy:
And you used to text me ten times a day. Looks
like we're both out of practice.

Me:
I'm not sure I want to see you.

Darcy:
Yes, you do. Or else you wouldn't have texted.
Just tell me when and where and I'll be there.

Me:
Fine. Noon, and you know where.

Darcy:
Done. And don't you dare stand me up.

I admit the absence of a location was a bit of a test. I
wanted to see if she remembers as much as I do. We'd found
this particular hideaway when we were ten, just past the
mass of trees bordering our neighborhood and down the hill.
The water had been high then, fresh off a long season of rain.
The creek is nearly dry now. Just a trickle of water runs over
the rock, catching on loose sticks and dirt.

I sit on the bank with my legs drawn up, my elbows resting
on my knees as I wait in silence. There's a slight breeze today,
but it's muted by the trees surrounding me. I close my eyes
and listen for the melody I heard in my neighborhood the
other day, yet it's lost in the anticipation that has taken over
every thought and instinct. I don't know what I think or feel,
only that I want to move forward with Lexie, and this rift with
Darcy is a weight that no amount of wishing away is going to
release.

I hear a snapping of branches behind me, and my breath inhales with such force I have to swallow not to cough. This is the one confrontation I never planned to have.

I stay seated even though I feel her approach. Feel her heat as she sits next to me, mimicking my posture and my silence. I've cried in front of her before on this very bank, staring at these very trees. And she draped her arm around my shoulders back then and never said a word. If you had asked me years ago, I would have said I could share anything with her. Feel anything in front of her and she'd understand. Now, every word between us feels dangerous.

We don't look at each other, but I don't need a visual to imagine exactly what she looks like. Brown hair in a ponytail, faded jeans, and a long-sleeved T-shirt that's likely a size too big.

"I'm sorry Bryson ambushed you," she says. "He didn't tell me you guys had talked until after you finally texted me."

"Well, I guess his plan worked. I'm here." My voice comes out colder than I want it to be.

"Yes, it worked, but I'd rather you be here because you want to be."

"Four years ago, you couldn't wait for me to be out of your life." And with that one statement I rip the Band-Aid clean off. I feel her tense next to me, feel the air shift between us from polite awkwardness to years of built-up anger.

"That's not fair, Cameron." She whips her head around to face me, and the turmoil in her eyes nearly guts me open. "You know we needed space from each other. Neither of us knew how to live without the other."

"I don't need a recap of the past," I say sharply. "What's done is done. I've accepted it, and I've moved on," I lie, continuing to look at her, the darker parts of me wanting my words to wound. "You and Bryson are the ones who can't seem to." It feels good to throw that fact in her face. To remind her it was them approaching me and not the other way around.

"Fine." Her jaw gets tight, just like it used to when Jerry Bingham would pull on her ponytail back in fifth grade. The flash of young Darcy is so sudden and intense that it rocks the wall I'm trying to reinforce. "Let's not talk about the past. Let's talk about the future, about how you were supposed to be in my life forever. How you were supposed to be at my wedding and know my son. How I was supposed to be best friends with your future wife and give her all the dirt on you. Those were all futures we were supposed to have together." Her voice cracks, and just like when we were younger, I feel the crack in my heart, as well. "But instead you cut me out of your life. I would have understood a month. Six months even. But years, Cam? Have you not missed me at all?"

I lower my head into my hands, having no idea how to respond to her. I'd shut out all those dreams just as much as I shut her out. "I have, but it was easier this way."

"Was it though?"

I sigh. "I don't know."

"Then let's start over. Get to know each other without confusion and feelings corrupting our relationship this time."

I lift my head and press my fingers to the ache at my temples. I don't know what I expected coming here, but it wasn't this. Darcy had been so lost and broken when we said our goodbyes. This woman is mature, assured, determined, everything I knew she would be one day. "I don't know how to start over with you."

"You could come to dinner," she says, her voice more full of pleading than sorrow. "Let me show you my home. My life."

I grunt a laugh. "And what? Hang out with you and Bryson?" The idea is so ludicrous it's funny.

"And Charlie."

Her son's name makes me pause. Makes me think of Bryson's words and the cruelty in which I said them so many years ago. "We're too old to live in childhood dreams," I say, my defenses rising again. "I'm glad you're happy, but I'm not sure today can change much of anything."

"Well, it should," she fires back. "Unless you're still in love with me."

"No," I say with absolute surety.

She doesn't even flinch at my tone. "Good. Then what's the holdup? What's stopping us from a new beginning on fresh ground? We have twenty-nine years of good history, Cam. History where we all cared for one another, even when it was hard."

"What do you want from me?" The force of my words knocks me to my feet. I need distance from her, now. "Is it not enough that I toured the country singing the love song Bryson wrote for you? That you have this fabulous life built on my talent? That I did exactly as you asked and made sure I wasn't a part of it?" I shake my head as she stares at me with open shock. "It isn't fair for you to come back now and demand I step into your world as if you weren't the one who pushed me out of it."

"First off, I didn't push you out. You walked away. And secondly, that song wasn't written for me."

"Please," I scoff, her words only ratcheting up my frustration.

"Have you ever even listened to it?" Her eyes narrow, her voice the calm of an adult trying to console a screaming child as she rises to her feet. "Have you ever stopped for one second to think that maybe you weren't the only one in turmoil back then? That maybe Bryson was also going through a complete life change?"

"It's called 'A Decade of Love,' written by a man who secretly pined for you for years. What else would it be about?"

"Honestly, when did you get so shortsighted? Bryson wrote that song for Charlie," she clarifies. "Not my Charlie, but the man who cared for him. Who challenged him and ultimately led him to Christ. The man who shaped Bryson's life. Cameron, that was a love song for a father, not a girlfriend."

I cross my arms and stare at her as four years of pain turns into confusion.

She watches me carefully. "We would never have done that to you. I know you and Bryson have had issues, but he would never have been so cruel." She steps forward, and I step back. She comes again, this time gaining on me as she grips my forearms locked to my chest. "Bryson gave you that song because you were the only person in the world he trusted to sing it. We didn't send you away, Cam. We set you free."

I can't speak because I don't trust myself not to break if I do. All this time, I'd seen that song as a slap. A reminder that he won. I never once considered it might have been a gift.

"Come to dinner," she says, more forcefully this time. "Get to know the real us. The people we've become. Please. I miss my best friend." Her eyes fill and so do mine. It's a reflective action, hurting when she hurts.

She swallows and steps back. "I'll send you the address. You don't have to call or text. If you feel even one moment of wanting to, don't hesitate. Just come over."

Even now, she knows me far too well. Emotion drives me. It drove me away, and now she's hoping it will drive me back to them.

"I'll think about it," I whisper, still trying to hold myself together.

"That's good enough for me."

I spend the next thirty minutes on that creek bank, listening to "A Decade of Love" over and over again. The first time still brought a sickening punch, but by the third time, I was able to focus. Able to really listen to the lyrics I've had memorized for years.

And slowly, as if the world were coming into focus, I began to see past the assumptions of romantic love. I think back to Bryson as a boy. The kid who was shy and timid. Then to the teenager with a giant-sized chip on his shoulder as if the world owed him a debt. I skip back to the beginning of the song and see that kid when I listen for a seventh time. I hear the pain in the words, the ache that has nothing to do with a girl, but a life spent feeling rejected.

I allow myself to remember the day he walked into my house, a duffel bag in hand, after his stepfather had kicked him out. His face had been pale, gaunt, and there was not an ounce of arrogance left in his straight back. Only a kid trying to hold it together. I press play again and listen to the next verse. This time I catch the gratitude. I understand the person he's talking about . . . is me and my family. The rescuers. I swallow down the sudden rush of emotion and blink away the rising tears.

The next verse is nearly my undoing. It's Bryson's salvation story, written with such amazement that I wonder how I could have ever missed the meaning. Wonder how I ever mistook this verse for being about the day he fell in love with Darcy. She'd been right to call me shortsighted. I'd been angry for so many years at the wrong person.

As I finish the song, I feel a smile come to my lips. Feel relief for Bryson. Feel the love I once had for him as a friend. A close friend. And that's when I realize my loss has been more than just Darcy. It has been them both. Not just a loss of a bandmate and musician, but a friend.

And then it happens. That moment I've been praying for. The moment I never truly thought was possible. But I feel it, deep in my chest, inside my heart.

Forgiveness.

I forgive him for loving her when I also did. I forgive her for loving him instead of me.

And to my shock, the act is easy. Because I wasn't lying when I told Darcy I was no longer in love with her. I'm not. And I'm not even sure if I ever really was the way I assumed. Because never, not once in any of my memories, do I remember feeling for Darcy even half of what I do for Lexie.

I stand, free for the first time in so long I can't even remember, and walk away from the creek and from the burden of living trapped in the past.

With each step through the thick brush, lingering questions and doubts clear from my mind. I don't want this thing with Lexie to be temporary anymore. Not that it ever really was, but I don't even want the illusion of it. I want her to know I've fallen in love with her.

And not just for Lexie to know, but the world to know. I want Cassie and Mason to stop warning her to be careful. I want to get down on one knee and promise her she'll never be alone again. I want to tug on Morgan's ponytail and tell her all about how wonderful Nashville is in the spring.

The decision brings a giddiness I haven't felt since childhood. I'd put Morgan in the best school and build a tree house in my backyard to mirror the one here. I'd have it done before they ever arrived; I'd surprise her. And Lexie could find work in property management. They have a massive rental market there. Of course, the move would have to wait until the school year finished and the renovation was completed, but that was only a few months away, six at the most. And the ceremony could be in my parents' backyard. Small and private.

A rumble of laughter pulses from my lips as I run a shaky hand through my hair. The future I'd all but written off is suddenly vivid and colorful and wide open in front of me.

I'll tell Lexie today. Right now. She deserves more than to wait and wonder about the two of us. I'll make sure she knows, without a stitch of question, exactly how I feel.

TWENTY-SIX

Lexie

I pull on the old thin cord connected to the attic stairs and turn my face away before dust can settle into my eyes. I should probably have stayed at the renovation house with Mason, but my presence felt unnecessary today. The plumbers are gone now, and the fact that Mason won't show me the final bill makes me wonder if our agreed-upon 60/40 percent split is really true. More and more of the bills have disappeared since his fall, and it doesn't take a genius to figure out that Mason is shouldering the greater financial burden.

At least he was in a somewhat good mood this morning. Cameron's friend Aiden is the gift that keeps on giving. He's there now, doing a walk-through. Like he did at Thanksgiving, Aiden has a skeleton crew of guys who requested extra holiday work. He's even agreed to let Mason function as their supervisor, forgoing the markup he should be receiving. If all goes well over the next two weeks, we'll still be on track to start the front porch construction and roof replacement after Christmas.

Which is why I'm even more sure I need to spend the next two days making my place feel like a home again. Mason has moved out, having gotten the news yesterday that his MRI was clean, and he was cleared to drive two days earlier than expected. And while I'll miss him, I am happy to get a little normalcy back into our lives. Morgan gets out of school tomorrow for Christmas break, and I want to surprise her by having all our holiday decorations put up. There's been this brick wall between us for months now, and I don't care if I have to karate-chop it with elf shoes and Christmas cheer, I'm determined to get behind whatever it is that's keeping her from opening up to me.

The springs creak on their way down, the weight nearly pulling my arm out of its socket as the folded stairs plummet to the floor. I gain control and unfold the accordion structure, praying the colder weather keeps little creepy-crawlies from coming out of their hiding places.

With a steeled spine, I climb the stairs and hunch-walk over to the corner of the attic where we keep the tree and boxes of ornaments. I did this all on my own for years before Morgan was strong enough to help me, and today will be no different. In fact, something about surviving that horrific anniversary makes staring at the tree a promise of new beginnings. This year, it won't be just me and Morgan, but Cameron and Mason, too. A family, just like the one I'd dreamed about with Annaliese ten years ago. Sure, it looks different, but I know blessing when I have it and I'm not going to let an old memory ruin it.

I heave the tree box as I walk backward, careful not to scrape my spine on the low ceiling. It's chilly up here, but I'm sweating, and only part of it comes from exertion. That feeling is back in my limbs, the same one that haunted me five days ago. Like my skin is covered in hives. I shake away the unease, convincing myself it's the anticipation of Cameron seeing Darcy today. Right now, actually. I stop and say a small prayer for him. I want so much for this to be the healing he's been searching for. Want to see those blue eyes light up again and his dimples appear deep and genuine. His true smile has been absent for days now, lost ever since Bryson stepped onto his front porch and reminded us both that the past never stays locked in a chest forever.

Unwanted tears prick at my eyes, and I shake them away. This pain should not still be lingering. I buried it five days ago deep inside my heart the minute I switched off my light and closed my eyes. Determination drives me harder, and I finally get the oversized box to the attic opening and crawl out until the floor is level to my chest. Once I have the box positioned, I slowly walk backward down the stairs, holding the railing while balancing the box against my body. With each careful descent, the edge of the box bounces down a step, and I re-adjust to keep us both from falling.

I'm three steps from the floor when my phone buzzes in my pocket. Pure adrenaline fires through my limbs, and I miss the next step. The box pitches forward, and by sheer luck or panic or maybe both, I somehow manage to jump from the stairs and miss being knocked out by a mere two inches. The box hits the floor with a thud at the same time pain sears through the length of my arm. I smashed it against the unforgiving stair rail in my quest for survival, tearing my T-shirt and leaving a bright angry scratch five inches from my elbow to my wrist.

A completely unnatural fury buds inside my heaving chest as I let out a curse word I never say. Next thing I know, the phone is in my hand and I'm staring at that stupid number again. The one that won't stop calling. The one that never, ever leaves a blasted voicemail.

Without thinking, I press my fingers against the keys.

> **Me:**
> If this is a client of Bradshaw's Property Management, I suggest you contact the office at 972-876-8900. If you continue to call my cell without leaving a voicemail, your number will be blocked.

I press send, feeling a surge of empowerment. Rarely do I ever engage in anything that could invite conflict, but this is getting out of hand. Satisfied, I shove the phone back in my pocket and walk toward the box to survey if the fall caused any damage to our already geriatric tree.

A vibration against my backside has me pausing. Why I hesitate to pull the device free, I don't know. And yet something deeper in my gut tells me this isn't a random caller. Slowly, I pull out the phone again, my hands shaking as I bring it to my face to release the security controls.

> **Them:**
> It's not a client. It's your sister.

I've never actually been shot, but I imagine it will feel much like this does. Like a hole just opened up in your chest, and the pain is so severe it rocks you backward. I feel myself stumble, knock once again into the blasted staircase situated right in the middle of the hall.

The phone rings a second later. Numbly, I accept the call.

"Hey, Lex . . ." Ten years of silence. Ten years of not knowing if she was alive or dead are felt in that one achingly long second. "It's me . . . Annaliese." As if I'd need that reminder. As if I couldn't pick out the tone and lilt of her speech in an amusement park.

I can't find my voice. Can't even form a hello.

"I know it's been a long time," she continues in a rush. "Too long. And that's my fault. I know it's my fault. I'm sorry, um, I haven't left a message. I've been too scared to."

Again, she pauses to allow me to speak, but I still can't. I'm barely able to lower myself to the floor without collapsing. I'd dreamt of this phone call for years, longed for it, dreaded it, resented its absence, and now I have no idea what the heck I'm supposed to say or do.

"You hate me." She sighs wearily. "And of course you do. I'd hate me."

But I don't hate her. I love her. I feel that love with every strangled breath. "I don't hate you," I finally squeak out.

"You don't?" The relief and agony in her tone hollows me out, and memories flood my mind of her curling my hair for Mom's funeral. Of her tucking me in bed that same night, only to stay and cry with me for hours.

Pain grips my chest stronger than I expect, stronger than I think I can handle. But somehow, I breathe. Somehow, I find the strength to say, "How are you?"

Her breath hitches, and I know, like me, she's trying not to cry. Suddenly I'm grateful we're not doing this in person. Grateful to have at least a modicum of privacy while I grieve the ten years we lost.

"I'm good. Better now that you're willing to talk to me."

Defensiveness and anger rise inside me. The same anger I've stuffed down year after year because I could do nothing about it. But now I can. I can say all the things I wanted to say to my sister since the day she abandoned me and Morgan. "Of course I'm willing," I blurt without any preconceived thought. "I have agonized over wondering if you were safe or in need or even alive. How could you ever think for one second that I wouldn't want to talk to you!"

"Because Morgan said—"

271

"Morgan?" Her name on my sister's lips feels like a hot poker is being thrust inside of me. "When did you talk to Morgan?"

"Yesterday . . ." There's an insecurity growing in her tone, a realization maybe that I'm about one word away from crawling through the phone line and shaking her. "We talk every day."

My vision blurs, not from tears but from shock, anger, utter and complete disbelief. "What?"

"She said she told you—"

"How?" is the only word I can seem to get out of my mouth. "How did this happen?"

"She found me on social media about five months ago and sent me a message telling me who she was and then asked for my email. I didn't ask a lot of questions about it because I was just so happy to get a second chance I knew I didn't deserve. But I promise, I asked her several times if you were okay with us communicating, and she said you were but only through email, so that's all we've done. But I'm guessing by your reaction, that isn't true."

I can't move. I can't breathe. My daughter has been lying to me for months. *Months!*

"I have to go," I say despite there being no air in my lungs.

"Lexie, please. I swear, I thought you knew about the emails."

I hang up, my hands shaking so badly I drop the phone at my feet. It clatters against the wood, toppling on its side. I can only stare at it.

I run to the back door, my hand covering my mouth, and barely make it past the concrete patio before I dry-heave onto the grass. But nothing comes from my stomach. I think of Cameron and wonder if this is what his panic attacks feel like. If his ribs are being cracked in two while his heart is being unceremoniously ripped from his chest. I press my palms to my face, lean over until I'm nearly breathing in the grass.

I shut my eyes against the truth I can't escape. My daughter has been talking to Annaliese for months without my knowledge. All the signs I've seen and ignored flow into my head. I should've spent more time at home, should've checked her phone better.

I sit back on my heels and stare at the rotting fence. That's the part that still doesn't make sense, because she doesn't have email on her phone. She doesn't have anything I don't monitor, and I never once saw a correspondence that looked suspicious.

Picking apart every day of every month, I sort through the possibilities. The where, the when, the how. It must have been at a friend's house. Morgan had said that Melissa was allowed email. Maybe she'd used her friend's account.

I scramble to my feet, pushing aside the heartbreak to a stronger, more productive action. With five fierce strides, I'm back inside the house, my phone in hand, Melissa's mom's number at my fingertips.

She answers on the third ring. "Hey, Lex! Sorry. I've been cleaning all morning." Her phone turns scratchy as she seems to readjust it. "What's up?"

"Hi, Amy. I just found out that Morgan has been emailing someone behind my back. I need to know if she's been doing it on Melissa's phone." I don't have time for niceties today. Not when it's this critically important.

Amy apparently understands because her response is quick and sharp. "I will find out and call you back immediately."

"Thank you." More than ever, I'm grateful for mothers who parent the same way I do. I know Amy monitors Melissa's phone through several avenues. We've talked about the different apps at length.

I pace back and forth through my living room while I wait,

trying to ignore the way my legs shake with each step. My hands haven't stopped trembling since the phone call, and it appears to have taken over other parts of my body, as well. I lean over and press my hands to my knees, willing the nausea to go away again.

Every time I think of Annaliese talking unsupervised to my daughter, I feel sick. Morgan doesn't understand the danger. Doesn't understand how addiction wrecks the person you love and also wrecks you if you're close enough. She doesn't understand that because I didn't want her to. I wanted to protect her from it. From the horrors of life that I had to face. That was my job as her mother. To protect her innocence.

The phone rings, and I spring back up, eager to see what Amy found. "Well?" I ask, biting my nail.

"Nothing. I'm sorry. I checked Melissa's inbox and her deleted files."

Disappointment punches me in the stomach. "No. It's okay. I knew it was a long shot. I just can't figure out how she got access. I check her phone daily. And the school blocks outside emails." I pace again, my mind wrestling with the dilemma.

"What about the iPad Mrs. Hardcastle gave her? Could she have downloaded email on that?"

My steps halt. "What iPad?"

Amy's voice hitches as she slowly answers. "The one she uses in the tree house. Melissa's mentioned it on several occasions."

The pit in my stomach widens as suddenly everything makes perfect sense. "Thank you, Amy. I need to go."

"Lex, I am so sorry. If I had any idea you didn't know, I would have said something sooner."

"Of course. I know. Thank you." I'm fumbling over my words as I end the call, but my mind is already racing ahead of me. I grab my keys, rush to my car, and speed the two blocks to Cameron's house. I know I'm not parked straight. I don't even care. I have to get to that tree house.

I grab the spare key from the frog container and rush up the slats nailed into the trunk. As soon as I fling the door open, I see the iPad and my heart falls to my knees. I crawl inside and unhook the device from its charging station. I recognize it immediately, down to the address label Mrs. Hardcastle stuck to the back of it. It's one of those free labels you get in the mail after donating to children's hospitals. The name *Betty Hardcastle* is printed in crisp bold font.

Settling against the wall, I tap the screen only to be blocked with a password request. I put in Morgan's lunch code. It's always the one she uses and doesn't think I remember it. I'd tried so hard. Fought to keep her safe from the evils outside of our home. Once past the firewall, I click through the apps. Everything is open on it. No parental controls at all. And why would there be? This iPad was meant for a seventy-year-old woman. I'd set it up for her myself. Downloaded all the apps she'd need . . . including email.

Touching the icon is like taking a knife and slicing a cut inside my wrist. The wound may or may not kill me, but it is sure to devastate me emotionally if somehow I survive. The sequence of lies is so long at this point, I feel crushed by them. Fury springs up again, hot and tight in my chest. I close my eyes, count to ten, and find the email that started this horrific chain of events.

August 7th

Dear Annaliese,

Thank you so much for answering my friend's DM. I know it was probably weird seeing a random person trying to contact you, but I'm so glad you were willing to give me

*your email address. I've wanted to know about you for a
long time now. And well, I guess I was nervous you may
not want to know me. But here it goes, just in case. I'm
thirteen now, well thirteen and a half to be exact. I will be
an eighth grader at Frank Seale Middle School next week.
I'm currently five-foot-five, but Mom, well, Aunt Lexie,
thinks I'll grow taller. She once said I have your eyes.
When I saw your pictures on Instagram, I saw she was
telling me the truth. My closest friend is Melissa, and my
favorite teacher is Mrs. Mendez. She teaches history. Well,
I guess that's it for now. What are your favorite things? I
hope to hear from you soon. Oh, and don't worry if it takes
me a few days to write back. My mom is strict about computer usage and I'm not always able to get to email.*

*Yours truly,
Morgan*

My throat burns as I read my daughter's words, hear the
insecurity in her flippant mannerisms, and worse, see *Aunt
Lexie* in script as if she's already shoving away from my
parenting. Any question on how Morgan found my sister is
answered. Social media. The very devil I worked tirelessly to
erase from our lives. And yet with one message on a friend's
account, my daughter upended our entire life. I close out the
email and click on the reply, likely as terrified as Morgan had
been to read my sister's response.

August 7th

*Dear Morgan,
    I cannot tell you how much your message meant to me.
First, please know that I absolutely do want to know you.*

276

I've longed to see you for years now but have felt unworthy to even begin to ask for your forgiveness. I'm glad you like history. It was my favorite subject at your age, as well. I'm also very glad you have my eyes. When you were born, I remember holding you and seeing those big blue eyes looking up at me and wondering how I created something so incredibly beautiful and perfect. No doubt you have only become more so. Do you have a picture you can send me? As for my information, here's the rundown. I am thirty-two years old. I don't count halves anymore because frankly at a certain age you stop wishing for the next to come so soon. I work at a cute little boutique in Arlington. It's only ten minutes from my apartment, and since I don't have a car, it's an easy commute by bus. I'm also five-foot-five, so I'm not sure you'll grow a whole lot taller. My best friend growing up was a girl named Amber. Not sure what happened to her. We lost touch in high school. Anyway, I'd love to know more about school. What other friends do you have? Any boys yet? And I understand Lexie's rules. You should listen to them. She's always been the more practical sister. Speaking of which, is she okay with us talking?

> *Write soon,*
> *Annaliese (You can also*
> *call me Annie.)*

A sting of grief hits me so hard I drop the iPad into my lap. My sister sounds healthy, mature even. She sounds like the person I once knew. She sounds like Annie. And I miss her so badly it makes my skin tingle with jealousy. Jealousy that she and Morgan had this connection I wasn't invited into. Worse, I wasn't even aware it existed.

Slowly, I pick up the iPad and read Morgan's response, see the first of many lies as she tells my sister that I've blessed their reconnection but am not ready to speak to her myself. Annaliese either buys the lie or doesn't want to dig too much into the truth, because she doesn't question Morgan's excuses. Instead, there begins a string of communication, each one becoming less formal and more comfortable. Some are simple one-liners, and others are long wordy stories. There is nothing deep at first, just small talk, until I halt on one Morgan sent the week Mrs. Hardcastle died.

August 29th

Dear Annie,

My neighbor died last night. She's the one I told you about. Mrs. Hardcastle. The one whose tree house I use. I feel like my heart got crushed in a shredding machine, like the ones they use in the school office. I had to run to the bathroom twice to cry. I don't like to do it in front of people, it makes me feel weak. I know you and Mom lost your mother when you were close to my age. I'm sorry. I don't think I quite understood how that must have felt until now.

Your heartbroken daughter,
Morgan

To my sister's credit, she wrote back the same day, though I imagine Morgan didn't see it for weeks since I ended the tree-house visits during that time to let the family grieve and wait to see what they did with the house. Morgan hadn't told me about crying in the bathroom at school. I don't know why that feels like a betrayal in itself, but it does.

August 29th

My sweet, darling Morgan,
I am so sorry you are heartbroken. I know exactly the feeling and it's terrible. I hope you deal with those feelings better than I ever did. Promise me this. You won't suffer alone. Lexie is there and she loves you so much. Talk to her. Talk to me. Talk to a friend. But don't think for a second that you lost your world today. Only a piece is gone. Trust me on this.

> *Your loving mother and*
> *hopefully your friend too,*
> *Annie*

This time I pull my knees to my chest as if the act might keep me together. It doesn't. I can't breathe through the sobs, the pain, all of it crashing down on me with renewed vigor. The words Annie quoted were my mother's. She told them to us in the hospital the week before she became too sedated to speak. Annaliese had barreled from the room in a fury, angry at the world, at God, at our mom for being so at peace with the idea of dying. I'd only sat there and cried, trying to wrap my mind around living my life without the woman who impacted me positively every single day. Never would I have expected the tragedies that were still to come. Never would I have imagined one day I'd be sitting in a tree house, wondering if tomorrow my daughter would be the next person I'd lose.

I glance at the bean bag next to me and wonder how many times she sat right in that spot and wrote. Wonder if even once she felt any guilt for what she was doing. I wipe my wet cheeks and continue to read. First, Morgan's apology after so much time, then the day she coerced Cameron and me into our agreement. The emails after that come daily, often in a string over the hour she was given, reading more like text messages than email. They tell jokes and stories like old girlfriends. Stories I was never told. Words I had begged Morgan to give me when we rode home from school in silence. She'd saved all of them for Annaliese. I nearly quit reading, convinced I can't possibly endure more. But I have to know what battle I'm walking into. Have to know who the enemy is or if there even is one. Cautiously, I pull up the next correspondence in the inbox and immediately find the enemy is someone I never once considered.

TWENTY-SEVEN

Cameron

Lexie doesn't answer any of my calls. I tried when I left the creek, then after I picked up some flowers for her, and again on my way into our neighborhood. It's not like her to avoid me, and worry presses in like a nagging old wound.

Then I see it, her car parked haphazardly along the curb in front of my house. I pull in and park behind her, confused, and check the house down the street. Mason's truck is there and so is Aiden's. But why would Lexie park two houses down? I pull out my phone and try her again. No answer.

I quickly exit the car and look around the surrounding houses for any sign that she got trapped in conversation by one of many chatty neighbors. The streets are empty, minus the wave I get from Mr. Sanders on his way out to check the mail.

My gaze snags on the side gate I know was shut when I left. It's wide open now, the backyard exposed and open for anyone to enter. I leave the flowers on the passenger seat and slam the door behind me.

"Lex?" I call as I walk toward the backyard. No answer. My steps turn into a jog. "Lexie?"

I pause when I reach the back porch, scanning the area for any sign of her. The only proof I'm not completely losing my mind is the frog container, which is open and sprawled on the decking next to the table it usually rests on. My gut sinks with the possibility that something has gone very wrong. Something that must include Morgan.

I'm climbing toward the tree house before I even register how I got here so quickly. The door stands open, and I spot Lexie the second I reach the landing. "Lexie." Relief spills through every limb at the picture of her safe and seated inside the small space. "What is going on?"

She looks up and meets my eye, and the hostility in hers rocks me back a step. "You've been talking to my daughter?"

I stammer out a "yes" that is nearly unintelligible. I don't know how to process an angry Lexie. I've never actually seen her this way.

"So you knew, then," she demands, her voice growing harder if that's even possible.

"Knew what?"

"That Morgan has been emailing my sister for months behind my back?"

"What? No. What are you talking about?" My breath catches as her words sink in. And then as if in slow motion, all the pieces to my earlier conversations with Morgan come rushing back. This was the friend. Her mom. The secret relationship she sought my advice on.

Lexie studies me, her eyes moving as if scanning my mind. "Then why did she write that she talked to you about Annie?"

"Because she did talk to me . . . but about her feelings toward wanting to know her mom," I say defensively. "She never said anything about emails or correspondence with your sister."

My words seem to make Lexie even angrier, or at least that's how I would interpret the scathing look she's giving me right now. "And still you said nothing to me."

"I'm sorry, Lex," I say, guilt piling up. Is this what parenting feels like? Always wondering if you're making the right decision or completely screwing everything up? "I thought I was doing a good thing in giving Morgan a safe person to talk to."

"She already has a safe person to talk to . . . me."

I open my mouth to explain more, but Lexie cuts me off.

"Can you please give me a minute." She adjusts from sitting against the back wall by the lamp to folding her legs in front of her. "I need to finish reading these emails, and I don't want to do it with company."

I feel the heaviness of her sorrow that is sheathed in too much anger to address right now and squeeze her hand. She makes no attempt to squeeze mine back. "When you're ready to talk, I'll be waiting for you inside."

She doesn't respond, so I quietly exit, anxiety growing with each step down the tree. How could I have been so naïve? I totally screwed this up. I focused more on being Morgan's friend rather than being a concerned parent. Which is exactly the roll I'll have if Lexie and I get the future I hope for. I'll be a stepfather. The weight of the responsibility lands with unexpected force, along with the nagging fear that Lexie may never trust me again.

TWENTY-EIGHT

Lexie

Cameron's excuses only serve to flame the fire in my belly. I reread the email again, trying to understand how he could be so foolish.

November 18th

Dear Annie,

My mom has a new boyfriend. Or almost boyfriend, I guess. You probably remember him. She's had a crush on him since she was my age. Anyway. He's cool. He gets me, you know? I can tell him things . . . I even talked to him about you a little. He doesn't say much, but sometimes that's better. Well, I have to go. Mason is coming home from the hospital today. He's fine, by the way. I know you were worried.

> *Talk to you tomorrow,*
> *Morgan*

That email was sent almost a month ago. A month! And he never said one word. I read the next string of emails. The ones where Annaliese tells stories of old family gatherings, complete with tug-of-war and piñatas. The anger in my chest builds. If I'd known, I would have seen the signs, would have stopped this long before it got to this point. I continue reading until my eyes snag on a three-letter word that completes the tearing apart of my heart.

December 8th

Mom (I hope it's okay that I call you that),
    You won't believe what happened today! Blaine, the boy who I told you about that has the curly hair, well, he sat by me at lunch. Totally out of the blue. Just sat there, ate his food, got up, and left, and that was it. What do you think it means? Oh, and write back soon. I only have fifteen minutes today.

Morgan

Morgan,
    I'm thrilled by that title. I know I haven't earned it, but I hope to. I think Blaine definitely likes you. Next time he sits down, say hi, and see what happens. Oh, and I had a thought. What do you think about spending Christmas break with me?

Forever grateful for you,
Mom (I really like how this looks on here)

Mom,
    I could never say hi first! I'd die of embarrassment. And

*I'd love to spend Christmas with you. Let me work on it
with Lexie. She's still really mad at you. But I'll talk with
Cameron this weekend when I have more time. Maybe he
can give me some advice. She's different when he's around.
Less smothering. I know that's a terrible way to put it, but
it feels that way sometimes. No promises. But . . . we'll see.*

> *Urg, time's up. I'll email
> soon.*
> *Morgan*

My legs go numb and not from the hunched position I'm
sitting in. Morgan had called Annaliese *mom.* Had told her
about Blaine, a boy I knew nothing of, had made plans and
assumptions all under my nose.

I press my palms into my eyes and will the tears to cease.
I can still fix this. I'm still in control, at least for now. And
until my sister takes the initiative to pursue custody, Morgan
is my daughter and I have the final say. There will be no more
secret messages and no more lies. I force myself to finish.
The last several emails are spent making plans. Talking about
restaurants they'd go to. Which stores they'd shop in. Morgan
gushes on and on. She doesn't even like shopping and yet,
with Annie, it's all giddy excitement.

For months, my daughter has lived a separate life from
me and I've been too distracted to notice. Didn't listen to my
gut when I should have. Didn't pursue those moments when
she came so close to confiding in me. Instead, I let a stupid,
childish crush consume me. I'd welcomed an entire third
party into our lives without ever really checking the conse-
quences.

Somehow finding a semblance of composure, I crawl
down from the tree house, my legs stiff and my back aching

from being still for over an hour. Morgan gets out of school in forty-five minutes, and I'll be there to pick her up . . . on time. But first, I have to know every detail of the conversation my daughter had with Cameron.

I walk through the back door and pause as he glances up from his spot at the dining table. He has only one more song to select for his new album. One song, a goodbye, and a plane ride are all we have left. What sad compensation for all I've lost.

Cameron removes the headphones from his ears and sets them on the table. He's watching me carefully, making sure I'm not about to break. There's no need. I've done that. Multiple times already.

"What exactly did Morgan say to you?" If I'd known what was going on, I could have stopped the planning. Could have stopped the days of building hope that I now will have to crush. Cameron's brow furrows in confusion, and I try not to grit my teeth as I clarify. "Last weekend. She wrote she was going to talk to you about spending the holidays with Annaliese."

"She never . . ." He scrunches his face, and I see him touch his fingers as if counting back the days. See the minute he remembers, and the fury nearly chokes me.

"I want to know everything. Line by line."

Cameron massages the back of his neck, visibly uncomfortable. "She, um, asked if she could get my advice on a friend. And then she told me the girl was in a secret relationship and that they wanted to go public with the news, but she was scared of hurting her other friend. She wanted to know if she should tell the friend to admit the truth."

"And you said?"

"I told her she should. That lies only get worse with time."

"Is that all?" I can feel the iciness in each question, even though I'm actively working to calm down.

"All what?"

"All she said in that conversation?" I growl, exasperated. I feel like a detective having to coerce and pinch out details of a life I'm solely responsible for. "Think, Cameron. Did she say anything else of importance?"

"I am thinking. That's all I've been doing while you were in the tree house," he bites back and then seems to rein in the small burst of temper. "The only other thing she told me was that you really liked me and she didn't want you to be alone."

"And you didn't find that a little concerning? She practically spelled the situation out to you, and you missed it. And worse, I missed it because I never knew. How could you have kept something like that from me?"

"Because she asked me to," he says, resigned. "And I didn't want to lose her trust."

I stare at him, mouth open, trying to reconcile how in the world I got here. And then it hits me. I'd done this. I'd allowed it. I wanted my two-month fantasy with Cameron despite the risk to my heart because he felt worth it. But I hadn't considered my daughter. Hadn't thought of the attachment she might have to him. And never in my life did I think he would keep information from me in favor of her.

I square my shoulders and press my lips together. "Starting today, Morgan is no longer allowed in the tree house. And if she comes by here trying to talk to you, I want you to send her directly home. No more secret conversations you conveniently forget to tell me about."

"Of course, I'll send her home, but you and I still need to talk about this." He takes two steps closer, his eyes steady on mine, but I don't care how determined they look or how blue they are. This thing we've had together has been a mistake.

"And I think it's a good time for us to part ways, as well."

"What? No. Absolutely not." This time he doesn't pause.

He takes my upper arms in his hands as if he can shake me out of my decision. "You have a right to be upset with me and okay, I deserve it, but you don't get to toss me aside after one misunderstanding. We need to talk through this."

"There is nothing to talk about. I told you my deal breakers from the beginning." I pull away from his grip. "And you obviously care more about being the cool guy with the tree house than you do about protecting my daughter."

"That's not fair. You know I love that girl. I would never intentionally hurt her."

"Intentions don't matter," I fire back. "Actions do. And your actions have ruined any chance of trust between us. Which is pretty ironic, don't you think? You. The man who stood there and told me you hated lies no matter their justification. Went on and on about how omitting truths and stretching information would not be tolerated, and yet you let my daughter confess her deepest, darkest secrets to you and never once told me!"

He steps back, a new tension showing in the set of his shoulders. "That's not how it was at all. I was just trying to be a sounding board for her."

"No, you were enjoying being adored. By me, by her. By the world. It's your pattern. It's what you do. It's why one stupid failed album has the power to break you." I know I'm hitting him below the belt, but I'm done pretending I'm still thirteen with a crush. It served no purpose, only made me jump in too fast and too recklessly. "You have this need for everything to fit into a perfect little box. Well, news flash, I am not perfect. Life is not perfect. What is happening with my daughter is not perfect. And you cannot turn a blind eye to the real world because you want to live in some dream that doesn't exist."

"You think *I'm* living in a dream world? I've spent the last year marinating on my failures. I have no illusions on my status, Lexie. You have the market cornered on that one." I turn away from him, refusing to hear his words, but they come anyway, searing my skin. "Why do you think Morgan came to me in the first place? Because you refuse to talk about anything hard. You can't fix every problem with a motivational speech. Sometimes you have to face it, dig in deep, and expose the pain." He takes a breath, and for some reason his calm, soothing tone only ratchets up the electricity in my skin. "Morgan wants to know her mom. She needs to be able to talk to you about it." He moves forward, and I feel his hands gently touch my arms. Feel the same inexplicable draw that put me in this horrible position in the first place. His voice is soft when he says, "If I could do things differently, I would. And I will in the future. Remember, I'm new at this parenting thing and I'm going to make mistakes, but I'll learn."

I whirl around, breaking the contact and its effect on me. "You are not her parent!" I shout. "You're a sixteen-year itch I finally got to scratch, and at far too great a cost. And now it's done. I never should have risked my daughter on a pointless relationship."

He rears back as if I've slapped him. "You think what we have is pointless?"

My eyes burn with unshed tears, and he blurs in front of me. "I think I should have listened to Mason when he said this was a bad idea."

At those words, his entire expression changes from shock to hurt and then to resignation. He steps back, finally releasing me to leave. But I feel no victory in the win. Only the heartbreak that I allowed a stupid fantasy to hurt us both. But I swallow down the burn in my throat and step toward the door.

"If Morgan comes by here, please send her home." And with those final words, I walk out of his house, and this time he doesn't try to stop me.

～♂

The air pulses with eerie silence as I drive Morgan home from school. It feels like a death has taken place. A quick, bitter one where you never even had time to say goodbye or express all the ways you loved that person.

She gives me a funny look when we pull into the driveway. It's been ten minutes now without a word from me, which isn't normal at all. From her, yes. The one-word answers are part of the wall between us. A wall I now at least have a name for. Annaliese.

Morgan tugs her overstuffed school bag from the front seat and heaves it over her shoulder. She's gone an instant later, rushing into the house to no doubt toss her things onto her bed, stuff down an afternoon snack, and head to the tree house.

"Morgan," I say calmly as I come inside, "I'd like to talk to you for a minute."

She pops her head out from her bedroom, the one she finally got back yesterday. "Can it wait, Mom? I really want to get to the tree house before it gets dark."

"No, it can't wait." My stomach is a writhing ball of nerves as I sit down, my hands shaking so bad I fold them on my lap. "Please come sit down."

Morgan's expression changes to the one she gets when she thinks she's about to get into trouble. I feel the tension rise in her shoulders, her mind preparing for a battle. But I don't want to argue today. I want to turn back time.

"I should have known something was wrong when you didn't talk on the ride home." She sits carefully. "What did I do now?"

I nearly smile because it seems to be the only outlet for my current anxiety. The last time we had a talk in the living room was after she was especially rude to Mason, and before that it was to remind her of boundaries since I felt like she was taking advantage of Cameron's generosity. How ridiculous I must have sounded to her when they were sharing secrets behind my back. I swallow down the hurt and proceed with my practiced speech. "First, I want to say I'm sorry."

Morgan's eyebrows scrunch together. "For what?"

"For not talking to you about Annaliese. I should have. And that wasn't fair."

Her breath catches, and I see the look of betrayal form in her eyes. "Cameron told you, didn't he?" She crosses her arms. "It wasn't a big deal. I just told him I wanted to know her, that's all." She looks away, because that's what she does when she's lying to me.

"Cameron didn't say anything. Annaliese did when she called me this morning."

Morgan turns back to face me, and a flash of fear lights her eyes as she realizes I've been informed of her long-term deception. "Mom . . . I . . . can explain."

"Okay." I watch her and wait for the excuses to flow. "Go ahead."

"I was curious, and I had this friend who told me she found her dad from a video on TikTok, and I just thought maybe . . . so I looked. And she was there. And she looked like me and like you a little and . . ." Her eyes fill with tears as she turns from my gaze again.

"And you didn't feel you could tell me," I finish for her.

"I didn't want to hurt you." She wipes her cheek with her palm, still not looking at me.

"But you did hurt me, Morgan. By lying to me. By talking

about your feelings to Cameron and Annaliese and everyone else but me. When did I lose your trust?"

"You haven't, but this is different. With other people you always look for the best in them, but with her . . . you sink into this dark place. And I didn't want to be the one to put you there."

"Again, I'm sorry I made you feel that way." I take a deep breath, feeling lost as to what to do or say. Finally, I settle for the best I can offer. "I recognize that it's very normal that you would want to know your birth mom. But there are reasons why I have shielded you from her. Annaliese can be wonderful when she wants to be, but she can also be dangerous."

Her face reddens as she listens to me, her mind already forming its arguments. "Annie is not dangerous."

"I know her emails would make you think that. But my sister is a master manipulator. You can never be sure of her state of mind."

Morgan's voice hitches with both outrage and surprise. "You read my emails?"

The audacity in her tone nearly unhinges me, but I manage to keep my voice calm. "Yes, because unfortunately, reading them was the only way for me to know what was going on. You took a huge risk by messaging a random person you didn't know. She could have been strung out. She could have had a boyfriend who saw easy prey and misled you." I shudder at the thought, but Annaliese's history with men is not a positive one. "This world is dangerous, Morgan. That is why I've spent my entire life protecting you."

"You don't know her like I do. She's my friend. She loves me." Tears swim in her eyes, and each ripple is a knife to my chest. The anger has leaked from her voice, replaced by the pleading of a little girl. "She's going to come at Christmas, and then you'll see."

I fight again for the calm I know I need to have. Do my best to put aside the hurt and the anger for the sake of her understanding. "I know this is going to be hard to understand, but I cannot allow you to be around her until I can be sure she is in a healthy place."

"Why are you doing this?" Her eyes turn pleading, and I can't help the matching tears that roll down my cheeks. "Is it because I lied? I know I should have told you the truth. Cameron told me to, but I didn't because I knew you wouldn't understand. But maybe if you talk to him about it, maybe he can help you see things I can't."

"Morgan." I close my eyes when her name comes out a growl. "Cameron has no part in this decision. Or in our lives at all for that matter. I am not doing this to punish you. I'm doing it because it's what's best for you."

She bolts to her feet, her mouth wide in horror. "What do you mean Cameron has no part in our lives?"

I realize my slipup too late. "It doesn't matter. That's not what's important right now. What is important is—"

"You broke up with him, didn't you?"

I rub my temples, my head in agony. "Yes."

"Why?"

"Because, Morgan, he's leaving in less than a month." And they were both getting far too attached.

"He was always leaving. You never cared before. Not until I talked to him." She shakes her head, the tears flowing now. "You're doing it again. You're stopping your life because of me."

"What are you talking about?" I stand, desperately wanting to shake some sense into her. "You are my life!"

"That's exactly the problem." She backs away from me. "I'm not you. Annie's not going to hurt me the way she did you."

Anger sharpens my tone. "She already has. You just love the idea of her too much to see it."

"Well, I don't care." Morgan wipes her eyes a final time, her mouth growing tight. "I'm going to stay with her over Christmas, and you can't stop me."

"Yes, I absolutely can."

"No, you can't! You're not even my real mom. You're just my stupid aunt who has a flimsy piece of paper from a judge."

How I'm able to speak when her words feel like bullets is beyond me. "Well, that 'flimsy piece of paper' says I'm your guardian, which means until the court tells me otherwise, you're my responsibility."

Her teeth grind together, and I catch her motion right as she goes to grab the phone she set on the table. I get to it first.

"There will be no phone. And no tree house."

Her voice hitches with both shock and rage. "You're grounding me?"

"In a way, yes. At least until you and I can have a real conversation about this without your being so defensive and angry." The phone is cold in my trembling hand, and I pray my face does not reveal the terrified, broken woman inside. The one who's internally collapsed to the floor in agonizing sobs. "Plus I need time to process this, and I don't trust your judgment right now."

"That's not fair to me or to Annie."

"You have lied to me for five months, Morgan. Lied right to my face, even when I begged you to open up. Tell me how that's fair to me?"

She stares at me, no rebuttal this time. I see the pain in her eyes, the pull between resentment and guilt. The tug she must feel between loving me and wanting to know her birth mom. I wish I could remove all of it, but I can't. I can only do what I think is best for her right now.

Eventually she looks away, and I know the shame of hurting me is the reason. It's why she hasn't been able to look at me fully since she started her deception. I walk near her, my heart pounding, and put my hand on her shoulder. "I love you, Morgan. We will get through this, just as we do everything . . . together."

But together is not what she seems to want anymore. Instead, she turns, disappears into her room, and slams the door behind her. The sound is a detonation to the relationship I thought we had.

TWENTY-NINE

Cameron

If I ever previously complained of time moving slowly, I officially take it back. Not one day of my life has ever felt as daunting and long as these past twenty-four hours have been. Lexie is gone. A ghost who exists in every corner of Mrs. Hardcastle's house.

Morgan never did come by pleading to talk to me, and it's killing me not to know how she and Lexie are doing with all the upheaval. I've started and deleted nearly a hundred texts to Lexie, but whenever I text the words *Sorry I didn't tell you* or *Forgive me*, they all feel too small. And the rejection and accusation she leveled on me still burn.

I lean back against the headrest and stare out the windshield at the mostly full parking lot. I'm at Walmart, even though I don't need anything. I've been here for twenty minutes in my cramped seat, listening to overplayed songs on the radio. My younger self would revolt. Between iTunes, Spotify, and Amazon Music, I had a song for every mood, every thought, and every hope. Now it's just noise, so I really don't care where or who it comes from.

My joints are stiff, and I've readjusted my seat at least six times, but I still remain parked, waiting for the call that has had my mind racing with doubt and the unknown. I sent Mark my song selections last night and confirmed I would, in fact, record the label's generic, uninspired album. He responded with several *awesomes* and notes of how proud he was of me. Really, he was just thrilled he wouldn't be dragged into court on breach of contract. The question remains, however, if they will reject these choices, too. If the offer of ten song selections was just another smoke screen to appease me while they map out the next twelve months of my life.

"One year," I whisper to myself. That is how long they still own me. Yesterday, that year didn't feel so dreadful. Not with the idea of coming home to Lexie and Morgan after a rough day of production. And rough I knew it would be. As of right now, I couldn't even play the ridiculously easy arrangements that go with the songs. Then again, they'd probably be thrilled to hire paycheck musicians and simply keep me as the pretty face and voice of a "commercially acceptable" song. They want me stripped bare, unoriginal. I suppose, to the label, I'm more palatable now than I ever was before.

I check my phone, wondering if I missed Mark's call. His appointment with the production head was an hour ago, and he was supposed to call me right after. But no, there are no missed calls. Not from him . . . or Lexie. Not that I was expecting the latter. Just hoping.

Willing my stomach to stop its incessant churning, I click on the Messages app and read the texts I haven't yet found the willpower to answer.

Darcy:
Did you know that some lipsticks contain fish scales? I just read that in one of Charlie's fun-

fact books. Not sure I will ever wear makeup
again.

Darcy:
Oh, and almonds are a member of the peach
family. So there's that . . .

Darcy:
Also, "stewardesses" is the longest word that is
typed with only the left hand. I tried it, and it's
totally true!

Darcy:
Hey . . . if you come over, you can read these all
for yourself. There are some really freaky things
in here. Just sayin' . . .

Despite not wanting to, I smile. These weren't the first
texts she's sent since our conversation by the creek, but they
were the first that felt natural. Years ago, I would have come
back with a snappy comment for each, and we'd spend hours
typing random, unimportant anecdotes to each other. Instead,
I do as I have all day and close the app without replying.

I close my eyes and squeeze the cold steering wheel. It's
weird how little we know our own hearts. At the wedding,
my secret desire was to have Darcy back in my life the way
we used to be. And to be able to look Bryson in the eye and
tell him how much he completely failed me. Both have occurred now. Neither, of course, the way I expected them
to. But gone is the pain and the hurt and the bitterness I'd
felt toward both of them. And yet my heart is hollower now
than it was the day I stepped off the plane from Nashville,
because for the first time in my life I finally understand why
Darcy continually said no. We would never have been able to
love each other in a passionate, wholehearted way. She'd seen

the truth I'd been too blind to see until the moment I experienced the feeling myself. The day I kissed Lexie by that tree and knew my heart would never again be the same.

And now she, too, is gone. And I have no one to blame but myself. The villain in my story, as Bryson so eloquently pointed out, has always been me. I've lived so long in the ideal, looking only to tomorrow and the next great thing I was going to accomplish, that I forgot to appreciate the now. Even with Lexie, I had planned our entire future without ever looking at what she needed in the present. A partner. A friend. A man who knew how to recognize when intervention with a child was necessary. For all the years I have on Lexie, somehow I feel like the one who desperately needs to grow up.

A horn blaring from the parking lot makes me jump and pulls me from my tormented thoughts. I stare at the phone once more. At Darcy's text, at Mark's nonresponse, at Lexie's grinning face on my home screen and decide right then that I'm done overthinking. Done living every day inside this brain of mine that has served no purpose except to encourage me to live in constant dissatisfaction. The time for introspection is over. That's all I've done since coming home.

"*Intentions don't matter,*" Lexie had said. "*Actions do.*"

And while she was right about many things I am determined to work on, she was wrong about this: our relationship was not pointless. And she and I were not built on some fantasy we wanted to play out in living color. Every moment and emotion had been real for both of us. And maybe that's what scared her into walking away. But I would get her back.

I may not have been the man Lexie needed right now, but I want to be. And if that means owning my faults and facing my past so that I might be whole enough to help her face hers, then I'll do it.

Eagerly, my hand slides to the keys dangling from the ignition, and I start the engine with fierce determination.

~

When I plugged Darcy's address into Google Maps, I didn't expect the route to take me twenty minutes outside of town to a place that had more farmland than roadways. I hope she meant what she said about my showing up without a text or a call because, according to the GPS, I'm less than a mile from her front door.

I slow down to a crawl on the highway, keeping my eyes peeled for any kind of landmark that indicates her house. Ahead on the left, I see a new metal mailbox by the road, the decorative base formed into a silhouette of a cartoon dog on its hindquarters holding the mailbox in its paws.

Familiar warmth spreads through me. The same kind of nostalgia I felt when Cassie walked down the aisle at her wedding. I turn left and follow a long gravel driveway down to what appears to be a brand-new house. The yard is still fresh soil, and the concrete in front of the garage is a pristine white. I stop and put the car in park, even though the gravel drive continues on to another home about one hundred yards away. That house is much older, smaller, and made of brick, whereas Darcy and Bryson's home is a two-story with vertical white siding, a beautiful wooden front door, and windows lined in black trim.

There's a covered walkway along the back of the house that leads to a large shop building. My eyes scour the area outside my car for any sort of furry creature that might attack on sight. But I don't see or hear any barking as I expect to. Either Darcy doesn't have any pets, which would be absurd, or every one of them has managed to find its way into the house.

I ease open my door and slam it shut. The sound seems

to echo off the quietness all around, disturbing the strange tranquility of this place. Bryson living in the country is hard to fathom, but I guess I didn't really know him as well as I thought I did. The meaning behind his song was proof of that.

I hear a grind of a screen door and look up as Bryson takes a step out of the front entrance.

If he feels startled or irritated by my presence, he doesn't give it away. Instead, he slides his hands in his jeans pockets and walks toward me.

"Darcy ran to the store with Charlie, but they'll be back soon."

I nod. I'm not sure I came here for Darcy. Not really sure of anything anymore. The hatred I'd once felt for him is gone, replaced now by admiration that he'd accomplished the one thing I hadn't been able to do. He'd healed from his past.

"Do you want to wait inside?" he asks carefully when I remain silent.

"I can't play anymore," I say out of the blue. "I mean, I can pick up an instrument and make sound come out, but it's all noise, all jumbled up in here." I point to my head and finally meet his eyes.

He stares at me, confused by my admission, and he's not the only one. I don't know why that came out of my mouth, but now that it has, I can't stop.

"I poured everything I had into that second album, and my soul never refilled again. I've been faking it ever since. Heck, I've probably been faking it a lot longer than that."

He studies me for a moment, and then his eyes flick to the shop. "I want to show you something."

I don't know why I'm surprised at his response. Talking about feelings is like swallowing acid for the man. "Okay," I say, resigned and wishing I'd kept my mouth shut.

He takes a step toward the shop, and I follow. It has a pair of huge double doors on the side. After he unlocks and swings them open, I see the building isn't for Darcy and her dogs. It's a music studio. Complete with stage and sound equipment and microphones.

I walk gingerly to the electric guitar on a stand at the far corner. I was there when Bryson bought it. In fact, I was the one to convince him to get that particular brand because I knew the quality of sound the instrument could produce. "You're still recording music?"

"Not recording so much as just playing. Messing around, really."

"Why did you do it, then?" I ask, stunned by this revelation. I assumed Bryson had given up music altogether when he left the band. Assumed he never played another note. Because otherwise none of it made sense. "If you still loved playing, why did you walk away?"

"Because Black Carousel wasn't me anymore. I'd outgrown it. Outgrown the foundation of everything it stood for. And honestly, it's taken me a couple of years to mentally detach the music from the band, but then one day I picked up my guitar and I just started playing and . . . I loved it again."

"Obviously," I say, glancing around the state-of-the-art recording space that would be coveted even in Nashville.

He laughs, sounding slightly embarrassed. "Yeah, I might have gone a little overboard when we built this place. I think I resurrected all those awful years of playing in my living room with frayed chords and secondhand speakers and went a bit too far in the other direction." He crosses his arms and watches me as I meander through the building. The drum sets look new, as does the sound equipment. The man must have made a lot more money on his songs than I realized.

I run my fingers along the glass booth intended to enhance

acoustics. "Can you even imagine what we could have done with this when we were starting out?"

"I'd rather imagine what we could do with it now."

I jerk my head in his direction and furrow my brow at the use of his word *we*. Bryson has always been a visionary, a natural leader. I hadn't realized how much I needed that part of him until he was gone. Jay, Harrison, and I fractured within months of going on tour without Bryson there to hold us together. Last I heard, Harrison had gotten married and settled down, while Jay was still playing the bar scene.

Bryson walks over to the far wall, where five guitars are hanging vertical on hooks that are spaced to look as decorative as they are functional. He unlatches his first acoustic guitar, the one he bought at age fifteen with the money he'd earned from mowing grass.

"Here," he says, holding the instrument out for me to take it. "For old times' sake."

I take a step back and shake my head. "There is no going back in time, Bryson, and trust me, you'll be haunted by what comes from these hands right now."

"Maybe, but I want to hear it anyway." He comes closer, still holding out the offending guitar. I know that stubborn set to his mouth; he gets it right before a fight he has no intention of losing.

"No," I say, adamantly shaking my head. I feel the tingle of panic at my heels and take another step back, only to collide with the soundproof glass I had just been admiring. "I told you, I can't play."

"No, you said it didn't sound good, not that you couldn't do it." He's in front of me now, the wooden instrument the only thing between us and our standoff.

It's odd—for as much animosity as there had been between us where Darcy was concerned, the two of us have never come to blows. We'd been professionals, pushing past the anger and betrayal to put on a show and solidify our futures. But there's no concert to prepare for now. No reason to hold back angry words and flailing fists, and yet even with that wide-open door, we stand silently and stare.

I square my shoulders, struggling to remain calm. "I'm not going to play in front of you."

"Why?"

"Because I don't want to," I grind out, pushing the guitar away when he shoves it closer to my face.

"Yes, you do. You're just afraid to." He presses with both his tone and his body language. "Now tell me why."

My temples burn as my voice rises. "Because it doesn't sound right. Something's off. It's always off."

"Who cares?"

"I care!"

"Why?"

"Because it needs to be perfect!" I shout, my chest heaving.

I wait for the caustic comeback, but instead Bryson blinks slowly and replies, "Music is never perfect."

A war wages inside me as I fail to keep the stinging out of my throat. "It was for me. Before you and the band. Before I left Grace Community. Before our worlds got spun around and twisted upside down." I shove my hands in my hair, trying to ease the pressure building behind my eyes. "Back then it *was* perfect."

"No," he says more gently than I expect. Almost like a father. "It only felt perfect because it matched your sheltered, easy life up to that point. Music is heart and soul and pain and loss. Life turns for everyone, Cam. You aren't immune to it. So instead of trying to fit yourself back into the person you no longer are, embrace the journey. Embrace who you've

become." His gaze drills into mine as he holds the guitar out
to me again. "There is no shame in struggle."

Who I've become? For a long time, I didn't like that person. Didn't respect him. But that has changed since coming
home. I liked who I was when I redid the backyard, and who
I was at Thanksgiving with Lexie and Morgan. I respected
the man who helped with the house renovation and hum-
bled himself to apologize to Mason. Maybe Bryson is right.
Maybe I've been trying to play with the heart of a twenty-
year-old kid when I need to play with the soul of a thirty-
three-year-old man who's been through the wringer and
survived.

I swallow hard and yet feel my hand move as if on a pulley
I cannot control. As soon as my fingers curl around the neck
and the strings press into my skin, I feel an awakening.

Bryson steps back and returns to his wall to collect a
guitar for himself. He waits for me, for my lead, the way he
used to when we were sixteen and practicing in my parents'
garage.

I lick my dry lips and strum. The rough, fumbling sound
pierces me through just as it has for months now, and I nearly
quit, but then Bryson comes in with a harmonic chord, the
addition a dampening splash to the usual bitterness. I pick
up the pace, my mind drifting to the song Lexie had called
her favorite. I switch the melody, and Bryson pauses, waiting
until he recognizes the song before coming in again.

His smile is proud when he lifts his chin at me. "I always
liked this one."

I pick at the strings, feel the vibration in my soul the way
I haven't in *years*, and I find myself humming, low and me-
thodic. Bryson matches my voice, his harmony nearly pitch-
perfect. But I don't think I'd care if it wasn't. Because he's
right. Music isn't perfect. It can't be. It's too unhindered to

stay enclosed in such an empty tomb. I look around at this majestic space and see the notes dance in the air around us. I watch them pirouette, watch them grow arms and circle between partners. I tap my foot to the beat and play honest and flawed—a freedom I'd never once allowed myself.

A car door slamming and the screech of a little boy in the distance interrupt our escape down memory lane, and when Bryson and I make eye contact, we're both out of breath and stunned. Somehow, despite the years, the distrust, and the angry words, we're still connected. The magic that existed when we played together had never made sense, and yet it's still there, stronger and bolder than ever before.

"Have you ever wondered what we might have done together if you hadn't walked away?" I ask without any subtext or accusation. It's a question I've wondered about time and time again, especially at the height of our fame. "It was your song that made us. Your music. Not mine. If you had stayed with the band, you would have had everything you dreamed about."

"Dreams change," he says without any remorse in his voice.

"So you've never regretted the decision? Not even once?"

He carefully places his guitar on the hook as a dark-haired toddler comes running frantically into the studio, yelling, "Daddy!" Bryson swings the little boy up into his arms and nuzzles his neck while the child writhes and giggles from the tickling.

"Mommy says we get a new puppy if we say *pleaaaase*."

"Oh, she did, did she?" Bryson turns, Charlie still in his arms, and holds my stare as if to ensure I understand he's one-hundred-percent serious when he says, "Not even once."

Charlie scurries down and runs back to the doorway, where I see Darcy watching us, her face twisted with emotion.

I set down the guitar as Bryson strolls easily to his wife,

kisses her hello, and then leaves the two of us to talk. Charlie's toddler babbling continues until I hear the front door click shut.

Darcy and I stand there, silently, and look at each other.

"I never would have done what Bryson did for you," I finally admit, being honest with myself for probably the first time. "I never would have given up the opportunity. Not for you. Not for anyone."

She crosses her arms and leans a shoulder against the doorframe. "I know. And you were never meant to, Cam. You were always supposed to do exactly what you did."

I nod and glance one more time around, then at the guitar Bryson forced into my hands. "You made the right choice," I say, looking back at her, hoping to convey my regret in ever doubting it. "Bryson is a really good man."

"I know that, too." And she had, even back then, when the rest of us quit believing in him. "Are you staying for dinner?"

I walk toward my childhood best friend and grin down at her. She's in baggy jeans, an old Midlothian High School T-shirt, and her long hair is pulled high into a ponytail. She's by far the most familiar thing I've seen since coming home, and the love I feel for her is immediate, welcome, and wonderfully platonic.

I tug playfully on her ponytail. "Yeah, I'm staying for dinner. But only if you stop texting me random facts that make kissing a woman wearing lipstick sound disgusting."

She bellows a laugh and slaps my back, pushing me toward her front door. "Oh, you just wait. I have four years of missed torture to make up for."

THIRTY

Lexie

*M*organ hasn't spoken to me in three days. I've tried being nice, mean, authoritative, and desperate, but nothing so far has broken through her wall of defensiveness.

I take a deep breath and stare at Annaliese's apartment door in front of me, my nerves a somersault of anxiety. I don't want to be here, but the horrific truth I've been forced to face these last twenty-four hours is that I'm simply too late to stop the train that's long since left the station. My discovery of their emails came after months of relationship building, and somehow, even though I'm the one who was lied to and deceived, I've become the monster, the bad guy, the wicked stepmom bent on destroying the young princess's life.

So here I am, facing a lose-lose situation. Either way, Morgan is going to be hurt, but at least this way, we'll both know the truth: Annaliese is not the shining hero Morgan thinks she is.

Shaking my hands out one more time, I press on the doorbell and wait. Morgan and I had lived in a similar apartment complex when I first came back to Midlothian. The area seems relatively safe, though knowing Annie, she'd bolt the minute Morgan got comfortable here.

The door swings open, and I instinctively stiffen when I face the woman who abandoned my daughter ten years ago.

"You came," she says, sounding nearly as breathless as I feel.

"I said I would." It's hard to hold back the sharpness in my tone now that I'm looking at her in person. Either I'll break down and fall into her arms or I do what I'm doing now and try not to feel anything. Try not to notice how much more Morgan favors her than I remember. How her smile brightens her eyes or how she chews on her lip exactly the same way my daughter does when feeling insecure.

"Please, um, come in." Annaliese steps away from the door and swings her arm wide like a cocktail party hostess.

I step over the threshold, feeling much like a social worker as my eyes dart to every corner of the room in search of anything that might be dangerous for a child. The quest is fruitless. Apart from two small couches, one end table, an old TV with duct tape on the corner, and the small table it's balancing on, there's nothing else in the room. I notice the small candle she's lit, along with the nauseating smell of linen that she's always been fond of. When we were kids, she said it was the only scent that could mask the smell of marijuana. A habit she picked up soon after Mom got sick. A habit I should have told my dad about months before I actually did. I inhale deeply and search for the pungent smell under the crisp scent, but it isn't there.

Annaliese must notice because she shuts the door and says, "I've been sober for eight months now." She passes by me to the only other thing on her end table—AA chips. Several of them. Each marking a month of sobriety. "I never would have emailed her back if I hadn't been. I decided a long time ago I never wanted her to know that person."

I look at her, my expression cold. While she hadn't been the one to outright lie to me, I still resent her interactions with my daughter. "And yet that's the only person I can remember right now."

"I know. And I don't expect your feelings to change overnight." She sits down on the edge of the couch, nervously. "Do you want to sit?"

"Not really."

"Oh, okay." She hops back up. "Then, um, what would you . . . ?" She trails off, unsure what to do or say next.

I cross my arms and cut right to the chase. "How was it that you didn't question Morgan's excuses about my not wanting to see you for five entire months?"

"I don't know." She bites the side of her fingernail the same way she always used to do when being interrogated. "Maybe I didn't want to know the truth. Maybe deep down I feared you'd stop the communication, which is exactly what you've done."

I shake my head, disgusted at the hint of accusation in her voice, but also unable to say the words I want to stab her with. The worst part of loving an addict is that I still feel responsible for her sobriety. I still fear that if I say the wrong thing, or push too hard, or hold her accountable for the pain she's caused Morgan and me, then it will send her spiraling and the fall will be my fault. But how do I skirt the hard subjects and then drop my daughter off unsupervised? I can't. Which is again why this entire thing is a lose-lose. "I would like to look around your apartment."

Her brow pinches. "What?"

"If you want to continue to communicate with Morgan, then I need to verify those chips were not bought off eBay."

Her lips press into a frustrated line, but she doesn't argue, mostly because she was the one who admitted to me she used that trick once to get our dad to loan her money. "Okay, fine. I have no secrets." With that, she leads me to the one small bedroom. It's only big enough for a double bed and a chest of drawers.

"Where is Morgan going to sleep if she stays here?"

"I'd give her my bed and take the couch. Or maybe we'll sleep slumber-party style and both crash in the living room. You know, the way we used to when we were her age." Her lips curve into a faint smile. "I think Morgan would like that."

I swallow through the pain that image causes and force myself to accept what seems to be inevitable. "Yes, she probably would." Without permission, I walk to the dresser and look through each drawer for contraband. I do the same in the bathroom, checking under the sink, behind the toilet, in the toilet, and even through the trash.

Annaliese watches without a word of correction. She knows I don't trust her, and obviously she's figured out that I'm not leaving here or letting Morgan come without total assurance that it's safe.

The kitchen is the largest room in the space, with a small breakfast nook and a round table. I open the refrigerator and for the first time feel surprised. There's food in it. Not just any food. Healthy food: milk, eggs, lunch meat, cheese, and a few containers of leftovers that imply she's done some cooking. The half-empty containers are the most comforting things I've seen yet, because when Annaliese is using, she does not eat. I open the oven door and check the bottom near the heating coil. There are more crumbs in there than my own. Finally, I once again search every drawer and cabinet for any sign of hidden alcohol. The investigation comes back clean, and I stand there, unsure what to do next.

I hadn't gotten past this part in my head. Truly hadn't expected my sister to be as she claimed to be. Or maybe, in my darkest of hearts, I'd hoped there was still a chance to end this thing between the two of them. Guilt singes me with that realization. Annaliese isn't a stranger. She's my sister. That should make this better, though somehow it doesn't.

"Can we sit and talk now?" She folds her arms across her chest, her voice curt and defensive. She's hurt, and I hate that I'm doing that, but I don't know how to stop. I walk into the living room and take the spot next to the table with the AA chips, my eyes glancing at them briefly as I sit down. "You can check those, too. I promise they're real," she says as she passes by me and picks one up, rolling it in her hand. She sits opposite me and stares down at the plastic that marks her continual victory over alcohol. "I never intended to leave Morgan with you for so long." Her eyes meet mine, clear and determined. "I tried to get sober so many times. Every year on Morgan's birthday, I'd make myself a promise to get well, knowing how much I was missing out on. And every year I'd fail within weeks. But last year, when she turned thirteen, it hit me . . . I was out of time. My daughter was a teenager, and if I didn't act now, I'd lose her forever. So this time, I didn't fail. I made it a month, then two, then three. I had it all planned out. I'd call at Christmas and I'd change the memory of the last night we spent together."

Despite what her confession does to my heart, my words are still sharp when I say, "You could have called me. I would have helped you."

"You were helping me. You were raising my daughter when I couldn't."

My chest burns with unleashed emotion, but I fight through and ask the question that has plagued me for days now. "What are you going to say when Morgan asks about her father? Because she will, you know. I get that it's been all rainbows and unicorns between you two, but Morgan isn't one to mess around with her words. She shoots it to you straight and expects the same back. She's a lot like Mason in that way."

Annaliese seems taken aback by my bluntness, her voice flustered. "I don't know what exactly I'm going to say. I haven't thought that far ahead."

"You need to think that far. You need to think five steps ahead of her at all times. You need to check for hazards and bumps that will hurt her, and try to navigate her fall as best as you can. That is being a mother. It's not fun emails back and forth. Do you have any idea how much I wish that's all it was?"

"Well, you tell me what to say, then. Because the last thing I remember about her father is him handing me cash to get an abortion."

I cringe at her words, cringe at the memory of the man who first introduced my sister to the numbing effects of the bottle. At least one question is answered. He knows about Morgan and never wanted her. I can't help my relief. The greatest gift God gave my daughter was keeping that man out of her life.

"Okay . . ." I lick my lips, my mind racing with what words would hurt Morgan the least. "You tell her that her father was too young and too stupid to know what an amazing girl she is. And then you tell her he's out of the picture and she's better off not knowing him."

Annaliese nods with absolute concentration. "And she'll accept that?"

"She'll have to. Under no circumstances are you to give her his name. I don't want her searching social media again for a connection she isn't ready to have."

The responding wince from my sister does send a twinge of guilt this time, but she doesn't argue or bite back. Again, a response that is far out of character for her. "Does this mean you're going to let her come for Christmas?"

"I don't know yet," I say, struck by the look of hope in her eyes. I glance down at my fingers, unable to stomach it, and take a deep stabilizing breath. "But . . . considering how sure I was that the answer would be no, you can feel a little good about the fact that I'm now undecided." Blinking back an unwanted rush of tears, I finally look back at my sister. "At a minimum, I will allow the communication to continue, but I will be monitoring your conversations."

Annaliese's small hold on control snaps. Her eyes turn red, watery, and her voice trembles when she says, "Thank you."

I simply nod and begin to stand when she stops me with words that punch me right in the gut.

"Will you ever forgive me?"

It takes an entire minute for me to answer. Because while I loathe the way in which I got Morgan, I don't regret a day I've had with her. Annaliese's failure gave me a daughter I might not even have known otherwise. And to her credit, my sister did the most unselfish thing she could have at the time. She let go of Morgan when she recognized she didn't have the capability to take care of her.

"Honestly I don't know that either," I finally say as I take in my sister's expression. Pain and loss are etched in every line of her face, and it makes me wonder what further punishment I could want heaped on her. She missed ten years with Morgan while we made a life together. What more restitution could I ask for? I close my eyes briefly as the first glimpse of forgiveness peeks through the darkness between us. "But I want to, Annie." And I do. I want to love and trust her the way I once did. "It's just going to take me some time."

Tears slip over her eyelashes while she wrings her hands together. "I understand."

Unable to remain in the room a minute longer, I stand. "I'll call you and let you know what I decide."

Annaliese doesn't walk me out. She doesn't say another word as I open the front door, exit, and close it gently behind me.

~9~

I turn the corner and slam on my brakes when I see Cameron's car parked in front of his house. He was gone when I left his morning, and a part of me was grateful not to see the reminder of what I single-handedly destroyed during my rampage. Cameron didn't deserve the things I said to him or the vicious way I said them. He had messed up, yes. But so had I. And he was right—he wasn't a parent. To expect him to read Morgan's thoughts was unfair and unjust.

I throw my car into reverse, turn the wheel, and pull in next to the curb. I don't know what I'm going to say or do when he opens the door and very likely shuts it right in my face, but I need him desperately right now. More than I should, more than I want to, more than I've needed anyone beyond family, and no amount of willpower is going to allow me to drive away again.

Each step to his front door feels terrifying as I rehearse the apology in my head. But when I knock and the door opens, all the words fly right out and leave me empty. I look up into his stunned face, watch how his mouth forms my name, and croak out, "I'm so sorry," right before a deluge of tears renders me incomprehensible.

Cameron gathers me up without a word and folds me against his chest, his arms tight around me. A strong base of security as I press my cheek against his shirt. I don't know when he learned the art of comforting another person so well—how he knows when to speak and when to just let me think—but he's a master at it. At reading me. Sobs rob me of speech, and I hear him whisper soft cooing sounds about how it's all going to be okay. And I want to believe him. I want to erase this aching fear warning me of another traumatic change I cannot control.

THIRTY-ONE

Cameron

Since reconnecting with Lexie, I've wanted to know every facet of who she is. I've now seen her happy, angry, embarrassed, and strong. Nothing prepares me, though, for the gut-wrenching pain of seeing her broken. This beautiful, wonderful, caring girl should never have to feel this way.

I hold her tighter in my arms and rub a hand down her back as she sobs into my chest. Her hair smells like honeysuckle, and the ache of missing her over these past few days triples. I don't know what this means for us, her being here, but it really doesn't matter, because I plan to hold her until I force a smile from her lips and see that unending delight return to her eyes.

"I'm sorry," she whispers again for the fourth time.

And again I tell her the truth. She has nothing to be sorry for.

When she finally calms enough to breathe normally, she eases away from my hold, and while I'm glad she's no longer crying, I don't want to let her go. I want this woman to stay in my arms forever.

She wipes at her face, which is red and blotchy and still harboring the agony she just unleashed. "I shouldn't have collapsed on you like that. Not after everything I said. I just wanted to—"

"Lexie, stop. I'm glad you came here. I want to be the person you collapse onto." I grin down at her, hoping to inject a small measure of lightness into the moment.

My plan backfires, and her eyes fill again. "Why are you being so nice to me? I was cruel and angry, and you were far too easy a target." She looks down at her fingers, now playing with the hem of her T-shirt.

I take her hand and kiss her delicate fingers. "I'm glad you said what you did that day. I needed to hear it. And you were right about many things. Just not everything," I add quickly. I tug on her hand, gently bringing her closer. "My feelings for you are not idealized. They are very, very real. And I missed you terribly." I brush away the strands of hair sticking to her damp face and rest my palm on her cheek.

"I missed you, too." She falls into me again, though this time it feels less like a break and more of a choice. I rest my chin on her head and hug her until the world feels right again. To think I'd gone thirty-three years not truly knowing her now feels like a tragedy.

We slowly let go, but only to make our way to the living room. I want to talk. Want to know everything that's gone on in her world while we've been apart.

"How's Morgan?" I ask when we're both settled on the couch. My one hand is still in hers while my other rests gently on her knee. Touching her feels like a necessity at this point, and I don't plan to stop anytime soon.

Lexie swallows as if the question pains her but doesn't

start crying again. "She's angry and confused, I think. She has all these feelings about her mom and me, and she isn't sharing them with anyone."

The tightness in my chest is immediate. I want so much to hug that little girl and help her navigate all these new emotions. The intensity of the protectiveness is not new or as surprising this time. I love Morgan. And even though I don't have my own children to compare it to, I know my need to help her could not be more significant even if she were my own flesh and blood. "What can I do? I mean, I know I'm not her dad or even a family member, but I . . ." My voice trails off because I don't know how to articulate these new feelings. The only real example I had of a stepparent was Bryson's dad, and the man never cared for Bryson the way I already do for Morgan.

Lexie's eyes soften in a way that makes my furiously beating heart settle some. "You're helping right now." She shakes her head. "I've spent the last two days going through every possibility with Annaliese, and none of them feel right. I don't think I can be objective enough to make this decision on my own." She squeezes my hand. "I guess I came here because I need a friend. I know I said we were pointless and done, but I don't really feel that way."

"Neither do I," I say, relief washing away the last of my tension. We started out as friends. If that is what she needs from me right now, then so be it. "I'm here for you in any capacity you'll have me."

Finally, a ghost of a smile graces her face. I wish it were more. Wish beyond the stars that her eyes weren't cloaked in sadness. "Morgan wants to spend Christmas with my sister," she says, her voice trembling the minute the words release. "I went to her apartment today to see if she really is clean and sober, because if she wasn't, the decision would be easy."

Lexie blows out a long exhale. "But . . . turns out, it's not going to be easy."

Which means Lexie believes her sister is safe, though I still feel my spine straighten at the idea of Morgan spending Christmas with a stranger, related or not. "No, I can imagine it wouldn't be."

She glances around the room as if it might hold some of the old wisdom she used to get from Mrs. Hardcastle. Her gaze lands on the chair in the corner. The one I was sitting in before she knocked on my door. "Are you playing again?" She rises to her feet as she asks the question, letting go of my hand in the process.

"A little," I admit. The breakthrough I'd had with Bryson has stuck, and even though I've yet to find the passion I once held for the instrument, the noise in my head has been slowly fading away.

Lexie walks over to the guitar and touches it like it's a talisman, with both reverence and mild fear. "How?" She turns to watch me as I stand, my hands quickly finding solace in the pockets of my jeans. "I mean, what changed?"

"You," I say, shrugging.

Her brows bunch, confusion masking every other emotion her face gives away. "I don't understand."

"When you told me I live in the ideal and break when things don't live up to my fantasy, I vehemently disagreed. I knew you were angry, and I wanted to blame all that you said on stress and emotion. But then a day passed, and your words kept gnawing at me until I finally could admit the truth in them. Could see how much that idealism had driven so many of my life choices. And I don't want to be that person anymore. And I never want you to feel like you have to be perfect to be loved."

She wraps her arms around herself in a hug and presses her

lips together, not in anger but to keep the teetering tears at bay. I feel them, too, crawling up my throat, hating myself for ever putting that kind of pressure on her.

"I went to see Bryson," I continue. "And for the first time in years, I spoke the truth about the music. I admitted all my failures to the one man who I genuinely feared would break the last part of me."

I smile at the memory of dinner, of little Charlie throwing his food on the floor and watching Bryson match will for will with his son. Of laughing with Darcy when we spent the next twenty minutes together cleaning up his mess. That was real life. And it was absolutely, fantastically beautiful.

"And he showed me that I'd been doing to the music the same thing I'd been doing to everything around me. I was stifling it. Putting it into a box of unachievable expectations. I thought I'd changed, but I realize now I've always done this. When I was at Grace Community, I remember judging Brent and his choices, and then with Black Carousel, I did the same with Bryson. And I could get away with it because I was just the guitarist. But then I became the guy in front, and it turns out I'm not prejudiced because all that criticism and pressure stayed right there, only now it was me disappointing myself. Me picking apart every move I made, every song I wrote. I thought the label had done it, but it was me all along. I single-handedly stripped away every part that was unique, all in my quest to be perfect." My voice cracks, and I have to look away from the admiration in Lexie's eyes or I'll break, too. And she doesn't need that burden. She needs me to be strong right now.

I feel her next to me seconds later, feel her warm breath on my arm as she takes my hand and kisses my shoulder. "I'm really proud of you," she whispers.

My arm slips around her waist, and I pull her back to the

couch, onto my lap this time. She peers down at me, strok-
ing my hair, and I picture a lifetime re-creating this moment.
"I know it's not the same, but Morgan is like me in a lot of
ways. She feels so intensely that I'm not sure she can recognize the difference between the ideal and reality."

"You mean with Annaliese?"

I nod. "She may need to be with her for a while to truly
dissect what exactly she wants."

"What if I let her go to my sister's and she loves it?" Lexie
asks, the heart of her insecurity and fear lacing every word.
"What if I lose her?"

"You won't." I've never been more sure of anything in my
life than I am of that.

"But what if she gets hurt?"

"Love is always a risk, Lexie. It's what makes it so terrifying. But do you really think at this point she isn't going to be
hurt either way?"

Lexie bites her lip and evaluates my question. Finally, she
agrees. "No, I guess not." Another tear slips down her cheek
as I see the decision that has been eating her up inside is
now made. I pull her close and lay her head gently on my
shoulder. Her cries are silent, but they seem to hurt even
more this time. "Will you come with me?" she asks. "I'm not
sure I can do this on my own."

"Yes, of course." I close my eyes and squeeze her closer,
wishing I could do more than just watch and support her.
Wishing I could fix every part that feels wrong about this situation. But I can't. "I'll be next to you every step of the way."

THIRTY-TWO

Lexie

*T*don't tell Morgan my decision until the next morning when I knock on her door. It's nine o'clock, much earlier than she's been rolling out of bed since Christmas break started, and I certainly don't expect a welcome wagon. Last night I'd gotten a grunt and a shrug when I asked if she wanted to watch one of our favorite Christmas musicals. When she was little, she used to beg for the movie marathons to begin—they were her favorite part of the holidays. This time she didn't make popcorn or sing along. She simply sat there stoic and icy as we watched Bing Crosby dance across our screen.

Just before the grand finale, I reached out and held her hand, saying the silent goodbye I wasn't sure I'd be able to get out the next morning. To my relief, she squeezed my hand back, and we stayed that way until the end of the movie, tears choking both of us. No matter what happened moving forward, life as it had been for the past ten years was over. We both knew it and grieved in our own ways.

324

When the other side of her bedroom door remains silent, I knock again, slowly turning her knob as I do. I peek through the slightly open door and see her stirring beneath the covers.

"Good morning," I say as she rubs her eyes and sits up. There have been many signs of her depression since our fight, but the excessive sleeping has been the biggest. "I wanted to talk to you." My decision to wait until this morning was fully selfish. I didn't want to see her joy and elation over leaving me for longer than I had to.

Morgan grumbles and crosses her legs on the bed, her tired body hunched over. "Can't we talk later? I was having a good dream."

I sit down on the edge and pull her phone from my pocket. It takes a hard swallow before I can hand it to her. "As of today, you are no longer grounded."

Her eyes widen and spark to life in a way that brings me both joy and pain, but then they dull just as quickly. "So I can talk to my friends, but that's it, right? No tree house? No email?" She still hasn't taken the phone, almost as if she suspects it's a peace offering devoid of the one thing she wants—contact with her biological mom.

"Actually, the tree house is no longer off-limits." Again, I force my aching throat to swallow. "Nor is email, but you may choose not to use it anymore."

Her eyes narrow, watching me for the left hook she seems to be convinced is coming. "I don't understand what you're saying."

"I just think you might want to text instead of email." I pull up Annaliese's contact information and attempt to give Morgan the phone again. "It seems like it would be more convenient."

Her mouth opens as she stares down at the phone be-tween us, then closes again. Gently, she takes it from my trembling fingers and looks back up at me, the pooling tears in her eyes matching mine. "What does this mean?"

"It means you should call Annaliese and confirm what you need to bring. I told her we'd be there by ten o'clock, and you have a lot of packing to do, especially if you're staying through Christmas." I deserve an Academy Award for not falling apart as the words come out. More impressive is that they almost sound lighthearted.

Morgan blinks, then looks down at her waiting phone and blinks again. Then she catapults herself into my arms, hugging me with enough force to break my heart in half. "Thank you," she chokes out. "I know I hurt you. I didn't want to, I promise. I just wanted . . ."

I pull away as her voice fades out. She's crying now, and I'm still clenching every muscle in my stomach to keep from joining her. "I know, sweetheart. You just wanted to know your mom." She nods, her face sorrowful and apologetic. "And you should." I brush back the hair on her forehead, taking a long look at my little girl, who isn't so little anymore. "I just love you so much that a part of me didn't ever want to let you go." I can't stop the burning that springs to my eyes. Not when she looks so brokenhearted. I wasn't expecting this reaction. I was expecting delight and excited packing. I think this sadness might be worse; it certainly feels worse. I clear my throat. "But you are thirteen and a half now," I say, pulling myself together, "so I think it might be time for your first sleepover. Just don't leave your bra too close to the freezer, and tuck your hands in tight when you sleep."

She furrows her brow in confusion, and it brings forth the first real smile I've felt in days.

"Let's just say that Annie was a pro at sleepover pranks. I'll let her give you the details." I stand from the bed and gently touch Morgan's cheek before leaving her alone to digest what's coming. "You should get started. Cameron's going to be here soon to pick us up."

"Mom," Morgan calls out right when I reach her door.

"Yes?" I turn around, willing myself to stay strong for just a few more seconds.

Morgan holds her pillow to her chest the way she used to hold her favorite stuffed tiger. "My loving her doesn't mean I don't love you anymore."

"I know, honey. Your heart is far too big for that." We smile at each other then, and I let myself out of her bedroom, the click of her door shutting behind me like a knife inserted right into the middle of my chest.

The car is quiet while we drive. Cameron is in front, using the phone to navigate us to one of the few areas in Arlington he's never been to. Morgan and I sit in the back, clinging to each other, neither of us saying a word as we both gaze out the windshield.

My heart squeezes the instant Cameron slows and turns right into the apartment complex. "This is it," I whisper when he parks in front of her building.

Morgan turns and looks out each window to get a complete view of the place. "It's different than I pictured."

"Different good?"

"Just different," she sighs.

I glance ahead and lock eyes with Cameron in the rearview mirror. He's been a rock this morning, hauling bags, bringing breakfast, making stupid jokes that had us both rolling our eyes. He'd taken it upon himself to fill the role I usually play, and the goal had worked, had made the heaviness lighten just a little. Unfortunately, the daunting weight came back the second we parked, more pressing than ever.

When Annaliese opens her apartment door and steps out, Morgan's entire countenance changes. The slumped shoulders rise, the frown disappears, and her eyes light up, big and blue. I can't imagine the ping-pong of emotion she must be facing. My heartbreak and my sister's hope.

Morgan snatches her backpack from the space at her feet and quickly opens her door. Cameron's already at the trunk, removing her larger suitcase when I finally emerge from the car. My legs ache, and my heart feels hollow, but I force a brave smile for my kid and walk to the rear of the car, where she and Cameron stand.

Annaliese, to her credit, waits by her door, giving us these last few minutes to say goodbye.

"I guess this is it, kid," Cameron says after slamming down the trunk lid.

Morgan jerks her gaze to his. "Won't I see you again before you leave?"

"Oh, yes," he says, ruffling her hair the way he loves to. "I'll make sure of it. But until then . . ." He pulls a large square box from behind his back and hands it to her. "Merry Christmas."

She stares down at the gift, and I almost want to curse Cameron for nearly making me lose all my concentrated composure. "What is it?"

"You'll have to wait till Christmas to find out. No peeking," he adds with a wink.

Morgan lunges into his arms, and he holds her tight the way I always imagined a father figure would one day. I just never thought it'd be under these circumstances. "Remember, you promised to take care of her," she whispers, though not low enough that I don't catch her words or their meaning.

"And I will," he says just before releasing her. "I'll take this up to the door and give you two a minute." He lifts the suitcase, takes her gift, and disappears around the car.

I'm grateful yet horrified that I'm not going to make it through this goodbye.

"Do you have all your toiletries? And a phone charger?" I ask, straightening the lapels on her jacket, which is unzipped and flopping open. She nods, biting her lip. "And remember what I said. If you feel nervous or scared at all, you can call me. I won't rush out here to rescue you or change any rules. I'll just listen."

She nods again, and this time I see a tear roll down her cheek.

I swallow and it feels like a boulder is lodged in my esophagus. "We'll have our own celebration when you get back. Complete with a movie marathon and the two of us stringing popcorn." We hadn't even put up the tree yet. I didn't want to do it with all the turmoil that had been surrounding us.

Morgan stares into my eyes for a long time as though she wants to say so much more than she's able to. Then she falls into my arms and squeezes as if this might very well be our last contact. "Thank you," she says softly, and I blow out a shaky breath because there is no regret in her tone. Only appreciation. This may be hard for both of us, but she wants to be here. Wants this time with the woman who hasn't spent one minute in the last ten years being her mother. I both resent and respect her for being so stubbornly brave.

"Merry Christmas, sweetheart," I say when we separate.

"Merry Christmas, Mom." She kisses my cheek and backs away.

I don't follow, only watch as she skips to Annaliese's apartment, and they engage in a reunion that includes hugs and laughter and my sister's hands on Morgan's cheeks as she examines the daughter she left behind.

Cameron helps me into the passenger side, my body suddenly going numb. My heart feels numb, as well.

"Where would you like to go?" he asks gently, squeezing my cold fingers.

"Home. I'm meeting Mason at the house in an hour."

Cameron backs out of the parking spot, his hand still clutching mine, making the process much more difficult than it needs to be. He stays silent until we hit the highway and then he glances my direction. "We can talk abo—"

"No." I shake my head. "I'm done talking. Now is the time for coping, and that's exactly what I'm going to do." My sister is back, and my daughter is gone. All the words in the universe are not going to change a thing.

THIRTY-THREE

Cameron

$\mathcal{E}$veryone deals with grief differently, and it turns out that for Lexie, dealing means working nonstop on the renovation for the past five days. But today is Christmas Eve, and both Mason and I agreed that we would not let her step foot into that house.

Our badgering won and she finally caved, agreeing to come with me to Dallas for our first-ever official date. It seems we've done everything backward, and this is no different. I made the reservation weeks ago for a special holiday six-course meal at the Mansion at Turtle Creek. I didn't mention to Lexie that I had made it for a party of three and not two but instead did my best to keep her smiling and entertained all evening. She tried her best as well, though often failing to hide the layer of sadness that has remained since we drove away from Annaliese's apartment.

I'm just praying this next surprise will be the one thing to bring the Lexie I have completely fallen in love with out of hiding.

"Thank you again for coming with me tonight," I say as I turn the corner into our neighborhood.

"Thanks for inviting me. The food was amazing, and the atmosphere was incredible."

We took several obligatory date-night pictures in front of the beautiful historic structure, but they just don't feel right without Morgan's sassy smirk staring back at me.

"What would you say to continuing our date just a little longer? I have a surprise for you at my place."

"I hope that surprise doesn't include food, because I could not stuff another bite into this stomach."

My heart springs at her sudden quick wit, something I haven't seen all evening. "No food, I promise."

"Okay then, yes, I'd love to extend our date."

I pull up to the curb in front of my house, my nerves lighting on fire. While Lexie had been working so hard on her renovation, I too had been working. Though each hour felt more like relearning how to play the guitar versus making any forward strides. But slowly I found myself muddling through the noise and allowing the freedom to guide me. The sound felt different, and it would probably never again be the same. I'd come to accept that piercing truth, even embrace the difference, but I wonder what Lexie will think. If she'll enjoy the new sound or if she'll wish she had back the man whose music she played for years. Either way, I am about to find out.

I take her hand when we both come around the car and walk with her to my front door. There's so much I want to say to her, so much I've wanted to say for days now, but I keep it locked away inside. Lexie doesn't need the complication of my feelings in her life right now. And the one vow I made was that I would never be selfish with this girl. I would not force her to deal with my emotions simply because I need an outlet. I would wait till she was ready to talk about our future, even if it killed me to remain silent.

I stop us before we walk through the front door and take her other hand, turning us face-to-face. "Is it going to upset you to be outside in the backyard?" I don't know what seeing the tree house will do to her. Last time she was up there was the worst moment of her life, and I don't want to do anything to re-create that feeling.

Lexie's smile is sad when she answers, "No, I think I'd like to be out there. I find I enjoy seeing anything lately that reminds me of her. I've even left her mess untouched in the bathroom." Her eyes glisten. "I've almost tricked myself into believing she's not really gone. Just at a friend's house."

"Morgan isn't gone," I reassure her. "She'll come back. I know it in here." I press our joined hands to my chest.

Lexie lets out a long sigh. "I thought she'd call by now. She's texted a couple of times but just to check in on me. I don't think she misses me like I miss her."

I pull her into a hug because I don't know what else to say. My lack of experience has reared its ugly head so many times these past few weeks that I've resented my bachelorhood like never before.

She pulls back and kisses me quickly. "I don't want to be sad tonight. Show me your surprise."

"Okay, but first . . ." I cup her cheek, not at all satisfied with that rushed peck, and pull her in for the kiss I've longed to give her all night. The one that makes her melt into my arms and reminds me exactly how wonderful it is to be alive.

Reluctantly, I pull away and open the door, guiding her through my house and out to the backyard to where it all started. Where I felt that first step of freedom toward becoming a new person.

I turn on all the dangling lights and grab a lighter to light the tiki torches. I have already strategically placed my guitar in the corner on the porch.

Her usual awe returns as she glances around the lit space. The ambience still takes my breath away, as well. This property is beautiful. So beautiful in fact that I had Kelly put in an inquiry about purchasing the house. The owners are still undecided on whether they want to sell but agreed to give me the first shot at buying the house if they did. I understand their hesitation. They grew up here. I'm sure it's like letting go a piece of history. Even I couldn't stomach the idea of some stranger moving in and tearing down the tree house or removing all the lights I painstakingly hung. My future is far too clear when I look around this property. I imagine laughing children, and for the first time the face of my wife is very clear. The face of the woman now walking toward the chair I had marked *reserved* with a handwritten sign.

"Wow, you've thought of everything," she says as she lowers herself into the seat.

I grab a blanket and wrap it around her shoulders, then light the fire pit next to her.

"Okay, the suspense is killing me. Stop stalling and tell me what you have planned!" I love how the jest has returned to her voice and that for a moment she doesn't seem burdened by all the unknowns.

"Well, I do believe you won a bet that has never been settled."

Her breath hitches, her eyes lighting up so brilliantly I want to fall down at her feet and beg her to love me forever. "Does this mean . . . ?"

Her question fades when I grab the guitar and stand in front of her. My hands tremble as I look at Lexie and see that hers do, as well. She's clutching the blanket to her chest, anticipation pouring off of her.

"I know you were supposed to get to pick the song, but I hope you don't mind if I take some liberties."

She smiles and shakes her head.

I stand there, our gazes locked, my left hand clutching the neck of the guitar, my right hand waiting. Suddenly I feel a slice of fear so debilitating I nearly drop the instrument, but I keep my eyes fixed on hers because I believe in my heart of hearts that this woman in front of me doesn't care if this moment isn't perfect. I truly believe she only cares about me, and that belief allows my fingers to move and my chest to suck in air right before I sing the first note.

The song I begin with is the one she said was her favorite, and I watch as she sways to the rhythm and sings along. This one is light and easy and probably why I chose to do it first. When I finish, she claps and cheers. Her cheeks are flushed, and the delight in her eyes makes every moment it took getting here worth it.

"Thank you, Cameron, I loved it." She goes to rise from her seat, but I stop her with a raised palm.

"You earned two songs, remember?" I say, and she lowers herself back down. My stomach flips around twice as I adjust the capo to the right position. "This one you haven't heard before. I wrote it for my solo album but ended up scrapping it because it wasn't good enough." I shake my head at how lost I was back then, how unwilling I was to be real. "Anyway, it's about surviving hardships, and I may have tweaked the lyrics just a little to fit a certain mother-daughter duo." When I first wrote the song, I'd stripped out all references to my faith. But as I dusted off the music sheets and practiced the melody, I was struck by how ridiculous that choice had been. There is no surviving hardships without faith. The song had felt empty because it *was* empty. I had removed the very thing that made it special. "I, um, hope you like it." I can't mask the insecurity in my voice and begin strumming before I change my mind.

Immediately, she scoots to the edge of the chair, her blanket dropping from her hands as if she wants no distraction at all. I finish the first verse and move to the second, watching every micro movement in her expression. She's fixated, lost in the sound as much as I am. The chorus comes, and I take one step closer.

This is the part I changed. The part that was driven by watching Lexie's courage, especially on the day she'd let go of her daughter. I'd been too angry and blind to see the way the Lord held me at my lowest, sustained me while I suffered, but I could see His fingerprints clearly on Lexie's life. He had brought her Mason and me and her renovation project at exactly the right time. He had strengthened her through all the adversity she'd faced. He'd fully and completely prepared her for this next challenge, and He would hold her all the way through the journey.

Those were the words I added. Those were the promises I knew in my heart were true.

She's crying when I finish, her face in her hands as her wails hollow me out. I carefully set down the guitar and kneel in front of her.

"I'm sorry. I didn't mean to make you cry. I just wanted you to see how brave I think you are."

"You think I'm brave?" She looks up at me, her cheeks wet, her eyes sparkling through the tears. "Cameron, that was the most beautiful song I've ever heard. The most meaningful song you've ever sung to me, in person or otherwise. You were the one who was brave tonight, and I cannot thank you enough for what you've given me." The relief nearly collapses me, but I remain steady in front of her. She brushes my hair as her gaze travels over each feature of my face. "I love you,

Cameron. I think I always have, even if back then it was only
with a young girl's heart. You have all of me. My heart and
my soul. I love you. And no matter what happens, I know I
always will."

I press my face into her hands, clutching her fingers with
mine. I'm so overwhelmed by her words that I can't speak,
can't get out all the declarations I've practiced and practiced
before tonight.

Being loved was all I'd ever wanted. I searched for it in so
many wrong places, had begged for it from people who didn't
feel the way I wanted them to. And now it's been given to me
freely by a person who still feels like a gift from heaven.

I look up at her, my heart full, my mouth ready to explode
all the plans I have for the two of us when her phone rings
across the charged air between us.

We both freeze at the sound, and Lexie quickly checks her
screen.

"It's Morgan," she whispers and swipes to answer. "Hey,
honey. Is everything okay?"

I back away, my heart a jackhammer, and try to stuff back
down the flood of emotions I was about to unleash.

"Of course," Lexie says, her eyes going wide with both
surprise and excitement. "I can be there first thing in the
morn— Tonight? Well, yes, of course." She gets to her feet,
listening and nodding her head. "Yes, absolutely. We'll do it
up special. Invite Mason and everything." She pauses and
then glances at me with a Cheshire cat smile. "Yes, and Cameron too. Okay, sweetheart, we'll be there soon." Lexie ends
the call and places her hand over her mouth before dropping
her arm in a daze. "You were right. She wants to come home.
Tonight. Right now."

Concern lances my insides. "Did something happen between her and your sister?"

"No, it doesn't sound like it. She was quick to assure me that she and Annaliese were good. She just said she missed me and that she wanted to wake up on Christmas morning in her own bed." She huffs out a sigh of utter disbelief. "She wants to throw a big party tomorrow with the whole family. You included. She wants it to be our new Christmas tradition." Tears well up in her eyes. Happy tears. Tears that mirror my own.

"I can't think of anything I would want more." I go to her and take her gently in my arms. Relief wraps around us both. For the first time all night, she feels whole. We feel whole. "Let's go get our girl."

THIRTY-FOUR

Lexie

I wake up to the smell of coffee and popcorn. It's a smell that might be off-putting to some, but it reminds me of every Christmas season that Morgan and I have ever shared.

I throw off my covers and swing my legs over the bed. It has been weeks since Morgan was up before me. Weeks of her lying in bed and disconnecting from our relationship. This morning feels like a rebirth, and I'm as giddy as a little girl waiting to see what presents lie under the tree.

Once clothed, I open my door and see my girl sitting at the dining table with two large bowls full of popcorn and a string of twine with a big needle on the end.

"What are you doing up so early?" I ask, padding toward the kitchen.

"Are you kidding me? We have a week's worth of work to do in four hours." She pats the seat next to her, and my grin spreads all the way across my face. There's my little worrier. I'd been concerned about what her state of mind might be this morning. But seeing her now, her face bright and energetic, her mind immersed in a new project, I feel complete relief that Morgan will find her way back to her old self.

"We can skip a few traditions this year, you know." I bypass the chair and hit the coffeepot instead. "No one will care."

"I care," she says adamantly. "This is the first year we will have our entire family here. It has to be perfect."

I consider telling her all the wise things that Cameron has learned over the past few months about expecting perfection from anything, but then add cream to my coffee instead. There are some lessons I can't protect her from. Some things she will have to figure out on her own. If this season has taught me anything, it has taught me that one cruel truth. I'm beginning to believe the process of kids growing up is harder on the parent than it is on the child. Who knew?

Cup in hand, I join her at the table. She quickly passes me my own needle and thread. "Tell you what, I will string all the popcorn you want, but I need words while I do it. You don't have to tell me everything, but at a minimum I would like to know what made you want to come home early."

Morgan looks down at the table and sighs as if she knew this moment would inevitably come, even though I gave her a pass last night. She'd been exhausted when we picked her up. And Annaliese hadn't been super talkative, either. They'd given each other a hug, saying they'd see each other again soon, and then Morgan slid into Cameron's back seat. She remained quiet the entire ride home, and while I wanted desperately to push for details, Cameron gently laid his hand on my knee and shook his head. For a man who'd only known my daughter two months, he seemed to read her even better than I did sometimes. So I held my tongue and didn't ask any questions, not even when we got home and she said goodnight, opting to go straight to bed.

But I'm not one to let elephants stew in the room too long,

so this morning we are definitely going to talk. "Did something specific happen?" I ask, hoping it gives her the runway she needs to open up.

Finally, she speaks. "No, not really. I enjoyed my time with her. But . . . in some ways, it was weird." She shrugs, and I get the sense she feels guilty about what she's about to say. "I couldn't be myself with her. I tried, and I know she wanted me to be, but I found that I wanted to impress her. Like what she liked, be the image she had for me. But it was too exhausting to continue."

I reach out and squeeze her hand, understanding perfectly how easy it would be to want to do that, especially at her age. "That's very normal, honey. All new relationships start out with a bit of a dance before they become real. You just have to give it time."

"Yeah. I figured, but I don't think I want to stay there too much, if that's okay. I don't feel like myself over there. But I would like for her to come here." Her brows rise, a question behind them. "If that's something you would consider?"

I curl the hand in my lap into a fist and try to reconcile the immediate jolt of anxiety I feel. Up to this point, there'd only been two tracks that I could see: losing Morgan to Annaliese or cutting my sister out of both of our lives. I hadn't considered the third alternative—the three of us coexisting as a family.

"Your face looks pained, Mom." Morgan snorts, her teasing a mild balm to my stress. "Does it really feel impossible to forgive her?"

My gaze darts to hers, my eyes narrowing. "Did Annie say something to you about it?" That question feels far too mature and pointed to be coming from a thirteen-year-old.

"No, not directly, but I could see her regret when she

spoke about you. Especially when she told me stories of you two as little kids. She misses you, Mom."

"I know. I miss her, too, but sometimes the choice is a little more complicated than simply wanting to forgive someone." Especially when that someone had hurt you time and time again. Had disappointed you, taken advantage of you, had lied repeatedly, and made you feel partially responsible for all of it. That is the agony of addiction. The person is two beings, and despite not wanting to, you find yourself loving one and hating the other. And since you never know which one you're going to get, it seems only right to protect yourself against both. "I'm not angry with her anymore." I smile through tear-filled eyes at my daughter. "I see God's hand in what happened ten years ago, and I wouldn't change the outcome for anything. But that doesn't mean I'm not wary of her presence in our lives."

Morgan swallows, but I see her eyes tear up, as well. I didn't realize she may have needed to hear that reassurance after all that has happened. "But I want the three of us to be a family, and we can't do that if you're constantly seeing her as the enemy," she says gruffly. "I know it's a lot to ask, but I don't want it to be like it was, all the secrets and separation. I want to be able to talk to you about her, about my feelings." A tear rolls down her cheek. "You're my best friend."

My fractured heart bursts into a thousand soaring but-terflies. I leap from my chair and rush over to her, pulling her into my arms in a hug of complete restoration. For her, I would risk it. For her, I would lay my heart out again and again, no matter the cost. "You're my best friend, too," I say as we squeeze tight and rock back and forth. "I can't promise I'll be faultless with her or won't be extra careful if I see warning signs, but I can promise to try. Starting today. Clean slate."

"Thank you." She pulls back and grins up at me, victory playing across her youthful face.

"You're welcome." I wipe both palms across her cheeks, drying the fallen tears. "Now, no more crying. It's Christmas and we have a lot to do. And I'm going to festive this up a little and play some music."

She giggles and drops back into her chair. I rush to my room, pulling myself together as I go, and search for my phone. When I find it, Cameron's text brings a warmth deep and full to my heart.

Cameron:
I'm going to assume you haven't had a grocery run in a while, and regardless, I am too much of a coward to try your infamous cooking after all of Morgan's stories. Would you mind if I take care of the dinner tonight?

I laugh like a schoolgirl and drop to my bed.

Me:
I am appalled by your lack of courage. However, since it seems to be your mission to keep us fed and healthy, I will allow the gesture.

He replies with a kiss emoji. But then three little dots appear.

Cameron:
How is she doing?

I didn't think it was possible, but my heart swells bigger.

Me:
She's good. We had a great talk this morning. You were right about waiting.

Cameron:
Yeah, well, I'm right about all sorts of things.

Me:
Don't get a big head. One win comes right before a lot of losses.

Cameron:
Hey . . . don't steal my victory. It may be the only one I get. Okay, got to go. I need to go scour the city for an open store.

Me:
Good luck. And get puffy Cheetos if they have some!

Cameron:
Puffy Cheetos? At Christmas?

Me:
Long story. I'll let Morgan tell you later.

Cameron:
Can't wait.

"Mom! Seriously, how long does it take to find your phone?"

"Sorry. Coming." I spring off the bed, the phone pressed to my heart. Cameron and I never got to finish our conversation after I professed my love to him, but I can't seem to find any insecurity in his lack of reciprocation. He's shown his devotion time and time again, and I value that far more than his speaking a certain four-letter word.

As I enter the kitchen, Morgan narrows her eyes at me. "What exactly were you doing in there? You have that goofy look on your face you only get when Cameron's around."

My cheeks immediately heat. "He texted that he's going to take care of the food. Apparently, you scared him away from my cooking."

"Awesome!" She stands so quickly from her chair that it nearly topples over as she walks to the counter. Seconds later, she is crossing something off a sheet of loose-leaf paper.

"You made a list?" My mouth drops open a little. "An actual to-do list?"

"Well, yeah. Mason does them all the time. That's how he gets so much done." She flashes me a grin, and the family resemblance is shocking. How is it possible I'm only now seeing that the family member she emulates the most is my bullheaded cousin? "And I even made a schedule!" She holds up the paper, bold and proud. The thing is color-coded and everything.

I press my face into my hands and laugh. Two of them in this world. Lord help us all.

THIRTY-FIVE

Cameron

The mood is festive when I let myself into Lexie's house on Christmas Day. I'm the last to arrive, mostly because I've spent half the morning searching for an open store before finally giving up and raiding my parents' freezer. After I told my mom the situation with Morgan, she had my car packed full of delicious, prepared dishes she'd been saving for our family's party tomorrow. I hugged her with the force of a bear. Both holidays now, my parents have come to Lexie's aid without a moment of hesitation. My eagerness to leave this city and never return feels insane to me now. Add it to the list of all the things in my life I once took for granted. Never again.

Lexie turns the corner and sees me struggling to get the front door shut around all the sacks of food. "Hey! Wow, let me help you with that." Her tone is full of wonder and happiness, and it blows my mind to think that just days ago she was crying in my arms.

"Sorry I'm so late." We finally get the bags inside and close the door. "After finding only two gas stations and a pharmacy open, I had to regroup. Mom says Merry Christmas." I grin at Lexie and shrug, knowing once again the hero status will be bestowed upon my parents.

She covers her mouth with her hand and eyes the two large brown sacks and three plastic bags at my feet. "Oh, Cam, you shouldn't have. Did we take all their food?"

"We didn't even put a dent in it." I slip my hand around the back of her neck and pull her in for a hello kiss that is far from quick. "Merry Christmas," I whisper against her lips.

"Merry Christmas to you, too," she says, her cheeks turning pink.

Together, we carry the bags into the kitchen and put the refrigerated stuff away. "Go ahead and turn on the oven to three hundred degrees."

"What is it?" Lexie asks, pulling at the foil covering one of three glass serving dishes.

"Ham, sweet potatoes, and green-bean casserole. She said to stick them in the oven covered, and we should be good to go in one hour." I fold the sacks flat. "I also have rolls we can warm up, plus two different pies."

"You really are the food fairy, aren't you?"

"Yes." I pull her to me and wrap my arms around her waist. "But I have many more talents I'm very much looking forward to sharing with you."

Her blush gets darker and reaches to her neck. I kiss the edge of the redness, relishing her smell and her skin.

"Do you want to meet my sister?" she asks after indulging me in a few more lingering moments together. "They're all out back."

"Sure." I haven't been in Lexie's backyard before. No doubt it's just as warm and inviting as the rest of her home. I slide my hand into hers, lacing our fingers together. "How receptive has Mason been to her being here?"

She grunts a laugh. "He's been on his best behavior. We had a long talk this morning, and really his resentment is on my and Morgan's behalf, so if we can forgive her, then he should be able to."

"Is that what you've done?" We halt in front of the door, neither wanting to continue this conversation outside.

"I'm working on it. For Morgan's sake, and I know it's what my parents would want me to do."

I brush a stray hair from her cheek. "Have I told you what an incredible person I think you are?"

"A few times."

"Well, it will never be enough."

She averts her eyes, embarrassed by the praise. I'm careful now not to use words like *perfect* with her, yet I will never stop telling her how amazing she is. If being in this place with her required all the pain and agony I've gone through over the past five years, I would live every moment over again.

She opens the door to the bright sunshiny day. This winter has been anything but cold, and though I always think I want a white Christmas, I am grateful for the low seventies we get to have for most of the day.

I let my eyes adjust to the brightness and then take in the small group. Morgan and Annaliese are sitting in patio chairs around a metal table, playing a card game. Mason is lounging nearby, his head bent back, sunglasses covering his eyes, looking as if he's either napping or sunbathing. I figure the former because he doesn't move when we join them. Lexie's yard is tiny compared to most I've seen in the neighborhood, but it's well cared for. My heart catches a little when I imagine her out here pushing a lawn mower by herself and hope Mason has stepped in and helped. Either way, I take solace in knowing she will never again be alone and squeeze her hand tighter.

Morgan jumps up from the table and rushes into my arms, her contact a gut punch but also one of my best moments of the day. "Merry Christmas, Cam!"

"Merry Christmas, kiddo." I kiss the top of her head and wonder if she opened the gift I gave her yet. "Did you like your present?"

She draws back, letting me go. "I haven't opened it yet. It's under the tree with the one I got for you."

My heart melts even more. "You got me a gift? You didn't have to do that."

"I know." She shrugs. "I wanted to. Here, come meet Annie." She takes my hand and pulls me away from Lexie at the same time Annie stands, looking both nervous and awkward.

"Hi, Annie. I'm Cam," I say and reach out a hand to her. I try to forget the pain she's put both Lexie and her daughter through. It's hard. I want to be cold to the woman, but then again, if I had been judged as I should have been for all my mistakes, I wouldn't be here either.

"Nice to meet you," she says softly, her grip limp and uncomfortable when she takes my hand. "Morgan has told me a lot about you. She even had me listen to a couple of songs."

"Really?" I raise an eyebrow in her direction. "I thought they all sounded the same."

"They do," she says, crossing her arms. "But that doesn't mean they're completely terrible."

"Morgan!" Lexie gasps, and I laugh out loud. She wasn't privy to that first conversation at Cassie's wedding and doesn't see the endearment in our bantering.

"It's okay. I know deep down . . . really deep down, she's a closet fan." I wink at Morgan, and she rolls her eyes, but the affection in them is not missed by me or Annie. She looks between me and Lexie, and I see a flash of pain on her face.

349

Our falling in love was just another thing she'd missed in her absence.

"Well, I bet that oven is ready," Lexie says when silence falls between us. "I'll go put the dishes in."

"No way! You will jinx the food with your cooking black thumb. I'll do it." Morgan rushes past Lexie, whose feigned outrage is so adorable I have to physically hold myself back from kissing her again. "And Annie brought stuff for cookies. Let's get that going, too."

"I, um, guess that's my cue," Annie says to me and eases nervously around the table to join them. She's not comfortable here, not yet anyway, and certainly not with me and Mason alone.

When the girls disappear, I walk to the edge of the patio, trying to picture the first time Lexie stood here and made the decision to make this place her home.

"We make quite the picture, don't we?"

I spin around at the sound of Mason's voice. He hasn't been asleep after all. "What do you mean?"

"Think about it. In one space we have two ex-best friends, sisters who haven't spoken in ten years, and a kid who's loved enough that we're all willing to put those things aside just to make her happy." He pushes up from the chair and comes to stand next to me. His arms cross as he looks out at the small stretch of grass. "And worse, I have a feeling you're planning to do something to make it all even more unbearable."

My nerves prickle, and I hate how he knows me so well. "I'm in love with her."

"Of course you are," he snorts. "You'd be an idiot not to be. The question is, what are you going to do about it?"

I turn and face him. "I'm going to ask her to marry me. And I'd really like your blessing if that's possible."

"It's not possible," he says with a frown. Then he puts his

hand up when I tense in defensiveness. "But not because of all the reasons I gave you in the hospital. Truth is, you've proven me wrong on many accounts since then."

My shoulders relax, though it doesn't help my confusion. "Then why?"

"I'll tell you, but first walk me through your vision. How do you see the next year playing out?"

I rub the back of my neck, wondering if this conversation is just a test he's putting me through. Mason isn't her father, but he's the closest she has to a protector, and I genuinely don't want him opposing us. It would hurt Lexie too much. "I was planning on asking her today. Then after school gets out and the house is done, I would fly her and Morgan out to Nashville. They could both tour with me, and I'd get whatever tutors I need to keep Morgan up to date with her schooling. Once my obligation with the label is done, we'd come back home."

Mason's silent as he listens to all the dreams I've conjured up. "And what about Annie?"

"What about her?"

He looks at me like I've missed a glaring neon sign. "They just found each other again. Are you going to pull Morgan away from her mom after they've been apart ten years? And what about Lexie? How is she supposed to navigate the house and all this emotional upheaval while trying to plan a wedding and support you?"

"I don't know. We'll figure it out. We love each other—that should be enough."

"Maybe it should, but it's not, Cam." His voice is softer now, almost regretful. "If you ask her, she will say yes. But I'm not sure you've really considered what you're asking her to give up. Who is actually sacrificing here? Her or you? Because right now, it looks to me like it's just her."

"So, what then? I just leave and let her go? How is that better?" I run my hands through my hair. "I can't get out of this album, Mason. Believe me, if I could, I would have already. I'm stuck for the next year."

"Exactly. You're stuck, but she isn't. She's happy here. Morgan is thriving. They finally have a chance at a family." He looks toward the closed back door. "Are you really going to take that from them because you can't be alone for one more year?"

I grind my teeth together. "So you're saying if I wait, you'll support this relationship? Or is this your way of ensuring we break up?"

He looks me in the eye, serious and direct. "If you wait until you are free to love her the way she deserves to be loved—not on some tour bus or at home alone in a new city—then yes. You will have my full blessing. I'll get a license and officiate the thing myself."

I grunt a laugh at the visual but feel an ache inside so enormous that it threatens to swallow me whole. "I'm not sure I can do what you're asking," I admit.

He doesn't bite back at my honesty. Instead, he sighs and looks to the sky. "I get it, Cam. I truly do. I've been at the same crossroads, and I wish I'd had someone there to wake me up to the mistakes I was making."

My head jerks in his direction, confusion apparently clear in my expression because he continues.

"I was engaged in Austin. She was Barry's daughter, my dad's friend who I was staying with. I knew from the first moment I laid eyes on her that she would be my wife. Felt it down to every nerve ending. I pursued her like a tiger does a gazelle. Finally, after a grueling six months, I got her to go on a date with me." His voice is both bitter and nostalgic, and I remain silent as I listen, riveted. "I convinced myself she was

ready. Allowed myself to be blinded only by what I so desperately wanted. And somewhere along the way, my inability to
see her needs broke us."

"What happened?"

"She walked away. Well, ran away was more like it. Two
days before the wedding. Left town, and the only indication
I had that she was alive was a social-media post of her posing
with a metal chain and a caption that said 'Dodged that bul-
let.'"

Horror slaps me in the face, followed by a rage that one
only gets when someone they care about is hurt. "She didn't
deserve you," I bark out. "You're the one who dodged the bul-
let."

"That isn't the point. What I'm trying to get you to see
is that it's a two-party dance, Cam. Both people have to
be considered. And in your case, it's three because there's
Morgan, too. Now, you can drag them out there with you on
that dance floor, but it's going to be a lot more painful for all
of you involved." His words are a spear into my heart, one I
can't ignore because of the raw truth he laced around it. He
squeezes my rigid shoulder. "If you two really love each other,
I have no doubt you will still feel that way in a year." With
those final piercing words, he leaves me alone to think and
returns to the house.

I shove my hands in my pockets and dip my head, defeat
and disappointment weighing on my shoulders. My fingers
curl around the small box I have tucked deep down, the
image I've had for days playing across my mind. Getting on
one knee, telling her how much I love her, and watching as
she screams yes and nearly topples me over in a hug. But
even as my heart swells at the beautiful picture, my soul reminds me of the lesson it took me far too long to learn.

Life isn't a perfect image. And none of my ideals so far

have brought any happiness or stability to my life. I'd been selfish back then. Unwilling to give up even one small piece of the vision I saw for myself. It was only about my dreams, my future.

And just like that, I understand how Bryson walked away from a life that would have changed his entire family dynamic. He loved Darcy and Charlie enough to put them first.

And I love Lexie and Morgan enough to do the same.

Decision made, I take a deep breath, let go of the picture I had of today, and join the rest of them inside the house.

THIRTY-SIX

Lexie

I t's the Christmas I've always dreamed of but never expected to have ever again. By the time we ate, the awkwardness had faded, and soon old stories came alive between Annie, Mason, and me. Morgan and Cameron listened intently, laughing and begging for more. They especially loved the ones that highlighted what a dreamy space cadet I had been growing up, but after one particularly mortifying story involving my schoolgirl crush on a certain friend's older brother, Cameron reached over, pulled me in, and kissed the side of my head.

"The guy sounds like a dolt if you ask me," he said playfully. "He should have snatched you up the minute you turned eighteen."

After that, I was too busy bouncing on a hundred cloud nines to be bothered with embarrassment.

We now sit in a circle around our small, leaning, dilapidated old tree. Only half the lights worked when we plugged them in, and most of the ornaments are handmade. Like us, the tree is a knit-together hodgepodge of torn and broken pieces, and yet together it's truly beautiful.

There are only two gifts left to give out. One for me and one for Morgan. The one for Morgan is from Cam, and she seemed determined to save it for the end. I touch the delicate necklace at my throat and understand why she'd want to savor the moment. When I opened his gift, I nearly choked at the decadence. The chain is made of 18-karat rose gold, the pendant a fan shape set with mother-of-pearl. The expense was obvious and far more outlandish than the custom throw pillows we had made for his outdoor patio. One said, *The Lee Porch, kick back, relax, and live simply.* The other one, Morgan's choice, said, *Life is better in a tree house.* Oh well, at least he seemed to genuinely love them both.

"Okay, Mom, you're next." Morgan hands me the gift, and I take it with trembling fingers. It's from Annie. And unlike Morgan, I am not looking forward to seeing what's inside.

Slowly, I unwrap the box, careful not to look at Annaliese, who's currently biting her fingernail. Once the paper is gone and the box opened, the item inside makes me immediately tear up. "I thought we lost this," I squeak out. I glance at my sister, and she mirrors my pooling eyes.

"I took it with me when I left that night," she admits.

Carefully, I pull the ornament free of its holder and study the picture embedded inside. Me, Annie, and Morgan at three years old. We'd bought this ornament together. Had taken at least ten photos before we were happy with the results and sent it to a one-hour photo shop.

"It belongs with the two of you," she says, her voice quiet but strong.

I reach out and take her hand in mine. "It belongs with all of us."

She smiles at me, and instinctively I glance at Cameron when I let go of her fingers. He's watching us with an expression I can't read. There's a softness in his eyes, but also something else. Pain maybe, regret, but I can't imagine why. Dragging my gaze away, I go and hang the ornament on the tree, front and center. I like how it looks there. It feels like hope, a new beginning.

"Well, hon, you're all that's left," I say to Morgan and pass her Cameron's gift. The oddity of the size has confounded us for hours. About twelve inches, perfectly square, and at least two inches deep. And it's light. Too light to even feel like a real gift.

She shakes it and looks up at him. "What is it?"

"You'll have to open it to see," he says, and I swear there's a catch in his throat, as if this moment is the beginning of an end. I look at him, my eyes questioning, but he doesn't spare me a glance. His attention is fixed on my daughter.

She tears open the paper, unwilling to wait any longer, only to discover a decorative box made of light cardboard. She lifts off the lid, and inside is a record. Old-school style, wide and made of vinyl. Her brow furrows. "You bought me NF on vinyl?" I know what she's thinking. She doesn't even have a record player to make it work.

"Turn it over," Cameron says with a devilish gleam in his eyes.

She does so and gasps. In black Sharpie is a personalized note from the artist himself, telling Morgan how cool of a girl she is and how she's going to take the world by storm. She gawks at Cameron. "You know him?"

Cameron winks. "We have a mutual friend. I have a record player for you, as well. It was just too big to wrap."

She squeals and lunges forward, hugging him while she chants "thank you, thank you" at least a dozen times.

"You're welcome," he says when she finally releases him. I see the affection in his eyes, the total adoration he has for my daughter, and I swear I fall in love with him all over again.

When we're all done cooing over our presents, the next

few minutes are spent stuffing a trash bag full of discarded paper. I tie the bag and get ready to haul it to the trash outside when Cameron takes the bag out of my hand.

"Mason can take this out. I need to talk with you for a minute." The look in his eyes is unmistakable, the sheer determination to get out whatever is going on in his head.

"Okay." I let him guide me out the back door. "Is everything all right?"

He takes me as far as the edge of the patio and turns me to face him. "Yes and no." He sucks in a breath and then takes both my hands in his. "The other night you told me you loved me, and then Morgan called, and I never got to say all the things I've been dying to tell you."

I reach out and touch his temple. "You don't need to say anything. You've shown me how you feel many times over."

"Maybe, but I want to say it. I want to shout it from the mountaintops." His gaze drills into mine, his voice hoarse. "I love you, Lexie. I'm pretty sure I have since that first night you came to dinner, but I had too much brokenness inside to see how much until recently." He lets go of my hand and reaches into his pocket.

My heart stutters and comes to a complete stop when he pulls out a small black box.

"I'm not going to ask you to marry me tonight," he says quickly, and I try not to deflate in disappointment.

"You're not?" I croak.

He smiles affectionately. "No. I wanted to, but doing so tonight would put an unfair burden of choice on you."

I look down at the box, completely confused. "Why are you telling me this now?"

"Because I'm leaving soon, and I don't want you to have any question as to how I feel or what our future holds. I am absolutely, completely in love with you. All of me." He presses our joined hands to his heart. "But we both have commitments we've made. You to Morgan and your sister. And me to my label. I'm tired of being a man who doesn't keep his word. I'm going to finish strong, and when I walk away, it will be with my head held high. When I return to you, I want to be a man both of us can respect."

Despite my yearning to see what's inside the box, I know he's right. There has been way too much upheaval these past couple of months to heap another life change on top of it. "But you do plan to ask one day?" There's an insecurity in my voice that I dislike but can't seem to shake.

"Yes. When I'm free from this contract. When I can come home and be a husband and father the way I'm called to be and not some ghost of a presence. And when I open this box and get on one knee, be prepared. Because it's going to be in the most obnoxious, public setting I can think of." He grins mischievously. "After a year of holding on to this ring, I'm going to want the entire world to know that this incredible woman is going to be my wife."

"Can I see it?" I move my fingers toward the box, but he grips it tighter in his hands."

"Nope." He shakes his head, and the box disappears back inside his pocket. "I need something to entice you to wait for me."

I work to school my annoyance but decide he's probably right to make me wait. Seeing it and not having it on my finger would be worse. Resigned, I lace my arms around his neck, and he wraps his around my waist. "No enticement is needed," I assure him. "My answer is yes. Now or a year from now."

He presses his forehead to mine, and I close my eyes against the pain. "I'm going to miss you so much it already hurts. Promise me you won't fall in love with someone else while I'm gone."

"Oh, Cam, don't you know by now? I'm destined to love

only one man in my lifetime, and you are that man. We'll make it work. I've loved you from a distance my whole life. What is one more year?"

"I'll fly home every opportunity I have."

I smile despite the sadness I already feel. "And Morgan and I will come out for spring break."

"It's a date," he says, lowering his head while pulling me flush with his body. He kisses me deeply and with promise. I relish the feeling, amazed at the security I feel in the two of us even while he's telling me goodbye.

"Mom! Cam!" Morgan's voice cuts through the air. "Are y'all seriously out here kissing again? We're all waiting on you to watch the movie." She has her hand covering her eyes like the vision of us embracing will scorch her irises.

I feel Cam's sigh as he pulls me closer. "I'm going to miss her like crazy, too." His voice is soft, wistful, yet he doesn't say more as he lets go and steps away from me.

"You guys are going to make me upchuck my dinner," Morgan grumbles, lowering her hand and folding her arms against her chest.

"Is that so?" Cam lunges forward and heaves my screeching daughter over his shoulder, tickling her. Her size and her wriggling make him release her quickly, and the two banter all the way into the house.

I stop and stare through the open back door at the family waiting inside. Two months ago, I thought my biggest dream had come true. But how small my vision was. I glance at the sky, knowing both my parents are up there and happy.

"Thank you," I whisper to the One whose blessings always exceed our greatest desires, then move to join my new family inside.

EPILOGUE

Lexie

The crisp night air is perfect, and tomorrow's forecast is even more appealing. I look down at the large square diamond on my left hand and revel at the knowledge that in less than twenty-four hours, I will be Mrs. Cameron Lee.

He was true to his word and asked me to marry him on-stage in front of forty thousand screaming fans and then serenaded me with one of his most popular new releases. The label had been right in their assessment of Cameron's cross-over potential. His pop album soared to the top of the charts, popular especially with teenage girls, to Morgan's chagrin. Cam did not share the same affection for the release, but he honored his commitment as he'd set out to do. And in a twist of irony, he was able to graciously turn down a third contract from the same label that had almost dropped him a year before. Poetic justice, if you ask me.

The concert in Dallas had been his final one. A goodbye to

the city that started it all. He sang "A Decade of Love" to end the show and choked up halfway through the song. There wasn't a dry eye in the house, especially his. But I knew his tears weren't because of the pain that song used to bring, but of gratitude for the chapter that had ended, however hard, and for the new beginning that was to come.

A squeal of laughter pulls me from my reflections, and I turn back to the crowd gathered outside of Bryson and Darcy's house. A joint bachelor and bachelorette party, they called it, and had showered us with a slew of embarrassing gag gifts that Cam assured me were a sign of their affection for us. Even Mason had come—with a date, to my complete shock, though he refused to give me any details when I asked. I'd wear him down later.

My eyes drift to Morgan, who's running around with Charlie and Lacey, January and Dillon's little girl. She's surprisingly gentle with the little ones, and I have a feeling she'll be spending the holidays with a lot of babysitting gigs.

"Want some company?" a voice asks from my right. In the darkness, it takes me a moment to make out Darcy's approaching figure.

"Sure," I say, rubbing my arms to ward against a cool breeze. The first time I met Darcy, she practically tackled me in a hug. Her warmth was intoxicating, and it took only moments for the two of us to connect. She was a major source of strength for me while Cam and I suffered through that last stretch of a harrowing long-distance relationship, and she was fast becoming one of my closest friends. Even Annaliese opened up when Darcy was around, and she'd been relatively shy when meeting the mass of people that came with the Cameron Lee package.

Darcy settles next to me on the wooden bench I've found and follows my line of sight to Cam and her husband. They're tinkering around in the studio, bickering over something they're listening to. "This new venture is going to be an interesting one," she deadpans.

I laugh, imagining she's probably right. Bryson and Cameron have started their own production label, and so far everything has been a battle. The name, the genre, the demos they have coming in by the hundreds. "Have they always operated this way?"

"Pretty much." Darcy sighs, but it's full of love for them. "Yet somehow, in the end, they'll create something brilliant together."

"I believe it."

She glances at me. "Are you nervous?"

"No. Just excited. Ready for it all to be over and for us to start our life together."

"Cam says he's moving into your rental while the house is being renovated."

"Yep." I shake my head in awe of his wedding surprise. He'd taken both Morgan and me to Mrs. Hardcastle's house two weeks ago and told us his sister-in-law had sold the property. The family had finally decided they weren't returning to the area, and it was time to let go of their childhood home. Morgan and I had linked arms, ready to say goodbye to all the memories that had occurred there. Instead, Cameron handed us a key and said, *"I feel pretty certain Nanni would approve of the new owners."*

"I still can't believe he bought you a house without your consent. I would have killed him."

"I thought it was romantic."

She grins. "Which is why the two of you are meant for each other."

I nod, agreeing with every ounce of my being. I love Cameron's spontaneity. Love his grand gestures and emotional speeches. Love his steadiness and the way he makes sure he's aware and meeting every one of my needs. "We want Mason to do the work, but it's going to take some serious convincing to get him to say yes."

"I can't imagine why. From what I heard, the two of you made a killing on the last property you sold in that area."

Satisfaction spreads through me. I had been right about the market being a gold mine, an admission that nearly choked Mason on the way out of his mouth. "We did, but I think he still has nightmares from the process."

"Don't worry. Between all of us, we can wear him down."

"I'm counting on it."

"Okay, no more isolation." She loops her arm through mine and pulls us up to stand. "The bride-to-be is supposed to be fawned over, not found hiding in the trees."

We walk side by side toward the group gathered out back, but Darcy stops me before we join the crowd and our men, who finally closed the studio doors and returned to the party. "This was a dream of mine . . . all of us here, reunited," she says, her eyes glassy.

"That is a very good dream."

"Yes, it is." She squeezes my arm one more time before we part.

Cameron quits talking when he sees me approach, his eyes glinting with joy and love. "There you are." He pulls me in and kisses me deeply, forgetting all about the crowd next to us.

Cheers and whoops filter through my ears, but I can't find an ounce of care.

"Are you ready for tomorrow?" he whispers against my lips.

"Yes, but more importantly . . . I'm ready for a lifetime."

ACKNOWLEDGMENTS

*I*t's hard to put into words how I feel about closing out this series. This journey has been full of highs and lows, but mostly God has given me a great message through every book that has ultimately brought me to a place of contentment and peace.

Readers often ask me which character I relate to the most, and in this series it has been Cameron. I'm not a musician, but as a creative it's so easy to fall into the trap of discontentment with our craft. When I started writing *Love and a Little White Lie*, I was in a back-and-forth struggle with the Lord over the future of my writing. Like with Cameron, there had been so many disappointments, so many unrealized expectations, and I was left frustrated and searching for answers. And then right when I thought I knew the path, the Lord gave me a victory I was totally not expecting. An amazing book deal and a Carol Award. The dream . . . realized.

But like Cameron, I too had to ask what happens after the dream comes true? When sales drop and publishing contracts aren't renewed. What's left when the rest of the world no longer values the art you are creating? Was it worth it? Was the laboring over every single word a waste? Why, and how did I get here?

And through those dark questions and moments of self-doubt, you, my wonderful readers, were my Lexie. You wrote me about how my stories touched your lives. You encouraged me and lifted me up when I honestly felt as if I'd let myself and the Lord down somehow. You reminded me that it wasn't ever about the numbers, but about hope and healing and that we serve a relentlessly loving God who gave me a gift I had the privilege to share.

Like Cameron's, my journey will probably look a little different moving forward. How exactly? I don't know yet. I'm still waiting on the Lord to answer that one.

In the meantime, I want to thank you for ten amazing years. Thank you for thirteen novels, one novella collection, two awards, two stellar publishers, several amazing editors, beta readers, and a group of friends who are now like sisters. Thank you for a family who never lost faith in me or the purpose behind why I write flawed, broken characters who experience the unconditional love of Christ.

I found immense healing through each story, and my hope and prayer is that you did, as well. Until next time, my friends . . . be kind and support those who are brave enough to put their hearts in the pages of a book.

All my love, Tammy L. Gray

Tammy L. Gray lives at the edge of the hill country with her family, and they love all things Texas. Her many modern and true-to-life contemporary romance novels include 2021 Carol Award–winning *Love and a Little White Lie* and the 2017 RITA Award–winning *My Hope Next Door*, showing her unending quest to write culturally relevant stories with relatable characters. When not taxiing her three kids to various school and sporting events, Tammy can be spotted reading her favorite authors and supporting her husband's ministry at their hometown church. Learn more at tammylgray.com.

Sign Up for Tammy's Newsletter

Keep up to date with Tammy's news on book releases and events by signing up for her email list at tammylgray.com.

More from Tammy L. Gray

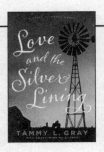

After her dreams of mission work are dashed, Darcy Malone has no choice but to move in with the little sister of a man she's distrusted for years. Searching for purpose, she jumps at the chance to rescue a group of dogs. But it's Darcy herself who'll encounter a surprising rescue in the form of unexpected love, forgiveness, and the power of letting go.

Love and the Silver Lining
STATE OF GRACE